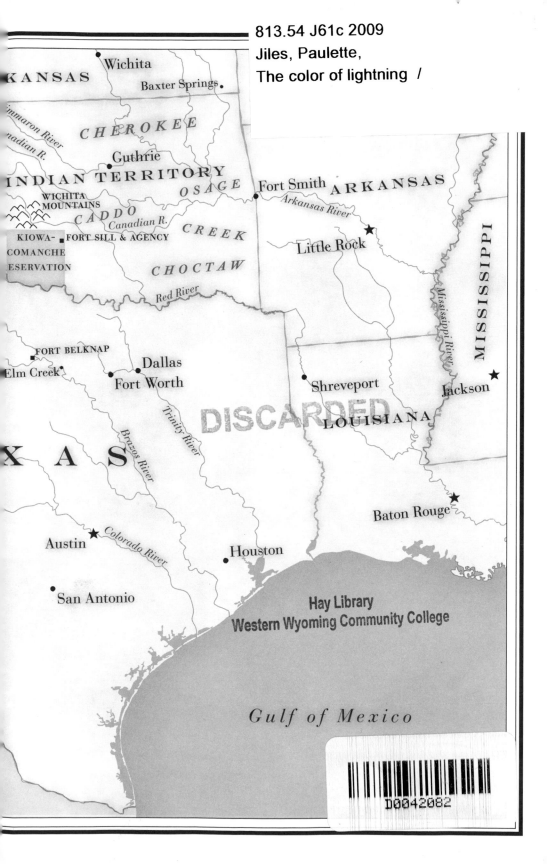

THE
Color of Lightning

Also by Paulette Jiles

Stormy Weather

Enemy Women

Sitting in the Club Car Drinking Rum and Karma-Kola

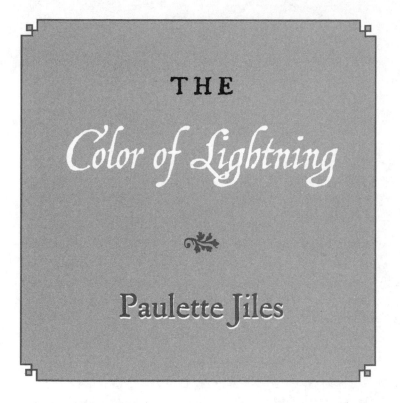

THE
Color of Lightning

Paulette Jiles

wm
WILLIAM MORROW
An Imprint of HarperCollins*Publishers*

THE COLOR OF LIGHTNING. Copyright © 2009 by Paulette Jiles. All rights reserved. Printed in the United States of America. No part of this book may be used or reproduced in any manner whatsoever without written permission except in the case of brief quotations embodied in critical articles and reviews. For information address HarperCollins Publishers, 10 East 53rd Street, New York, NY 10022.

HarperCollins books may be purchased for educational, business, or sales promotional use. For information please write: Special Markets Department, HarperCollins Publishers, 10 East 53rd Street, New York, NY 10022.

FIRST EDITION

Designed by Nicola Ferguson
Endpaper map by Nick Springer

Library of Congress Cataloging-in-Publication Data

Jiles, Paulette, 1943–
     The color of lightning : a novel / Paulette Jiles — 1st ed.
        p.   cm.
     ISBN: 978-0-06-169044-0
     I. Title.
   PR9199.3.J54C65   2009
   813'.54—dc22   2008046339

09 10 11 12 13   OV/RRD   10 9 8 7 6 5 4 3 2 1

For my brother, Kenneth Jiles,
and my sister,
Sunny Elaine Holtmann

Acknowledgments

MANY THANKS TO my agent Liz Darhansoff and editor Jennifer Brehl for their unfailing encouragement and support. To my brother, Kenneth Jiles, for advice on firearms; all mistakes are mine. To my niece Denise Jiles Pollard for genealogical researches on Britt Johnson and his family. To nephew Matt Jiles Holtmann for the 1886 copy of *My Story of the War*. To June Chism for accompanying me on travels to the Red River and hiking the Wichita Mountains and for introductions to ranchers Loretta and Lane Corley in Oklahoma and De and Clint Brown in the Cross Timbers, and many thanks to the Corleys and the Browns for their hospitality and guided tours of the Red River bottoms and Spanish Fort. To Caroline Raskin for the loan of an original signed copy of Elizabeth Custer's *Boots and Saddles* and for the literary loan of her Mount Vernon Street house in Philadelphia, to Sky Lewey for the Wilbarger book. Thanks to Sergeant Lee Coffee (USA Ret.), Buffalo Soldier re-enactor, for the story of Emmanuel Stance; and in memory of Melody, the Buffalo Soldier horse. For listening to long descriptions of a work-in-progress, thanks to Susan Lawson and Donna Stoner, and for an early read, thanks to Laurie Wagner Buyer. Much appreciated.

THE
Color of Lightning

Chapter 1

WHEN THEY FIRST came into the country it was wet and raining and if they had known of the droughts that lasted for seven years at a time they might never have stayed. They did not know what lay to the west. It seemed nobody did. Sky and grass and red earth as far as they could see. There were belts of trees in the river bottoms and the remains of old gardens where something had once been planted and harvested and then the fields abandoned. There was a stone circle at the crest of a low ridge.

Moses Johnson was a stubborn and secretive man who found statements in the minor prophets that spoke to him of the troubles of the present day. He came to decisions that could not be altered. He read aloud: *Therefore thus saith the Lord: Ye have not harkened unto me in proclaiming liberty, every one to his own brother, and every man to his neighbor. Behold, I proclaim a liberty for you, saith the Lord, to the sword, to the pestilence, and to the famine, and I will make you to be removed into all the kingdoms of the earth.* That's in Jeremiah, he said. So they left Burkett's Station, Kentucky, in 1863 in four wagons, fifteen white people and five black including children, to get away from the war between armies and also the undeclared war between neighbors.

Britt Johnson was proud of his wife and he loved her and was deeply jealous of her because of her good looks and her singing voice and her unstinting talk and laughter. Her singing voice. All along their journey from Kentucky to north Texas he had been afraid for her. Afraid that some white man, or black, or Spaniard, would take a liking to her and he would have to kill him. He rode a gray saddle horse always within sight of the wagon that carried her and the children. She was as much of grace and beauty as he would ever get out of Kentucky.

Before they crossed the Mississippi at Little Egypt they stopped and there at the heel of the free state of Illinois Moses Johnson caused Britt's manumission papers to be drawn up and notarized by a shabby consumptive justice of the peace who looked as if these papers were the last ones he would notarize before he died from sucking in the damp malarial air and the smoke of a black cigar.

The justice of the peace said it was a shame to manumit the man, look at what a likely buck he was, a great big strong nigger, and Moses Johnson said, You are going to meet your Maker before long, sir. You will meet him with tobacco on your breath and smelling of the Indian devil weed, and what will you say to Him who is the Author of your being? You will say Yes I did my utmost to keep a human being in the bonds of slavery and robbed of his liberty, and moreover I spent my precious breath a-smoking of filthy black cigars. Here is the lawyer's signature on his papers and his wife's papers as well. You will have your clerk copy all of these and then deposit the copies in the Pulaski County Courthouse. And from there they went on to Texas.

You could raise cattle anywhere in that country. At that time there was very little mesquite or underbrush, just the bluestem and the grama grasses and the low curling buffalo grass and the wild oats and buckwheat. When the wind ran over it they all bent in various yielding flows, with the wild buckwheat standing in islands, stiff with its heads of grain and red branching stems. The lower creek bottoms were like parks, with immense trees and no underbrush. The streams ran clearer than they do now. The grass held the soil in tight fists of roots. The streams did not always run but here and there were water holes whose edges were cut up with hoof marks of javelina and buffalo and sometimes antelope. Ducks flashed up off the surface and skimmed away in their flight patterns of beating and sailing, beating and sailing.

Mary had been raised in the main house with old Mrs. Randall who was blind in one eye, and she had not wanted to come to Texas, even on the promise of her freedom. Britt said he would make it up to her. As soon as the country was settled and the war was over he would start in as a freighter. He would break in a team from some of the wild mustangs that ran loose in the plains. There had to be a way to catch them. Then he would buy heavy horses. And then they would have a good house and a big fenced garden and a cookstove and a kerosene lamp.

The people who had come from Burkett's Station built their houses with large stone fireplaces and chimneys. They rode out into the country to explore. The tall grass hissed around the horses' legs like spray. Feral cattle ran in spotted and elusive herds, their horns as long as lances, splashed in red and white and some of them dotted like clown cattle.

They had come to live on the very edge of the great Rolling Plains, with the forested country behind them and the empty lands in front. Long, attentive lines of timber ran like lost regiments along the rivers and creeks. Everything was strange to them: the cactus in all its hooked varieties, the elusive antelope in white bibs and black antlers, the red sandstone dug up in plates to build chimneys and fireplaces big enough to get into in case there was a shooting situation.

There were nearly fifty black people in Young County now. Britt said soon they could have their own church and their own school. Mary was silent for a moment as the thought struck her and then cried out, She could be the Elm Creek teacher! She could teach children to sing their ABCs and recite Bible verses! For instance how the people were freed from Babylon in Isaiah! Britt nodded and listened as he stood in the doorway.

Mary planned the school and the lessons aloud and at length, and lit the fire and sang and talked and made up rhymes for the children that had been born to them, Jim the oldest and Jube who was nine and Cherry, age five, who had wavy hair like her mother. She told the children stories of who they were. That their great-grandfather had been brought from Africa, from a place called Benin, and that he was the son of a great king there, taken captive when he was ten, because he saw in the distance a waving red silk flag and had gone to see who was waving it in such an inviting way. He had sung a certain song he wanted all his descendants to remember but it had been forgotten. From time to time Mary said she dreamed about Kentucky and the rain there, and her mother and her aunts. She dreamed that she and Britt and the children had gone home.

BRITT TRIED NOT to favor Jim over the other two but already at age eleven the boy was both manly and kind. Jim bent over the pages of the Bible by firelight, entranced by words like *reigneth* and *strowed*. His mother made him spell them out. That spring Jim rode with his father searching out the wild cattle that grazed along the Clear Fork of the Brazos and when they came upon buffalo they sat on their horses and watched them, looking for some clue as to their nature. One of the white men who had lived in the country for ten years led them to see a herd moving north in the cold spring rain. They were dark and woolly and stood high at the shoulder, they moved down the slopes of the Brazos Valley wreathed in their own steam and water dripping from their half-moon horns, free and un-tended. No human beings owned them or directed their movement. They went where they meant to go in their own minds. They spread to the bald horizon under a drifting animal mist, and they smelled good.

"I wonder if they have regular teeth," said Moses.

"Like cows," said old man Peveler. "They just have regular teeth like cows."

"How do they eat?"

"They eat very well. The tongue especially."

Young Jim wanted to ride down among them but Britt laid his hand on the boy's forearm and shook his head. A calf turned to stare at them. It was a bright rusty red. Its mother turned and called to it and the calls from the herd of thousands in low explosive grunts made a ceaseless web of sound as the herd made their way north by the notions they held unspoken and secret, some ageless living map written out invisibly in their hearts.

They turned back toward Elm Creek. Old man Peveler had been in the country a long time and carried the scar of an arrow wound in his neck. The red men live in the north, he told them. Past the West Fork of the Trinity and on beyond the Red River, which is four days' ride north of here. That is their land and this is their raiding country. They raid for fun. The young men love it. Then they ride back north across the Red and they are safe there, so keep your firearms loaded and to hand.

And so they stayed. In Kentucky there was nothing but war and no safe place. To the north and west were the wild Indian lands of plain and canyon. Now that they had arrived they found that there was no other place to go. There was no retreat. No going back.

Britt worked for old man Peveler, driving freight, carrying supplies from Weatherford over the rolling prairies to Fort Belknap and Concho, supplies to the Ledbetter Salt Works. This way he learned the roads and the freighting business. The men at these places told him that he should be careful. But Moses Johnson said he hadn't seen a red man since they had arrived. Judge Wilson said it was true, there had been some kind of Indians close by at some time but he did not know of what persuasion they were and they were gone now, and with nearly two hundred civilized people in the county it was not likely they would return.

They were alone now. All those who had come from Burkett's Station, Kentucky, were alone, each family in its own house on the ocean of grass. Their cabin windows sparked in the night like the distant ports of small craft on unfamiliar seas. They were not sure what lay to the north and west, perhaps some veiled landscape or nation of people who had once owned the land where they themselves now lived. But these people were gone and were not coming back.

BRITT LAY DOWN his tin shears and listened. It was a heavy dark night with a haze about the three-quarter moon, hot and close. The dog stood up and stalked slowly into the yard with the fur of his back rising hair by hair. Mary and the children were asleep. The trumpet vine crawled down over the doorway and in it some persistent ticking insect clocked the seconds. Britt stepped to one side of the open door, into the shadow where he could not be seen, with a half-made candle sconce in his hands. A wind came up out of the grasslands and moved down into the valley of Elm Creek and rattled the cottonwood leaves over the cabin. The dog stood stiff-legged, staring at the far bluff of the creek where the stone circle was. A man stood there. In the blue moonlight Britt could see that the top half of his face was painted black. His hair drifted in the wind. Then he was gone.

THE MORNING OF October 13, 1864, Britt bridled his team of horses. The men were going to Weatherford for supplies and a few other things like hard candy and Mrs. Fitzgerald's hair dye. There are no mornings anywhere like mornings in Texas, before the heat of the day, the world suspended as if it were early morning in paradise and fading stars like night watchmen walking the periphery of darkness and calling out that all is well. Mary's lessons scraped clean from the thin boards, and bread baking in a skillet.

Britt came in and took up a smoking hot triangle of cornbread from the skillet and lifted it to his mouth. Then he bent forward with a confused expression to a piece of paper lying on the clothes trunk. All over the margins of the paper were sums.

Their freedom papers.

She had been using the margins of their freedom papers to teach the children to write sums with a pen.

Britt slung the cornbread back into the skillet and shouted her name. How did she ever think she could do such a thing? What white man would now believe these papers were real? Mary shouted to him he could go and get another set. How were the children supposed to learn how to use a pen? There wasn't any other paper. She stalked across the cabin with her chin in the air and her hair coming unpinned from under her headcloth. She banged the skillet onto the hearth and pieces of cornbread flew up and scattered.

Britt stormed outside and threw his dray whip across the yard. He turned and went back in again. How could he go and ask Moses Johnson for another set? And let him know how he did not value them, but let the children scribble and blot ink all over them? Moses Johnson nearly got himself lynched for wanting to free his slaves, his life's mortal end could have been in those papers. Look at them. Just look. He held up the manumission papers. Seven times nine equals sixty-three, seven times seven equals forty-nine. Divide by three. A hot feeling rose into his chest and then to his face.

"You were looking for a better life than I could give you," he shouted. "You'd rather be a house slave to old Mrs. Randall than to be free in Texas with me."

If she didn't like the way he lived his life she could go back to Kentucky to her mother and take the children with her, war or no war. The children hid in the washhouse and spied with fixed stares out the cracks between the logs and whispered to each other about the progress of the fight between their parents.

Britt lowered his head and bit his upper lip to keep from saying anything more, and when he raised it again Mary had run over to the window and thrown open the shutters. Her arms were crossed and she was staring out at the grapevines draping over the heavy green water of Elm Creek.

"And stop looking at yourself in the mirror," he said. "And when you go, leave Jim with me."

Mary took the mirror from the wall and threw it on the floor. It broke up into many angled pieces. Each piece reflected something of their house and the clothing of their children hung on pegs on the wall, and one large piece shone with the image of the sky and its early-morning adornment of cottony clouds overhead tumbling southeast in the early breeze and the bright dots of cottonwood leaves.

Two married people found themselves on separate and barren planets, alone in a place called Young County in the remote land of Texas. In an instant they realized that the bonds between them were not strong at all, but very fragile, and if these were broken they would be solitary and isolated for all eternity, and all that they had made together and the children they had made between them would be thrown out on long orbits like minor comets.

"I don't want the damn thing and I never wanted it the minute you brought it home. Don't ask me if I'm sorry because I ain't sorry and I never will be sorry." She kicked at the broken pieces. "There ain't nothing wrong with those papers because I could scrape it all off if I wanted to, Britt Johnson, and besides they are going to end the war and free everybody and those papers won't mean nothing, nothing, listen to me. You never listen, Britt. You are half deaf, I don't know which half, maybe it switches from one ear to the other depending which side I am standing on. And I wouldn't mind going home at all, no sir I would not. Next wagon going east I would, I can cook and earn my way as well as anybody."

"Woman, will you never shut up?"

They were both caught up in a rage of destruction, both hoping that at some point the other would realize how serious this was.

Britt turned and left. He walked straight out to the corral and pulled the lead rope from its pullaway knot and got on Cajun's back. He caught up Duke's lead rope in his right hand. He bent his head for a moment and thought about the other black people he would see in Weatherford. He named them to himself as if the names were a kind of secret, personal magic against the desolation he saw in front of him which was his life, if she indeed were to leave, without her, and without Cherry and Jube. At the last moment young Jim bolted out of the washhouse and in one clean leap sat himself on Duke's back.

Mary stood in the doorway. She was crying.

"And don't bring me back nothing," she said.

He turned the leader out onto the road. "All right," he said.

"I don't want to go back to Kentucky," she said.

"All right."

AT THE FITZGERALD home Britt slid off his saddle horse Cajun and lifted his hat to the people gathered there. Young Jim lifted his hat as well but remained on Duke's back.

"Mrs. Fitzgerald, Mrs. Durgan," Britt said. "Good morning, Mr. Johnson, Mr. Peveler, Judge."

"Good morning, Britt," they said.

"Well, Britt, I hate to see you hitch up that good saddle horse," said old man Peveler.

"I'll have me a team," said Britt. "Before too long." He lifted the harness onto Cajun's back.

Mrs. Fitzgerald was a large woman who had been married in East Texas to a man named Carter who was half black and then she was widowed in some dubious way, and had come out to the Red River country with her son and daughter and son-in-law and two granddaughters. After Carter died then she married a man named Fitzgerald and then he died of tertiary fever. Her ranch house was two stories, built of horizontal logs and plastered over an eggshell white. It had a wide veranda all around and immense cottonwoods sighing overhead now illuminated by fall leaves the color of lemons. She had a view toward the architectural arrangements of red stone in the bluffs of the Brazos and Indian Mound Mountain. Her son-in-law had been shot dead in some kind of argument over property lines. Elizabeth Fitzgerald now ran the place single-handed with her powerful, carrying voice and bottomless energy. Her daughter, Susan Durgan, and the two granddaughters stayed close to the ranchhouse while Mrs. Fitzgerald rode out sidesaddle to harass her hired hands all day. Her twelve-year-old son Joe Carter rode out with her but stayed twenty yards behind. At present Elizabeth was boxed into a stiff, loud dress, and her vast waistline was armored with a whalebone corset.

"Don't you give Mr. Graham any more than five cents a pound for that dirty salt of his!" she shouted.

"Yes ma'am," said Moses Johnson. His voice was low and re-signed. He cleared his throat.

Two of Fitzgerald's heavy wheelers stood in the corral unhar-nessed and calling out to the other horses. The Fitzgerald team were solid bays and when they sweated the sweat came out in rosettes on their necks like leopard spots. They were her best horses and she would not permit them to be used for a short trip to Weatherford and so instead they backed a pair of half-broke chestnuts into the traces and then placed Britt's light leaders in front of the two-ton freight wagon.

Jim jumped down and stood aside as his father's horses were backed into place. The men got aboard. They would cross Elm Creek and the water would swell the wood of the freight wagons, the felloes and the axles. They would journey on for a day to Weath-erford with tight wheel spokes and undercarriages.

"Didn't Mary send you with no dinner?" Elizabeth Fitzgerald stormed up to Britt where he sat on the wagon seat and peered at the space at his feet. Her big yellow-and-pink-checkered skirts flew out around her feet.

"No ma'am," he said.

"Well, Britt." Elizabeth nodded. "Y'all been fighting. I won't have it, I won't have it."

"Mrs. Fitzgerald." He lifted a hand. "I can fight with my own wife if I want."

"Leave young Jim with me," she said. "I'll get something for you." She turned back to the house. When she came out with a par-cel of food wrapped in a tea towel she said, "Leave young Jim here. I'll send him over to bring Mary and the little ones to stay with me while you're gone."

"Yes ma'am," said Britt. "Jim, you hear?" He watched as his son Jim, in bitter disappointment, wrung his hat between his hands and stalked off to the house.

"Joe ain't going either so no sulking!" Elizabeth shouted after him.

Joe Carter and Jim slunk away toward the creek in a loose adolescent walk and kicked at stones and horse manure.

Moses Johnson glanced at Britt and then to Judge Wilson.

"I guess she don't care for you going all the way to Weatherford." Moses' raspy low voice was thick with the heavy pollen in the air. His lips worked with the effort of not saying anything more.

"It ain't that," said Britt.

"Well." Moses shifted the reins from hand to hand. The two lead horses shifted the straight-bar driving bits in their mouths. They were impatient to go. The cool wind was inviting.

"You could bring her back something fine from Weatherford," he said.

Britt looked ahead at the road. "Maybe that would help. I don't know."

And so they started and the water of the creek flashed up in sprays around them, flew out in arcs from the passage of the wheels, the pools dotted with cottonwood leaves. Overhead the sandhill cranes and the great white egrets drifted like ash in shifting planes, heading south.

Chapter 2

❧

THAT DAY OF October 13, when the men were in Weatherford buying supplies, a combined force of seven hundred
Comanche and Kiowa poured down into what the white people
knew as Young County. The force split up on the drainage of Rab-
bit Creek, and several hundred Kiowa and Comanche men turned
west and rode down both banks of Elm Creek. The first people they
came upon were Joel Meyers and his son Paul and they killed both
of them. A lance went straight through Joel Meyers and as he fell he
clawed at it but within seconds his lungs had filled with blood and
it poured out of his mouth so that although inside his head he heard
himself calling for his son, no words came out.

Paul ran for a hundred yards or so until Hears the Dawn caught
him by his home-knit suspenders and dragged him for a long way
while others shot arrows into his left eye and his abdomen and his
chest and at last Hears the Dawn dropped him because the others were already galloping toward the Fitzgerald cabin. On the way
they shot down Joseph Meyers. He spun backward over the cantle of
his saddle and turned a complete somersault and lay dead facedown
in the grass. Two men stopped to disembowel him, and take his

scalp, and divide his body into quarters as if to drive every last sign of humanity from his remains.

As they came on toward the Fitzgerald place on Elm Creek Mary talked and talked and sang and had done so all morning, but had never said a word about what had taken place between herself and Britt. Susan quietly told her mother to quit asking and not to get involved in black people's affairs. Lottie Durgan, age three, refused to share a June bug on a string with Cherry Johnson, age five, calling her a nigger, and was heartily slapped by Elizabeth for saying nigger, and the June bug flew away high, high into the cool air trailing a thread, the last length of red thread in Elizabeth's sewing kit, trailing it like a tiny line of blood.

The women heard them coming. It was unmistakable. The roar of more than a hundred horses at full gallop. There was no other sound like it in the world. It was like some giant piece of machinery bearing down on them from the north along the creek. Elizabeth Fitzgerald dropped her sausage grinder and grabbed for the powder horn and the ramrod but she spilled the powder. *"Susan, Susan!"* she screamed. Pieces of beef and slithering entrails spilled from a pan and flopped writhing on the kitchen floor.

Her daughter Susan Durgan had already loaded the forty-year-old Kentucky long rifle and ran out the door and on until she was out from under the roof of the veranda. She lifted the heavy flintlock, standing on the stones of the path. Mary grabbed the smaller children by their wrists and flung them inside the door so hard Millie Durgan, who was eighteen months old, fell on her face and skidded into the washstand. Elizabeth scooped up the gunpowder with a page she had torn out of Deuteronomy. Jim Johnson and Joe Carter were both now twelve years old and they knew they had to act as men but they were without weapons. They had entered into another life within seconds. All that they had been thinking of and talking about moments before were now things that might have been written down in some ancient text that told of life long ago.

Susan stood on the path stones and aimed the long rifle carefully. She brought down Little Buffalo with one shot but then they were on her and hacking at her. Elizabeth saw that her daughter was dead and shut the door as Susan Durgan was cut to pieces by the first men who reached her. She was dragged out into the yard by one leg and her clothes stripped from her. They hacked at her white breasts. She had life enough left to try to turn toward the door to see that it was shut and then all her life and her blood erupted from her chopped neck arteries. Elizabeth and the two larger boys threw the table and the chests up against the door but it could not be held.

Hears the Dawn and a man named That's It smashed through the door and kicked away the remnants of boards and hinges. Suddenly the cabin was full of men. Their hands reached out and took hold of flesh and balled up into fists and struck. A Kiowa and a Comanche each took one of Jim Johnson's arms and claimed him. Then they began to fight with one another until at last Aperian Crow, a Koitsenko of the Kiowa, turned in exasperation and shot the boy dead. In the crowded, violent confines of the room the explosion was deafening.

In the thick gunsmoke Comanche and Kiowa dragged the little girls and Jube out of their hiding places in the other rooms. They tied Joe Carter's hands and beat him over the head with their rifle barrels. They smashed all the crockery and tore the featherbeds apart and threw up handsful of drifting down into the air. They ripped open the last bag of flour and scattered it and poured dirt and sand into the cornmeal bin. Mary and Elizabeth were tied to horses. The children were held in front by men. Then they were out and on the open prairie, riding hard. Susan Durgan's scalp and its tangled brown hair bounced on the pommel of a man named Eaten Alive. As he rode, the bobby pins and the comb came out of it and fell into the grass.

They ran the Texans' stolen horses before them, the saddle horses and the gasping great bay draft horses, and then finally they halted beyond the Clear Fork of the Trinity. Three or four men stripped both women of their clothes so that they could not run away. They threw fuel on a great fire. In the bright, manic and arid night air thorn branches were seized by fire and burned into black script. The men danced in a delicate, lifting step as if the earth no longer anchored them. Each man danced for himself alone, and the men at the drum sang in a high, tenor plainsong about war and the quick, beautiful horses that they owned and loved, horses that had brought them out of the northern mountains and carried them against their enemies. The men sometimes left off the dance and raped Elizabeth Fitzgerald and Mary Johnson. They tied the women's legs apart and bound their ankles to brush while one man after another forced himself into the heavy white woman and the black woman. Mary tried to shove the first one away by grabbing his chin and forcing his head back, screaming. A man who moments before had been singing at the fire smashed her head with a rock. It sounded like someone had dropped a melon from a great height.

Then after many men had had their turn the younger boys came. A twelve-year-old Kiowa boy got up smiling and his groin was covered in blood. Mary lay very still. The Kiowa boy wrapped her dress around his shoulders and said *yabba-babba-wuh-huh* as if he could imitate Mary's speech. He then looked over his shoulder at the older men who had tired and were sitting by the fire on packsaddles. They laughed and so he began kicking Elizabeth in her dense, padded flesh.

No, said Elizabeth. No, no. She fought to pull her legs together.

Joe Carter, who was twelve and also naked, rose up with his wrists tied and threw himself at the Kiowa boy, screaming. *"You fucking Indian, you goddamned red nigger!"* He bore the boy over backward and kneed him in the balls and the boy doubled up, snorting. Joe Carter was on top when Hears the Dawn brought down his knife on Joe's neck, severing his spinal column. For long moments Joe Carter kicked and trembled spasmodically. He lay on his face in the dirt, his arms beneath him and kicked out one last time like a mechanical toy and then lay still.

In the slow dim moments before dawn the Comanche named Esa Havey came and cut the cords that tied Elizabeth and Mary. He sat down and looked at both of them and the children who had come to sleep beside them in the night; Cherry, age five, and Jube

Johnson, age nine, Lottie Durgan who was three, and little Millie who was eighteen months. The children were silent and still. They knew that they might die at the hands of these men and their mothers could not protect them. Elizabeth looked back at Esa Havey. He slapped her hard and her nose began to bleed. He did not like a woman's direct stare. Elizabeth looked down. It seemed that she would be able to travel. If she were not able to stay on a horse they would kill her. Mary sat up and smiled. Esa Havey watched her. He looked closely at her eyes. Both of her eyes were open and focused so she would probably not die from the blow to her head but she was strange. Mary blew a kiss to him from her bloody mouth. He stood up and walked away in the dark.

"Mary?" said Elizabeth. She was whispering. "Mary."

The outline of Mary's cheekbones shone in the starlight. Her eyes wandered. "Night, late," said Mary.

Elizabeth was silent for a long time. If only Mary would not have a seizure, if only she could ride, they might live.

"Yes, we're out very late," Elizabeth said, and watched as Mary stroked her hand over Cherry's wildly waving hair. "We'll have to get home, here, one of these days."

Mary nodded but said nothing.

"We'll have to do some hard riding, Mary," said Elizabeth.

Mary nodded.

"Mary, can you talk?"

"Yes."

"Do you understand?"

"Yes."

"Well, tell me what I just said."

Mary turned her large dark eyes toward the flames that cracked up around twisted wood, around the hard dry brush that left little scent or smoke. Sparks floated upward to the yellow stone of the low bluffs of the Dry Fork of the Trinity River. The men moved among the horses. They pulled out their war stallions and let them go to rest and graze and follow as they would. One of the men brought out a stumbling, lamed pinto. There was a shot. Something heavy fell with an earthen crash. The men began to cut pieces from the pinto.

"I don't care what you just said." Mary said this very clearly. Then she bent down and pressed her cheek against the top of Cherry's head. "Undin Jim," she whispered. "Un Jim din."

Elizabeth pushed back her bloody hair and she felt her nakedness against the world. One man had grabbed at her nipples and wrenched them repeatedly, as if he were trying to tear them off, and now there were knotted swellings under both nipples. Her breasts hung down heavily, weighted with bruises and pus. Her son Joe's body lay in the brush where someone had dragged it. Now flies were lighting on it, and she knew flies were buzzing about the bodies of young Jim Johnson and her daughter Susan where she lay in the yard with a bald and bony skull. Maybe the dogs had come to them already and she understood that she would have to think about whether she wanted to live or die. She couldn't think at the moment. Her two granddaughters sat awake and silent with their hands gripped around her arms. She would have to live for now.

"Mary, Jim is dead."

Mary put her hands to her eyes. "Half and half," she said. She pressed her hands against her eyes and tears ran down between her fingers.

Elizabeth understood she meant something about when the two men who had grabbed him each by one arm.

"Don't let them hear you cry," she said.

"Half and half," whispered Mary.

THEY WERE THREE days riding and on the second day Esa Havey came and threw bundles of cloth at Mary and Elizabeth. The women pulled on the remains of their underclothes and dresses and pulled them between their legs so that they would not rasp and chafe against the horses. The men would not give them saddles because they were war saddles. They would be ruined and polluted by the women's blood. On the second and third nights ten or so of the men came to them and took their fill of sex but they stopped beating them although one man with otter-wrapped braids could not resist smashing Elizabeth across the breasts when he saw she was trying to protect her swollen nipples against his rough pounding. She did not scream. He wanted to make her scream and so he took up his bow and once again hit her across the breasts. The pain was so deep and fundamental that she fainted. After that loud words came from a man, shouted at another group of men. The men seemed divided in some way. They were arguing. Two men stood face-to-face and shouted.

Mary sat up and watched them with interest. She did not seem to care about the men who came to her and shoved themselves inside her. Now she watched their faces in the firelight and their gestures and listened to their edged, dangerous voices. She sat beside Elizabeth and absentmindedly patted her head as if she were a child or a pet. Then she turned and circled little Millie under one arm and Cherry under another. Jube sat with Lottie. Then Mary took Cherry's hand and made her pat Elizabeth on the forehead. Mary hummed a little and then as Elizabeth began to make groaning noises she pressed her hand over the white woman's mouth. She knew the men were arguing about them; that the men had begun to lose the luminous aura that had sustained them in their ride and their attacks and their war-fury. It was drifting away. They were like men who had been very drunk and were now falling into the gray and ashy world of sobriety and were not yet hungover. To get out of that gray and ashy world and back into the wild light of sheer aggression they might rape the little girls. But somehow she could not put this into words, even in her mind.

Mary kept her hand tight over Elizabeth's mouth and after a few moments the older woman stopped groaning. She sat up and held her arms across her breasts as if the pressure might help relieve the pain.

"Mary," she said. "I want to die."

"Too, too, when too," Mary whispered, and lifted a hand to her head wound.

Elizabeth could not make sense of this. Esa Havey and another man spoke loudly and signed to a crowd of the other men and boys in front of the fire. They used the Plains sign language. They did not all have hair alike. A tall man with a slightly receding chin got up and started on a determined walk toward the captives. Even though Mary threw out both hands above Lottie Durgan's head he grasped Lottie by the arm and knocked Mary aside. Esa Havey came up and shoved the man backward until he let go of Lottie. Elizabeth crawled forward and took hold of her granddaughter's skirt and drew her into her weakened arms.

They stopped arguing. The silence was chilling. Each man turned and saddled his own horse and they threw the women onto barebacked ponies. By this time Elizabeth's arms and face and throat were blistered with the sun and netted with bloody hash marks by the stiff creosote and blackbrush stands. Esa Havey took Lottie Durgan and put the little girl behind him. Lottie did not cry or look at her grandmother. The man with the receding chin came and handed the eighteen-month-old Millie to Mary after he had glanced at Elizabeth and saw her barely clinging to the pony's mane. Then he took Cherry behind him and someone else took Jube. They went on in the night without moon or starlight and the horses carried their heads low to see the ground before them. They moved north under heavy cloud cover, in damp, thick air that seethed with incipient lightning.

IN THE CHILL and rainy dawn the men from Elm Creek came to the formations known as the Stone Houses. The segmented stone cores jutted up out of the rolling steppe lands and from a distance they seemed to be the remains of some sort of ancient structures. They were a mile apart and around them sandstone slabs like paving stones lay half-hidden in the long grass. Britt Johnson, Moses Johnson, the Peveler brothers, and the Wilsons climbed to the top of one of the stone knobs that so resembled a fort or place of sacrifice, a ritual city half begun and then abandoned and gone to ruin.

They stood at the top in the rain, looking north. The rain streamed down out of heaven, obscuring and filling every crevice, dripping from their hats, pouring down the fractured stones, destroying the tracks they had been following for two days. They had come nearly a hundred miles with only a brief rest at night in a fireless camp. They had no more food and the rain was washing away all sign. The horses below were trembling and had trouble walking. Out there in the flatlands and the low swaley valleys the Comanche and the Kiowa could be waiting in ambush and so they could go no farther.

Along the way they had found remnants of the flesh of Susan Durgan's scalp and hair where someone had trimmed the scalp into a small round thing to be fitted onto a hoop. To be tanned and decorated with beads and small hawk bells, carried on a pole like a decoration, a heraldic banner.

"We have to turn back," said Britt. He felt himself subject to a rage he had never known. It was like a strong fever that burned his lips and forehead but left him poised and still. Contained like some kind of unignited explosive. He turned and slid down from the top of the Stone Houses from rock to rock, smeared with yellow and red clay mud. The others followed him.

He walked through the heavy, wet grass to his bay horse and for a moment he was outlined against a gray wall of rain. He put his hand across the saddle seat and leaned his head on his forearm.

"It was Comanche," he said. "The ones they call Comanche."

"Probably." Old man Peveler nodded.

Rain drifted to the south in long columns. Then the sun came clear of the eastern horizon, reluctantly, as if its red light somehow adhered to the level earth. With full light a flock of great birds came up out of the valley of the Red River to the north, their calling noisy and joyful. Hundreds of sandhill cranes lifted from their feeding places out in the flooded bottoms, kiting in the updrafts with laborious upstrokes.

Britt watched them, streaming overhead, towing their insubstantial shadows behind them, and he heard the low, flat call of their archaic voices as they sailed along some million-year-old migration path. With long necks stretched out they skimmed overhead and called out in their hoarse voices of the joy of air and light and their simple lives of clouds and wind and death by predator at every hand and still they soared and sang. Then there were only a few stragglers and then they disappeared toward the south.

Chapter 3

*T*HE MEN WHO decided the fate of the Red Indians lived in the east, under roofs of slate and shingle. There were windows paned with large sheets of glass that looked out comfortably on a dense and busy world. The roofs lined up in slanting layers of coal smoke on each side of narrow streets and these streets were full of hurrying people and vehicles at all hours. Around these great cities, fields like chessboards in snowy whites and tans and the orderly drift of orchards with naked winter limbs. The bells of Philadelphia called out daily in measured peals of the arrival of important ships on the Delaware River. January of 1865 and four degrees of frost. The ice was thick enough on the Schuylkill River at Lemon Hill to support skaters and sleighs and fires made of scrap lumber. Quaker ladies moved across the ice in sweeping skirts. The skates gave them the treasured illusion that they had no legs. They were afflicted with a sort of shy and happy vanity with their own gliding in the smoky snow.

One of the younger Quaker girls waved at Samuel Hammond, whom she had last seen at the Orange Street Meeting in a trance of praying with his eyes open or thinking of something secular. He did not see her and stalked on through the snow with his collar up and a tall, cold silk hat pulled low on his forehead.

Samuel Hammond was a small man who had just come back from the war. He walked on and caught a streetcar and then disembarked. He entered the house at Fourth and Delancey with a stiff feeling, as if he were breasting a hard current coming from a distant spillway. He did not like to refuse the men whom he had come to meet and speak with, and especially he did not like to be seen to refuse a work of such necessity and such urgency, work that had been allowed to fall into the ruinous hands of oily grafters who thought of government money as loose miraculous treasure that came from nowhere and nobody. Money an alchemical miracle come from nothing, without labor. He handed his tall, formal hat to the small butler at the door. The young man grasped the hat and bowed with a jerk that made his reddish bangs fly out.

"They are upstairs, sir!" he said.

"I will follow you."

"Very well!" The boy paused as if disoriented and then laid Samuel's top hat on the hall table with a careful gesture and then began a precise walk up a flight of stairs. Samuel Hammond followed him up the stairs, into a hallway. The January light poured in at the far end through a tall window and the panes danced with the disquieted shadows of bare limbs.

The boy butler headed into the library at a tilt; he took hold of the door handle and paused and said, "Samuel Hammond!"

Samuel knew all of the men in the room; for the most part he knew them from that leisurely life before the war when people were sure of things. Merchants, a government accountant, all of them of the Society of Friends Indian Committee except for Lewis Henry Morgan, who was of some other Protestant denomination and had become an Indian expert. The young butler paused and then turned himself precisely 180 degrees until he was facing the hallway and marched out and shut the door behind him.

Dr. John Reed held out a fragile hand. He spoke to Samuel in the old-fashioned informal second person.

"Thou hast a grim expression on thy face, young man."

"Dr. Reed," said Samuel. To the rest of the men who had risen, smiling, he said, "Lewis, I am glad to see you. Peter, Absalom, Joseph, delighted."

The fire in the library fireplace had burned down to coals. They had been here an hour or two before his appointed time. He took a chair. Samuel was in his mid-thirties, five foot seven, thin and clean-shaven, without scars or wounds despite a year as a volunteer ambulance driver with Sherman's army in Georgia. Some near misses. No real hits. Samuel had a habit of lowering his head slightly and gazing up at people from under his eyebrows. It made him seem considering and grave and mistrusting. Over the fireplace was the full-length portrait of Thomas Cope with his hesitant smile and a wall of books behind him and beyond the books in abstract space a merchant ship in a storm.

"We have invited you to plague you once again about the agency," said Peter Simons. He was nearly sixty and heavy in the waist and shoulders, a draper and importer. His white hair stuck up in a cowlick that was coming unplastered, and it made him look like a red-cheeked toy. Simons and Samuel had twice shared their consignments in the same ship's holds. Simons laid his hands on a stack of folders on the library table. "But this time we have new horrors for you to think about."

Samuel smiled and pinched up his trousers at the knee and sat down.

"What?" he said. "More corruption?"

"A great deal more," said Absalom Rivers. He had a permanent ink-stain on his forefinger from filling out government forms in triplicate. "We are shocked, of course." He seemed to be counting up the number of shocks and dividing them by four. "Their depravities are without number." He reached for a folder. "The latest: the superintendent of the Office of Indian Affairs has spent twenty thousand, four hundred and ten dollars and, ah"—he flipped over a sheet of paper in the stack—"forty cents that was to have gone to a farming project for the Osage tribe in Kansas on a home for himself in Westchester County." He looked up. Absalom had a full head of dark hair, and it seemed to Samuel that he was such a complete accountant that, as it was said in Matthew, every hair of his head was numbered. He had been elected clerk of the business committee at the Yearly Meeting of Friends for his dry obsession with columns of figures as well as his occasional visitations of the Inner Light. Samuel wondered if he had attempted to calculate its speed.

"That's terrible," said Samuel. "The army contractors were nearly as bad." He jiggled his foot and then stopped and placed both shoes flat on the floor.

"Yes, yes." They nodded and murmured. It was a subject loaded with explosive and combustible matter.

Joseph Kane slid forward in his seat. "The war will be over in a few months. We must not only live in the present but look ahead." He raised one finger. His brown and gray hair glistened in the winter light and his voice was a high, thin tenor. "Looking ahead, we have succeeded in urging the Peace Policy and appointing Friends as Indian agents." His eyes were brown too, or hazel; his coat was chocolate-colored. He turned to Lewis Henry Morgan. "Lewis, say something."

Morgan was a handsome, restless man. "Samuel, they have me in a headlock. I am supposed to be the final clinch in convincing you to take the Indian Agency out in Indian Territory."

"Not quite. Not quite. In a way." Kane's rich browns were like imported cocoa. "Not quite the final one. But Lewis is here to give us some of his insights into the nature of the red man. Having spent so long among them." Joseph Kane owned three merchantmen and had just bought his first steam-driven bottom a month ago. He was related several times over to the Cope family and had that family's sturdy probity; he shared their long history in both the Society of Friends and in Philadelphia's shipping community. Thomas Cope smiled blindly from his frame over the mantelpiece. Quaker, shipowner, railroad magnate, who proved that a man could serve both God and Mammon. A deeply kind man. An example to them all, except he had not been faced with a civil war.

Samuel twisted in his chair. "I see. Lewis is here to give us some insights into the nature of the red man." He paused. "Why not ask a red man?"

He watched them sit back in their chairs and make very small wavering, defensive gestures. Their minds turned somersaults down the center aisles of their egalitarian beliefs. They turned to one another but no one said anything.

Morgan laughed. "You are cruel, Samuel." He put both sets of fingertips on the library table and shifted the papers. "We had a wonderful summer among the Seneca when you were fifteen."

"We did." Samuel smiled.

"I am free now to travel up the Missouri River, and pursue my studies, my deepest interest, and I urge you to do the same." He removed his fingertips and folded his hands together. "Your year was hard. I know."

Samuel nodded. "The title of your work is *Systems of Consanguinity,* isn't it?"

"*Systems of Consanguinity and Affinity of the Human Family.* Miraculously saved." Morgan had been prepared to deliver his monumental work of fifteen years on the nomenclature of personal relationships of various Indian tribes to the Smithsonian when a great part of the Smithsonian building had burned down a month past, in December.

"God had other plans for thy work," said Dr. Reed, "than to be consumed in a fire." Morgan bowed slightly to the aged doctor. "And Samuel, he has other plans for thee."

Samuel inclined his head in a short nod. "It is the same as last time. I have business interests to attend to after my year's absence. I find that I must look to the future as well as all of you." He shifted again in the chair. Everything was so clean. The year with the army had been several centuries of mud and blood and uniforms in rags, a time of smoky campfires and rain falling unregarded on the eyes of the dead, men nodding in comatose sleep with their socks over their rifle muzzles. Hospital tents smelling of dirty flesh and excrement. He had come back amazed at the cleanliness he had always taken for granted. The spotless, ironed cuffs of the men before him. His own spotless ironed cuffs. The clean suits and the noiseless room, a shining wood floor and the sparkling glass of the lamp chimney. Everybody's shoes of unbroken leather and two pairs of whole shoe-laces. "Is this supposed to be good for me or good for the Indians?"

"The Indians," said Dr. Reed. "God is asking thee to serve yet more."

"Who else from the Friends?"

"Two, both in Indian Territory. Kansas and the area they call Oklahoma."

Samuel shook his head. "I must look to the future."

He was on the very edge of saying something more, that some-day he would marry and have a family and must think about pro-viding for them. But Peter Simons, the red-cheeked and glistening draper with his sober-colored, rich coat, his spiky white forelock, was the grandfather of a young woman who a year ago had sent Samuel's ring back to him. This because he had volunteered as an ambulance driver. Her letter was acerbic and replete with single and double underlinings on such phrases as *the sinfulness of supporting this barbaric war in any way and I see you have abandoned your Quaker upbringing to aid and comfort those who fly in the face of God's com-mandments.* Quakers had the gift of making people uncomfortable. Especially other Quakers. Especially himself. He would have said the same thing two years ago.

Peter Simons knew what he had been about to say and slowly closed his eyes and then turned to the library fire and opened them again on the red piling of coals. He ran his hand through his spiking snow-white hair. Simons was her grandparent and could not tell the little beast to keep her opinions to herself.

There was something more that no one was saying. Samuel waited them out. He waited, and so did they, in the comfortable sort of silence to which they had all become accustomed. Four of them because they were Friends, and Lewis Henry Morgan because he had spent so many years traveling among the Seneca, the Ojibway, the Sioux, the Crow, and the Mandan, people who often sat in total silence, like a species of violence-prone Quakers, while thoughts and images streamed through their minds. The Indians seeking a sign from their dream spirit and Friends waiting for the Inner Light.

The door creaked open, and the young butler tilted forward into the room and straightened himself smartly with a chair back.

"There's lamb," he said. "And tea and all."

Joseph Kane sat back so that the butler and another serving-man could lay his plate of lamb in front of him. Kane shifted and tugged down his brown coat sleeve and seemed about to say something but then didn't. He touched his watch in its watch pocket in a habitual, compulsive gesture. His mind seemed to tick over like the works of his timepiece.

Dr. Reed talked about the new Indian Bureau. He ate sparingly. Who could keep an eye on what was happening in the distant western lands when Atlanta was burning and a million freed black slaves were following the Union armies and men were dying by the thousands all over the South? It was not the kind of thing that had a high priority in 1865.

He spoke of the incredible corruption in the Office of Indian Affairs and what had happened to the men who ran it.

Nothing. Nothing, not a thing. Nobody was ever charged. They promised the red men clothes and they sent out two hundred men's summer suits and every one of them was large enough for a three-hundred-pound man, and so the Indians cut the sleeves from them and made leggings for the children. They had sent flour that was full of weevils and bacon that had turned green and portable soup in chunks that boiled up into something like wallpaper paste. How could they expect human beings to remain at the agency and live on remnants, leavings, garbage?

The new Indian Bureau was going to be handed over to the various religious denominations, and that would take care of the corruption. He hoped. A man can always hope. Dr. Reed had some doubt about the Methodists, but the Episcopalians were fairly solid. However, the Baptists might end up holding wild camp meetings with the red men out there somewhere in the Rocky Mountains and who knew what would happen then? He thought about asking for some regulations that Indian agents not be allowed to speak in tongues.

"The salary for the Indian agent at the Comanche Agency will be provided by the government and managed by the Society of Friends Indian Committee," he said. "We have convinced this Congress to dissolve the Office of Indian Affairs, and so assign each of the tribes, or tribal areas, to various religious denominations."

Samuel looked up with his fork in his hand, surprised.

"I would have thought it impossible that Congress would ever dissolve any government agency," he said.

"Well, they have. Now, the Episcopalians are taking the Sioux."

"Really?"

"And, let's see, the Methodists have—" The shipowner paused.

Peter Simons said, "They have the Ojibway."

Samuel was surprised in a reserved and expressionless way. They had convinced the government to disband the Office of Indian Affairs and then the government, out of its ability to call into being these bureaucracies as if conjuring them up from some book of magic, invented the Indian Bureau.

"And what tribe does the Society of Friends have?"

"The Comanche and the Kiowa, and a group called the Kiowa-Apache," Lewis Morgan said.

The green mint jelly sparkled on the tender meat. Samuel was hungry, and so he ate steadily and quietly.

"And what do we know about these tribes?"

Morgan lifted his fork. "Ah, let's see now. The Kiowa are one thing, and then there is this group of some kind of Apache that lives with them and has for many years. They are called Kiowa-Apache. They don't speak the same language but they always live together."

"The salary is adequate," said the accountant. "We want an honest agent who does not have to make up years of absence from his home by illicit trading. It is five thousand a year."

"That's very generous," said Samuel.

Dr. Reed nodded his white head and put his papery hands into his lap. "This committee has met now for a good many years. Our hearts have gone out to the suffering of the Indian people." He thought for a moment. "I was born in 1789. I remember my parents talking about the Shawnee Wars in Ohio, and the Pennsylvania militia's murder of ninety Moravian Christian Indians at Gnadenhutten. Used hatchets on them while they knelt and prayed. Lord Amherst's distribution of smallpox-infected blankets. What treaty have we not broken with these people?"

"Yes," said Peter Simons, and there were murmurs of assent around the table. "Have you read the reports about the massacre in Colorado? Colorado State troops falling upon a peaceful village of Cheyenne."

Morgan nodded. "I read them last week."

"Did you know any of them, Lewis?"

"No. What does it matter?"

"All women and children. They did fiendish, fiendish things. How can this go on?" Simons looked around the room. "The colonel should be taken under arrest."

"And the Georgian's attacks on a civilized, literate people, the Cherokee," said Dr. Reed. "Our Meeting raised funds for them and sent relief, and they died and wept all the way to Oklahoma Territory."

"I know." Samuel laid down his fork.

" 'What owest thou unto thy Lord?' Psalm Fifty-two. And so Elizabeth Fry asked of us all."

"Yes, of course."

Beyond the library window came the sound of the great bell in the Swedish church. The clanging wavered over the rooftops and drifted in troubled tones through the glass of the windows. Some important ship had come into the docks on the Delaware. Then a rooster shrieked in the stableyard behind the house, again and again.

"That is a fighting cock," said Rivers, the accountant. "That boy. He was warned he would be fired."

"I would imagine," said Simons.

"He fights them down there with the Irish in Southwark."

"Well, he is young and Irish himself," said Kane.

"What ship would that be?" said Samuel. "That they are ringing the bell for?"

Dr. Reed waved away the ship and the fighting cock and the Irish boy butler.

"Samuel, our confidence in thee is very strong. I have prayed about this. I have taken it to the Lord."

"Confident in what way?" said Samuel.

"Thou hast not wavered in thy beliefs in this past year?"

"No." Samuel said it without hesitation. His beliefs remained true and perfect in an icy, remote way. And he, Samuel, had observed with interest as his own former personality contracted and then realigned itself and changed. After a while he became a skilled and fearless ambulance driver who had no idea who he was. His beliefs turned, suspended in the air, lit by another light in crystalline majesty, and in quiet moments of exhaustion or sleep and the dreams that came to him then, he saw them shining beyond his reach. There was always a sort of grieving in his mind.

"We know, first of all, that you would be that person which you would ask another to be. That you would help the red man to question his distance from God and point out that the distance might be closed. Only after the Indian people confess to their Creator, *I have used violence in my life to carry off what was not mine*, would they come to see that violence keeps mankind from God's own light and His presence, and that light, and that presence, is far beyond anything we might value here below. Far beyond."

"I understand that," said Samuel.

"Thou art needed," said Dr. Reed. "These people have need of thee."

Lewis Morgan watched Samuel while Dr. Reed spoke in that ancient, thready voice. Everyone nodded. After a long pause Morgan turned to Samuel and said, "These are unsettled tribes you would have to deal with. I believe they only came onto the plains when they got horses from the Spaniards. Before that they were apparently on foot and unable to penetrate the Great Plains where the buffalo lived. Now they have become rich and strong. They have a tight, and I would say almost impenetrable, network of kinship. Their lives are lives of action."

Samuel nodded with a polite expression. He was the youngest man at the table, and the less he said the better. He lowered his head and gazed up at Morgan. "But I have not said I would deal with it at all, yet."

Morgan nodded. "I understand."

Joseph Kane raised a finger. His hands were speckled brown with age. "By kindness. By reasoned argument."

"Of course," said Samuel.

The shipowner said, "So much violence has been used against the red man. The Texans will be coming home from the war, in-ured, accustomed to scenes of slaughter and violence we still have trouble comprehending. They have driven the red man from his own hunting grounds before the war, and they will continue to do so after it. An enormous reservation has been set aside for our red men, the—" He paused.

"The Comanche, the Kiowa, and the Kiowa-Apache," said Mor-gan, patiently. "And I believe some Wichitas."

"Who has the Wichita?" The elderly doctor leaned forward.

"I think they are more or less tossed in with the others," said Morgan.

Joseph Kane still had his finger in the air. "As I said, an enormous reservation set aside for these tribes. The Texans are to leave them alone, and not to encroach on their hunting grounds. Now, there will be a military presence." His hand fell to his side and touched the ticking watch. "But the soldiers are for the purpose of prevent-ing the Texans from taking the Indians' land."

"What if they decide they don't want to be on a reservation?" said Samuel.

"They will see that it is to their advantage. It is to prevent them from being abused by the white settlers." He sat back. "Samuel, at last we have a chance to do things another way than by military force, or any force."

Samuel glanced at Lewis Morgan, but Morgan regarded Samuel with a blank, steady stare.

"Is this not what we believe in?" Kane shifted his brown coat and looked around at the others.

"It is," said Samuel.

"In no way will you present them with guards or with punishments."

Samuel glanced down at his plate as the manservant took it away.

Dr. Reed said, "Early in the fifties a large force of Texas Rangers attacked a perfectly peaceful reservation and slaughtered women and children sleeping in their beds. Now it will take a long time before the Indians of Texas ever trust a white man again. But that trust can be regained."

Samuel said, "I want to thank you for considering me." He moved the salt cellar around in a circle and lifted his head as the furious rooster beyond the window hammered at the windy spring air.

"And we have especially considered you," said the accountant Absalom Rivers, "because you have lived through the violence of Sherman's campaign for ten months and several weeks. Some disagreed with your decision to drive an ambulance, but I did not. I certainly did not. You will not be terrified or unstrung by loud explosions, gunfire, or expressions of violence, or the art of bookkeeping."

Samuel stared at the crystal salt cellar. "The art of bookkeeping." Then he said, "But I have my life to put back together again. I have invested in a cargo for England and half-interest in a ship. That is money committed."

"I know," said the shipowner in his brown suit. He waved one hand. "I know."

"And when these things are taken care of and my finances secure, perhaps in a year or so, I would consider it."

Joseph Kane nervously took out his watch and didn't look at it and put it back. Peter Simons the glossy draper with his white hair looked down at his shoes. Dr. Reed coughed like the burning of paper. Lewis Morgan looked around curiously.

Joseph Kane said, "Samuel, the ship you have invested in, the *Monongahela*, is on the rocks of the Cape Tipman bight. I received the telegram this morning. The cargo is thrown overboard. I don't believe any of it is salvageable."

Samuel said, "No."

"Yes."

The great bell of the Swedish church rang on and on, a warning that a Philadelphia ship was reported in peril on the sea.

Chapter 4

❧

THE *MONONGAHELA* CAME into the docks with four inches of freeboard and three jets of water leaping out of her innards into the Delaware River. The bells of the Swedish church rang out once again in celebration of her return home, in whatever condition. The pumps belowdecks kept her afloat long enough to creep into docking, throwing out great arcs, a ton a minute. She had come to grief on the rocks of Cape Tipman, bilged with sixteen feet of water in the holds. The two hundred passengers were got off safely, but her cargo was lost. It had been thrown, barrel by barrel, into the sea. Salt and flour streamed out into a gale-force wind.

She had been raised by hiring a salvage crew to force empty, sealed oil barrels through the gaping underwater hole and into her hold. They then fothered the hole with one hundred and eighty feet of canvas in an enormous bandage around the entire waist of the ship, and as it passed over the wounded strakes the canvas was drawn in and clung to the hole in an interior bulge and sealed it. The pumps and the barrels full of air began to lift the rocking body of the ship. This during a storm. The men who went down into the water could hear the grinding noise of the *Monongahela*'s keel on the stone ledges. A terrifying sound, the noise of the Atlantic itself, as it ground up men and ships on unseen rocks and then tilted them over into the bottomless sea. The divers were hauled shaking to the deck and offered hot tea. Since the ship's owners belonged to the Society of Friends, they were not allowed spirituous liquors, and the divers cursed the goddamned Quakers and drank their scalding milky tea in offended silence.

After the meeting with the Friends' Indian Committee, Sam Hammond had received telegram after telegram in his office at the Old London Coffee House at Front and Market concerning the *Monongahela*'s progress past one port after another. Now he could see her coming in like a whale about to beach itself, her broken mainmast lashed down on the deck with only a foresail and a sprit-sail flying. The ship's lee rail foamed five inches above the Delaware. He had raised the money to purchase the cargo and had borrowed the money for an interest in the ship itself.

Below his window on Front Street an entire circus was unpacking itself. They had come from England to gladden and entertain the people of Philadelphia now that the war was nearly over, to amaze them with women in tights and men with red noses. The Liberty horses staggered in the street from the unaccustomed feel of solid ground after their sea-crossing, and some predator in a draped cage was being loaded onto a dray. Samuel would also be liable for the repair of the ship as well as the lost cargo and the cost of the ship's recovery. He pressed his hands against his eyes as the circus disentangled itself and went off down the street with trumpet and drum. He thanked the Lord for this chastisement. He prayed he would learn and understand whatever it was the Lord meant for him to understand by this, and by many things when you came to think about it.

He would sell his experimental farm in Germantown. Its ordered, quilted little fields and the regimented orchard. Then he would accept the position of Indian agent to the Comanche and Kiowa and the Kiowa-Apache in Indian Territory.

Perhaps this was what the Lord was trying to tell him with the wreck of the *Monongahela*. This was Providence at work in his life, taking him in charge for its own great purposes. A rainy February wind, spangled with drops, drove over the waterfront. The jury-rigged foresail and spritsail of the ship rattled down from their yards and the anchor chain roared like a metal waterfall and the sloshing sailors flung ropes to the bollards. Other sailors in other ships watched the *Monongahela* come sloppily in and greeted her with jeers and bits of rude songs.

Samuel rode the horsecars down Fairmont. From the window he listened to the shouts of the street vendors, selling fish and white wine by the glass to passersby. Small Irish boys cried out *'Ot paday-das, 'ot padaydas!* The car rumbled over the granite cobblestones. He jumped off at Twenty-second Street and walked to Mount Vernon Street, its row of elegant brick houses. The three-story structures with their neat white steps, their brightly painted doors and brass knockers, pressed close to one another. They were both small and long, and elegant as miniatures.

He came into the house on Mount Vernon and rested his arm on the gray granite mantelpiece. The girl had lit the fire not long ago. The fireplace was elegantly carved, and he thought how before long he would be sitting in the open again before a heaped pile of burning sticks.

He went to the back garden to sit in the cold on the cast-iron bench under the one slim walnut tree. Around his small garden tall brick walls looked down. He held his grandfather's Bible between his two hands like a great directory, himself a man trying to recall a certain address before opening it. The *Monongahela* and its ruined strakes and the tons of good New England flour heaved into the Atlantic sent outrage like a small tidal wave into his brain.

People did not really understand who they were until they had been tested, and then came the terrible surprise that they did not know who this new person was either. A succession of strangers, interlopers, banged through the door of the mind without knocking. He recalled the pressurized sound of a mortar shell, and sometime later he found himself wandering peacefully about in the Georgia woods singing a filthy song about a widow from Baltimore. A thoughtful, quiet soldier with a head injury woke up in the Mac-Guire mansion among the other wounded and turned into a loud and aggressive man who could not count to ten. If God meant for us to praise and worship Him, why did He not give us a single self?

When he was twenty he stood up in the Orange Street Meeting on First Day to denounce John Joseph Gurney's idea that justification and sanctification were two separate things. Now he could no longer remember the dispute. It had been intricate and consuming but he could not well recall it.

He did not doubt that Christ had died for him, but which one of him? The adamantine young man bright as a blade and full of theological certainties, or the Samuel Hammond on a wagon seat, worn and brown and chewing tobacco in the rain, waiting for the wounded? And what of himself now, an urban man of Philadelphia in a prewar suit and deeply in debt?

After a while the light filtering through the leaves fell around him and into his very self. If you ask and ask sincerely you will be granted that inner light. He had to ask and ask again. Time passed. Finally he opened his Bible to Psalm 139.

> You have hedged me behind and before and laid Your hand upon me. Such knowledge is too wonderful for me; it is high, I cannot attain it. Where can I go from Your spirit? Or where can I flee from Your presence? If I ascend unto heaven You are there; if I make my bed in hell, behold, You are there. If I take the wings of the morning and dwell in the uttermost parts of the sea, even there Your hand shall lead me, and Your right hand shall hold me.

A FEW WEEKS later Samuel took the horsecars to Front and Market, where the cars stopped because the grade of the street down to Water Street was too steep for the horses. He and Lewis Morgan walked down the slippery cobblestones on a bright March day.

Samuel's hair stood up in brown peaks and low sea-clouds scudded overhead at a rapid rate and bars of sunlight flashed between them. The waterfront smelled of salt and sewage and the piercing odor of creosote.

He carried brown paper packages of stout serge cloth, portable soup packed in squares between sheets of waxed paper, hard, unmelting spermaceti candles. The sailors' arms were hideous with tattoos from the Sandwich Islands, dark and strawberry-colored designs of naked women and the names of ships and wives and girlfriends, anchors and palm trees, blue-black on human skin.

"And their language?" said Samuel.

"I have no idea," said Morgan. "I can't think of the name of the fellow who is trying to classify the Indian languages. Schoolcraft has done quite a lot on the Chippewa."

They walked past the ancient salt and fish warehouse with its checkered English brick, and stopped to stare up at Irwin and Young's ship carvings, fastened to the outside wall of the second story. There were women with naked breasts and pink nipples and a grim, toothy sailor in bright paint that seemed to have thrust himself through the window and was grinning at the far shore of the Delaware with teeth like piano keys. Third and Dock was dense with warehouses and markets and foot traffic, donkeys lifted from their feet between the shafts as more and more layers of stiff, papery dried mackerel were thrown onto their carts.

"And their beliefs?" Samuel stopped to look in the window of Bingham's Fish and Provisions. "Does this dried soup look better than the stuff I bought at Levin's?"

Morgan put his hand over his forehead like a visor and leaned against the glass and squinted against the reflections. "No, it's got flies in it." They walked on. "No one knows. We have studied the tribes on the Upper Missouri because they are accessible. We can get to them, you see. You can take a steamboat. These southern plains tribes lie great distances overland with no water transportation. No water. One creeps from waterhole to river to waterhole, as I have heard."

"They take scalps," said Samuel. "What in God's name for?"

Morgan lifted his eyebrows and held up a forefinger. "Now that is interesting. At our latest meeting a fellow named Gaynor, Charles Gaynor, he is a natural philosopher and antiquarian just come back from the Russian Far East. He went there with Gennady Nevelskoy to the Amur River. Lord, how I envy him." They strode onward on the smooth rounded cobblestones. "Myself with a recently bereaved family."

Samuel touched his arm. He could think of nothing to say that would not have to be shouted over the noise of the passing vehicles.

"It's all right. Thank you. Anyhow . . ." Morgan cleared his throat. He paused. Then he said, "Gaynor did some excavation there on the coast of Sakhalin in Siberia. At the risk of his life. Shoveling around in the ice and dirt in a burial mound. Found four mummies of very ancient provenance that had been scalped and the scalps sewn back on."

"Really."

"Just so."

"I see."

"He said his thought about it was that the mummies, you know, when they were live persons, had been scalped in some sort of war, or attack, and then their own people or tribe had most likely gone to a great deal of trouble to recover the scalps and sew them back on. Thus it is a safe conclusion that it has something to do with a person's soul, ascent of the soul and so on."

They dodged a coal wagon and walked on. Samuel said, "There must be some similarity between the Comanche and the tribes you have visited."

"What I have heard from the Mandan and Sioux is that the Comanche are perpetually in a state of war with everybody. A Brulé Sioux man, an old man, said they had come from beyond the Rocky Mountains and simply leapt on everybody like tigers. Now you need a spirit stove and a sou'wester."

"No I do not, Lewis. I need a broad-brimmed hat. A good hat you can live under. My old one was lost going into Savannah. It was the best hat I ever had. I miss it."

They found one on Dock Street at a slop draper. It was brown, of beaver felt with a grosgrain ribbon around the edge of the three-inch brim. Samuel set it firmly on his head. "I am ready for arrows and runaways."

They trudged upward again, back up Market to the horse-cars. Samuel and Lewis Henry Morgan stood back while laughing young women fought with their skirts on the step, and filled their seats with their packages and budgets and gloves and yards of skirt hems. The air was heavy with sea mists, and the sliding tilt of gulls overhead in their ash-colored jackets. A sea breeze sprang up out of the northeast, and on Queen Street white curtains were sucked out of the open windows and gestured frantically with embroidered hems.

Samuel was refreshed by the wind. He was going somewhere unknown, the western lands that lay beyond the politics of religion, the interminable splits of the Society of Friends. Beyond prisons, beyond cities, armed with a good hat and portable soup.

In the silence of his little house on Mount Vernon Street he went over the map. It remained resolute and graphic in its inked lines for towns, cities, railroads, until it came to those western lands beyond the Missouri River, and then it faded into vast unmarked spaces, like a door left ajar with a storm coming and the wind blowing in at will.

He went to Germantown to visit his mother and father, his sturdy farmer brother and his brother's wife and children. Their hundreds of acres of wheatland and orchard near Lancaster. They nodded and said very little when he told them he was once again leaving Philadelphia. At prayer together that night his father asked the Lord to make clear His purposes and to help him, Nathaniel Hammond, to understand the paths of the wayward.

Samuel sat with the men of the Society of Friends Indian Committee and went over the paperwork he would be required to complete. Every draft of money and all orders had to be written out in triplicate to avoid the corruption of the old Department of Indian Affairs. He must receive, verify, and then distribute the annuities.

He must see that the annuity goods were shipped out of Leaven-worth in due time. He must hire a clerk, workmen, perhaps a physician, with luck a schoolteacher, and all of these employees' names must be submitted to the Superintendent of Indian Affairs and approved.

The Kiowa and Comanche were to receive $30,000 worth of goods according to the treaty they had signed. These goods were to consist of blankets, brown muslin, satinet, calico, hosiery, needles, thread, suits of men's clothes, butcher knives, iron kettles, frying pans, hoes, and small axes. In addition, rations were to be issued every two weeks; beef, bacon, flour, coffee, sugar, soap, tobacco, and soda. These would be given to the chiefs, who would distribute them among the women of each family. The beef was to be issued alive. The live cattle were to be given to a headman of each family, who had a signed receipt in hand.

The members of the committee went over these stipulations carefully, as if what were written there would bring order and obedience. As if the issuing of calico and sugar would cause the Comanche and the Kiowa to become content, delighted, grateful. That it would inspire them to take up farming and eat vegetables.

"The Indians are what we have made them," said Dr. Reed. "Every war between us and the red man has been precipitated by broken treaties. If they have attacked the settlers, it is because we have made them what they are."

Samuel said, "God made them, sir. I do not think we of Philadelphia have taken on the task of creation."

Dr. Reed stared at him in silence. The kindliness shrank out of his face. After a moment he said, "I see."

Samuel flushed. "I'm sorry, sir. I have spoken out of turn."

Dr. Reed nodded. "It is all right, Samuel. I have known thee from thy schooldays." He turned in his chair and turned back again. "If the Texans would cease to crowd them," he said. "If they would leave the red man alone. There is room out there for all."

SAMUEL BEGAN TO pay attention to newspapers. He read every news report from the far West that he came upon. The stories were brief and vague, half a column here and there in between headlines about Grant's disjointed army piling up, one regiment after another, in Richmond. The *New York World* and the *Times* both had correspondents with Grant, and their headlines ate up the front pages. News from Texas consisted of clips from other papers. Union troops landing in Indianola and Corpus Christi. Savages shot down in their villages. Long quotes from local officials about exterminating the red vermin.

Samuel understood that the Society of Friends was troubled by the Texans because the Texans were so clear and straightforward in their speech. They did not seem to need to hide their intentions behind deceptive and gentle phrases. They came to take the land and they meant to keep it. They would take it from red men as they had taken land from the Shawnee and Cherokee in the Carolinas and before that the wild Irish in Ulster and before that whatever croft or patch of rocky land they could hold against the lairds in the lowlands, and if they could not hold it they rode with the lairds against the neighbors to raid other neighbors' cattle and had been doing so for centuries before the birth of Christ, who was the Prince of Peace, and they intended to keep on doing it, for as long as it took.

Chapter 5

❧

LOTTIE BECAME RED-CHEEKED and feverish. Elizabeth knew the men would not abide a sick or crying captive child, and the days after they were taken she carried Lottie in her arms. She made a sling of her shawl and wrapped the ends around both of them. She carried the three-year-old from the first great rise in the land until they came to a large encampment, where the men were greeted with shouts and singing. Women and girls danced alongside the men with their heraldic scalps, the confused and frightened stolen horses. A great bonfire burned and in its light the horsemen rode around the camp to the songs and the cheering. They held up the things they had taken from the houses they had raided, they waved blankets and quilts, and a Kiowa warrior turned a hand mirror back and forth so that it flashed in the firelight.

Two old women came to them and seized Elizabeth by the arm and led her away into the dark and violent night. They shoved her and Lottie into a small stand of live oak. Mary and her two children and little Millie, eighteen months, were hidden by the elder women in some other place. They stayed there all night, watching the stars, as the celebration fires flared up and the singing went on and on. The elder women sat between them and the firelit village of tipis. They watched from their old eyes, black with blue casts in them, old in their knowledge of the nature of men and raiding. They sat hooded in their blankets. Elizabeth held Lottie until the girl fell forward in sleep. Then she found herself waking up faint and hungry in a gray light.

That next day they went on. A light rain fell for two days, and it was cold. At some point they stopped and the traveling band of two hundred Comanche and Kiowa split up. The captives were divided between them. Elizabeth saw a young Kiowa woman sweep Millie up in her arms and stroke her hair and smile. The young woman pressed her cheek to the little girl with tears in her eyes. Elizabeth thought she would probably never see Millie again, and she was right.

The rain dropped thin as mist on the trees in the draws and painted their trunks dark as some unrefined ore, dark as slag coal. Elizabeth pulled her shawl over her head and over Lottie's head when the two groups parted and she was shoved ahead with the Comanche. She could not see Mary or Jube or Cherry or Millie as they went away northwest with the Kiowa.

She walked on with the Comanche and their long, easy march of hundreds of horses and travois. The ends of the travois poles bore down to make deep wavering tracks in the wet earth and the heads of children with hair in stiff spikes stuck up out of bundles and blankets on the travois, jiggling like dolls. All along the trail were things that had been taken from houses on Elm Creek and then thrown away; a tobacco cutter soon abandoned because of its long, awkward handle, curling irons, a shoehorn, a flatiron, a pair of women's high-laced shoes, a tintype of Jeremiah Durgan in its velvet frame and starred, cracked glass, all scattered in the grass. *They don't want any of it*, thought Elizabeth. *They stole it and then they threw it away. All those things mean nothing to them.*

Elizabeth found enough to eat as they went. She caught a painted terrapin and pried its shell apart. Inside there was meat and autumn fat. At the noon rest she boiled it inside its own shell and fed Lottie first and then herself. She took up the bitter buffalo gourds and dug out their flesh and made drinking cups of them.

When they first came into camp Elizabeth was claimed as a slave by a skinny woman with a drawn and hostile face and elaborate tattoos around her mouth, who quickly taught her the Comanche words for *water, wood, bring it*. Elizabeth endured the woman's blows without a sound. The skinny woman was the wife of one of the men who had raped and beaten Elizabeth, and he had a thunderbird painted on his tipi, an audacious claim to great power. His name meant Eaten Alive.

He had two wives, and the skinny woman was the older one. Elizabeth called her the Dismal Bitch. The younger had a round, plump face with a broad smile. Elizabeth saw her turn that happy face away when the Dismal Bitch turned on Elizabeth with her pony goad and left long bruises the shape and color of burned sticks on her arms.

Elizabeth Fitzgerald worked to make herself useful and needed so she could save Lottie's life. The women's lives were very hard. They were hard on others and hard on themselves. Eaten Alive's skinny first wife lifted the massive fresh buffalo skins that weighed close to a hundred pounds with hands whose two forefingers were missing at the first joints where she had cut them off in grief over dead relatives. A brother whose raw half-broke pony ran him into a copse of trees on the drainage they called the Caddo's Hand and knocked his brains out on a live oak branch. Her mother and father had perished in the great die-off of the spotted disease when wagon trains came through Comancheria on their way to California, and brought with them a killing fever, spirits that burned up so many people that there was hardly anyone left to hunt or pray. It left the people diminished and angry as hornets and perpetually hungry.

They came upon a small group of buffalo walking southward with their breath smoking from their wide muzzles, with their sweet and grassy smell. Their beloved outline of humped back and low-carried heads a template in the mind for tens of thousands of years. The men ran them down and killed them for the heavy autumn hides, to make moccasin soles and rawhide boxes and the stiff mittenlike horseshoes for the stony plains ahead. For winter robes and buckets and rope. The women ripped off the weighty hides as they would strip blankets from a bed.

Elizabeth had diminished within the ragged remains of the yellow-and-pink-checkered dress. She was lank and hungry and forty years old. She lifted the moist, bloody skins onto travois at the killing grounds and walked behind them to the camp. She went around the edges of the skins and hammered in small stakes and then raked the skins clean with a cast-iron scraper. She tore off the white connective tissue in great swaths. She broke into skulls with a stone and pulled the brains out and folded the shivering gray pudding into the damp skin. She was silent and furious at this filthy work and the primitive process. Why didn't they get themselves a tanner's beam and a big two-handed fleshing knife? They liked to kill themselves working, that's why. She ripped at the skin as if it were one of the men who had raped her.

Every evening she was weary beyond feeling and still she carried water in buckets made of buffalo stomach until it was dark. Somewhere in camp were captives from villages in New Mexico but Elizabeth knew she was not to speak to them or see them and how she knew this was hard to say but she kept her head down with an acid feeling of willed subservience. She fed Lottie pieces of raw marrow out of her greasy hands. She did not know what was wrong with the child. The three-year-old's head lolled on her shoulders as Lottie struggled to hold her head upright. Perhaps it was some spiritual collapse, a shrinking of the mind against the world in which she found herself.

Lottie did not cry. She was silent. No one adopted her because they were afraid of what disease she might have. Perhaps she was inhabited by some hostile entity, something living in her and looking out at the Comanche encampment from behind her gray three-year-old eyes. They made her sleep at the tipi entrance, and people stepped on her and shouted at her when they came inside. Eaten Alive's youngest wife lifted her hand and told people to be careful but the Dismal Bitch turned a blank, predatory stare on the Happy Wife and so the young woman deflated in a breath and went back to her stitching.

When they moved on northward that November of 1864, it was the fourth time they had shifted. Elizabeth was tiring day by day and hour by hour. She ate anything; meat scraps from skins and broth found at the bottoms of kettles. If she could stay strong and work she would live, and perhaps Lottie would live as well.

Elizabeth carried wood to the tipi and sharpened the frail old fleshing knife she had been given. She wondered how she could manage to have Lottie taken in and adopted by the Happy Wife. Even if she were adopted and learned Comanche and were tattooed, Elizabeth did not care, only that the child would live, under this cold, remote sun that seemed to burn the trail before them, mile after mile of open rolling plains and the tangled vines of buffalo gourd at her feet. They walked on from one river bottom to another, the ribbons of timber lacing the plains. Elizabeth walked resolutely with Lottie in her arms. When Lottie cried, she held her hand over the girl's mouth. *She will live, she will,* thought Elizabeth as she walked.

The second buffalo kill was on the north bank of the Wichita River, at the falls. Elizabeth knew they would not be rescued. They were too far north, out in the plains, and any party that came after them would be outnumbered and outgunned. The Indian men had repeating rifles and bandoliers of ammunition, lances with foot-long steel heads, and every man was a warrior.

At the falls of the Wichita River where the water spilled five feet over a lip of red stone, Elizabeth slid into a pool to cool her injured breasts. Cottonwood leaves drifted from the great, calm trees. The leaves were the color of primroses and butter. They fell like rain and dotted the red water that boiled up at the foot of the falls in rusty foam. She left Lottie on the bank on the stinking greasy shawl. The girl's face was skeletal. Her nose holes were as big as eyes and her gray eyes were sunk back into her skull to gaze out from the very center of the child's self, that which is otherworldly and hard and bright and indifferent.

Elizabeth stood up and the red water cascaded down her spare body.

"Lottie darling," she said. "Don't leave us."

"All right, Grandma," Lottie said. "Grandma, you wet."

"Yes," said Elizabeth. She looked up. The skinny wife she called the Dismal Bitch came running down the sloping bank with her lips drawn back. She raised a heavy digging stick of bois d'arc in one hand and she had the handle of a fleshing-knife in the other. It was of soft cast iron and very old and it had broken off in Elizabeth's hand two hours ago. The Dismal Bitch was shouting with rage. She kicked Lottie aside and strode toward Elizabeth and then waded into the water.

The Dismal Bitch kept on crying out in Comanche as she sloshed through the water and waved the broken handle in Elizabeth's face. Then she struck Elizabeth over the head with the digging stick. Bois d'arc is a yellow, dense wood, hard as iron. Lottie put both hands flat over her eyes.

Elizabeth had taken her beatings without a word all the long walk from the Brazos to the Wichita River. Now she threw up both her hands. The Dismal Bitch smashed the stick onto her palms with such force that rays of fire burned from Elizabeth's finger joints to her shoulders. Elizabeth shut her hands in a tight grip around the stick, and turned both wrists and jerked the stick toward herself, onto her own collarbones. She snatched the Dismal Bitch off balance. Then Elizabeth twisted to the right and tipped the stick over and threw the woman on her back into the shallow water. Elizabeth bore down. She fell to her knees on underwater stones and crushed the stick across the woman's throat. The Dismal Bitch would not let go the stick. *But you will soon enough*, Elizabeth thought, *when you are drowning you witch of hell.*

The Comanche woman's hands jerked loose and she reached up out of the foaming water for Elizabeth's hair. Elizabeth heard a light voice calling "Grandma, Grandma." She stepped back with the stick in her hands.

The bois d'arc wood was bright yellow and smooth, barkless, and shaved to a chisel shape on one end. When the woman stood up with the red water streaming down around her, Elizabeth drew the digging stick back like a baseball bat and struck her across the throat and then again across the top of the skull and again on her forearms as she lifted them in defense. Then again across the back of the head, a terrific blow, as she fell into the water and began to scramble away.

Elizabeth yelled and raised the digging stick above her head and shook it. Her broad heavy face with deep lines cut like parentheses around her shouting mouth. She yelled in triumph.

The Dismal Bitch reached the bank and ran toward the horse herd, beyond the encampment. She did not know where she was going except away from the river. She was seeing double and so ran into a travois and then tripped over a dog with puppies and then lay there.

Elizabeth stood breathing hard and silently. The tipis had blossomed in white cones all along the banks of the Wichita, and there was laughter and the dogs barking at something and the smell of woodsmoke. The tall red grasses were tipped in shakos of white cotton lit by the late sun like spirit hair.

On the grassy bank the second wife, the young happy wife with the pleasant face, sat down beside Lottie and patted the girl's shoulder. Lottie lowered her eyes and began to open and shut her dirty hands and then a spreading stain appeared on the grass as her urine ran down in yellow streams, over the grass and cottonwood leaves.

After a while the Dismal Bitch got up and wavered into the horse herd, and then vomited. She went back to the tipi with the thunderbird painted on it and collapsed.

Happy Wife came and gave Elizabeth and Lottie pemmican wrapped in some fibrous inner bark and a wooden bowl of prairie turnips. Elizabeth and Lottie sat beside the fire outside Eaten Alive's tipi. They ate the greasy mass, ate it all, relishing the bits of agarita berry. They drank from their cups made of the bitter buffalo gourd. Then Happy Wife came out and signaled that Lottie should sleep inside the tipi, just inside the entrance, and the three-year-old collapsed like a small dirty figurine and people coming in stepped over her carefully when Happy Wife shouted at them. She shouted at them and then turned and picked up a heavy red blanket and laid it over Lottie.

Eaten Alive sat up on a bluff of the river far away from the arguments of the women. He poured songs from a bone flute. They had passed the Wichita and would soon pass the Red. They had captives and horses and a harvest of winter skins. Little Buffalo and several others were dead, but they had died honorably, in battle. Eaten Alive tipped out a lilting current of mourning from the bone flute for Little Buffalo. All men must die and we must rise into the other world with a self whole and unchanged with the hair streaming uncut from our heads and so he had died. Eaten Alive owned five songs now, all love songs, love of winter and rain and horses and the morning sun and love for his young second wife. The humpbacked trader of the Tewa people came invisibly with his delicate music. His name was Kokopelli, and he bore melodies and seeds and he lived beyond the ages in the plains air, drifting with clear grace notes and tremolos.

Chapter 6

A<small>S THEY WALKED</small> on, Elizabeth recited silently all she had ever memorized in school. Bits of speeches on Independence Day, verses of the Bible, the names of her neighbors, her children's birthdays, whispering to herself under the chill sun of the November plains. Pillars of dust the color of madder rose up to mark their passage.

Overhead vultures wheeled high on the updrafts over the Red Rolling Plains, some rising and some sliding downward, descending in an airy mobile whose center shaft was in the remote blue zenith. They circled at great heights, mile upon mile, when heavy clouds white as glaciers sailed up from the northwest.

One early morning there was a heavy fog. They broke camp in a strange isolate stillness as if in a world just formed and not yet emerged into definition. Every limb adorned with lines of tiny drops and the grass wet. They walked on with soaked, dark legs, and they covered many miles in silence, going nowhere in the same spot with the blurring fog all around them. By midmorning the fog had separated into phantom banks lying apart like grounded clouds among the *ekasonip*, the stands of red grass. Then it rose up and fled away overhead in a low, rolling tide. At every draw Eaten Alive's two wives slid from their ponies to collect deadwood. Elizabeth gathered as much as either of them. She packed it with great crashes onto a travois. The Dismal Bitch avoided Elizabeth and would not look at her. Elizabeth picked up a heavy stick and stuck it in her belt. She secretly marked the days on it, one notch after another. Her checkered dress grew larger as she shrank inside it and the hem tattered into fringes.

After the Wichita they came to the Red River, and Elizabeth knew that beyond the Red was these people's dwelling-place. Where she would be beyond help and beyond anyone's reach in an alien country whose landscape was known only to a very few. The Happy Wife, Pakumah, had taken Lottie to herself now, maybe to spite Tabimachi, the Dismal Bitch, who sulked thin and bitter in her own eight square feet of space beside her parfleche boxes, packing and unpacking obsessively.

Elizabeth slept outside or just inside the tipi entrance, which she learned must always face to the east. But she did not care because Lottie was now wrapped in a four-point blanket beside Pakumah and ate from Pakumah's bowl and slept soundly all night. She had begun to smile again. They had tattooed a star on her forehead. Pakumah and her sisters gave Lottie anything she asked for. When she screamed and threw things they smiled and tried to soothe her with little gifts of egret feathers or a pinch of sugar or a prairie chicken's air sac dried and blown up like a small transparent balloon.

Elizabeth knew she herself was spending her life force like a running stream but she had ceased to care.

They came to the Red River bottoms at a place where the river made a loop to the south and so the current was slow and there was a tall forest in the flats. There were open stretches of pure white sand. The cottonwoods and the sycamores grew to great heights. Banks of jaunty Carrizo cane with its plumes and shakos. The water itself red as rust, as brick, red as wine. They camped on the south side at a place where it was clear they had always camped, and the men herded the horses through the trees and urged them into the river.

The horses hesitated and dodged and turned back, and then the leaders went in, and then the rest. They poured over the bank into the water in erupting sprays; pintos and duns, gruellas of dove gray, bays and blacks. They were stolen Texas horses with long backs, or the Comanche mustang ponies with trim clean legs and heavy manes and tails. Their tails floated behind them as they swam and then they footed themselves in shallow water and stood drinking greedily. The men and boys rode in after them and slipped from their horses' backs into the water, unbraided their hair and ducked themselves again and again.

Elizabeth walked a long way in search of firewood. Pakumah gave her a worn little mare and a travois, and so she left Lottie in the young woman's care and went more than a mile in a wandering route through the woods. The vines and saplings made dense thickets and the trees were skirted with heaped driftwood brought down by floods. Elizabeth delighted in the shade, the scattered sunlight, after the relentless sun of the open country. She loaded branch after branch. Her hair hung down in separate dirty locks and several of her fingernails were split, her shoes held together by thongs. She prayed aloud. Eaten Alive had hit her with his quirt for praying aloud, so she had learned to say nothing in English and to puzzle out Comanche words. She prayed that Lottie would get well as she lifted smooth gray deadwood onto the travois. She said *sycamore* and *driftwood* and *taibo* and *esakonip* and *haamee*.

She walked on up a sandy rise to a stone bluff that stood a hundred feet or more above the river. Above the bottomlands everything changed. Now there was only dense thickets and short trees. She went on, pressing through the rigid branches. They all seemed to be made of thousands of strands of twisted, coarse wire. She tied the little mare to a limb and went to the top of the bluff.

It was good to be up high. The level horizon all around her had begun to give her a lost feeling of stalking earnestly and without end toward a vanishing horizon. It was good to look out over the floodplain of the Red and the curve of the river and the wind turning the water's surface into a weaving of light. No smoke anywhere, on any quadrant of the horizon, except for the big camp upstream where the tipis' pale cones rose out of the high trees, where the campfires were lit and children ran shouting in play and the men were bringing in the wet horses through the blue evening air.

Elizabeth went along the bluff and before long she came to a mound of stone blocks. They were squared. They bore chisel marks. She reached down to touch them. They were of weathered sandstone, worn down by heat and rain until they lay in heaps and were shoved aside by ancient post oaks grim as trolls.

She walked among them looking for some sign or symbol. On one was a Spanish cross with bulbous terminals on each arm. Beyond the remains of the Spanish fort was a ruined cabin built of upright logs that leaned in all directions. The stone chimney was blanketed by greenbrier and passionflower, gray and dry and noisy, seedpods shaking in the wind.

Grapevines tangled over the leaning wheels of a wagon. The Spanish had come and built something of stone and after them, people of her own kind, and neither could hold this place against the arid country or the Comanche and the Kiowa, so here their efforts lay in ruins. Inside the fallen walls she saw disintegrating cloth caught beneath several logs and within that the long bone of a leg or arm. It did not frighten her. She was too tired and had come to think of this as her end as well. Elizabeth thought, *I could well die in this country. I could die in the next five minutes.*

Weighty clouds built up in the northwest now, lit from behind by the sunset light, and their topmost towers glowed with an internal light. She pushed aside the planks of the wagon. The place had long ago been scavenged, the wagon's metal tires gone to make fleshing knives or beaten into arrowheads.

She sat on the stone blocks awhile to rest. She was being worn down, faded and weathered like schist, suspended between two languages so that words came to her out of an unstable white space where nothing seemed to hold meaning. She was not sure of the meaning of anything.

From downstream came a low and powerful sound. A deep

coughing roar. She raised her head, and across the river in the last of the November light a jaguar slipped out of the intricate netting of greenbrier vines and cane. He stopped to smell a limb of deadwood as if a message had been left there for him. Then he lifted his heavy head with its mouth open, panting. His beautiful rosettes were an extravagant adornment in the monotonous colors of the Red River and the white beaches and black trees, gray drifts of winter grass. He called out, singular and lonely, far north of his common range. He walked out of the trees and made a swift passage like a great spotted fish through the grass to the edge of the river in a slow moving tide of spots and when he reached the bank a covey of black ducks rattled up off the water. In the next second the jaguar had launched himself into the air and twisted upright and snatched a duck out of the clattering mass and fell, fell, with his long body writhing and sent up plumes of red water as he struck the surface.

He came up with the drake in his mouth and swam to the bank, his banded tail floating behind him. He heaved up on the bank streaming water and shook himself, a windmill of spray. His rosettes shivered in waves down his body as he shook himself, and the duck wings flapped wildly in his mouth.

He dropped the duck and called out, *Hough! Hough!* Then he turned and looked up at her with his golden eyes. The stripes ran off his face like water.

Elizabeth was at the edge of starvation and near a fatal exhaustion, and in her weightless daze she felt he was speaking to her. A creature at the far edge of his range, or beyond it, solitary and lost but somehow surviving. A vision. She had been granted a vision.

Chapter 7

❧

A COLD FRONT CAME down upon them from the north, great layers of chilled air revolving one over another. It tore leaves loose and tipped over a drying rack and the dogs seized upon the meat and bolted away with it in the wind. Tipis flattened against their poles on the north sides and the horses were unsettled and milled and shouldered into one another. It took all the men and boys to hold the herd and keep them from drifting back south over the river before the punishing wind.

Elizabeth helped chase the dogs away with her stick and to set up the racks again and secure them. Now she was permitted to sleep inside the tipi. She listened to the light rain that came with the cold and fell asleep for a while. She woke up again and lay sleepless in the smell of woodsmoke and wet fur. She was visited by a pure and constant rage she could do nothing about. Lottie had another name now, and Elizabeth forced herself to accept this and to remember it. Siikadeah. Her name was now Siikadeah. When they broke camp the next morning to continue on to the north they left dry circles in the grass where the tipis had been.

That day they ferried their travois loads across the wide flat surfaces of the Red River in boats made of skins stretched over willow frames, like tubs, wallowing and unstable, boats like bowls that tended to spin in circles when paddled. In places it was so shallow the women waded alongside. The boats were loaded with the women's possessions and on top of a pile of these rode Lottie and two other children. Lottie threw pecans into the water, laughing and chattering in small phrases of Comanche. Pakumah kept a firm hold of Lottie's ragged dress and the girl screamed in irritation and Pakumah let her scream. Lottie threw Pakumah's digging stick into the water and Pakumah only laughed. The men swam the horses over in a pawing, blowing mass. Then they were on the far bank and in Indian Territory.

THEY CAME UP Deep Red Creek with its vermilion sands, and then they cut to the west and came upon the timbered loops of Blue Buffalo Creek, searching for West Cache Creek, which would lead them into the Wichita Mountains. They had been joined by more and more traveling bands of Comanche and Kiowa until they numbered in the hundreds, walking through the cool November plain of yellow grass. Ahead in the mountains they would find plentiful water and timber for the winter, and elk, and antelope, and nut trees. They were happy and lighthearted. Susan Durgan's scalp waved in a terrible, playful way from a man's shield. There were many other scalps in various colors of hair from nameless dead people now buried or left to the scavengers far to the south from Mexico to Oklahoma.

The Wichitas began as a distant blue like a bank of clouds. Then they rose higher day by day. This was their winter camping place, these red granite mountains rising up alone in the great plains, foothills of nothing. A place of deities and shadows, sacred to the diminishing Wichita tribe, whose numbers had fallen and fallen and now they lived in one valley in their red-grass huts and grew corn and beans and ate the white man's food when they could get it. The Comanche and Kiowa had reduced the Wichita to a fearful client people.

As they came up West Cache Creek into the mountains Elizabeth saw their beehive grass houses, with thready trails of smoke rising from haystack crowns. There were people there but they scattered so quickly they were like mourning doves surprised at their feeding and they vaulted into the brush and the tangled black trees.

They traveled up West Cache Creek. This led them to a wide prairie that lifted in elevation mile by mile into the heart of the Wichita mountains. As they went on higher and higher the travelers were surrounded on both sides by rocky peaks. On one mountain a pair of enormous stones stood by themselves staring down at travelers. The descending song of the canyon wren spilled down the granite slopes. Then they came to the forests of post oak and Spanish oak in between the peaks. They came upon a wide stony hole of water and despite the chill the children plunged in like otters.

This was where they would spend the winter or not, as the spirit moved.

They halted in a valley of tall post oaks and Elizabeth walked among the shading trees of a true forest searching for campfire wood. Pools of water ran one into the next like beads on a string. Nervous killdeer darted around the edges of these pools, and they found the heart-shaped tracks of antelope.

Lottie kicked around in the travois blankets and went over one side and fell on her two hands. She got up again and was narrowly missed by a young boy galloping past heedless of anything but catching up to the other boys. Elizabeth shouted to her granddaughter but Lottie's two hands were taken by older girls and they went off with the other children among the clutter and flying poles and the men sifting quietly away from the women's work to rest in the sun and smoke beside West Cache Creek.

The children chased a pet antelope fawn and brought it back to the woman who had adopted it. Then they lost interest and found the dog with spotted puppies who had been allowed to ride in a travois and was grateful. Lottie picked up a writhing puppy and gave it a Comanche name. *Tuaahtaki*, cricket.

Two young men went up a nearby peak to keep watch. Elizabeth, too, had begun to fear the soldiers. The Comanche often killed their captives when they were attacked. Elizabeth did not know if she could save both Lottie and herself if this were to happen. She helped unroll the tipi cover from its pole and decided she would die trying. She saw herself smashing the digging stick over a man's nose. She made herself stop thinking this by humming a vagrant melody that she recalled, a ballad about drowning Scotsmen, and then straightened up and admired the bony, subdued horse that Lottie and two other children were riding about camp.

Camp life surged around Elizabeth. A heavy older woman stood and sang in a loud, quavering voice with an expression of great happiness. A baby had just been born. Two men shouted at one another in anger and the civil chief stepped between them and separated them. He sent the younger man away from camp with a herd of fifteen horses; a young and handsome man with copper bracelets up his arms. The young man galloped away behind the horses, pouting and flashing his bracelets. Another group rode off to the northwest with loud flourishes and shouts; they were going to visit the Comanchero traders out of San Idlefonso.

The tipis rose one after another like mushrooms. Fires crackled, the men ran the horses to water in the shallows of West Cache Creek, and so they lived life as it had been given to them for thousands of years, both here and in another creation, in the legend time and perhaps even before that, when God so made the world and set the stars in the heavens and the waters below and from those waters some aquatic being had brought up earth. A force had formed the hot and smoking blood clot that became the buffalo. Had set the ramparts of Medicine Bluff and the Wichita Mountains and smoothed the plains as if fleshing a great hide, and set the sun overhead on its indifferent burning wheel that dragged the Comanche's crawling shadows behind them like dark and sacred hair over the wide earth.

Rain came again in heavy downpours, wave after wave of it. The firewood Elizabeth and the two wives, happy Pakumah and the sullen Tabimachi, brought in was tangled with greenbrier and the last of the autumn flowers, purple asters and dog daisies. Elizabeth slept to one side of the doorway of the tipi instead of in the entrance, because she worked hard and did not look any man in the eye and because she could brain-tan buckskin as well as any. She took up a dull knife and tore the hair from a deer hide down to the skin, which was white as paper. They had never heard of a currier's blade with a recurved edge that would have had the hair off in a minute. Idiots, an idiot people. She watched as the Dismal Bitch built a fire under it to smoke the hide brown. The thin wife threw a handful of oatmeal into the flames so that the deerskin took on an ochre color. Elizabeth saw the snowing handful of oatmeal and wondered where she had got it and wished she could have some to eat.

She watched as Pakumah beaded a new buckskin dress for Lottie. Pakumah had left the deerskin in its natural white and beaded it in blue and black chevrons around the neck. Pakumah lifted it over Lottie's head and sat back to admire her in it.

Elizabeth learned the pattern of moccasins and cut them out and sewed them together and then stitched the heavy bull buffalo hide soles on them with very small waterproof stitches. She rammed the awl in as if she were piercing the heart of Eaten Alive with every stitch. Her anger had become a fixed and hidden constellation, and its cold fire warmed her heart. Elizabeth then handed the moccasins to the young wife Pakumah to see how it was she beaded the vamp.

In the first week of December there came a heavy snow that started in the early morning, before dawn, and in that dark snow the thin and now silent older wife Tabimachi removed the door cover and stepped out. She walked along a narrow trail up the mountainside. She came to a great bluff where the waters of West Cache ran choked and foaming far below in a narrow chute. She tied the rope to a twisted post oak and put a heavy loop of the rope around her neck and fell over the edge of the cliff and so died.

Chapter 8

THAT SAME SNOW fell upon Mary and Jube and Cherry and little Millie living with the Kiowa far to the north, along the Canadian River. They had passed out of that part of the country where the men raided and were now in the territory of hunting and living and shifting in slow considered moves from one part of the plains to another, and so it seemed to Mary that they would not now kill her or her children. They might be abandoned. If they were left alone on the plains without tools or weapons or blankets, she would die and the children would die. She and her children were in an immense and beautiful prison, limitless on all sides.

Mary held Cherry in her arms and Jube walked alongside, watching everything around him with alert and narrowed eyes. His dead older brother had left an empty space and Jube came to fill that space within days, flowing into its blank silhouette like powder smoke. They walked behind the travois of Aperian Crow's wife in their tattered clothing and broken shoes. All Mary had to cover her was the remains of her dress and her long chemise. She had torn up several yards of the skirt to make a kind of shawl to cover her head and shoulders against the cold wind and the sun. Jube had more clothes;

they had not been interested in tearing off his clothes. He had a shirt and a pair of pants of coarse wool and his unraveling stockings. His shoe soles were coming loose at the toes but that could be fixed if only they would stop traveling.

There were two other captives, Mexican boys of about seven and nine who every day fell farther and farther behind. The men had gone through battle and hard riding to capture them and now they seemed to have forgotten their existence. The Kiowa went on as if they were caught up in some cosmic rapids and Mary and her children too were caught up in it and borne along with them and where that impelled and violent current itself came from no one knew.

The bald sky overhead filled with a cool invisible wind that turned the seed-heads of the grasses in waves of silk toward the southeast, and thin cirrus clouds poured in streams in the same direction, curled like question marks. Words would not come to Mary. They shattered inside her head and then reassembled on her lips in strange combinations. So she had begun to learn sign.

The two thin ends of the lodgepoles that Aperian Crow's wife used as her travois poles dragged and bumped along behind the pony and sent up little rooster trails of dust that hung for a long time in the dry air. Mary tried to keep herself and Cherry directly behind these two traveling spouts of dust. If she kept her eyes focused on them she could walk a straight line. Jube turned again and again to see if his mother and sister were keeping up. All around them the Kiowa moved across the face of the north Texas plains like fish in water, the familiar and sacred straits of grass that had been their own for several centuries and in which their songs and wars and marriages and births had taken place in moments of intensity while the wheel of the year revolved around them.

Aperian Crow's wife turned and looked back. Her unbound hair lifted and fell in black strands. She made a come-here motion to Mary and pointed to the travois where eighteen-month-old Millie Durgan sat wrapped in a blanket.

Mary ran forward and put Cherry beside Millie on the heap of blankets and furs on the travois. The two girls crawled under the

blankets together and slept. And so the youngest, childless wife of
Aperian Crow took Cherry to ride on her travois during the day. She
would have adopted Cherry as well, but here, trudging along in the
dirt, determined, unbeaten, tenacious, was Cherry's own mother.
Millie was hers alone. So they went on and Mary noticed that now
only one of the Mexican boys stumbled along behind them, wounded
and inarticulate. Late that night a woman gave the boy some shattered fragments of jerky and he sat and ate them at the far edge of
the firelight, slavering like an animal.

Mary and Jube kept on and as they walked they scavenged.
Whenever there was a halt they collected mesquite beans and scuffed
in the dirt of old campsites where Mary found a piece of a broken
bottle and Jube discovered a jumble of things half-uncovered at the
root of a short and twisted cedar. An armadillo had dug a hole there
and brought up the remains of a broken wooden box. Jube dug it
out with his hands. He found a stiff boot of a very old design with a
square toe and a high rotten heel, and under more layers of red soil
he found two tarnished silver spoons and an ancient Spanish spur.

With the broken glass bottle Mary cut off the needle tip of an
agave leaf as she had seen the Mexicans do and then drew it down so
that a long string of fiber came with it. With this needle and thread
she sewed their shoe-soles back on and made herself and Jube col-
lecting bags from the rags of her skirt so that they might carry their
finds with them and leave their hands free. She found a clay pot
that was only broken at the top and could still hold water. A fan of
windblown dirt streamed around it. It was very old, with odd figures
on it. A lizard repeated many times in black and a squared spiral; a
twisted cross in angles. She tried to show this to Jube but her words
came out *crissin crissin crissin.*

"I can see it, Mama. It's all right Mama."

Aperian Crow was a Koitsenko, a war leader, and now he was
no longer the man to whom people listened. The landscape of war
and raiding was behind them, south of the Red River, and they were
in another frame of mind, another social arrangement, all of them
content to be on the move in the galloping wind. The man whom

they now followed was First Wolf, who would tell off the days of march between one water and another, and which wandering roads the buffalo followed. Somehow he had made a mistake, and now the buffalo could not be found.

This was their promised land, and they learned it as one would learn the face of a beloved, every line and blink of eyelash, every turn of the head, motion of the hand. Tone of voice. Starvation was the unkind parent of the horse Indians of the plains, and its memory never left them. This time First Wolf had made a mistake or the mistake had made itself, and then the mistake had lain in wait for him and his people.

They went on for a week without game and ate up whatever they had. Mary and Cherry and Jube went without food for two days. Mary sat outside the lodge of Aperian Crow and begged of whoever passed them by and Jube said to them as they passed, *"Hei gow meen a tau hêimáh,"* we are very hungry, and because he said it in his clumsy mispronounced Kiowa people gave what they could spare. The knobby end of an old antelope thigh bone that Mary crushed with rocks and then boiled and fed to the children. A strip of rawhide. Half a pilot biscuit. Around their camp near Rainy Mountain the men found old buffalo skulls out on the prairie, and brought them in and turned them to point at the tipis. A message to the lost buffalo to show them the way to the starving Kiowa, who loved them.

At the end of a week several men rode in saying there were three buffalo carcasses ahead. They had killed them and had left them for the women to skin and cut up. Mary ran forward with the other women and with them fell upon the carcasses with whatever came to hand. They lay in heavy dark mounds and a ragged calf skipped and bawled near his dead mother. Three young girls ran the calf down on horseback and one of them roped it to cheers and shouts, and dragged it along in a fan of dust and then it was cut to pieces.

Mary had nothing but her broken piece of glass but she knelt down beside two other women and helped to tear at a stomach and lay open its hot interior. They tore out the still-moving entrails and ate them as they were. They handed the livers to the hunters.

In a short time all that was left were the white bones, slick and glistening, enameled with designs of red tendons. An old woman chopped off the ends of the greater bones with an axe and handed them to Mary. That night Mary fed her children on the rich, heavy marrow. She roasted the ends in the fire and broke them open with a rock, and the tubes of marrow slid out and she dropped these into Jube's and Cherry's hands still smoking. She broke open another and ate as much as she could and then roasted more. She meant to save some for the Mexican boy but in a moment found she had eaten it all and was ravenous for more and so she bent her head and hot tears streaked her face and she was bitter at what she had done, what she had become. A speechless, famished creature sitting in the cold dirt with smeared hands.

That night Aperian Crow's youngest wife took Cherry into the tipi to sleep with Millie because Millie had cried for her and called her name over and over.

Then they went on.

Jube dropped back beside his mother. Mary pointed toward Aperian Crow's wife and tried to say something. Jube grasped her hand and pushed it down.

"They don't like you to point," he said.

Mary nodded, and kept walking.

"Jin, jin. Jin," she said. Then she bowed her head and tears of frustration came to her eyes. The strange word kept coming to her lips and she could not stop herself from saying *Jin jin jin jin jin* until she pressed her own hand against her mouth. Last night it had made Old Man Komah so nervous, this repeated syllable, that he had left the campfire and had come to where she and the children sat together on a piece of blanket and hit her across the face with the ends of his quirt.

Millie started screaming. She held her hands out toward Mary and cried "Mar-ee! Mar-ee!" Aperian Crow's wife had spoken sharply to Old Man Komah. The child was not to be upset, she was to be given whatever she wanted if it were in their power to give. Old Man Komah said nothing but went back and sat down by his own fire. The young wife then stood up with Millie in her arms and came to Mary and the children and made a motion with her hand that they were to move their little piece of blanket and to sleep close to the tipi. Then she took both Cherry and Millie inside, singing a low song to them.

The night sky was cloudless so that the cold fell out of it like dew and in the morning Mary and Jube found themselves curled nearly in the ashes. Her longing for Britt was so intense that she felt utterly vacant. But she lifted her hollow self upright at dawn and staggered and then waited for her balance to return and went to gather buffalo chips and brush and whatever she could come upon that would burn and warm herself and Jube.

As they walked along Jube said, "Mama, don't try to talk no more. Listen, just make the signs they make."

Mary signed *yes*. In the distance was a rise and the foremost riders coming to it appeared briefly as cutouts against the hazed yellow sky. They jogged downward and then others lifted to take their places. Then Mary signed *name*.

"Yes, Mama, we got to know her name." Her polite name. Neither her secret spirit name nor a joke name. It was not information easily come by. Jube had learned quickly.

Mary nodded furiously, and reached out to put her hand on Jube's thin shoulder.

"I'm going to do that," he said.

Jube ran ahead. His strength was rapidly leaving him and there was a kind of trembling in his interior but because of all the marrow he had eaten last night the weakness had not yet reached his hands or legs and he must keep going while he could. He dodged around the travois legs and the dogs and was careful not to run in front of any mounted warrior's horse. He ran on until he came to Old Man Komah's two-wheeled cart. He called to him in Spanish.

"Mister Komah. Here I have you a present."

The man looked down at Jube. "Where did you get that?" he said.

Jube held up the Spanish spur with the great spiked rowel. "I found it back there. I was looking for mesquite beans. It was in an armadillo hole."

"Why is it not rusted?"

"I rubbed it with sand." Jube held it up toward Old Man Komah as he ran alongside. "I saved it for you because you're Mexican."

Old Man Komah sat with the reins in his hand and said nothing while Jube continued to walk and then run a little and then walk alongside his *carreta* wheels. The axles sang in a disjointed noise, a phrase in a high whine repeated over and over. He made Jube wait awhile.

"Get up here," he said.

Jube calculated the roll of the spokes and then stepped on one and was carried upward and grasped the rails and made it to the seat. Old Man Komah laughed. He held out his hand and Jube put the spur in it. Komah turned it over and looked at it carefully. His mule swiveled one ear and then the other, and hoarded the world in its dark eyes.

"Those Spaniards," he said. "When there was a king of Spain." He handed it back to the boy. "Keep it. What else did you find?"

"Spoons. I think they are silver."

"See if you can make some kind of jewelry out of those spoons. You can trade them to that man there." Komah lifted his head and stuck out his lower lip toward a man ahead of them on a three-color paint horse. The man had rings of tattoos around his upper arms. "Nocteawah. He likes things for his ears."

"What does Nocteawah mean?"

"Find out for yourself. Learn to speak Kiowa."

"Yes sir," said Jube. "I'm trying."

"How do you speak Spanish?"

"All of my family spent a year in Nacogdoches, working for an old Spanish man."

Komah still did not look at him but off across the prairie. Komah was an important person in this little band. Jube was not. Jube was a runty little captive child who might not live much longer. "An old Spanish man in Nacogdoches."

"Yes sir. They spoke Spanish."

"Who did you live with?"

"Señor Esteban Arocha."

"Well." Komah then turned to Jube; to his lifted face, his torn, nappy hair with the lice streaming through it, the silver spur trembling in his hands. "And now, what do you want?"

Jube sat suspended between several choices with held breath and the spur grasped hard to stop his hands' shaking.

He said, "Sir, my name is Jube Johnson."

"Chon-son, Chon-son," said Old Man Komah. "Um-hm."

"Could you tell me the name of Aperian Crow's wife? She has little Millie."

He nodded.

"And now she has my sister Cherry."

"Yes, you should call her Gonkon." Old Man Komah took out his tobacco bag and a small book of papers cut from the *Dallas Clarion* newspaper. The small square of paper had a picture of a woman's hat and the price: fifty cents. "When you speak to her, call her Gonkon." Komah rolled a cigarette and lit it and drew on it. "Now get down."

Jube dodged between the women on horseback with their loaded travois and the men on horseback and dogs and other children. He came back to his mother where she walked, trudging, one foot in front of the other. She was growing weaker. Her hands swung at her sides as if they were loose weights. That morning they had eaten some of the torn bits of flesh from a new buffalo hide and he did not know what they might get to eat tonight. They were not offered any of the meat from the three buffalo because it had been shared out among all the people in the band and there was none left for the captives. They had been given a throat and a tail.

"Her name is Gonkon," Jube said.

Mary nodded.

Jube said, "I am going to make some earring things for Nocte-awah and get a knife from him."

Mary smiled. She reached out to touch his hair. She made a

wiping motion. She did not yet know the sign for *cut* so she made a scissors with her fingers.

"And you going to cut my hair."

Mary nodded again and closed her eyes for a moment. She stood still and wavered and then sank to her knees and fell forward on both hands. Jube cried out and got his hands under her armpits and pulled his mother to a sitting posture. Her hands were dotted with sandburs and she turned them palm up before her face. Jube knocked the burs away and begged his mother to get up and keep on walking. People passed them by on either side among sailing strands of grass and thin valances of dust raised by travois poles. Mary stared ahead at the golden striated levels of the plains that lay at the bottom of the sky, an absorbing pale yellow haze without definition in which there was neither work nor struggle nor hunger nor fear. Then she closed her eyes again and turned her head away from it.

Then everything settled and fell into place. She got to her feet and stood and swayed for a moment from one foot to another. Jube looked up at her with open lips and horror in his eyes.

"Mama, please."

She grasped the piece of skirt around her neck and nodded and patted his shoulder and walked on. She pressed forward on will-power alone. If she were left behind, the children would stay with her and so endanger themselves and so she must keep up at any cost.

That night Mary tried to help Gonkon put up her tipi poles. First they laid the three center poles flat on the ground and tied them together near their tips. Then they lifted them upright and walked out the legs to make a tripod. Mary held to one of the poles to steady herself for a moment when Gonkon was not looking. Then they began to lay in the others in the crotch of the tripod one after the other so that when they were all up they made a mounting spiral of pole tips. Then they brought the cover: it had been rolled on a pole like a giant ancient manuscript and they unrolled it foot by foot around the tripod and secured it. Mary's knees shook. She sat down outside the tipi and folded her hands in her lap. Aperian

Crow's wife came out of her tipi with a graceful step and Mary said, "Gonkon."

Jube looked up with a terrified expression. His mother was going to say "Gonkon, Gonkon," over and over again until Old Man Komah came and hit her. But his mother clamped her lips shut and pressed her hand against them. Gonkon laughed.

"Mar-ee." She handed Mary a wooden bowl full of meat and broth and hominy and waved Jube away. When Mary had eaten, Gonkon brought Jube another bowl, which was all she had in her stores. That and no more. Then the two of them collapsed in sleep. Gonkon brought out two worn blankets that had been used as harness pads and threw them over Mary and Jube.

They took up the trail beside the white sands of the Canadian River, traveling northwest. Before long First Wolf and his scouts came upon a streaming band of buffalo that numbered perhaps three or four hundred. The beasts smelled sweetly of grass and the bulls had grown the long shaking pantaloons and beards of winter. The men ran them down and shot them with bow and arrow, which were more easily handled than the long guns, and the bow and arrow were silent. Men like Aperian Crow and other warriors like Satank and That's It and Kicking Bird could get off five arrows in the time it took to reload a long rifle. Their arrows were tipped with steel hunting arrowheads, without barbs, long and slim, which could be pulled out easily. The barbed steel arrowheads were for people.

"Mar-ee."

Gonkon handed her a butchering knife and then signed that it was only a loan and Mary signed *thank you,* or some gesture that meant appreciation. Mary took a great bolus of meat in her hand and cut down through the middle of it and stopped short of halving it by half an inch. Then she spiraled her knife through one half of the chunk of meat until it was a long thin strip, and then the other half, spiraling around and around the inside of each half to the end, and thus it made a ribbon a yard and a half long. This was hung on the scaffolding and then she took up another and another, alongside all the other women, and by nighttime the scaffolding covered an acre of the white sands of the Canadian River valley and fires glowed beneath the thin ribbons of flesh. Quavering flames shone through them as if the meat were red paper. Gonkon saw that Mary was given good pieces of tongue and hump and kidney fat.

It was a kind of great fair held out in the distant plains, a carnival of buffalo meat, of bones, of people singing in Kiowa of the immense being who had lifted the stone, and of the hole beneath the stone where the buffalo came streaming out in their millions to populate the earth.

And so they went on into winter and Mary began to hope that she and her children would survive and that they would live to see Britt again and abide once more in their own house down in Young County. She tried to tell Jube that his father would come for them, that his father loved him dearly. Jube nodded and bent to his silver spoons. When Mary could rest she collapsed to the ground and stared out at the endless auburn and biscuit tones, the oxblood-colored earth, the lampblack hues of the leafless trees.

She had dreams about Kentucky, where she had been born, about the two walnut trees that stood on either side of the well path that led from the back of the house into a countryside rich with water and rain. Old Mrs. Randall speaking to her in admonitory tones out of that white and angled face. Soon the true cold would set in; she and Jube must be allowed into a lodge, or they would not make it through the winter.

Jube worked hard on his two spoons. He bent off the handles and put them away and begged a nail of Old Man Komah. The freighter had been born to a Mexican father and a Kiowa captive mother and at some time in the past decided to come and live permanently with the Kiowa as their interpreter and storyteller and blacksmith. In the *carreta* he carried a stack of old newspapers and pieces of leather, buckles, birds' wings, jars of colored beads, and a toolbox. From this long box he held up a tenpenny nail to Jube as if he were granting him his dearest wish, as if the nail were the keys to the kingdom. Jube took it and thanked him and then ran.

Jube shaped his fire coals as he thought best and heated both the nail and the dishes of the spoons. He made himself a pair of tongs of green mesquite. The tongs smoked and burned and only lasted a short while but there was no shortage of mesquite. He drove a hole through the spoons and used a stone to wear down the broken edges where he had broken off the handles. Komah sat and watched him and said nothing. He rolled cigarettes out of square pieces of the *Dallas Courier* with its fragmentary news of Grant and Lee at each other's throats in Virginia and its advertisements for hair dye, and smoked silently and offered no advice.

Jube let the silver cool. He reached into his mother's carrybag and found the piece of broken bottle. With great care he broke off small points and then more points of green glass.

Komah nodded and then at last bent forward. He held out his hand for the chips of green glass. Jube gave them to him. Komah pulled a small leather sack out of his back pocket and filled it with sand. Jube sat on his heels in the kindliness of this man's regard, his interest and care. It was like being someplace warm and out of the wind.

"Too sharp, *ya veas?*" he said. "If you put these on an earring it's going to cut somebody. Now here." He poured all the glass chips in and shook it, rolled the bag of sand and glass between his hands. "So."

Two days later the sharp edges of the green glass were dulled and Jube strung his spoons on agave-fiber thread, and Old Man Komah boiled a glue for him from buffalo hooves. Both of the concave discs glittered with emerald-colored glass chips. Jube had quickly learned Kiowa words, and the most important was *ahô,* said with a falling tone at the end, which meant *Thank you,* not to be confused with *ahó,* said with a rising tone at the end, which meant *Kill him.*

Nocteawah was a young man who had been on only one raiding trip into Texas and had never taken any scalps and was somewhat boyish still so that he could not entirely hide his delight in the earrings. Jube saw his eyes widen slightly and then Nocteawah looked away. Jube had learned the Kiowa word for *knife,* and he said it. He started to hold up one finger and then changed his mind and held up two. Nocteawah would not take the earrings from him by force because everyone could see that Old Man Komah had begun to help Jube. Had boiled up the buffalo hooves for him. Had rolled a cigarette for him and let him smoke it.

Nocteawah waved his finger back and forth in the Mexican way for *No* and held up that one finger. *"P!ah,"* he said. One knife.

Jube waved his finger back and forth as well and then said, *"Yii."* Two.

Nocteawah looked up into the brilliant yellow cottonwood leaves, held up one finger again; *P!ah*. Then he made himself busy with a goose wing. He carefully chose two feathers for fletching. Jube put the earrings in his carrybag and stood up. He turned away. Then suddenly he turned around and thrust his arm out straight and held up two fingers and then began to dance around and around his own two fingers. He held them to his face with a puzzled expression as if he did not own them. He grasped them with his other hand and tried to force down one of the fingers but it wouldn't fold. He spoke for the fingers in a piercing irritated voice in garbled Kiowa: *Yii! Yii! Thae hohn noh hon dai!* and then fell to wrestling and dancing with his fingers so that Nocteawah laughed and laughed, threw his head back and shouted with laughter and so saved face. He gave Jube two good knives and took the earrings and the next day rode with them sparkling and tossing in his ears. *Ahô, ahô.*

Chapter 9

WITH HER KNIFE Mary could now help Gonkon inside the lodge. She could trim stew meat and snap off the points of porcupine quills. She was better at the heavy work with the skins. Jube set to work with an antelope skull and his own new knife and made his mother two bone combs with very fine teeth. They stayed near the broken red ridges where Punta de Agua Creek came into the Canadian. The ridges bled red sand into the river, ridges edged with brush and stunted cedar. In the valleys, scattered groups of buffalo were still moving south in the autumn cold. The band of Kiowa stayed there for two weeks. The buffalo carcasses seemed to lie in hills and heaps of hills. Mary cut through the heavy hide from neck to vent and along each leg, stripped out the good liver and entrails and kidneys. Getting the head off was like hewing down a small tree. The meat was cut into round pieces that could be spiraled out into jerky. Gonkon told Cherry to tell her mother that someday they might be so hungry they would come back here to boil up the bones and the feet.

The work was very hard but now Mary had all she wanted to eat and she was stronger and if she was careful she could hide the fact that she sometimes lost her balance and that her vision was blurry.

The man who had smashed her head with a rock after he had raped her often passed her by without looking at her. He had a sun tattoo on his chin as if he spoke to this deity daily, and maybe he did. She pretended not to see him. She made him invisible.

A group of men rode toward them one day and stopped a distance from the encampment. The crier came through the tipis with that jaunty and important way of walking that criers always have and shouted that they were Kiowa-Apache. They came to visit and smoke and after a day or so they and five or six men rode off to the Alibates flint quarries to see what they could find. Everyone was far away from the soldiers and the Indian agent and all the irritation and frustration that came from dealing with those people, and so they would enjoy themselves. Jube stood and watched them ride off. He wanted to go with them very much. To ride in that careless company of young men. Old Man Komah walked past him and then stopped and touched Jube's shoulder.

"Someday you can go with them," he said. "But you have to get your dream first. You don't have any protection now. You got to get your dream person."

Jube stood in the dry grasses as they went past, and saw that every one of them had some invisible phantom riding with him, a transparent being that shone in transient sparkles around their heads, over their scalp locks. A protector and guide. Jube deeply wanted one of those beings to come to him and tell him, *I will be with you always.*

AMONG THE KIOWA-APACHE was a young white captive. Jube saw him sitting on his horse among the other warriors when they returned from the Alibates with pieces of flint striped and spotted in many colors like layered candy. The boy was burned brown by the sun but he was somehow pale beneath this and very thin. His body had no fat on it, and his long bones were prominent and his kneecaps were like cylinders. His stomach and abdomen were flat. His fair hair hung in two braids to his waist, and he wore the stiffened bangs of the Kiowa-Apache, and heavy earrings. He spoke their language easily as if he had no other and moved among the young men of that tribe as one of them. They laughed and rode past one another to bang the convex fronts of their shields in a kind of play-fighting. The young white warrior's shield had a tossing light-brown scalp pendent from its center like a tassel.

When he slid from his horse into the cold pools of Palo Duro Creek his elongated reflection shimmied in the breeze as if it were his spirit detached from himself, paler and thinner and lost. Among the other young men he seemed the replica of a plains warrior that had somehow been left unfinished or perhaps something not yet begun. He stood stroking the horse's neck while it drank.

Jube followed him and sat on an outcrop of red stone. The young man looked up.

"Hello," said Jube.

The young man said something to him in a language he had never heard.

"Can you understand me?" said Jube.

The boy said *underwater person* in Kiowa. He stared at Jube with a wide hostile stare.

"Where are you from?" said Jube.

The boy bent down and picked up a handful of rocks and with a quick bend of his wrist shot them at Jube.

"I no English," he said. "No."

Jube ducked and jumped off the rock and ran backward.

The young man sat down on the ground then, cross-legged with his parfleche boxes, and drew out a rawhide-wrapped package of steel lance heads. He selected one and turned it over in the sun along the sight of his right eye, and its edge was clean as a razor and shone like a line of fire.

Jube approached him again as he would a feral animal. He stepped carefully over the crackling shallows of new ice. The boy suddenly sprang to his feet in one motion and slashed at Jube with the lance head. His eyes were like blue glass.

Underwater boy, he said in Kiowa. *Go, go.*

Jube turned and ran a few yards. He turned back again.

"What is your name?" he said. He said it in English.

The young man lifted his chin and stared downward at Jube from half-shut lids, his eyes fringed in bleached lashes. "Mat-thiew." Then he laughed and turned back to the lance heads.

Jube stood for a moment and then walked back to the village of Kiowa lodges and he was disturbed and he did not know why.

UNDER MARY'S HANDS the thick winter hides changed from something that had come from a bloody wreck of an animal to soft pliable blankets. In them a person would be safe against all the winter snow and cold. If she worked hard enough she might be allowed to keep one. Mary turned the edge in her fingers and saw that the short hairs of the buffalo were thick and dense, more so than any other animal hide she had ever seen.

Gonkon had already chosen two hides from seven-month-old cows for Millie and Cherry and worked several hours making them a Kiowa bed, a couch of basketwork. The little girls were like dolls to her. She combed the lice from Cherry's and Millie's hair with a porcupine-quill lice comb and with a quick flick of the wrist snapped the lice into the fire where they burned up in sparks. She oiled Cherry's hair with fat and twisted it into ringlets. Mary and her daughter both had wavy hair. Jube's hair was a mass of kinks like his father's.

Mary walked out into the cold shallows of the Canadian. She went in the late afternoon when the sun was warmest. She made soap from the yucca root and soaped Jube's hair. Then with her sharpened butcher knife she shaved it off very carefully. "Mama you scalping me," he said. Mary smacked him lightly on the back of the neck and kept on. They would be more welcome in the lodge if they looked better, she and Jube. These Kiowa were a vain and cleanly people whenever it was possible. They admired good looks and shining hair.

She was not called upon to work that day because the other women saw what she was doing and one came down with the loan of a kettle. It was the older woman who seemed to be related to Gonkon and was called in Kiowa *grandmother*. But all older women were called grandmother. Mary boiled their clothes. She stirred the water with a sycamore sapling pole and she and her son stood wrapped in their ragged blankets. She made an ointment of the poisonous mountain laurel beans, boiled and then mashed into fat. She plastered her head and her body with it and then washed it out. The powerful toxic alkaloid made her tongue tingle and her hands shake and the lice all died. Thick wads of Jube's hair wafted off across the sandy flats. They looked like the clustered tatters of the buffalo bulls' forelocks that were sheared off when they fought and crashed into one another head-on in the spring.

Aperian Crow rode by. He was magnificent in large abalone shell earrings and a bright plaid turban, a new soft buffalo robe thick with winter hair, moccasins to the knee beaded in the distinct Kiowa floral patterns. His shirt had been freshly boiled and his flashy dappled gray horse wore an embroidered saddlecloth. The band had shifted suddenly from poverty to wealth now they had found the main buffalo herd. Everyone was well fed and strong. They were celebratory and kind, they wore their best clothes. He said something in the tonal Kiowa language that made him sound as if he were singing, or beginning some melody that was never completed. He smiled and lifted his chin and gestured toward Jube's sheared hair that the wind was taking away, toward Jube's now-bald head. And so Jube got the name Fights in Autumn. This was a joke that it took Jube some time to understand.

Mary and Jube stepped into the open oval entrance of Gonkon and Aperian Crow's lodge. Mary's vision underwent some strange shift as she entered, in that everything became many times larger in some indescribable way, and then shrank down to normal again, but she maintained her balance and they stood quietly to one side without moving. Aperian Crow laughed at the sight of them, their newly boiled ragged clothes sewn together with the agave thorn and its thread, Jube's shaved head shining and Mary's tightly waved hair twisted and packed into the two combs. Their brown arms and legs shone with oil. Aperian Crow indicated that they should sit down in the place of lowest status, to the left of the door, and they did so and then she and her son ate from the bowl that was passed around from hand to hand, meat and dried wild peas and mesquite beans. Mary turned to look at her daughter.

Cherry sat with Millie on their bed made of willow withes, thick with buffalo robes. Cherry tossed a dried, inflated grouse air sac to the two-year-old. She felt important and petted since she was now six and had also been adopted. They batted it back and forth. It was thin and light, a transparent balloon. Two small elegant people decorated with tiny bone rings on their hands and glass beads in their ears and bright red paint dotted all along the parting of their hair. Millie was now called Sain-to-odii.

When they had all eaten, Gonkon handed two buffalo robes to Jube and Mary and indicated that they should spend the night and Cherry called out, "Mama, she says you-all are sleeping inside."

Mary signed her thanks.

"Mama, you pretty," said Cherry.

Mary nodded and smiled.

When the fire had burned low a man stepped inside and waited to be acknowledged. Aperian Crow looked at him carefully and made a gesture for him to sit down. It was one of the visiting Kiowa-Apache. He wore straight bangs over his forehead that had been stiffened until they stood out in a spray. He began to sign to Aperian Crow and so the two men smiled and talked and told jokes in sign language. Mary watched the signing as long as she could, trying to understand and remember, but then her head drooped forward as sleep overcame her. She jerked upright again as she heard them laughing and over the crackling of the fire she also heard Cherry's laughter. Mary looked up, alarmed. Gonkon had said Cherry's name, which was something about a fish, "Ohn pi."

Cherry was signing rapidly. She was making the two men and Gonkon laugh. Her hands signed a story out of the dense and smoky air, threw shadows on the hide walls. She signed with fingers that spoke of falling in the river and chasing the grouse and Gonkon chiding them. She imitated Gonkon's frown and her admonitory finger. The men laughed again. Then with the wisdom of a child who had seen her brother shot dead, watched her mother raped and beaten to the edge of death, who had been dragged along the ground by one arm by a man on horseback until he finally decided to throw her up on the horse behind him, she folded her small hands and quit while she was ahead.

After a moment she turned back to Millie and the balloon, and they bunted it into the warm air with their fingertips. Mary watched the glinting air sac. Is this not how people speak with one another? Is this not the way those who can speak lift and balance words between them and send them into the air to one another and keep the speaking afloat? Mary sat quietly outside the gates of any language. They were closed to her. She watched as the air sac floated and drifted in the currents of hot air from the fire and tumbled back and forth between the girls' fingertips.

THE BUFFALO WERE moving south again. Back to their caves in the remote south and so the people harvested them while they could. They took down enough buffalo to see them through the winter and although it seemed a great deal to Mary she also knew that this supply would dwindle down to starvation levels before the herds came back in the spring and she would try to survive until then because then Britt would come and get them. Mary did not reason out how this could come to be. When they crested a low, sloping ridge she could see the immense distances of relentless plain that lay between her and Britt. He was now a faint image hard to recall, his face and voice were fading and elusive.

They moved west along the Canadian River through white sands and heavy trees parallel to the water, lengthy groves of cottonwood and sycamore and snarling vines; grapevine, greenbrier. Like a four-hundred-mile oasis narrow as a snake. Above this valley yucca and sotol spiked all along the bare slopes. Clear drops on each needle in the foggy mornings. Cherry and Jube took up the singing language and its fluting tones easily and said the names of things and what the things did. An old man whose right hand shook all day and even in the night when he got up and walked around the lodges as if he carried an invisible rattle was called by words that meant *possessed, inhabited, he counts out with that hand the remaining days of his life.*

Jube sharpened his mother's knife every night on a stone, working with an intent look on his face. They had their small space just inside the tipi entrance with their two buffalo robes. It was their space and no one stepped into it and they did not step into the space of anyone else, and as they settled themselves and cooked what they had to cook in the ancient pot they did not look at anyone else, nor did anyone look at them, and so they all lived in their own privacy, inside invisible rooms.

In the mornings Mary got up early to help with the corn. It was blue and red and yellow, the beautiful grains like jewels. It was soaked in ashes whenever they stopped for a few days so that the grains slipped their glassy indigestible hulls, and then had to be rinsed in the river with a net over the mouth of the skin bag and then pounded into a mass and then cooked in the ashes in a square of cornhusks. Old Man Komah called it *tamal.* It was so good, so hot on a cold morning, the thick, yellow pudding smoking from its cornhusks.

Jube thought about where he could go out to hunt. He would make himself a man in this small band. Those who were important and respected were hunters and thus far he and his mother were considered among the poor, the lost, those without status because they had no man to hunt for them, and so he would become that man.

He ran with the other boys his own age and learned to shoot with bow and arrow. It was a simple child's bow made of a single piece of Osage orange. He learned by watching. To hold the bow in his left hand with his thumb cocked up and the arrow laid in that notch and drawn smoothly back to the head so that he could feel every imperfection along the shaft. He saw its yawing flight and how it shunted and missed and struck awry.

He spent a long time sitting near the men to watch them make their shafts and how they straightened and smoothed them, how they were fletched. He learned to use the round shield and dance in front of five or six shooters and stop their blunt arrows. The shield was a toy shield of thin scrap buffalo hide but Jube learned to keep it moving in a figure-eight pattern and bunt off the stob-headed arrows as they came at him. From time to time he was allowed to ride an elderly gelding that had once been white but was now heavily dotted with cedar-colored roaning. He was freed of all heavy chores and the women of the camp always had something for him. A grouse wing or pecan meats crushed and scattered over a fresh tamale or antelope eyes popped out of the head, smoking hot. Once Nocteawah signed that he wanted to see Jube argue with his fingers again, but Jube turned away.

He fought with the other boys. Jube was a hard fighter. He didn't care what they did to him. He and Kiisah smashed each other with rocks and then sank their hands into one another. He took hold of Kiisah's hair and tried to wrench it from his head but Kiisah could get no grip on Jube's hair because he didn't have any. They fell into a dead campfire and wallowed in sand and ashes, silently, rib bones flying up around them. Two grown men came and pulled them apart. One of them signed to Jube, *We are moving. There is no time for fighting. Fight later.* And as they walked away the men were silently laughing. "Fights in Autumn," one of the men said. Jube's left eye closed in a round leaking bulb and blood ran out of his nose but he held a handful of cold wet sand from the river packed over his face for a while and refused all help from his mother.

Kiisah became a silent observer of all that Jube did with pieces of bone. The fish carvings that were to dangle on the line and attract calico bass and carp that lived in the river, the white bone rings with lizards and galloping snakes and fishnet designs etched into them with ashes. Kiisah asked for one and Jube gave him a hair slide made of a ring of antelope thigh bone with dangles made of mother-of-pearl. Making the tiny holes in things was Jube's greatest problem. Then Komah taught him to use a bow drill.

The creatures that lived on the south Texas and New Mexico plains each had their own guarded lives to live on certain trajectories that moved between the seasons and above the earth and below it. Fox fur would shed frost like no other, and Jube wanted foxes. They lived in holes where they kept their young ones away from the world until it was winter, and now was the time to take them. He spent a day and a night watching at a hole in the bank of the Canadian. He did not eat so they would not smell him. When at last the mother appeared he stood up and when he drew his bowstring he also drew in his own breath to suck away the life he wanted to take. He shot her and left her lying with an arrow through her ribs, her jaws snapping like a machine, and ran to the hole and began to dig. He dug into the frozen red soil with his bare hands and then with a stick he found to one side, until he got the kits and clubbed them to death and then the mother. He thrust a sharpened stick through their back legs and put them over his shoulder. They were heavy but skinning was women's work. He walked and ran for an entire day until he caught up with the moving village of Kiowa, running in the cold dust, following the long snaking lines of travois tracks and the beaten paths of horses, until far ahead he could see smoke and the mist of horses' breath lying low to the ground. He could see the poles rising and tipi covers flying out and up, a village appearing like magic among the bare cottonwoods alongside the Canadian. He walked among the expanding tipis with the mother fox and her kits over his shoulder and did not look to one side or the other.

Old Man Komah sat on his cart and called to him.

"Give me one," he said.

Jube turned toward the cart and without a word handed up one of the fox kits with its rich pelt. Old Man Komah took it.

"I will give you something for this," he said. "In return."

"Never mind," said Jube. He waved his hand. "It is a present."

Old Man Komah turned his attention to the dead fox kit so that Jube would not see him smile.

The foxes were put between the liner and the tipi wall to stay cold until his mother could skin them and tan the skins. Jube sat and ate all that his mother and Gonkon gave him. He felt the fat and meat enter his bloodstream in a hot rush and then lay down and slept a long time.

There was a pleasant feeling that night in Aperian Crow's tipi. The Koitsenko called Jube by his name, Fights in Autumn, and made a come-here motion. Jube went around by the tipi entrance to avoid passing between the others and the fire and sat down on his heels beside Aperian Crow. The man took Jube's hand and held it palm up and poured into it five good steel hunting points. Jube understood that Aperian Crow was saying something about asking someone whose name was something about a face in the sky. That he should go to that person to see about a good horse.

Gonkon was the wife of an important man. So far she was the only wife with him. He had two other wives but they had begun to fight between themselves and Aperian Crow had tired of it. He wanted to be alone this winter with Gonkon and so he sent the others back to their families on the Arkansas River far up in Colorado.

Since Gonkon was a rich woman she had a tipi liner: a six-foot-high band of canvas that was strung all around inside and the skirts of it were pegged down to the floor with parfleche packing boxes and stones or whatever came to hand. Then Gonkon could lift the outside tipi skins a few inches between each tipi pole and fresh air roared up between the liner and the outside wall, drawing the smoke up with it. The people in Gonkon's tipi sat warm on the draftless floor. So that night when the blizzard came, they of all the people slept lying with their legs out straight.

It began with a hard, single blast. This was in the late evening when the sun was already down but not all of the light was yet gone. It was very still. The bare cottonwood limbs lifted and floated in black nerve patterns against the fading pink and magenta sky. In those dramatic and discrete slashes of black, Fights in Autumn could see Kokopelli with his cedar flute and hear his songs of love and desire ringing across the drifting nighttime planes of the great world. Suddenly the northwest side of the tipi belled in with the force of the blast and then slackened and then a few moments later it flattened again against the tipi poles and the liner. Aperian Crow lifted his head. He was thinking about his horses.

With a series of shrieks the wind hit again, and this time it carried snow. The sound rose into a sustained howl. Mary stood up and went out with Gonkon to bring in armfuls of wood. They fought with the round hide door, snatching it shut, and tied it down. They stacked the wood against the liner all around the circumference of the tipi and then it was full night and the wind and snow bore down on the Kiowa and all their animals with a great noise.

Mary lay half awake all night to watch the flickering light of the fire shifting on the tipi walls and the liner, a hypnotic and incessant dashing of light and shadow, the noise of the tipi cover and liner belling in and out accompanied by the unpredictable stanzas of the wind. The fire smoke shot upward, carried by the chimney of air that rose between the liner and the walls. It blossomed up into the smoke flaps and out. Whirling eddies of snow sifted down between the flaps and flashed in the light of the fire, and vanished. The fire threw shadows of moccasins hung up to dry so that they seemed to walk against the tipi walls, the fire threw shadows of a fishnet and a gourd dipper snaring the evaporating snowflakes.

Mary lay warm under her buffalo robe. Its dense hair circled her neck. She could hear Jube breathing, deeply asleep, and Cherry in some dream, whispering in Kiowa. All their possessions so hardwon in their places: the knives, the moccasins, her combs and the box of bone and shell and bits of silver that was Jube's workbox, the silver spur and now his arrowheads. His foxes stiff and cold between the liner and the outside wall. Mary closed her eyes. She had ceased to dream in language. She dreamed now only in images.

She dreamed of buffalo skeletons reassembling themselves, walking disjointedly through the snow and wind. They walked in jerky articulation into the world of the storm, striding forward with eye sockets bald as moon craters looking out of their earless heads. The flakes passed through rib cages and the eyeholes of skulls as the skeletons of buffalo walked on and on through the blizzard, undaunted, determined, heading back to where they had come from, far to the south, to the cave of winds where they were endlessly reborn. Where they would re-form over the long winter and then come north again in the spring as they always had and always would.

Chapter 10

❧

THROUGH THE WINTER of 1864 and 1865 Britt Johnson
lived in the cabin by himself. His son Jim lay buried a hundred yards away, above the flood line of Elm Creek, on a pleasant
small bluff with a view northward so he could forever watch for the
Comanche and the Kiowa who had killed him, where he could lie in
sleepless vigil, watching under the full moon, listening for the sound
of a hundred horses at full gallop, a sound that was like no other.

Britt's shadow fell on the plastered white walls, restless and
without comfort. He was impatient with the chore of cooking and
so he ate little and there was little to eat. The bare limbs of the cottonwoods and the sumac, the twisted mesquite, were like iron cal-
ligraphy against the cold sky. The Indians raided only when there
was enough grass to feed their horses, but now and again two young
men or three would cross the Red River on a winter lark and ride
south into Young County, singing about their wish to come away
with Texas horses and Texas captives and to bury their steel points
and bullets in enemy bodies. He kept watch against their coming to
take away what little remained to him.

Britt walked away from his shadow in the house. He went out

to Jim's grave and talked to the boy. Jim had said, *Dad you never say much. Dad tell me about how you all came from Kentucky. Tell me about Nacogdoches.* And he had said, *Well there's not much to tell.* And he remembered the disappointed, frustrated look on Jim's face.

He had told Mary to go away with the little ones and leave Jim with him, and that was what had happened.

And so he talked; he asked Jim how the grass would be, for now that Jim was in the otherworld all things were known to him. He told Jim that he would set the old grass afire in two months, as soon as the cold and the random freezes were gone in late March, and then the new green grass would grow up thick as a carpet. Duke and Cajun would have plenty of grazing then, and they would grow fat and strong and then he would leave for the Indian country and he would bring back Mary and little Cherry and Jube and whoever else he could get hold of. He said that the flames might sweep over Jim's grave but the boy would not mind that.

Around him the slow lifting prairies of grass like old straw. But when those remains were set afire the grass came back. It came back like the fulfillment of some ancient promise, a treaty made with the world time out of mind. It seemed that the new grass even now was forming and trembling just under the surface of the earth. That it moved in flashing sequences beneath the soil and when it came up in spears his horses would grow strong on it and he would leave this house, the only one he had ever owned.

In the distance Britt saw a man on horseback coming from the east. A white man. Britt could tell by the way the man carried himself and by the way he rode. His horse was in poor condition. It slogged along, throwing its hooves one by one as if they were as heavy as cannonballs. He had come a far distance and little to feed the horse.

Britt stood up. He had nothing left but one sack of corn but he would offer it. He walked back to the house against the wind.

His horses had seen the traveler and came galloping down the wide sloping draw, tossing their heads and calling out to the strange horse. Britt called "Come boooooooys! Cope, cope!" and opened the corral gate as if he would feed them, and they dashed in and he shut the gate on them.

Britt went inside the house and opened the last sack of field corn and poured a bucket full and went back out.

The man sat on his trembling horse and regarded Britt.

"Who are you?" he said.

"My name is Britt Johnson."

Britt put the bucket on the ground beside the tie rack and the man dismounted and pulled off the bridle. The bit was an army bit, stamped CSA on the button. He rebuckled the bridle around the horse's neck to hold him because Cajun and Duke were calling out to him from the corral in a storm of noise.

"Who do you belong to?"

They watched the ravenous animal crush down on the corn grains.

Britt said, "Moses Johnson. Ten miles from here." He said that because it was the least trouble and spared explanations.

"Why ain't you there?"

He looked up at Britt. Britt was taller by nearly a head, and he was gazing out over the creek with his long, perfectly black eyes. Finally he said, "Mr. Johnson and I have an agreement."

The man was very thin and when he took off his hat he had a deep scar that circled half of his head on the left side. His eyes were black and his stiff, greasy hair was black and stood out in spikes. His boots were sewn together crudely and the stitches were giving way. His trousers were some indefinite color and were held together with patches upon patches.

"The war's over," he said. "They got Lee boxed up."

"Has he surrendered?"

"Not yet. Won't be long, though."

A slow caution overtook Britt as he stood there and watched the horse eat but he gave no sign and there was no change in his demeanor. He was thinking as to what was the best thing to say and at the same time he wondered if all black people were now free. What was to become of them, especially those in Kentucky where he knew his mother lived still, or had been living when he last had word.

"We don't get news out here," Britt said.

"How are the Johnsons?"

"They are all right."

"What about the Durgans and the Fitzgeralds? The Hambys?" The man looked up and saw the headboard on the bluff on which was written, *Jim Johnson Age 12 Kilt By Indians 1864*. He didn't say anything about the grave but turned and looked intently at Britt. "I am Thornton Hamby's cousin. I am just come back from Virginia."

Britt said, "There was a raid in October. We think they came down across the Red. We were gone to Weatherford, the men. We went for supplies."

The man stood silently and his hand tightened on the horse's mane.

"They killed my boy there, and Doc Wilson, and Susan Durgan, Joel Meyers and his boy, and some more people there near Fort Murrah. Eleven all told. The Hambys and Pevelers are all right. They took my wife and my two children captive, and Elizabeth Fitzgerald and her two grandbabies. Little girls. They killed Joe Carter on the trail. That was Mrs. Fitzgerald's boy from her first marriage."

Britt thought about saying more but he didn't; it was more than he had said to another living human being in weeks. The man listened silently. The horse lifted his head from the bucket and looked around for more. Since there was no more he called out to Cajun and Duke. His mouth was wide open and bawling right beside the man's ear.

"Hush," the man said. "This is the loudest horse I ever had in my life." He unbuckled the bridle from around the horse's neck and slipped the bit once more into its mouth. "They never got any of the Hambys?"

"No sir. They are on high ground. They saw them coming. They hid the women and the children in a cave there on the creek and went back to Bragg's place and held them off for five or six hours. Pete Harmonson was hit and he died here a week ago. Tom Hamby was blinded. Thornton Hamby was home on convalescence. Susan Durgan shot Little Buffalo before they killed her." Britt gestured. "That's what old man Peveler said. He looked at the body. He knows them."

"Killed him?"

"Yes sir. Killed him graveyard dead."

The man turned and looked up at the sky. His nostrils flared out as he took deep breaths. He absentmindedly patted the horse on the neck and said, "Hush, hush." He turned back to Britt. "Any word about the women and children?"

"Not so far."

"You know the things they do to white women."

A slight pause. "I know." Britt put his hands into the pockets of his coat and clasped them tightly shut against the bitter words he was about to say but didn't.

The man got back on his horse. The thin gelding staggered a little as he stepped up into the stirrup. He had two different stirrups on the saddle; one was steel and the other was made of wood. He was using a piece of carpet as a saddle pad.

"Have they asked at the agency?"

"No. Too dangerous to go up there." Britt paused. "I am going to look for them when the grass is up."

"You are?"

"Yes."

"Alone?"

Britt lifted his palms to the air and then once again put his hands in his coat pockets.

"Well I'll be damned." The man looked around the house and barn, the washhouse and pens, saw the brush cleared along the creek. He raised his hand. "Thank you for the feed."

"I have a little coffee and some buffalo that's still good," said Britt. "If you want to stay to eat."

"I better get on." The man fooled with the reins. "My name is Vance Hamby. I knew Thornton had come home wounded. Other than that we got no word."

"No. Never hear anything out here."

"And you're going by yourself."

"Yes."

Vance Hamby sat silently for a moment and then he touched his hat brim. "Well, take care, Britt."

"Yes sir. I will."

IN THE MIDDLE of March Britt was visited by Paint Crawford and Dennis Cureton and Vesey Smith. The three were also free men. Paint was free because old man Crawford had died but before he died he had written the paper that set him loose, and Dennis Cureton was free because he had been free back in St. Louis before he ever came out here with the Cureton family, and Vesey Smith was free because he had the manumission papers from somebody named Smith that had been killed in the Plum Creek raid back in the forties. No one had ever noticed that Smith's dated signature had been written ten months after his death, but there were so many Smiths around, and so many people killed here and there, that nobody gave it much attention. North Texas was a good place to be a black man; slave or free, they were all expected to carry arms. Every hand was needed to a gun or a plow or a branding iron and there were no records and what with the chaos of the war and incessant guerilla warfare with the Comanche and the Kiowa a person could pretty well do what he liked and he could be whatever he took a mind to as long as he had a strong back and a good aim. Britt walked to meet the men out of the smoke of the grass fires that burned in long, thin lines across his pastures.

They saw young Jim's grave and the shambles of a womanless house and Britt's lonely bed slept in only on one side. Mary's yellow print dress hanging on a peg. Jube and Cherry's wooden tops on their spindles to one side of the hearth. Tears came to Vesey Smith's eyes, but he turned away before Britt saw him.

They asked about Tom Hamby and how he was and Britt said he was as blind as a posthole. Vesey Smith asked how it had come about that he was blind and not dead because to be blind you have got to be shot in the eye somehow and usually it will go on through to your brain. Britt thought about it for a moment, and then said that when they had all forted up there during the raid, forted up at Bragg's place, Tom Hamby had stuck his head out the door to grab at a dead Comanche who had fallen against it because he wanted the man's cartridge box. When he did that, he was hit in both eyes by a load of pebbles. Some Kiowa had run out of buckshot for his shotgun and had loaded it with pebbles and caught him in the eyes and burst his eyeballs.

They got into a discussion as to whether all the black people were now free or not. Britt sat and listened. They had come out with some homemade wine. Not very much, and it was acid, but it left him with a pleasant glow. They asked him over and over again for his opinion since he was a man very much honored and respected in the small black community of north Texas and in many ways in the white community as well, but Britt was not a talker. All he said was that they should wait until they heard one way or another. Just live your lives and be careful, he said. I think there is going to be trouble but what kind I don't know. He said he was waiting for the grass, and then he had a job to do, and after that job was done then he would think about it.

"Hear him," said Paint. "The man has talked for five whole minutes."

"I was born to listen," said Britt.

"You going after Mary and the children," said Paint. He lifted his fingers to his chin. His hand and the left side of his face were turning white in eccentric, random blotches.

"That's right," said Britt.

"Britt, we want to start up a freighting business," said Cureton. "We can't do that if you dead." Dennis shifted his long knobby bones around on the cowhide stool. He was tall and thin and had a long neck and a face with high cheekbones, a collection of angles.

"I'm going to bring them home," said Britt. He tore off a strip of newspaper from a publication called *The White Man*, from Jacksboro. He rolled a thin cigarette of crisp tobacco leaves, a Mexican custom he had picked up in Nacogdoches. He lit it and smoked and turned up his tin cup of cloudy red wine. It was as sharp and caustic as the mustang grapes from which it had been fermented. "Whew!" He wiped his mouth. "God almighty."

"Britt, it might be too late," said Dennis. "I hate to say them words." Dennis lifted his long thin fingers to his mouth and then dropped them like spiders on his knees. "If you'll pardon me."

"We'll see."

"Well, we want to talk about this freighting business," said Vesey. "If you don't mind."

"Talk on," said Britt.

And so by the light of the fire they conjured up wagons and teams. They predicted entire divisions of the United States Army that would arrive in Texas now that the war was over, when they came to reoccupy the deserted forts. The army would need everything from horseshoes to black pepper and one of these days there would be a railhead at Fort Worth carrying these things. Things that needed to be off-loaded and then transported to Fort Belknap, Fort McKavitt, all the towns that would spring up when the war was over. A man needed to learn how to pack glass panes, trail one wagon behind another, how to waterproof canvas for the wagon sheets.

Britt nodded. He thought about the great tall wheels of a freight wagon and their intricate shaping. He liked the thought of them rolling forward over the land and the land falling out behind like a glossy, brass-colored substance or a textile woven out of the earth itself. He and Mary and the children with a few luxuries, and more children to come. Money to buy some great draft horses with feathered fetlocks and heavy necks. Mary chattering away in some little schoolhouse where she would delight black children with her stories, her alphabet, her *strown* and *reigneth*.

Vesey said there would be the men coming home, towns going up. That's the place for a free nigger, is freighting. That's what the free niggers did in the South, done it for years. White men don't care if you freight or barber. Now I don't want to be a barber. I'd cut somebody's ear off by mistake and they'd lynch me.

"Don't make jokes like that," said Britt.

Vesey hastily poured him another cup of the bitter wine. And so his three visitors imagined a business; a fleet of freight wagons that they would own themselves and not be held down to a little farm. A little farm on some creek bottom was about all they could get if they could even get that, since they did not know what their status was now. Hard work, busting dirt. How much better it would be to sit on the high seat of a freight wagon traveling under a wide sky and calling out the names of your team. And so Britt listened and said nothing and when the thin moon came up and they were asleep in their blankets in front of the crackling fireplace he walked out and sat down by Jim's grave. Out of the dark plains to the north came the liquid, collapsing sound of some night bird casting about in the air. The two of them sat for an hour and watched to the north and listened for the sound of horses.

IN EARLY APRIL the grass came up bright green out of the burned-over pastures and Cajun and Duke walked slowly with their heads down, tearing up great mouthfuls of it. Britt began to stitch his boots together again. He cut away the shredded leather around the seams and pieced them back together and hoped they would hold out. If not he would have to go barefoot. He had his jerk meat drying before a great fire in the yard. He had ten dollars in silver money and with this he would ride to the Johnsons and ask to buy enough field corn to make into hominy. The hard corn and hominy might last him to the Red River and it might not. The rest was ransom money. There was nothing he could do about his coat or his pants. His most valuable possession was Cajun, a dark bay with a white snip on his nose. He was close to sixteen hands and well-built and kept his weight, his black hooves were solid and took the shoe nails easily. There was very little that frightened him. As long as he had Cajun Britt felt he might make it. He would use his big slanky gray horse, Duke, as a packhorse.

A little after sunrise on the day that he had planned to start, Thornton and Tom Hamby, Moses Johnson, and the Pevelers rode up with a loaded packhorse.

"Are you going, Britt?" asked Moses.

"Yes sir," he said. "The grass is good. It's time to go."

Thornton stepped down and tied the packhorse to Britt's yard rail. "There's as much as you can use there," he said. "Flour, meal, biscuit powder, bacon grease. There's my .36 Colt. It's the police model but I put a Navy cylinder in it. Two extra cylinders, loaded. There's powder and caps and such as that. And my holster."

Moses Johnson came and laid a package on the chair in the yard. He laid it down carefully as if it contained secrets or prophesies. He was silent a moment and then regarded Britt. "'Thus hath the Lord God shewed unto me: and behold a basket of summer fruit. And he said, Amos, what seest thou? And I said, A basket of summer fruit.'" His long upper lip worked. "That's in Amos. Not many people know that."

"No they don't, Moses." Britt used the man's first name and it went unremarked.

"There's boots and pants and a coat and two shirts. Some jewelry and Mrs. Fitzgerald had about fifteen yards of figured silk so we threw that in too. Whatever interests them."

"Well," said Britt. "Y'all didn't have to do this."

Moses hesitated a moment and then said, "Well, we did too." He touched his brown beard and drew out the thin ends of it.

Tom Hamby said, "And there's dresses and things in there for Mary and Elizabeth should you get them back. If they are alive I don't reckon they will have much left on in the way of dresses."

Britt nodded. There was an acid feeling in his throat. "I packed her yellow one," he said.

"We talked about it and if we go this leaves the women and children with no protection," said old man Peveler. "That's what happened last time. And if the Federals catch us armed they'll say we're in rebellion again and they'll send us to jail in Austin."

"When did that come about?" said Britt.

"It's the new rules," he said. "The Union army come and occupied Texas now, well at least they're in Austin. And they are laying down some new laws. They don't want people forming ranger companies."

Britt shook his head. "That ain't going to work," he said.

"That's how it is."

Britt wondered if this applied to black men as well but said nothing. "How are people going to hold off when they come raiding?"

"I don't know, Britt. They ain't no arguing with them." Peveler gestured toward Duke. "Leave that horse with me. Take that pack pony. He's thrifty and he'll carry a quarter his own weight. I just shod him."

Britt nodded. "I'll do that. Thank you."

Tom Hamby sat on his horse with his hands atop one another on the saddle horn and his blind face turned in their direction.

"Britt," he said. "I wish you wouldn't go. If you go I never expect to see anything of you ever again except your hair." He stretched out a hand into the unseen world and his eyelids trembled over the caverned sockets. "And I wouldn't be seeing that I would be a-feeling of it."

"Well, I got to, Tom," said Britt.

When they left, Britt stood in the yard to see them off and each one rode past him and bent down from his horse to shake Britt's hand as he went by.

Chapter 11

꩜

HE STARTED OUT in a spring windstorm and made thirty miles by evening. As he came into the low, even valley of the Brazos, he turned into the shelter of the trees. Tall white-bodied sycamores whipped toward the southeast and their new leaves streamed like sequins into the wind. Lightning forked out of the clouds and in its brief catastrophic flash he saw the tree trunks become incandescent. The heaps of crumbling flood debris and jittering small leaves of the chokecherry lit up as if with pale fire. He unsaddled and sat with Moses Johnson's good slicker over his head under the drumming rain. It sprang into glassy bars as the lightning flashed again and again. The wind tore at the slicker as he grasped its edges around himself and the horses stood like stoics with their heads down.

When he woke up the wind had died and he could see stars overhead through the leaves. The Dipper stood at midnight when he re-saddled and laid his hand on the packs and checked all the wet knots and stood into the stirrup and went on.

He splashed into the Brazos River in a blaze of moon reflections at a ford that he had used before. Beyond this he only knew to go northward toward the Stone Houses and the Red. The trail led him out of the valley of the Brazos into a landscape of new grass colorless as ash under the tearing clouds with a half-moon breaking through and the incessant, sulky noise of draining water. On his left side a low escarpment sat in black shadows thick as a pool of tar. The world smelled of earth and wet grass. The moon washed the land-scape with an intense light. The clear plains air made it seem as if it were light that came out of the landscape itself. A great yellow star hung in the northeast and it turned on a sparkling axle over a world of moonlight and grass and a northern horizon drawing away even as he and the horses rode toward it.

He did not know where the trail led but it went on straightfor-wardly through the world of winter grasses bent and broken, pierced by spears of new green. Stands of prickly pear cactus were blacked with ominous and suspicious shadows until he rode past, and then ahead appeared yet another. He was cold but he didn't stop to get out the heavy wool blanket. He rode on with the lead rope in his hand and the packhorse coming after. He came up yet another rise. When he stopped, Cajun lifted his head and pointed his ears. Britt searched back along the trail where they had come. In the remote distance several rising stars spread out as if they had been spilled, and the three stars that shone in a line together lifted up out of the eastern horizon.

He rode slowly through a broken landscape that seemed clear to the sight but yet it was not. Something large and spotted loped slowly and without concern across the trail a hundred yards in front of him. It paused with its head turned toward the horses and the long tail moved back and forth. It watched them come on for a long time. Then it went on at the same pace.

The trail wavered faintly on, due north.

Finally in the midst of a great stony flat with the horizon on all sides only an indistinct and darker line he stopped and patted Cajun on his heavy neck. He was in the war land where no one lived but only traveled through. It was a strange and peculiar place. It was a land designated for murder and captivity and flight. An arena where men came to contend with one another and kill one another. He had to make it through to the other side where they lived and ate and swam in the rivers and slept easily every night.

This was a world unto itself that lay between the Canadian River and the Rio Grande as if it had been designated on the day that God made it as the place where men would come to fight and kill one another. The Texans had brought their women and their children and their slaves right into the middle of the war land and expected to set up houses and fields and herds and live as if they were in Maryland, and were surprised on moonlit nights like this when Comanche arrows sang through the air in the dark.

A swarm of stars appeared against the eastern horizon as the moon went on westward. To the north stood two broken rises of caprock. In the dim moonlight it seemed that sand and gravel were draining down their sides from under a crown of dark stone in a stealthy movement, but as he stared at it nothing moved. When he turned away it seemed to start up crawling again.

There were no house lights anywhere, from one horizon to the other. Only the yucca standing with streaks of moon reflection running down the glossy spiked leaves. Hope was very strong in him, as strong as his two hands, and he turned his mind toward the woman who was waiting for him at the end of all this. He thought of her kind face and it was like conjuring up a lighted window in this heartless landscape, a lighted window in an inhabited and comforting house.

Then at some time during this long night he saw far ahead of him the minute winking of a fire. The fire appeared and disappeared, flared and then subsided. Britt felt the wind in his face. It was blowing toward him but he could not detect the smell of woodsmoke. Whoever was there, and whatever animals they had with them, could not take up his scent, either.

He made out to his right what seemed to be a patch of low scrub and went there and found a sturdy stand of brush where he could tie the horses. He fought his way through the cranky limbs to the bole of something big and tied them there. Then he went forward on foot.

The enormous belt of stars poured across the black meridian. He could see by their light. He walked and watched where he put his feet and then stopped to look at the firelight again. After a while he stood at the edge of a gentle slope and a drainage below him of cracked stone layers in starlit stripes. Along the side a flame burned out of the rock and a star glinted on the surface of a black pool that wallowed in dirty stains down the incline. It burned alone and untended.

Oil. It's rock oil that has caught afire.

If it had drawn him to itself then it could draw others. Britt eased himself down on his heels and searched out every jittering shadow. The entire slope was alive with them and they seemed to flow and crawl, surfaces blazed and shone red and then disappeared as the flame sank to a sapphire blue and then rose again. As he sat he could smell sulfur and the reek of oil.

He got up and paused to listen for a moment and then turned to walk back to his horses. His spurs made a low chinking sound. He then stopped and was confused. All around him the flame threw out long faint bars of moving light and shadow. He did not know where he had left his horses.

He thought of himself alone and on foot in this immensity. On every side a deeper darkness marked the horizons of the earth and above the night sky alive with stars. He should have counted his steps. He did not want to wait for dawn and be caught afoot wandering in this no-man's-land. He did not know where his horses were. He started walking again because it was the only thing he knew to do. This time he counted his steps. From time to time his spurs rang on stone. At six foot one he was the tallest object in this dark and limitless world. He had become the center of the universe because the only reference point was his lost self.

Lord look down and have mercy, he said. *Have mercy on my wife and children.*

God now seemed to be a cold force, a great wheeling being, the world's axletree turning above his head in worlds upon worlds of light.

He walked on with his ringing spurs and the light damp wind at his back.

He called in a low voice, *Come boys.*

There was no answer. Not even that of his horses loose and walking away or grazing. Britt stood without moving for a long time. He released a long, nervous breath and began to walk again, south, with the Dipper at his back. He counted a hundred paces. He stopped and then he called again, louder, *Come boys! Cope, cope!*

Cajun nickered to his left. An anxious sound. The packhorse called out as well.

Britt turned toward them and called again and heard their worried voices. In a few moments he was with them. He stroked Cajun between the eyes and laid his hand on the big horse's solid muscle of chest and shoulder. Then he tightened the cinch by feel and stepped up and they went on north.

After a long while the moon sank into a straw-colored haze and a great gray battleship of cloud stood in the north, wired with repeated strobes of dry lightning. It had to be near sunrise. Then it would get warmer. Britt was very tired. At the horizon in front of him a thin line showed the faint gray of coming dawn.

HE CROSSED THE Red River into Indian Territory late the following morning. He rode to the edge of the floodplain. Below him were the bottoms. The tall trees were all on the north side. On the south bank where he sat and watched, the post oak was stiff and short. Their leaves whispered in wet sibilants. He was uneasy and exposed here on the river and at a crossing frequently used.

Across the broad Red River Valley lines of pelicans slid away to the windward in the blue air. The river itself wound and shifted among white sands. The pelicans were newly arrived on the springtime plains and had a thousand miles yet to go. When Britt rode to the water they rose up reluctantly and sailed away a short distance in orderly rows. Britt searched up and down the bank, looking for a trail where people crossed. He had heard that the quicksand was deeper than a man was tall.

He came upon a wide track. It was beaten down by the flat round prints of horses that had no shoes. It led through the short trees down to an unlikely-looking place at the river's edge. He did not like the appearance of a sand and gravel shoal on the far side. It seemed washy and unstable. The trail showed that this was the crossing, but springtime floods could well have changed everything.

He got off and reset the pack on the packhorse's back. The pack harness was a good one with a breast collar and a crupper. He tightened these and tucked in the ends of the straps and the knots over the two packs. He was satisfied that it was balanced evenly on both sides and would not pull the horse to one side or the other. He took off his boots and fed a bit of string through the pulls and hung them around his neck. He unloaded the revolver and the Henry and wrapped the loads and the two extra cylinders tightly in the slicker. He put this over one shoulder. He pushed the Henry into the scabbard and wrapped it and the revolver in a piece of ducking. He tied them on top of the pack. Then he hung his holster and belt on the saddle horn.

Britt spurred Cajun down the short, steep bank and into the water. Cajun had flat hooves like paddles and the big horse plunged in, thrashing through the water with walled eyes and Britt off to one side, clinging to the saddle horn. Cajun went under once and the Red River poured into the horse's mouth and eyes and he came up snorting. They were all right until they came to the farther bank and its shoal of gravelly sand. Cajun began to sink and flounder. He clawed at the watery gravel and it gave way beneath him and the water clouded with streaming sand. Britt staggered alongside and sank to his knees and then sank even more.

The horse surged forward. It was as if he were digging out a canal. The whole bank ran with water around and under the gravel and it continued to collapse under them. It was worse than quicksand. Britt sank to his thighs alongside the horse and felt the myriad clickings as the small stones gave way under him and muddy red water filled the holes that Cajun stove in the shoal. Britt forgot about the packhorse. Cajun fought so hard to get clear that he was bucking; his legs and hooves made sucking noises as he charged forward. It nearly broke Britt's hold but his large hands gripped the saddle horn and held, his veins seeming to lift and burst out of his wrists and arms.

At last Cajun struck on an underlying layer of stone or hard clay with his front hooves. He bent his back in a high curve and clawed up onto it, still up to his knees in the soupy gravel but his front feet were on some buried hard surface and he charged forward, dragging Britt alongside.

The packhorse was already across and stood calling to them in a shivering high whinny. He had got across and run up the bank among the trees. Britt came to him, streaming water, and patted his wet neck and then unwrapped the revolver and the rifle. He wiped them carefully and then broke open the barrel of the Henry and blew it out and then snapped it closed again. He ran his hands down Cajun's legs. He had pulled them both out of that collapsing sink and there he stood unhurt and ready for travel. Britt loosened the cinch for a moment and let both horses rest and then went on. They passed through the belt of tall sycamores and cottonwoods of the north bank, then into brushy bottoms and up onto the plains again.

As he went on he felt in his back and knees how tired he was, and he rode with his feet out of the stirrups to relieve the pressure on his knees. He saw that the land on the north side of the Red River was a country of long waves of land that sometimes rose to broken ridges. Here and there a dark streak where a few trees grew along a dry watercourse. He rode on with a chill April wind in his face and shivered uncontrollably in his wet clothes, but he did not stop.

BRITT CAME UPON Tissoyo at noon on the day he crossed the Red. Just beyond the lifting prairie stood the Wichita Mountains, blue and remote, dreamlike. In front of these distant peaks the young man sat on his horse combing his hair, keeping watch over a herd of more than a hundred horses. Britt stopped immediately, pulling back on the packhorse's rope. The horses were going to call out at any moment.

Tissoyo drew a quill comb through his hair. He had parted it behind and had thrown each half forward over his right and left shoulders and was combing the right part, the silky black hank in his hand, stroking the comb through over and over and singing. Above his head chill and massive ranges of clouds blossomed upward, tier upon tier, and among them vultures sailed effortlessly.

Britt had heard that the Comanche and the Kiowa and the Kiowa-Apache possessed some kind of bottomless and efficient magic that carried them through all the years of their wars on the settlements, that kept them ahead of Rangers and cavalry alike, and this magic had to do with their hair and with other people's hair. He watched for a few moments as the young man tied up the right braid with a thong and then wrapped it in a long shank of otterskin. Before he could dress the other braid the packhorse called out in a wild, long whinny and Cajun called out as well. Britt held both hands out into the air on either side of himself.

They sat and looked at each other for a long time. The Comanche sat on his horse with one braid done up and the other loose on his breast. He had stopped singing. Britt sat without moving and his hands out to either side. The young man searched the country behind Britt but it was wide open and no concealing trees or brush in sight, only the bending new grass and the horizon and great clouds soaring upward, white as porcelain and crisp at the edges. The black man was alone in all that wide and limitless space.

Slowly Tissoyo began to wrap his undone hair. When his second braid was wrapped in otter like the other he lifted his hand and made a come-on motion, cupping his hand toward himself.

Britt rode slowly toward him. The herd of horses grazing on the side of the slight rise lifted their curious heads to Britt's horses and several called out with their ears pointed. Britt was not sure what to do. There was no telling what he ought to do. Neither man reached for a weapon. The distance between them closed.

"Unha numuu tekwa eyu?"

Britt shook his head. He stopped within speaking distance.

"*Habla español?*" Britt said.

"*Ah, si, si.*" The Indian watched him for a moment. Then he said in Spanish, "Are there others with you?"

"No one."

The young man sat on his buckskin horse and considered. He wore a revolver in a holster and a bandolier over one shoulder, a buckskin shirt and moccasins with leggings.

"Where are you going?"

"Here," said Britt.

"Hm. Where do you come from?"

"The Brazos River." Britt placed both hands on his saddle horn, one on top of the other. "Tell me your name."

The young man told him his everyday name, Tissoyo, and said that he was a Comanche, *Nemernah*. He continued to gaze at Britt and Britt knew the man was trying to place him in some category where armed and mounted black men took up their social space but could not.

Tissoyo wanted to know if Britt had brought things to trade. Britt said that he was not here to trade, but was looking for things that had been stolen and wished to recover them, and he told Tissoyo his own name as well. Britt.

"No lead bars? Do you have caps for a Nah-vee Golt?"

Britt shook his head. "No."

"Then you are not a Comanchero. We are waiting for them to come from Santa Fe with ammunition. It's spring, it's good grass time and time for people to travel." He gestured at the land, and then bent forward with one forearm on the saddle horn and inspected Britt closely. "What lost thing are you looking for?"

"The women and children that were taken on Elm Creek south of here, near Fort Belknap."

"Ahhhhh." Tissoyo nodded. "Brrreet." He said Britt's name over and over. Britt sat quietly and brushed away the mosquitoes that had begun to land on his horse's neck and his own neck. He did not know what sort of customs this man lived with or how he thought inside those customs and traditions and so he proceeded with great caution into an alien landscape of the mind and the mind's eye.

"It was the fight where Little Buffalo was killed," Britt said.

Tissoyo lifted his eyebrows very high. "So I heard," he said.

"They have my wife and two children and they are black like me."

Tissoyo lifted his eyebrows once more and once more said, "So I heard."

Britt loosened his hand. He had shut his hand around the saddle horn in an iron grip and his fingers were cramping. That was what the lift of the eyebrows meant; it meant, *So I heard*.

The Comanche stuck out his lower lip and lifted his chin toward the northwest. "There. That is where they are," he said. Britt nodded. "Your wife and two children. A week away. With the Koi-guh."

"The Koi-guh."

"You have come a long way," said Tissoyo.

"Yes."

Tissoyo smiled brightly. "Stay with me," he said. "I was sent out here to look after Esa Havey's horses because I threw flowers at his wife. Do you understand Via Láctea?"

"No."

"The Mexicans say Via Láctea." Tissoyo threw his head back until he faced the cool blue spring sky overhead and stuck out his lower lip. That was how they pointed at things, Britt thought. You never knew in what gesture or sign or object did magic lie, hidden maledictions or a bewitching that might be started up unawares like a jackrabbit bounding out from under your horse's feet. Sprinting toward trouble and horrors on the grassed earth. "That up there, at night, stars without end in a long river across the sky, the Mexicans call it Via Láctea."

"Ah," said Britt. "I understand." He meant the Milky Way.

"We Nemernah, we say, Esa Havey. Same. Via Láctea, Esa Havey."

Britt lifted his eyebrows in the assenting gesture. This seemed
to make Tissoyo happy.

The Comanche dropped both hands and patted his horse on
either side of its neck. He said, "The camp chief, the civil chief, said
I was a troublemaker and making eyes at Esa Havey's wife was im-
moral and immodest and somebody would end up having to pay a
great many horses to make somebody else feel better when his honor
was wounded. So I might as well look after Esa Havey's horses until when the strawberries are so big like the tip of my little finger
because if this kind of thing kept up I would end up in debt to him
anyway. And here I am all by myself. What do you have to eat?"

Britt smiled. "Probably about the same as you."

"Do you have sugar?"

"Yes, I have brown sugar." The horses shifted beneath them, trying to touch noses and smell of one another's breath. Britt glanced
toward the horse herd. Several horses had Moses Johnson's brand
and others carried the brand of Elizabeth Fitzgerald. In the noon
sun they had broken out in a slight sweat that looked like leopard
spots on their necks. He said nothing.

"Do you have coffee?" said Tissoyo.

"Yes. But it is green."

"We will roast it. I have a square of metal so big, thus, it is from
an army train. It was the top off of a box of ammunition. We can
roast it on that. Come with me."

Chapter 12

❧

THEY RODE TOWARD a shallow valley in the distance. A small and shallow little creek valley with pecan trees, the grass grazed short by the buffalo until it seemed it had been carefully mowed. Not a stick of underbrush. Just the naked smooth grass and the stand of pecans and here and there fallen limbs. The gray trees with their bark as corrugated as runs of ancient lava. The pecans lifted brilliant, lime-green leaves no bigger than a snail's shell up to the sky as if washing them in the cool air. The two of them set about gathering wood and when the fire blazed in transparent blue flames they stood in the smoke to rid themselves of mosquitoes. Britt unsaddled Cajun and lifted the pack from the pack pony's back. The two of them shook themselves and then dropped down on their front knees carefully, like old people, and then flopped over on their sides and rolled with deep grunts of pleasure. Cajun wallowed on his back and his big hooves pawed with delicate gestures in the air. They got up and shook again and sent grass and dirt flying. Then they trotted over to the Comanche horses.

When the fire was down to coals Tissoyo set the metal lid of the ammunition box over them and Britt shook out green coffee beans onto the lid. They banged and jumped as they roasted. Britt took up a stick and began to turn the beans and shift them around.

She was alive. The children were alive. Britt felt as if he stood before the opening of a deep cave in which a great treasure was hidden. A treasure made up of all the things that made life worth living. If it would get his wife and children back he would have taken up his rifle and shot his new friend in the back without a moment's hesitation but he had to enter this perilous and occult cavern with his hands empty of weapons.

"How are we going to grind them?" Britt asked.

"Here, I have this thing." Tissoyo turned to a rawhide box and poked around in it. The pack box was painted with careful and brilliant designs along each seam. Loving work. Tissoyo held up a sausage grinder.

Britt nodded. It was Elizabeth Fitzgerald's sausage grinder. The wooden handle had a chip out of it at a certain place. He had seen Mary use it many times.

"All right," he said.

So he sat and ground up the roasted beans in the sausage grinder and although it was very coarse they still got good coffee out of it.

"The Americans do excellent things with wheels." Tissoyo turned the handle of the sausage grinder.

"Yes, they do."

He saw that Tissoyo had not bothered to set up a tipi. He was young and unmarried and he did not have a wife to set it up for him and so he was living the bachelor life in the way of bachelors all over the world and in every age; things in a muddle and careless with the remnants of food and his extra moccasins and a shabby wool coat hung on a tree limb. The Comanche drank the black coffee out of a tin cup and gestured toward dried meat hanging from the rack in cinnamon-colored ribbons.

"Now take some of that and put brown sugar on it and eat as much as you like and tomorrow we will go out and find a buffalo calf."

"Good," said Britt. He saw a Spencer repeating rifle in a decorated rawhide scabbard and a hard box of untanned leather beside it for the ammunition.

"You came through the raiding country," said Tissoyo. "The place where we raid."

"Yes, I did." Britt took a pinch of brown sugar out of its bag and sprinkled it on a strip of jerky. "Honey is even better," he said.

"Yes, but we don't have the hives up here like they do down in the hills," said Tissoyo. He pinched up a sticky clump of brown sugar from the bag that Britt pushed toward him and dropped it on the dried meat. He crushed up the sugared jerky between his strong white teeth. The fire reflected on the small pools of water that lay in the shelving creek bed.

"Yes, there are plenty of hives down there," said Britt. "Down where there are big trees. Where are the white women and children?"

"The white woman? White. Ah, *taibo*. She and the little girl are with Esa Havey, with us Comanche." Tissoyo swallowed. "Very good. The *taibo* woman is a slave to the first wife of Eaten Alive. The first wife of Eaten Alive is my mother's sister's child. They got into a big fight. The big loud *taibo* woman was in the water, on the Washita River, to bathe her tits because her tits were so big and swollen where Hears the Dawn and That's It had beaten on them down in the raiding country. She was sitting in the water to cool her tits and Eaten Alive's wife came and told her to get out of the water and threw a digging stick at her and hit the *taibo* woman over the left eye." Tissoyo tapped himself over the left eyebrow. "So then the big loud woman got up and took her stick away from her and smashed my cousin in the head."

Tissoyo began to laugh.

"Um-hum," said Britt. He reached for more of the jerky.

"The big loud woman was yelling something. Hears the Dawn said she was saying 'Kill me.' Hears the Dawn can understand their speech, but he can't speak it very well. Everybody was laughing. Maybe she said, 'I will kill her.' Somebody took up a rifle and said he would kill her, the loud woman, if it would make the loud woman happy, but Eaten Alive threw the man's gun barrel down and said he could get a hundred dollars for her and so not to kill her. Now then, Eaten Alive's first wife lay there for an hour and then got up and went and got her digging stick and walked away from the camp for turnips. She walked like this."

Tissoyo laughed and with his hand made a wavering motion.

Britt laughed as well and then choked on the sugar and cleared his throat. He smiled briefly and then took up his coffee cup. Maybe God had sent him into the camp of this talkative, gossipy, lonely young man who had been sent into temporary exile because of his frivolous behavior and who would probably talk the entire night. He had not been shot at. He must not lose any of these advantages. He nodded and smiled.

"And the captive girl?"

"Yes, yes, she is so big." Tissoyo indicated the height of the three-year-old with his hand. "She has gray eyes and black hair."

"Yes."

"She is sick. The loud woman tends to her. The girl sleeps in Eaten Alive's tipi but she sleeps by the entrance and it is cold there and there is always wind coming in when somebody comes in and so she is still sick. People step over her when they can but they don't always look where they are stepping and sometimes people step on her. She is too sick to get out of the way."

"You just came from the Wichitas."

"Well . . ." Tissoyo looked up and squinted one eye. "It was a half-moon like this three times when I came."

Three months, thought Britt. *She could be dead by now. But they were alive three months ago.*

"There was nothing I could do. Maybe things have changed by now."

Britt nodded.

"How could I tell Eaten Alive how to run things in his own tipi? He says I saw the *rinches* shoot my little brother in the head when they came down on our camp on what you call the Llano River and so what do I care about one of theirs? If she lives she lives."

"When was that?"

"I am not really sure. No, it was when Eaten Alive and some others of his same age rode down the river they call the Nueces and shot up the red-bearded man's *ranchito*. They tried to stab the redheaded girl to death, but she wouldn't die. Before they started his little brother begged to go along." Tissoyo lifted a hand. "What can you do when a child begs you? So he took him. And then after the fight at the redheaded man's *ranchito*, they came back north, and Eaten Alive and all of them camped at night there on the Llano and the *rinches* came upon them. What a fight that was!" Tissoyo slapped his hands together. "I only heard about it. I was too young to go. How I wish I had been there. When they all came home they were streaming a kind of fire around them."

Tissoyo ran his hands down through the air, each to one side of him, with waving fingers.

"They sang as they came into camp. Fifty men all singing of what they had done and how they had charged into the farms and ranches of the enemy. And somebody started up a mourning song for Eaten Alive's little brother, ah, it made me cry to hear them singing as they rode. You could hear their voices for a mile. They had a red scalp and two blond scalps, very long ones that waved and shook in the wind, and in that hair was the soul of the enemy held tight, tight. There was light all around them and all around their war horses and it was as beautiful and dangerous as the color of lightning."

"Think of it," said Britt. *Fijate, hijo.*

It was now fully dark. A light wind carried the odor of new grass that speared up through the stems of winter growth. A dry pelt that sulked heavy and brass-colored and fallen. Enough new grass that before long the Indians could ride out of their safe and comfortable camps and into the war country where everything was permitted and everything was done.

"But the one you call a black woman and children and the very smallest *taibo* girl are with the Koi-guh," Tissoyo said.

"The Kiowa. Why?" Britt said.

Tissoyo looked at him in surprise. "We always split up the captives," he said. "So they can't talk with one another and plan to escape." He gestured and his copper bracelets rattled. "You say *Kiowa*. Very well."

"I see, yes." Britt picked up a stick and pressed it on the coals. "Where are they?"

"Farther north. They went far up the river you call Canadian, north of the Wichita Mountains. Past the Antelope Hills. Aperian Crow doesn't want the agent to bother him about things that are no business of the agent's. The Kiowa are tricky people. I will help you. You are a slave yourself."

"No," said Britt. He thought of how to explain it. "They let me go."

"You paid them," said Tissoyo. He turned to Britt expectantly. "Dollar."

Britt considered again what to say and after a moment he said, "Yes. I paid them."

"Well, in the morning we will talk and I'll tell you how to deal with the Kiowa. They are stingy people, and they are tricky to deal with, but I am going to help you. The *taibo* baby girl is the one adopted by Aperian Crow's wife. His youngest wife is in love with her. You see I will tell you everything, how you are to act and so on."

He loves intrigue, thought Britt. *It is meat and honey to him. He loves to get in the middle of something and keep secrets and to outbargain people and to know things other people don't know.*

"I will do whatever you say," said Britt.

"Good, then."

They fell silent. In the east there was a faint flicker of lightning on the horizon. There was no moonrise except for a thin and milky light filtering through the overcast. Tissoyo lifted his head toward the east.

"Now, there are four Thunders," he said. "There is Copper Thunderbird and Walking Thunder and Falling-to-pieces Thunder and the last one is Shy Thunder, which is what that is, and it may come to us and it may not."

Britt lifted his head to the ancient pecan trees and their brittle limbs. All the leaves were lit up on the undersides by their campfire and when they moved there was a flickering quality to them. The great fragile limbs arched above them.

"If there is a wind we'd better move out from under."

"We will see."

Britt called his horses and fed them a handful of corn and then hobbled them by the fading light of the fire and left them to graze on the new grass. They nosed busily through the overlay of dead stems for the lime-green bouquets that had started up, spray after spray. He sat down on his saddle blankets and turned his saddle upside down so that his head was against the fleecing of the underside. He was not afraid of Tissoyo or that Tissoyo would change his mind. He was wary of what could change Tissoyo's mind for him. There might be some sign, some portent that would tell the Comanche that his guest was dangerous, that his guest harbored secret designs and needed to be shot. It could be the appearance of a flock of ravens in a certain pattern, or the appearance of one of the four thunders bearing a warning and speaking in an imperative voice. Britt was as alert to the possibility of signs and portents as was Tissoyo himself. He lay himself down carefully under his blankets and left his revolver wrapped up in his coat under his saddle and commended himself to God and fell asleep.

HE AND THE young Comanche sat on their horses downwind as a herd of two or three hundred bison walked deliberately down the long slope of the world and its tissues of wavering new grass. Britt crossed his hands over his saddle horn and watched. They were good to watch. They smelled like cattle, warm and rich, and their deep grunting calls made a web of sound almost below hearing. Their upright horns curved out of the mass of their dark heads so low to the earth. They paced toward the banks of Deep Red Creek for their morning drink. Ravens overhead sailed along with them calling *tok, tok.* He saw a raven alight between the horns of a shaggy bull and with a quick motion settled its tail and crossed its wings behind and began to hammer at the bull's head, pecking up ticks. The bull stared off at the creek waters and continued to chew. He was ragged. Patches of winter hair fell away in wads and the scissortails carried these away in tufts for their new nests.

The ravens had seen Britt and Tissoyo but they did not raise the alarm. They were busy. The cows and bulls walked grazing toward the water. When they came to a low place in the bright red sands of the bank they slid down and they splashed into the current, the cows weighing a ton and the bulls a ton and a half, sinking to their bellies in the brilliantly colored water. They were the divinities who ruled the intricate progressive movements of the year on the high southern plains, and other animals walked along in their passage. Wolves trotted patiently at a certain distance and the light-headed buffalo birds darted at their hooves as the buffalo flushed up insects and the prairie voles and the ferrets drank from their tracks. Cajun stared at them with a fixed look of intense interest, his ears pointed toward them.

"There," said Tissoyo. A cow and a calf came up behind. Belated and unprotected. "The milk in its stomach is very good." He lifted the Spencer and squinted his left eye and fired.

The other buffalo kept on grazing without a pause. Tissoyo circled behind the herd and roped the calf carcass and dragged it away. Then he dismounted and slashed into its stomach and lifted out the bloody cheese of buffalo milk and rennet. He scooped a handful into his mouth and then offered another handful to Britt. Britt took it and swallowed it like a gory custard without blinking.

He wiped his mouth on his sleeve.

"Excellent."

THAT NIGHT TISSOYO began to pack his saddlebags. Tissoyo was moved and excited at the idea of following the Kiowa into the north and bargaining for captives. He shook out his blankets and packed small bags of face paint.

"Now, what do you have to offer them?"

"A few things," said Britt. "Some gold coins."

"Ah, they are going to want more than that."

"We'll see."

"Your horse is excellent. But they have horses as good."

Britt waved his hand impatiently. "We'll see."

Tissoyo went out into the evening and roped two paints and led them up. A Medicine Hat paint with a white face. Above his white face, red ears and forelock like a red cap on his head, and a splash of red across his chest like a shield. A patch of red on its rump and a red tail slashing at flies out of the red patch. A strong horse with hard white legs and good bones. The other a mare nearly all black except for a white stripe down her nose and a patch of white on the near side and trim white ankles. She had a curved neck. She was graceful and delicate.

Tissoyo wiped grease out of a small hard box of rawhide and applied it carefully to the Medicine Hat's nose.

"He gets sunburned," he said. "I have to look out for him." He fussed over the horse, drawing out the red mane between his fingers. "It's his white nose. His skin is white under the hair and he gets sunburned. Mmm, mmm, mmm." He blew his breath into the horse's nostrils.

"Why are you taking them along?"

"I don't want them to get stolen. Somebody would steal them right away if I were not with them."

That night Tissoyo drew a map in the dirt. First they would cross flat country northward and travel around the west side of the Wichita Mountains. Then on northwest, to the Washita River, and then on to the Antelope Hills on the Canadian. After the Antelope Hills they would go northwest to the Black Mesa country. Tissoyo gestured to the northwest. In the far north the Great Plains were very wide, but as you came south the plains narrowed and it was not far from the Black Mesa country across to higher mountains. They would be there. If not, somewhere else. In the morning he would ride to camp and get some boys to take the herd and then they would go. Nobody would care. Just so long as he stayed away from Esa Havey and his young wife.

Chapter 13

⚜

THE TRAIN RATTLED through the flat country in the April rains. The roadbed of the Illinois Central was only a few feet above the level of the Wabash River, and Samuel could see the long low wetland shimmering and speckled with floating islands of trash and the sun shining in a dull haze on the spring earth. Early the next morning they came to the Illinois shore of the Mississippi at East St. Louis. He and other passengers and freight crossed the great river on a wallowing ferry that fought clumsily against the spring floodwater. They tied up to an iron ring as big as a cartwheel on the St. Louis levee and then they went by hansom cab to the clanging railheads at Chouteau Pond. The passengers boarded another train there and continued westward.

Going through the Ozarks he saw people who had not seen a razor or a bar of soap since the dawn of time. He sat in the dining car and stared out the smoky windows with a book in his hand. The track and roadbed were very bad; the car swayed from one side to the other and Samuel closed his eyes and shut his book.

The porter staggered to his table. Behind him was a wide

amiable-looking man with his hat in his hand. The porter asked Samuel if he would mind another gentleman sharing his table.

Samuel looked up. The man held a large portfolio under one arm.

"I am interrupting your reading." The man turned to the porter. "I will wait in the smoking car."

"No, no," said Samuel.

The porter bowed over the white napkin on his arm. He said, "This is Mr. James Deaver, he is a correspondent and he is very hungry."

"Do please sit down," said Samuel. "My name is Samuel Hammond."

"As he said, I am James Deaver." The man sat down across from Samuel and glanced at him and then out the window and then back again to the menu in front of him. "Well, you are going west somewhere," Deaver said. He ran his finger down the menu. "Somewhere exciting and probably dangerous."

Smoke erupted in thick and separate puffs at the window. The train jumped again and a man across the aisle with his bowler hat lying upside down beside his fork snatched at his soup bowl. The waiter came down the aisle touching each table for balance. Samuel nodded to him and said he would have the catfish and rice. The man across from him said beefsteak.

"Yes, I am going to the Indian Agency in southern Oklahoma."

"There. I was right." The whistle howled as they smoked past a road crossing and a small village of frame and log houses. Broad signs in heavy black lettering demanded that people vote for Bellingham For Mayor and crowds of men arguing with one another from wagon seats and on foot barely looked up to see the train rush past. Cinders came in the window. "Which Indians?"

"I believe they are called Comanche and Kiowa."

"Ah!" Mr. Deaver was interested. He smiled and flaunted his napkin in the air to shake it out of its folds. "They are in the news lately. Now that the war is over, editors are looking around for mayhem. And here you are traveling to the middle of it. The very middle."

Samuel considered this for a moment and then nodded. "And you?"

"I work for the *New York Herald* as well as some Chicago papers. I am to team up with another correspondent in Omaha." He wagged his fork. "I hope we do not report any news of you, Mr. Hammond."

"I would hope not."

They sat back as the plates were laid in front of them. The waiter took his napkin and flicked away cinders, making a sound like *um um um!* and then left them. The train jolted and the waiter sailed along in his erratic walk, undeterred.

"They have invented a new bureaucracy, I have heard. The Indian Bureau. And they have given the various tribes out to several religious denominations. To pious and deserving people. Am I right? I am usually right."

Samuel laughed. "Yes, you are right. I am to be the new agent there. I am of the Society of Friends, and I try to keep my piety in check."

"No offense, no offense!"

"None taken."

"And how are you going to manage them?"

"Oh, I think we want to try some unusual methods in dealing with the Indian people. Honesty. Honoring our treaties with them. We will not use the military. Not on my agency."

Deaver nodded and then reached out to seize his water glass before it turned over as they hit a particularly bad stretch of track. They both held to the arms of their chairs and the car tipped to one side and then the other and then finally righted itself.

"Yes, novel and untried," said Deaver. He took up his knife and fork. "So they have given the most warlike tribes on the plains into the hands of Quakers. The most warlike and the least known. How interesting life is. How strange." He ate a large bite of his steak. "How peculiar are the ways of government."

"Are they so warlike?" Samuel said.

"Yes."

"How do you know this?"

"I am a newspaperman. Actually I am an illustrator but I am in the company of reporters and other illustrators. We love warlike and exciting things. It's how we make a living, our little mite, such as it is."

"And where are you going beyond Omaha?"

Deaver had a broad face and a wide nose and the sort of build that would become fat on good food, but at the moment his collar was somewhat too big for him. His mustache was short, reddish, and severely trimmed, and so was his hair. The tips of his fingers were spatulate, and there were ink-stains on his forefinger.

"After Omaha? To Denver. Along with my colleague from the *Herald*. After the story broke about Chivington's massacre of the Cheyennes, eastern papers were very interested. Savage doings. Outraged women. You can only hint about it, of course. Then, I think, I will make my way south if I can find a writer to go with me. Down to Indian Territory, same place as yourself. To report on the red men of the southern plains." He dropped a piece of his steak and expertly stabbed it up again. "Wild times in the wild west." Deaver wiped his mustache on his napkin and settled back in the racketing chair that trembled with every rail joint that clattered past beneath them. He tapped his fingers on the table. "I think you have a kind heart, Mr. Hammond."

"If I have, it is God's gift," said Samuel and smiled. He had known an engaging infantry sergeant in Sheridan's Fifteenth Corps who was an expert in both gossip and theft who somewhat resembled Deaver. Samuel gestured toward the man's portfolio. "How long have you been an illustrator?"

"Oh, seven years or so, which is probably a mystical number or something."

"You must have worked during the war, I imagine."

"I did, I did."

He waited but Deaver said nothing more but turned in his chair to lift a hand to the waiter, who was bolting down the aisle with a lidded pot of coffee, taking advantage of the comparative steadiness of the train to shoot coffee into people's cups before they hit a bad stretch again.

"Where?"

The coffee splashed into the cups, and the waiter swiped at the stains and then hurried on.

"I was in Tennessee with Grant for the *New York World*. I missed the battle of Pittsburgh Landing. Some people say it was the battle of Shiloh. And then on with Sherman. And on and on. I suppose your denomination worked with the Sanitary Commission?"

"They did. I met Mother Bickerdyke, that remarkable woman."

"Ah well, so did I! January of '64. I had switched over to the *Chicago Tribune*. I was there outside of Chattanooga when she tore down the breastworks for cooking fires. Saved the wounded from freezing entirely. It was a terrible storm."

"Yes." Samuel ate his fish. "Wounded on both sides suffered extremely."

"She was a singular woman, Mrs. Bickerdyke. So we know someone in common."

"Yes, so we do," said Samuel. "And then where did you go?"

"Oh, then where? Yes, I shifted over to *Leslie's*, because their reproduction plant is so much better, and stayed with Grant all the way into Virginia and Richmond. Lord, Lord, I am glad it's over and done."

"Yes. We all are."

"I thought for a while when Lincoln was assassinated it was going to start up again, or something was. Jeff Davis thrown out a window, Lee drowned in a butt of malmsey."

Samuel said, "It seems to me the nation was too weary."

"I think you are right." Mr. Deaver finished his steak. "Far too weary. I was up for three nights running doing sketches of the mourning drapery in St. Louis. I looked into people's faces. They were crushed. Exhausted. As for me, the black drapery on everything was a great deal of trouble. You have to keep in mind your sketches go to an engraver, which is how they reproduce them on the printed page."

"I didn't know that."

"No, people don't. They think it's done with magic lanterns or incantations."

It occurred to Samuel that Deaver was a sort of messenger who shifted shapes and locales, traveling from one human tribe to another and introducing incongruous images to each, an outsider who loved being outside. "So an engraver copies your sketches."

"On wood, yes. And then they are printed."

They turned to the window, to the bewitching flow of the landscape. How poor these people were. Horse harness made up of rope and pieces of carpet for padding. Men walking down the road barefoot with their ankles and pants legs brown with dust. One small town was a ruin of brick shells and standing doorways without walls and all around these doorways and sometimes windows glittering black heaps of burned wood and brick at odd angles.

"That looks as if it were shelled," said Samuel. "Are we in Missouri?"

"Yes, there was quite a lot of fighting around here," said Deaver.

"I knew nothing of it."

"No. Fighting in the east crowded out all the other news."

After a few moments Deaver laid down his knife and fork and drained his water glass. "I must find my berth. Must jot down a few notes."

"It was good meeting you."

"Indeed! Fortuitous. I may come upon you down in the Indian Territory one of these days."

"It would be my pleasure." Samuel stood up and gave a slight bow.

"Good luck to you, Mr. Hammond. I wish you well and a safe journey," Deaver said. "Guard your possessions from the army and the Indians both."

SAMUEL HAMMOND ARRIVED at Baxter Springs, a small town in the farthest southeastern corner of Kansas. It lay just west of the Missouri line and just above the Oklahoma border. It had huddled in these rolling hills against the ravages of guerillas and partisan warfare since 1857. The people appeared comatose with the effort and blood expended to no known purpose. The train station was still draped in black in mourning for the death of Lincoln. It had faded to gray. From here he would go by wagon to the Indian Agency in Oklahoma.

He was to be accompanied to the agency by a cavalry unit from Fort Leavenworth. Loose bands of young Comanche and Kiowa men drifted through the Territories and also road agents and unsurrendered Confederate guerillas. Samuel had reluctantly agreed to the guard.

He went to see that every basket and box and trunk was properly shifted from the train to the wagons. The spermaceti candles, his winter clothes, the extra boots, crates of dishes, chamber pots, medical supplies and reams of paper and bottles of ink. The people at the train windows watched with faces pressed against the glass like fleshy dots as a soldier heaved up a leather-strapped trunk and dropped it. It fell on its side and broke open. Quires of paper slid out in planes. The soldier gathered them up, dust and all, and said, "Sorry sir, sorry."

The soldiers were dressed in worn uniforms that had seen much marching in the East. They were lank and dusty and weary of conflict of any kind. They sat on barrels or the edge of the train station platform with reins in their hands or went into the Baxter Springs General Merchandise for barley candy or tobacco. Their horses splashed their bit shanks in the water troughs.

At last the convoy of five wagons was lined out under a bland late-April sky. There was a remuda of forty or so horses and a cavalry escort. The officer in charge said they would not likely be attacked; they had twenty mounted and armed men. He said, "They will soon hear about us, they will know where we are every day and every night."

Samuel said, "Must we go armed?"

The captain, a youngish man named Robert Dearing, stared at

him for a moment and then said yes. It was best to go armed. The two mounted soldiers on either side of them glanced briefly at each other and then off into the distance with blank stares. The horses leaned into their collars and the wheels flung gravel in sprays and they left Baxter Springs behind.

The landscape around them gradually drifted into rolling timbered hills that seemed to move in waves as they went past. The wagon smashed from rock to rock. The detachment of soldiers rode along in a column of two. From the scabbards their walnut rifle butts with brass butt-plates shone in the sun. It was spring, and he was far to the south and west of Philadelphia, and the sun was warm.

That day as they journeyed on beyond Baxter Springs they passed some few cabins and once a settlement of five buildings. Along the road they met a man driving a wagon full of immense bones. The captain stopped as he came toward them and stood up in his stirrups to look into the wagon bed.

"What have you got there?"

The man pulled up and said it was a mammoth skeleton broken out of the side of a creek bed bone by bone, and he was taking them to Baxter Springs to telegraph somebody somewhere, if he could figure out who and where, to see if he could not get some money for them. He was smoking a pipe in the figure of a man's head. The skeleton lay heaped in the wagon bed in a chaotic puzzle. The leg bones were big around as a small tree, the half-skull the size of a steamer trunk. Part of a curved tusk rolled upward and then was broken off. The creature must have stood fifteen feet at the shoulder.

Samuel walked alongside for a few yards to look at them. The mammoths had stood on these great bones in some age beyond ages. Unaccounted for in Genesis or anywhere else. There were giants in the earth in those days, and here were the white remains.

The man said he figured there were two worlds long ago and these mammoths came from World Number Two, which was also lived in by werewolves and the Great Black Dog and the sheehies, which his grandmother from county Fermanagh had told him about.

"This son of a bitch must of been as big as the Capitol dome." He knocked the dottle from his pipe, which made it look as if the carved man's head was losing its smoking brains. "What do you figure it ate?"

Samuel walked alongside and puzzled over it.

"I don't know. They must have needed a lot of sustenance."

"Well, whatever it ate, it must have eat it all up there in World Number Two and left his bones here in World Number One."

"That could be."

Sometime in the distant past the Indian people had known these immense beasts. Maybe they had hunted them or prayed to them. For the first time he understood that the red men had myths and histories of their own going back to the beginning of human time. That these myths had nothing to do with Europeans. Nothing.

He wished the man good luck and then wrote down Lewis Morgan's name and direction in Albany, New York, for him on a scrap of paper. He told the man that Mr. Morgan studied Indians but he might know someone who would be interested in these bones. The man thanked him and carefully folded the paper and tucked it in his vest pocket.

As they traveled, the timber shrank down to isolated stands and then appeared only alongside the stream beds. At night several soldiers set up his tent, and put up a folding bed and a table and chairs. Beyond the walls of the tent the crude and brutal world rolled broken on every side. He ate hard pilot biscuits and pemmican, which was sticky and thick, and once in a while the company cook brought in a plate of boiled gray vegetables.

"What is this?" said Samuel. He sat at the folding camp table with his hands each to one side of his plate.

"Prairie turnips, sir. We dig them out of the ground. They eat like potatoes."

"Thank you, Mr. Cardwell," said Samuel. He had carefully learned and remembered most of the officers' and the cook's names so he did not have to use their military titles. "Much appreciated."

One soldier was disciplined for brawling. The captain had him brought up on charges. His sergeant spoke for him, on his behalf, and said that the argument was caused by his theft of a silver whistle from another soldier but he was a good man and worked hard and was always sober. It did him no good. Samuel walked out on the prairie when they tied him to a wagon wheel and ignored the sounds of the long thin rod slamming into the soldier's back and his astonished and helpless shouts. That night out of the clear dark air he heard the triumphant tooting of the silver whistle in the hands of its proper owner until the sergeant shouted for silence.

The next day the soldiers closed around them as they passed by an encampment of plains Indians. The white cones of their tipis rose up from a draw of post oak dotted with new leaves. Thickets of smoke drifted around the camp. Indian men in a state of near nakedness sat on their horses alongside a herd of long-horned cattle. Samuel sat up, rigid and still. He saw a white woman, naked from the waist up, carrying a load of firewood on her back. She walked with a slow, determined walk between two tipis. The woman's breasts were ringed with tattoos, circle after circle right down to her nipples. Her hair was a bleached-out brown color thickened with some kind of clay plaster and she had tattoos at the corners of her mouth. She saw the soldiers and dropped her load and disappeared among the tipis.

"Mr. Dearing! Mr. Dearing!"

The captain in charge came riding back. He touched his hat.

"There is a white woman back there." Samuel leaned forward on the wagon seat. "There is a white woman in that encampment."

"Don't say anything," the captain said. "We will be lucky to get through here with no trouble."

"Why is she there?" Samuel clasped his hands together. "Surely we don't allow that."

"Allow what?"

"Allow American women to go about the tribes as common women."

The captain paused and then said, "She's a captive, sir."

"Well, why don't you take her back?"

"They won't sell."

"Sell?"

"We have offered two hundred dollars but it was refused."

"Go and insist that they release her." Samuel stood up on the jolting wagon seat and held on to the backrest.

The captain leaned out of his saddle and spit his quid on the ground.

"That would mean we'd be in a shooting situation, Mr. Hammond. There would be a lot of shooting and everybody would be really unhappy." He paused. "And it's possible she wouldn't want to come back."

"And why not?"

"She may have been with them since she was young, and if that's the case then she's married and got Indian children and she doesn't speak English."

Samuel sat down again, confused, caught between the iron blades of several conflicting facts.

"Do you know who she is?"

"We think she's Martha Hudnell. If that's who it is, she was taken from Fredericksburg in 'forty-four. She would have been about five at the time." He bit off another chew of tobacco. "The people down there have been trying to get her back for years but unless you just go in and shoot everybody you are probably not going to get her back for any money."

"Where is Fredericksburg?"

"In Texas. South of the Red. Down there in the hills."

"It's impossible that we can do nothing about this."

The captain nodded. "Yes sir, I will make out in my report that she has been sighted."

The wagons went on, all their canvas covers lurching in different directions as they came upon a dip or a shelf of stone, each in turn. Two of the cavalrymen sang, *It's your misfortune and none of my own.* Samuel's wagon and himself as well now were weighted with paperwork and worry. The image of the woman with the blue eyes and plastered tawny hair came back to Samuel in infinite detail, the woman taking long steps, her unbound breasts wobbling and her head bent against the tump line on her forehead.

It was outrageous to have a white woman walking around with her breasts exposed and those breasts ringed with dark tattoos, her brown hair in sticky strings bouncing about her shoulders with a great load of firewood on her back. But then why would it be acceptable for an Indian woman?

Samuel knew he was going to have dreams about this.

And so he did. That night Jesus appeared to Samuel in a business suit and asked him to sign something with a strange pen made of hair. To sign it would be fatal. He was resigned to this when he woke up in thick down layers under an early-May prairie dawn. In spite of his dream he felt very peaceful and quiet. He listened to the men shouting orders, orders that had to do with feeding the teams and who should be hitched with who. The military bugle calls tore out through the blue air and smoke rose up through the cranky limbs of the timber belt where they had camped.

That day they came to a traveling people strung out for half a mile, people a soldier said were Osage, taking their horses to the new spring grass in the Sans Bois Mountains of eastern Oklahoma. The women and children passed them riding in wagons. The men's heads were shaven bald except for a scalp lock bursting with feathers, and small spotted dogs trotted importantly alongside the wagons.

Then after five days when the land was empty of people of any kind and only miles of dim, rainy prairies where the wind bleached currents in the grass, they came to a group of Kiowa-Apache men, blinking in the rain. There were ten or twelve of them.

The soldiers talked their way past the Kiowa-Apache on the strength of the treaty and the fact that there were twenty soldiers along with the wagon. The two groups rode past one another in a state of humming tension with no weapon unsheathed but ready to hand. The Kiowa-Apache men held their blankets hooded over their heads like monks' cowls. Samuel looked into each face as they passed. At their rifles wrapped in pieces of canvas and their hands loose on the reins, the dark tattoos. Their reserved faces.

That night Samuel thought about the captive woman. That she had been taken but now lived, probably quite happily, with the Indians and had an Indian husband and children and so he resigned himself to it. The reports of white women and children killed might well be exaggerations of the Texans, who exaggerated everything. It was how they were. All you had to do was to listen to the Texans' tall tales, their songs, which were full of bloody revenge stories. Only hear them. The army teamsters and buffalo hunters that had joined in with them for a while, sitting at the campfire singing "Down by the Ohio."

I held a knife against her breast, as into my arms she pressed, she cried O Willie don't murder me, I'm not prepared for eternity.

Chapter 14

❧

SAMUEL MADE AN office of the front room of the new agency house, set out his forms and pens and papers. Placed his worn Bible atop the mantel. The house stood fifty yards from the banks of Cache Creek under the newly leafed cottonwoods. The trim was bright with new paint. A schoolhouse was being built as he had requested, and the agency warehouse repaired. He would set men to work on a sawmill and a blacksmith shop. Two miles away was the rudimentary army post, with buildings of adobe and picket housing three companies and their horses. Restless troopers shot dice, repaired tack, and smoked. They drilled on the dusty parade ground. They lost things and went hunting for them, cut hay in the bottoms, and once in a while found something alcoholic and high-proof to drink. Civilian contractors had begun to lay out the foundations for the stone buildings that would become Fort Sill.

Samuel sat down with Colonel Grierson. Dotted leaf shadows bounced in the dirty window lights. How good it was to be under a roof again.

The colonel said, "You have about two thousand, five hundred

Comanche, and one thousand, nine hundred Kiowa and five hundred Kiowa-Apache. There are three hundred Wichita." Grierson handed him a sheet of paper. He sat with a military posture. Grierson's upper lip was covered with a brown mustache. He still wore the insignia of Griffon's Tenth Division, Cavalry. His uniform was somewhat faded, especially at the knees of his trousers and at his shoulders. The yellow stripe running down the outside of his pants denoting cavalry was threadbare where he habitually tucked his pants leg into his boot. "Those are approximate. A great many of them are living as they always have, out on the High Plains, and they don't come in to be counted. So let's guess at maybe four thousand all told."

"Is that all?" Samuel cocked his head.

"Yes. From what I read in old reports, at one time they were ten times more. Maybe thirty thousand. But reports of cholera and smallpox epidemics on the plains started to come in in the fifties. I guess it was when the gold rush wagons went through. Nobody heard about it until about 'fifty-one. 'Fifty or 'fifty-one."

"Then they lost most of their people."

"Apparently. Much reduced."

Samuel bent his head to the desk before him and thought about it. Tried to imagine it. Then he said, "Very well." He went over the figures. "And you are clear as to your duties?"

"I believe so." Grierson had his hat on his knee and both boots side by side on the floor.

"And would you go over them, please?"

"Sir, I am under your command. We are allowed only to ask the Indians to remain here on the reservation, and we are not to confront them in any way. If they leave we might ride out and ask them to return. We are never to engage." He lifted his hat from his knee and replaced it again. "That's about it."

"Just so. How do you feel about that?"

"I am perfectly content, sir."

"Good."

"It was a long war, Mr. Hammond."

"Yes, it was."

"And as a Friend you had no part in the fighting, but I can tell you the men sent here are fairly worn down and they are willing to forgo any hostilities. And so am I."

Samuel inclined his head and glanced up at Grierson from under his eyebrows. "I understand perfectly well. I drove an ambulance for Sherman's army medical corps. I know very well they are weary."

"Ah." Grierson glanced at Samuel and something about his thin body relaxed beneath the uniform. "I see. A Howard?"

"No, the Finley. I was at Chattanooga and then on down to Savannah."

"The Finley was a good machine. Got carried off by one myself. How long were you driving?"

"A year. 'Sixty-four. It was instructive." Samuel hesitated, and then said, "It was humbling."

Grierson bowed slightly. "My compliments, sir."

Samuel folded his hands together. "Entirely unnecessary, Colonel. Unlike yourself I was rarely in the line of fire."

"Still." Grierson reached into his pocket and drew out a scrap of paper. "Now, I have a young man I can assign you as a clerk. He is with the commissary and his term of service is completed. He understands very well the intricacies of the paperwork requirements of the federal government. It is a style all its own."

"Excellent!" Samuel said. "That will relieve me of a great deal of worry. And his character?"

"He has a good-conduct medal."

Samuel nodded. "Awarded to enlisted men who have not absconded with unit funds, attempted to seduce the commander's wife, and have not contracted more than the company average of venereal diseases." Grierson laughed and Samuel smiled. "Does he use spirituous liquors?"

"Every chance he gets."

"Well, send him. We will see."

"There is a Mexican woman to cook and clean for you. She was rescued from the Comanche."

"How was that managed?" Samuel lifted his head.

"Last winter. There was a big blizzard in January, they tell me, and a band became scattered. The last agent sent patrols out to look for them and they came upon her."

Samuel thought for a moment and then said, "I don't think it would be appropriate. Since I am unmarried."

Grierson leaned back. "Then I will send you a dog robber. He'll carry your washing to the post for the washerwomen there."

"Good."

"Also a translator. Onofrio Santa Cruz. Another Mexican captive, he was with the Comanche. Fluent in Comanche, Spanish, and English." Grierson turned to look out the window where his sergeant stood with their horses. "And I would like to leave five men here with you at least for a while."

"I will not have armed guards here at the agency," said Samuel.

"I understand that. But until you get settled in, let's say five men and a sergeant to help out with your buggy horses and hauling in forage and so on. A work detail."

Samuel frowned. "All right. And now, about captives."

Grierson spread his rein-callused hands. "They want money or trade goods. I don't know if this new Indian Bureau has a budget for that. Or if your denomination has."

"But that's ransom money."

"I know," said Grierson. "Agent Donelly who was here before you was paying two hundred dollars and once fifteen hundred to get someone back."

Samuel lowered his head and stared at the floor, thinking. There was a long silence. Then he said, "Colonel, what is that?"

Grierson lifted his head and craned, his hands on his kneecaps. "A scorpion, sir." He stood up and walked across the room and stepped on it. He came back and sat down. "Stuff your shoes and boots with something. They like hiding in shoes and boots. It is painful but not fatal."

"All right." Samuel regarded the spiky, twisted clot. "Did Donelly then receive some of that money back, under the table?"

"It's possible." He paused. "With Agent Donelly anything was possible."

Samuel put his head in one hand, briefly. "And they expect to continue this traffic in human beings."

Grierson lifted his shoulders and turned his hat in his hand. "As far as I have heard the red men have always taken captives. It's a kind of custom. Sometimes the captives survive and sometimes they don't. Sometimes the red men themselves survive and sometimes they don't. Life is hard for everybody out there."

"Especially if your people are reduced to a tenth. Imagine it."

Grierson nodded. "Various realities out here unknown in the East, as I have learned." He cleared his throat. "Here is the legal situation. It is illegal for Texas state troops or ranger companies to cross the Red River into Indian Territory and onto this reservation. It is against our orders to pursue raiding Indians over the line as well, even in hot pursuit. Once they come onto the reservation they are not to be confronted. In addition the reconstruction government in Texas is forbidding any state militia or ranger companies at all. The new requirements are that we cannot use force in any way. I am very happy with that. Believe me. But they do raid down into Texas, and they take captives. They say that was their hunting and raiding country long before we came. Then the parents and relatives come here to the agency and want the agency to get their children back, or whoever, but unless we offer money and trade goods we're bolloxed."

"This is all new to me," said Samuel. He crossed one boot over the other and dust sifted into the air. "I was never told about this when I agreed to take on this task."

Grierson lifted his shoulders. "I can't imagine why not."

"Well. Can you give me an idea of how many captives are out there?"

"Well, most seem to be children." The colonel pulled another worn and folded paper from his pocket and opened it. "Let's start with boys. Let's see, here. Joe Terry and the Elams boy from the hill country. Adolph Korn from the same area. All about the same age. Rudolph Fischer, grown by now, a warrior. Cherry and Jube Johnson, Millie and Lottie Durgan, they were taken along with two adult women last fall. Another girl, Alice Todd. Martha Day, a girl. Minnie Caudle, same, Temple Field, Dorothy Field, Martin Fielding, Elias Sheppard, let's see. Various reports here and there of children sighted, names unknown. We get reports here and there. Communications are so poor . . ."

Samuel started to say something, but Grierson went on reading.

"There were three white children seen by a trader named Charles Whittaker with some Comanche up in Kansas, one of these could be Fremont Blackwell, aged seven, then an unknown white girl, and then there's Elonzo White, Thomas Rolland, Ole Nystrel, a Norwegian boy, Dave Elms—"

Samuel raised his hand. "Stop."

"Yes, sir. Excuse me, but I might add that over the years, from what Onofrio says, they have taken thousands of Mexican captives."

"What has the Mexican government done about this?"

"I'm not sure."

Samuel stared blankly out the window. Then he said, "Make me a list of those you know of, with their ages. And who has them, as far as you know." He paused. "I am appalled."

"As best I can, sir."

"Are they all young?"

"That's what I hear. They seem to take children from around two years to thirteen or so. Adults and babies usually don't make it."

"Any adults at all?"

"Well, as I said, this Elm Creek raid last October, they got two adults. Women. A colored woman and a white woman. They may still be alive."

"Very well," said Samuel. He stood up.

Grierson rose as well. "Let me know what it is you want me to do about it." He paused. "People say they are different when they come back. The captives."

"I would expect so!" Samuel reached for his hat. "After their experiences."

"Ah, yes," said Grierson. "Yes. But I have to tell you that some-times they don't want to come back."

"No," said Samuel. "How can that be?"

Grierson paused for a moment to think. "I don't know," he said.

A WEEK LATER Grierson came for breakfast and then after they had eaten, he bowed and extended his arm, inviting Samuel to pre-cede him out the door. And so they walked out together to inspect the construction. The schoolhouse was blank and clean, of new-cut stone. The stone had been prised out of a sliding bank of sand-stone on Cache Creek. Boluses of coal the size of kettles tumbled down with the ledges of broken rock and were knocked into pieces and burned in the stoves at the military post and in the buildings of the agency. Stonemasons banged the sandstone into squares and these into walls and veranda floors. The window frames were sawn from oak from the Wichita Mountains. The raw wood had a marshy smell. In the springtime light, clear and watery, things stood apart from one another. Everything around Samuel seemed provisional, temporary, and indifferent.

They went to the blacksmith shop and the farrier greeted them with a quick wave of his hand and went back to the strap hinges he was hammering out on an anvil while his helper squinted and dodged.

Samuel went to bed at nine. Then there was a tumult in the night, the night of a damp, lukewarm wind that brought a fine rain with it and a distant howling. Samuel bolted out of bed and struck a light into a hurricane lantern and ran toward the corrals. The gate was open and fifteen horses and mules had been driven off. He stood there in his nightshirt and the coat of coarse ducking that had been waxed and oiled and was called a slicker. Five enlisted men and their sergeant came up in the dark.

The sergeant held his lantern down to the tracks. Samuel heard a fluting tone; it was the wind singing in the windows of the stable like a silver whistle.

"Well, sir," said the sergeant. "They do it for fun, you know. The young men. Sometimes the old men too." He was shouting into the wet dark wind.

"But my wagon team was among them."

"Well, there you are," said the sergeant.

"Do they do this often?"

The sergeant nodded. "Yes, sir."

"I want my team back."

"I'll see what I can do." He lifted his shoulders. "If you offer them something for them. Like maybe flour, sugar, that kind of thing."

"But those are rations."

"Yes, sir, that's right. Rations." The sergeant wiped rain out of his eyes. "I will put a guard here at the corral for the rest of the week if you don't mind."

Samuel went back to the agency house and dried himself. For fun. Surely there were other ways they could have fun. He would put a chain and lock on the gate. That was not punitive, it was not unreasonable force. He sat at his desk and began writing a report by candlelight. It helped. His anger drained away in the specifics of official language.

Finally at two in the morning he was back in his bedroom. It was not the horses and mules he minded so much as the paperwork. He opened his Bible for a moment. The wind had a slow resonance and it sang at the ill-fitting window frames in several tones, one after the other.

When I remember thee upon my bed, and meditate on thee in the night watches. Because thou hast been my help, therefore in the shadow of thy wings I will rejoice. My soul followeth hard after thee: thy right hand upholdeth me.

SOLDIERS CLIMBED UP on wagon beds and barrels to watch. At the gate of the corral a hundred or so Comanche and Kiowa men sat on their ponies with rifle butts resting on their thighs. A Kiowa man with a loud voice stood beside Samuel. As each Texas longhorn was released from the corral it ran for its life out to the plains and the Kiowa shouted out the name of the man to whom it belonged. That man bolted forward on his horse after he had given the steer a running lead and shot it down.

Samuel sat silently and watched as the prairie earth before him for half a mile was littered with dead animals and the women slashing open their bellies to drag out the liver and the gallbladder and the long intestines. They and the small children ate these things on the spot. A young woman stood up in the watery spring sunlight and her silky black hair floated like a banner and her mouth and chin and hands were covered with tattoos and blood. Her fingers were slim and elegant and several rings gleamed out of the blood that covered them. She bent down with sweet words and soft whispers to her child and opened her hand to him so that he might take the piece of liver that trembled there like a jelly.

"Esa Havey!" The gate was thrown open and a piebald longhorn bolted out. The longhorn tipped his head from side to side and the great horns like turning spears shone in the sun. A man galloped out after him and the steer hooked his horse. It was not Esa Havey. It was a young male relative of Esa Havey that the older warrior had sent in to kill beef on his behalf. The man named Milky Way in the English language did not want to come in and be bothered about his captives. He did not want to have to sit and be lectured by the annoying new Indian agent.

The longhorn handled his massive horns like a desperate man with a saber. When the pony went down the longhorn turned within seconds and caught him in the gut and ripped through the cinch. The pony got to its feet with its entrails trailing.

"Shoot him, shoot him!" yelled the soldiers.

Esa Havey's nephew ran from the longhorn on foot. The piebald bull hooked at him and turned and spun with the agility of a deer. Esa Havey's nephew was unable to stop dodging long enough to cock his rifle. Then with the rifle in one hand the young man bent down and grabbed a handful of sand with the other and flung it in the steer's eyes. This gave the boy enough seconds to cock his rifle and shoot it in the forehead. He shot standing on his toes, a lean and beautiful body upheld on sinew and bone with his long black hair loose from its braids and flying in heavy shooks. Then he turned and shot the pony. The little buckskin fell straight down, its legs folding under it, and then rolled to one side in a sliding glitter of intestines.

Samuel Hammond and Colonel Grierson walked back to the agency warehouse for the clothing issue. They passed a tipi where a woman in a brilliantly ribboned shirt slashed the throat of a small spotted dog and then held it out at arm's length to let the blood drain.

"Kiowa," said Grierson. "The Comanche don't eat dog."

"I see," said Samuel.

He thought it would be better with the clothing issue. The coats and shirts and hats at least would not be shot or have their throats slit.

Samuel had asked that a great washpot of coffee with sugar be served out, and pilot biscuits and meat roasted on spits. Grierson had told him that the Indians believed one should never talk to a hungry man. The army was happy to butcher the beeves and serve up the feast since the enlisted men got to eat a great deal of it before it reached the trestles. The young people fell to play-fighting with the serge suit jackets and tore the arms off. Esa Havey's nephew ran after a lovely young woman and pretended to beat her over the head with a pair of argyle socks. She grabbed them away and filled one with sand and circled it around and around her head as if winding it up and flung it at him and missed. A little boy pranced past with the seat of a chamber pot around his neck, singing in Kiowa, *Here is a good-looking young man.* Two elder women nearby who were eating pilot biscuits laughed themselves helpless and had to beat the cracker flakes from their breasts.

The translator Onofrio Santa Cruz was the son of a Mexican trader and a Comanche mother, raised in San Idlefonso, New Mexico. A jaunty short-brimmed hat sat on his narrow head. He had some sort of a vision problem; he squinted and stared around himself with narrowed eyes.

Samuel gave a speech through Onofrio to bored and impatient headmen. Some of the men were old, and sat regarding him from under drooping eyelids, with noncommittal faces. Behind them were the younger men with paint in artistic and intriguing designs, and hawk and eagle feathers in their hair. Onofrio named them, but Samuel could not remember their names. The little boy with the toilet seat around his neck had fallen asleep in the lap of a big bony warrior with a receding chin.

Samuel said that when the annuity goods arrived he hoped more of the people would come in. He was very glad to meet them and his heart was turned to them and he wished to do right by them. The soft wind was heavy with grass pollen and the smell of frybread cooking in kettles. Samuel would, as their agent, see that the settlers no longer intruded on Indian land. They had been crowded and dis-possessed but things were going to change. So there was no need to raid the agency for horses. No need. Now he would like to have his team back. Today he had added fifty pounds of rice and fifty of cane sugar, to say how much he wanted his team back.

Onofrio translated. Several headmen spoke among themselves in short sentences, in which language Samuel could not tell.

Onofrio said, "They say all right."

Samuel hesitated, and then asked, "Was that all?"

"That's about it."

That night Samuel sent the guards back to Fort Sill. He would not have uniformed army soldiers anywhere near the agency build-ings. He would win over these people with patience and kindness. They would understand that white men were no threat to them and would not attack them, or take their land, and thus they would leave off their raiding. He sat for a while and read *The Pickwick Papers* and found himself laughing aloud in an empty house, transported to the wet, rich fields of Kent, and fell asleep in the chair, and forgot to turn to Psalms.

Chapter 15

THEY RODE OUT on the broad plains with nothing to sleep under, nothing to make a roof against the weather. Only themselves and the horses. Tissoyo rode a small buckskin, and his two spotted horses trailed along behind. It was possible that he simply liked to look at them, that they were like some fine embroidered linen, too beautiful to use. The loose horses paused and grazed and then when they found themselves left behind called out wildly and ran to catch up and stopped to graze again. Britt kept his revolver clean and the Henry carbine loose in the scabbard. They rode to the northwest. The air was fine and damp and the grassland rolled away for mile upon mile, differing in the colors and textures of grass as the soil changed, as they rode down northern slopes and up the southern ones. The big-headed brushy bluestem had broken out in stiff shakos, the Indian grass in violently swaying plumes. Everywhere the central stems of yucca burst out into tall stalks of flowers and sometimes an entire hillside would be covered with their waxy white candelabras.

"What is up there?" asked Britt. He lifted his chin toward the northwest. "How far can you go before you reach the ocean?" Cajun moved along steadily and sometimes broke into his easy, smooth trot.

"The what?" Tissoyo turned and squinted at him.

"*El mar, el gran mar.*"

"Never heard of it."

"Well, how far can you go the way we are going?"

Tissoyo thought for a moment, his clean expressionless eyes flat to his face, staring toward the northwest. One hand lay on his thigh and the other across the bow of his saddle with the reins in it. The constant wind lifted the tasseled ends of his braids.

"After a long time you come to very high mountains. There is always snow on them. The peaks rise up so." He lifted his hand, bent at the wrist, the palm upright. "Straight up. There are no antelope or buffalo there. But there are a lot of elk. The truly big bears are there." He lifted a forefinger to his lips and then dropped his hand on his thigh again. "They say the half-a-men live in the rocks. *Nenapi,* they fade in and out of the rocks." He opened and shut his hand. "Dangerous little *pendejos.*"

The blue slopes of the Wichita Mountains fell away behind them. They were passing around their western end and riding slowly higher and higher as the level of the Great Plains rose with every mile. In a long stretch that was floored with small sand dunes and bear grass they came upon the wreckage of several wagons. Weathered wood and unburied bones. Tipped wheels degraded into sections that had bleached to the color of burnished steel. There were scattered planks and round skulls half buried like kickballs with hopeless eyes.

Tissoyo sat and studied them for a while and then wondered if these were not the remains of the men who had been in the fight on the Little Robe River in his father's time. He slid from his horse and watched as a snake of some sort made a wavering in the grasses and noted where it went. He pressed away the rags of leather from a heap of human bone that had grown glossy from the things that had gnawed them. Whoever they were, they had been somebody, he said.

Britt knew the bones should be buried. He sat on Cajun and thought about it, but then they went on.

At the crossing of the Washita River they found shallow pools of water among flat stones where they could safely wade in. The main current was a choppy, fluent gray stretch of water that hissed at the banks. On both sides the great fragile cottonwoods with their chattering leaves. Tissoyo gathered handsful of buffalo grass and threw them into the pools and then took up his water skin and filled it as the grass filtered the water. Britt pressed his canteen down into the matted, floating grasses.

"They call you the underwater people," said Tissoyo. "You black skins." He pinched up a fold of Britt's skin on his forearm.

Britt stared at Tissoyo's hand until he removed it.

Then he asked, "Why are we underwater people?"

"When you lean over to look into the water your water-shadow is dark, like you are, and the one who is bending over the water is surprised." Tissoyo stood up and gazed around himself in a casual and untroubled manner, and then bent over to look into the water at his dark shadow or reflection that appeared there, with rays of the sun lancing all around the shadow's head like the halos of the Mexican saints. He pretended to gasp and jump back.

Then he turned to Britt with a theatrical gesture.

"You see." He held out one hand as if introducing Britt to his underwater self.

Britt leaned over. His dark shadow looked up at him as if it had lain there in the pool of water all along, suspended in infinite time, waiting for him, to rise up now and glimmer on the surface as he bent over to it.

"Yes, there I am," he said. "Interesting." Britt lifted his full canteen and it dripped on the stone. "So what do you call the people who are like me but they don't have black skins?"

"Ah, the *taibo*. The Indian agent and soldiers and people who live in log houses and the Tejanos, and French and Spanish and all of them." Tissoyo waved his hand toward the east.

"What does that mean?"

"Captive. It means captive. Sometimes it means a boy from the sun or soldiers. And so on."

Britt drank from the canteen and screwed the cap on. He leaned over the water again to see his underwater self rise toward him in shadow with his head outlined in luminescent rays. He said, "There are fish there." He bent to the surface. "That's supper."

Tissoyo made an elaborate gasping noise with indrawn breath. "Don't touch them! You can make people angry like that. Eating fish."

They stood into their stirrups and went on. The two spotted horses and the pack pony waded into the pools and drank their fill and then ran to catch up. Their wavering reflections disappeared into stone and then they were churning across the main stream. It was only breast-high on the horses. They splashed out the other side.

"What's wrong with fish?"

"Something. I don't know, but something." Tissoyo waved one hand. His copper bracelets flashed. "We cannot eat them. It makes something become resentful. A being."

Britt listened to the light jingle of his spurs in the stirrups and the lilt of the wind that never ceased on these high plains. It made Tissoyo's hawk feathers move forward and then flatten as if they were making statements. A wind vane. Overhead, streaks of cirrus clouds streamed, pure and seraphic. Before them a flat-headed misty bluff stood out where the Washita River had carved around a headland. Cajun's step was steady and quick. His black mane lifted and fell.

"Why don't you know?" Britt said.

"They all died. The people who knew died."

"What about the Kiowa?"

"Eh, the Kiowa will eat *anything*."

As they rode Tissoyo spoke of the death of all the old people when his father was young, from the sickness that had come with the wagons that were going west. The wagons were all full of men and they were anxious to get to someplace called California. The fever was a malediction that grew and spread and ate people. It was invisible in the plains air but slaughtered whole villages nonetheless. They lay down and died and rotted in their tipis and whoever could walk or get on a horse left them there. Once a small girl lived through the fever in one of those decaying tipis, alone among the dead. She walked out on the empty land and a man called Twisted Horn came upon her but did not know whether she was still inhabited by the hostile, acidic beings, and so he left food and blankets for her, and stayed by her at a distance for days until it was clear she was going to live and that the fever had left her. Then he took her up behind him. Her face was full of holes as if she had been shot with birdshot. She was now an old woman. She doesn't remember the names of her mother and father. It was like fleshing a hide. Tissoyo made a sweeping motion. All the people of that generation gone and raked off and flung aside. When the sickness had passed over, less than half of the Comanche were left alive.

And so there were no old people left to tell the young men when to raid and when not to raid or even the reason for raiding. None to restrain them. The Comanche had no clans; the names and the structure of the clans had been disassembled and left behind in pieces when they ran from the California fever. The wagon fever. Anyone who remembered the names of clans or why we do not eat fish or dog had died. There was nothing to stop the young men from killing or to calm them. The Kiowa have a lot, they are rich. They all own a lot of songs, and they have a way of making counts of days and years, and some small manlike images. They have songs and year-counts and the little images and stories. They are rich with ritual and legend. They know the names of the beings that are stars. They have the story of their beginning. So we stay close to them, it is like being beside a good fire.

The people who survived forgot where it was we came from except it was said we came from far to the north and we know this because we speak like the Utes speak and they say they came from the other side of the Rocky Mountains many months of travel from here. All they could do was fight and now every year we lose more and more young men in battles and so we diminish.

When all the people got sick and died, they say it was like the end of the world. A world with no Comanches in it. That would be evil. Without us to inhabit and think and to mourn for what was lost. For who we were. That would be evil.

Britt thought about this for a mile or so of steady walking and the loose horses flaunting their tails. They bit one another on the withers and once one of Tissoyo's horses lay down to roll and so Britt turned Cajun and caught up the pack pony's halter rope so that he would not lay down and roll as well, on top of the pack, and bust all his knots and rigging.

They came to a place not far from the Canadian where some people had thrown up their tipis in a snowstorm. Nothing goes unmarked or unrecorded in the dry air of the plains and the edges of the plains. Tracks and marks of habitation remain for decades, for centuries. Along streambeds, among the spiked crowns of yucca, long leaf-shaped flints eroded out of the soil and some of these flints had been made many thousands of years ago. But someone had made them, an individual like no other, who had a guardian spirit and a wife and children. And so with the immense bones of buffalo who were as high at the shoulder as a tipi, wolves as tall as a man. From time to time a person could find the lower jaws and skulls of these giant wolves lying open and hungry. They had been big enough to devour the man who made the flint in a few moments of gore and noise.

And so they easily found the circles made by people who had thrown up their tipis in a snowstorm last fall. Had stayed a week or so. Inside the circles the grass was shorter, unwatered, but at the edges it was much greener where heavy banks of snow had slid from the tipis and had given more moisture to the roots of the grasses.

"Were they the Kiowa with my wife and children?"

"I don't know," said Tissoyo. He walked around one circle. "The Kiowa use three main support poles for the tipis. We Comanche use four. But I can't tell which marks were the support poles." He bent down to touch a buffalo skull and then looked up and saw another.

"They were pointing the skulls toward the people," he said. "To ask the buffalo to come. They were hungry. Very hungry."

At night Britt and Tissoyo lay across the fire from each other and the horses ate their way through spring grasses with tearing sounds. From time to time one of the horses would snort an alarm and the rest would gather to him and then they would come close to the fire, shifting and nervous. Their eyes were lucent, glowing and deep in the firelight, as if they had some intense illuminations inside their skulls. Then Britt and Tissoyo sat up with rifles in hand and listened. The nighttimes were alive with distant noises, with disembodied beings, with great stars wheeling overhead.

They went on northwest on some trail that had been cut by the bison and also by people and horses. They came to the flat-topped Antelope Hills and then a few miles north of them, the Canadian River. They crossed the Canadian, gray as iron with spring rains, wide and shallow. When they passed a dry watercourse giving into the river, Britt saw something on the far side of it. He and Cajun scrambled up the bank, and he saw the remains of a child's body. A skull with some patches of skin and hair on it, the spine a jointed white puzzle, the immature pelvis. He dismounted and reached down to the skull and saw that the hair was straight and black. Some child that had grown ill and weary and had been left behind, and the only children the Indians would leave behind would be captive children, and this abandoned small creature was not his child. Someone's child, but not his.

"Mexican," said Tissoyo. "Maybe he was sick." The Comanche lifted one hand and threw a braid over his shoulder. He took the other braid and bit the end of it. "The Texans and the Nemernah don't think the same way about captives."

"No, we don't," said Britt.

"You can get another wife," said Tissoyo.

"She is my wife. Mine. I don't want another one. They took what was mine and killed my son." Britt's hand tightened on the reins.

"Yes, yes, understood." Tissoyo waved one hand anxiously. "But it is curious."

"What is?"

"The Texans never stop until they get their women and children back. It makes them so angry they become like beasts, when you take their wives and children."

"And also when you kill them," said Britt.

"Why do they take it so hard?"

"Just different," said Britt. "Just different."

BY NOONTIME A great wind came up out of the northeast. It began with one hard gust that almost blew Britt's hat from his head and then stopped and it was calm again but in another fifteen minutes came another gust and then another and another. Then it blew straight and hard. The wind roared in their ears so they had to turn their heads to one another and shout. Tissoyo's braids blew out behind him and his headdress writhed and fought to escape its pinnings. After an hour or so Tissoyo pulled up.

"I smell fire."

They saw it after they had traveled another five miles in the battering, glassy wind. First the smoke lifting on the horizon as if the whole world were afire and the tall rollers booming up and then bending in the wind toward them. Blossoms of ochre and gray that the sun shone through and turned blue on the edges. As they went on they saw at the bottom of this smoke the first appearance of flames, bright red and erratic, appearing and disappearing. The wind was in their faces and driving the fire toward them.

"We'd better get back to the river," said Tissoyo. "We are in the path of it."

It came on very fast. It boiled forward over many square miles of dried winter grasses and then they could see objects lifting in the air in the updrafts, limbs and flaunting webs of burning grasses. Before long the smoke covered the sky overhead. A running form flashed out of the fire and then three and four. Antelope bolted past with their little ears laid back and several fawns leaping behind them on knobby, angled legs.

They turned and went at a run for the Canadian behind them. The hot, smoking wind was at their backs. Britt's arm was nearly jerked out of its socket as he hauled at the pack pony's lead rope until it finally broke into a gallop. That distance seemed very long. He heard behind them a sucking, roaring sound. Before they rode down onto the sandy flats Tissoyo jumped off his horse and handed Britt his reins.

Tissoyo sat down on his haunches and gathered a pile of grass. With his thickened, muscled hands he ripped a dead agarita from the ground. He ignored the tiny thorns. He threw this on the pile of grass and mashed it into a ball. He tied his rope around it. Then he took up his flint and steel and struck a shower of sparks into the pile while loose strands of his black hair streamed out around his head in the searing wind. The packed ball of grass caught fire. The wind took up the two small heads of flame within it like a transparent magician, a dextrous invisible being, and sucked fire out of it. Tissoyo vaulted onto his buckskin. Fire leaped to the grass alongside as Tissoyo rode dragging the ball behind him. Then he threw the flaming ball into the stands of dry bluestem. The fire caught and ran sideways and then toward the water. They rode out onto the white sands of the Canadian River and the porous sandstone flats that clicked beneath their horses' hooves. The backfire spread and ate the dry grass along the bank and the smoke rolled into their faces.

Britt pulled the pack off the pony in case he could not hold him and then they would lose all that was in the pack. The ransom money and gifts, his ammunition and what supplies remained to him. He threw the pack onto a layer of sandstone that looked like petrified broadcloth and soaked a blanket and threw it over the pack and the ammunition inside it. He hobbled the pony and then Cajun, and wet his second blanket and threw it over Cajun and the saddle. He turned to help Tissoyo.

The two paint horses trembled in waves all over their bodies as they stood staring at the darkening sky and there was white around their eyes. Their tails blew between their legs and their manes stood out ahead of them.

"Throw them down," said Britt. "Blindfold them. They'll run."

Tissoyo roped both of the spotted ponies and then tied up a fore-foot on the Medicine Hat paint, so that he stood, three-legged and helpless. Then he laid a loop around the other forefoot and jerked him down on his front end and then they did the same with the black-and-white mare, and blindfolded both of them. Tissoyo wet his blankets and draped them sticky and soaked over the paints.

The backfire had now burned along the north bank of the river and died out, leaving a landscape in the negative. Here and there a stand of big bluestem still burned like a handful of crisp red signal flags. The main fire came on and with it the smell of cooking meat and sulphur. Britt and Tissoyo soaked their neckerchiefs in the water and tied them over their faces. They lay down in the stone pools of the riverbed. The smoke came upon them with a killing chemical smell, carrying in itself the gases of some remote burning coal bank and seared flats of cactus. Cajun stood steady with his blindfolded head down and his skin shivered as sparks fell on him.

It grew very dark. Vagrant sheets of fire blew into the air like burning laundry and disappeared. Other flames crawled low to the earth and roared when they fell upon fresh fuel. Sparks shot forward out of incandescent green brush whose stems were full of spring sap. In the middle of the hottest flames long thin ropes of fire tornados moved, bright pink and alive.

The fire stopped at the edge of the backfire but the smoke came on. Sparks cascaded down on them. Britt beat them out and they left black holes in his coat. Tissoyo had dipped his head in the water. Britt could smell the scent of burning flesh and closed his eyes. *Don't let me come this far and hope and have Mary and the children die in this.*

Long streamers of fire leapt the river. Britt glanced up and it was like shimmering red silk vibrating over his head. It jumped to the grass and brush on the far bank and flashed into a brief inferno and ate everything there was to eat, burned everything there was to burn, and then on the back of the windstorm it roared on.

BRITT AND TISSOYO waited until the following day to move. It was blowing a hard wind yet. The earth ahead of them would be hot and full of glowing small cinders of burned brush. They took the blindfolds and ropes off the spotted horses; they struggled up to drink and then Britt and Tissoyo slept on the stone of the river-bank that night. The water was thick and dark. The next morning they strained it through their dirty handkerchiefs and then went on, walking and leading the horses. They had to get through the burned area to find grass. If they did not get through the burned area the two loose horses would begin to range for grazing and be lost.

They passed smoking carcasses of antelope and the charred bod-ies of two wolves lying with their tongues sticking roasted and fleshy out of their mouths. They passed a raised, bumpy area that had been a prairie dog town. The small creatures lay dead in their entrance holes where the fire had sucked the air out of their tunnels and they had crawled up to breathe and died in the burning. A blackened armadillo looked like a Dutch oven someone had abandoned.

By the end of the day they had not reached the farther limit of the fire. They and the horses walked on with black and ashy legs. A cold front came down on them, out of the north, a hard spring chill in a transparent wind and a cloudless sky. It blew Britt's coat open and he had to grasp his hat to his head.

They were black to the knees and clouds of ashes like a charcoal mist blew along the ground. Britt strode forward like a machine, his head down against the wind and the haze of ashes rising around his feet. Ahead was a low draw. He and Tissoyo and the horses headed down it and stumbled over the broken plates of yellow sandstone. Up on one side they saw the shallow protection of a long cave. They scrambled up and into it, out of the wind. They let the horses go. Above the cave, in a ledge of stone, a thin seam of coal had caught fire. The seam was in round deposits, each the size of a fist. It ran all along one layer of limestone like a string of beads and each bolus burned fitfully with a blue flame.

Chapter 16

❦

BRITT WOKE UP some time later. The horses were gone.
Tissoyo lay facedown at one side of the cave. A great pain in
Britt's head shot all around his skull and burned behind his eyes.
He was very weak. Britt pulled himself forward through the dirt
and rocks of the cave floor until he was beside Tissoyo and then
managed to roll himself over the edge. He fell down several layers of
stone and boulders and through a stabbing yucca and came to rest in
a sandy fan where water poured when it rained. He began to breathe
slowly and deeply. His eyes burned. It seemed to be the middle of
the day. The northern wind was still blowing and cold and a mist
of ashes sailed and snaked like ropes above them still. A translucent
daytime moon looked down on him from the blue sky with an astonished face. He felt very sick. It was the coal fumes.

Britt shifted his long body until he was sat upright. There
seemed to be so much of him, terminating in weighty, unman-
ageable hands and large feet encased in blackened boots the color
of cast iron. The coal gas was drifting downward; coal gas was
heavier than air and it had soaked their lungs and blood all night.
It was a miracle he had awakened. Some driving, alert part of his

mind had reached through the coma and shook him and said *You must live, you must.*

He turned over onto his hands and knees and began to crawl slowly back up the slope. In a clumsy motion of his hand he turned over a rock. The scorpion beneath it whipped up its thin tail and stung him on the heel of his thumb. Britt smashed it with a rock and felt the deep pain rocketing up his arm and shoulder and this drove him on, it wakened him and made him angry. He placed his large unwieldy hands flat on the broken stones and dragged his heavy feet after him over the rock and at last reached the cave. He bent his head and took a deep breath of air and then closed his mouth and laid his scorpion-stung hand on Tissoyo's tangled, ashy hair. He closed his hand tight and then fell backward. He dragged Tissoyo over the lip of rock and they fell over each other until they came to rest in the sand and stones at the bottom of the draw.

The wind howled. Britt's head hurt so badly he felt as if fire were shooting out of his eyes. He was torn by thirst. With his thumb he lifted Tissoyo's left eyelid and with the other forefinger, touched the eyeball and Tissoyo blinked.

Then the Comanche's lips moved and his head turned one way and then the other. Britt fell back and clasped his stung hand to his chest. He lay there for a few moments.

He sat up, slowly, and tried to call his horses. No sound came out. His mouth and lips were so dry they stuck together. His tongue was as big as a bolster. He pulled his knife out of the scabbard and slashed a wound on the back of his wrist, and lifted it to his mouth as if it were a chalice and took the blood into his mouth and swallowed. He wiped his lips on his shirtsleeve. He lifted his head and called "Come boys!" He called several times and then fell back again. Tissoyo did not move.

After a while Britt heard a horse's steel shoes clicking up the draw toward him. It was Cajun. Lost and hungry and thirsty and without anything to eat in a world of drifting ash.

Britt got to his feet and walked slowly toward Cajun. Once he crossed one foot in front of another but recovered. He pulled the canteen off the saddle horn and drank and drank. Cajun smelled the water and pushed him with his nose.

Britt carried the canteen back to Tissoyo and poured water on his face. Tissoyo's hands reached up for the water with a Comanche word. He opened his eyes and drank the rest of the water. Then he leaned forward and threw up the water and the pemmican he had eaten and then green acid slime. It shot out of him, over his thighs, and ran off the buckskin in rivulets.

Britt stood up and said, "Wait. I will come back."

His voice was better now that he had drunk half the canteen. He went off down the draw with Cajun's reins in his hand. Where the draw fed out to a wide wash he found the pack pony with the pack off to one side, standing braced against the weight of it, and the two spotted horses. The fire had jumped the wash and left patches of stiff inedible bear grass and sotol. Even so the horses ripped at it. They saw him and called anxiously.

Britt got Tissoyo and himself mounted and the pack straightened on the pony. They started out across the burned country. Tissoyo fell forward from time to time and sank both hands in his buckskin horse's mane and then straightened and then slumped backward and caught himself again.

On a rise Britt saw ahead a horizon of shifting grass, the tossing new leaves of cottonwoods floating and lifting over some watercourse. As they went on toward it they passed the place where the fire had begun; a great spiked flash of black, the earth exposed, where lightning had struck.

That night they ate the rest of the pemmican and four pilot biscuits. The water lay in shallow pools but it was enough. The horses stayed near them to graze and search out the buffalo grass where it sprang up in tight curls under the winter bluestem.

Tissoyo's head fell forward into both hands. He was silent for a long time. He was crying without noise. Britt watched him. His head still hurt and when he moved too quickly he saw the cottonwoods ambulating in a queasy and uncertain way. He wondered if the coal fumes might have damaged Tissoyo's mind. Britt held out the canteen.

Tissoyo drank and drank and then wiped his face, his eyes and nose.

"Now I have to give you the horses. They are the best horses I ever owned. They are so beautiful." Tissoyo's voice was thready.

Britt raised his head. "Why do you have to give them to me?"

"For my life."

"Hm." Britt watched him in the firelight as Tissoyo pressed the heels of his hands into his eye sockets.

"I love them," said Tissoyo.

"But you owe them to me." Britt clasped his hands together and leaned back on one elbow. This was a new development and it was very interesting and he did not want to interrupt Tissoyo's train of thought.

"Yes. Otherwise a being would be offended. Somebody has already sent down the fire. Because of the fish."

"But I didn't catch any fish."

"But you spoke about it where they could hear you. It could get worse."

"I don't see how."

"Oh, yes. Much worse." Tissoyo wiped his hands on his buckskins.

Yes, thought Britt. *I could shoot you and take them.*

Tissoyo looked up at him suddenly and his eyes narrowed. "You could have left me to die and taken the horses. Or shot me and then taken them anyway."

Britt nodded. Despite his long day of ash and smoke he groped in the pocket of his burned coat and brought out his tobacco and squares of newspaper and rolled a cigarette. The heel of his thumb still burned from the scorpion sting and a hard, round knot had formed with a tiny red dot in the middle of it. He would have given a great deal for a drink of Paint Crawford's acidic mustang-grape wine.

"I need you," said Britt. "To help me with the Kiowa."

"Ahuh." Tissoyo lifted his hands to his head. "My brain is burning."

"But it seems to me to be true. You have to give me your horses. I gave you your life when I could have left you, or I could have taken it." Britt leaned back and smoked and regarded Tissoyo out of his long black eyes.

Tissoyo nodded. It was as if he had lost at gambling with the red-and-blue sticks. He had lost and there was a debt to pay.

"I love them," he said. "They are the most beautiful horses I ever owned."

"I will trade them to the Kiowa for my wife and children and whoever else they have captive," said Britt. "Then you go and steal them back."

"But we are friends and brothers, the Comanche and the Kiowa. I can't do that. We raid together and make war together. It can't be done."

"I have underwater power," said Britt. "That is how I woke up when you were still asleep in the coal gas."

"Ah." Tissoyo lifted his head. "So one would think." He turned his head to the jumping campfire. A cedar root had grown in a tight circle so that the fire poured out of its ring. "I wondered."

Mucho poder, said Britt. He gave the Spanish words a soft and urgent sound. *Un poder suave como la seda, como seda obscura cuando lo veas bajo del agua. Un poder que tienen tambien los seres que viven allí abajo en el agua.*

Tissoyo clapped both hands over his ears. "I don't want to hear it," he said. "Be quiet."

Tissoyo drank more water and poured it on his face despite the cold and then wrapped up in his fragmented, burned blankets and fell asleep.

THE NEXT MORNING they found the horses in a draw where two hackberry trees grew, and a stand of horseweed where they stood eating the tender shoots so rapidly Britt saw Cajun rip off ten bites before he stopped to chew. The Medicine Hat was black to the knees of his white legs and there were thin black marks on his hips where he had whipped his ashy tail. They loved horseweed, they would eat it even when the leaves were dried and rusty on the tall stalks, and here it curled up new and green. Britt and Tissoyo stayed there the day to let the horses finish the patch. They lay in the sun and slept like dead men. Then they got up and drank more water and slept again. From time to time Tissoyo counted in some language, pressing his forefinger to the fingertips of his other hand. He said that the Kiowa counted in strange ways and he was practicing. Also he wanted to see if his brains were right. Then they slept again and all the long cold night and in the morning saddled up and went on.

They had crossed the Red Rolling Plains, always moving north-west, until they had come to a broken country on the north fork of the Cimarron River where mesas rose up and were topped with black lava. They had ridden gradually, level by level, into a high country that had mesas and cones of hills and granite so tumbled into rockslides and standing columns it seemed the rock was still in movement. The nights were colder and the air sharper, thinner. Streams and watercourses ran snaking between the low mesas. The grasses were different, and Britt saw around him rapid, tilting flocks of birds with rosy heads and yellow stripes in their tails. There were marks where black bears had clawed the short oaks, plum trees with the fruit still small and green ripening on branches. Tissoyo said they were near the *estado* of Colorado, what the *taibo* called Colorado.

"And so what is an *estado*?" said Tissoyo.

"A place, the name of a place."

Tissoyo nodded. "There is supposed to be a line nobody can see."

"That's right."

Tissoyo was impatient with this. "How do they make a line if it can't be seen?"

Britt thought for a moment. It was a good question. "I think they mark it down on paper. It's only on the paper."

"You never know what the *taibo* will think of."

They came upon a marked trail where people had crossed the Cimarron. Tissoyo rode up and down along the wide trail of unshod hoofprints, and the sinuous grooves travois poles had made in the dirt, and the deeper cuts of wheels.

"This is them," said Tissoyo. "See, here is Old Man Komah's *carreta* wheel marks. This off to the side, this is Aperian Crow's best horse. That horse has big round feet like buckets. I wanted him but Aperian Crow wouldn't trade."

Fan-shaped streams of dust that had blown off the sharp edges of the prints. The remains of shattered rib bones that had been thrown to the dogs and that the dogs had carried along for a little while, a lost hair slide, desiccated human waste, torn brush.

"They would be here, in the Black Mesa country," said Tissoyo. "This is a good place to get out of the wind and there is plenty of grazing."

They left the horses at the bottom of a steep, broken slope of red granite and eroded lava and climbed to the top. It was like the Wichita Mountains. Old volcanoes now quiet that had poured their lava over a granite landscape, standing up out of nowhere. Britt's hard-soled boots slipped on the stone and he hauled himself up by grasping cedar branches and dwarf oak trees. At the top they lay down on a shelf of red granite in order not to outline themselves against the sky. They could see a long way. In the remote distance to the west the Sangre de Cristo Mountains of New Mexico and the cone of the Capulin volcano. And beyond them were the Mexican settlements, Santa Fe and San Idlefonso.

"There." Tissoyo lifted his head and stuck out his lower lip.

They lay on their elbows and watched the rising columns of campfire smoke. The smoke stood up in the windless air like flag-staffs. Somewhere would be men watching, as they were. They might have already been seen. His wife and children might be there alive, or they might not be.

"We must be prepared," Tissoyo said. He turned and ran low and then slid and scrambled back down to where they had tied the horses. Britt followed.

"For what?"

Tissoyo mounted and he turned his buckskin horse back toward the river.

"The Kiowa like to look good," he said. "We have to bargain with them. They are offended by dirty people. We are all burned and dirty."

At the river Tissoyo and Britt pulled off the saddles and stood their horses in the stream and raked their backs with wet handsful of wadded grasses. Cajun made a low sound of pleasure and then shook himself. Then they stripped and washed themselves and their clothes. Tissoyo was suddenly busy and purposeful, he was alive and delighted. There was intrigue ahead and trickery and a lot of talk and one had to be both beautiful and cunning. Then there had to be elaborate braiding and wrapping of braids. He polished his brass-button earrings and his copper bracelets. He broke out yucca root and beat it with a stone until a thin foam appeared in the fibers. They used this for soap, and Tissoyo scrubbed his head with both hands until the saponin left his hair shining. Britt let his clothes dry on the bank and sat naked and rolled a cigarette.

"How do we go up to them?" he said. "Should we make a white flag?"

"No." Tissoyo's head was still covered in suds. He spat. "First the lookouts will see us. We hold out both hands. I call out to them in Kiowa. I say we are friends." He stood up and the suds rolled down his long copper-colored body. He threw out both hands. " 'Friend!' I say. 'Comanche!' I say. And then I say, 'This man is also a friend!' And then they come riding up looking, looking . . ." Tissoyo stared narrow-eyed on all sides, bent over, suspicious. "To see if some people are behind us, lying in ambush. But no!" He straightened up and slapped yucca suds under his armpits and scrubbed. "No one in ambush. And I say, 'Tell Aperian Crow and Satanta and Satank and First Wolf and whatever headmen are here that here is coming Tissoyo with a man who is an underwater man.' They will already have sent all the captives off into hiding."

He fell straight backward into the shallow water and came up squinting and spitting and then fell backward again until he was rinsed off. He sat waist-deep in the water and wiped his eyes.

"They will say so much this and so much that for the captives. Well, then, you agree. Then they bring to you only one captive. They say, 'Now for the rest, we want more.' They do this all the time. They have always done that."

"I will tell them that I offer one price and I am sticking to it," said Britt.

"Yes, but they know how badly you people want your wives and children back. They know you will agree to increasing the price. And they will increase it for every captive." Tissoyo came splashing out of the water.

"We'll see."

"They already know why we are here. We don't have to tell them anything. First we eat, and then we start bargaining." He stood up and wiped water from himself, and his face was sober. "With my horses. But they are your horses now."

"I need them," said Britt.

"It is all right. I am still alive. You pulled me out of the coal fumes."

"You will get something for doing this," said Britt.

"It is whatever you think." Tissoyo pressed his lips together. He waved away Britt's words. "It doesn't matter."

"If I get back my wife and children someday I will see you have a horse as beautiful as the Medicine Hat."

"If I live," said Tissoyo. "Maybe someday."

WHEN BRITT AND Tissoyo rode in, the headmen of the camp were already wearing their best jewelry. Women pushed burning ends of wood farther into the fire to keep a large brass kettle on the boil, and from another fire rose the smell of roasting meat and burning feathers. They were cooking trumpeter swans and grouse breasts packed in clay. The long flexible necks and black bills of the trumpeters lay in a heap to one side. A woman took up a grouse and held it by the feet, made a quick shaking motion to make the wings flap open. Then she held it to the ground and placed a foot on each wing and pulled upward and the feet and breasts came away from the rest of the body. She laid this on a grill of green sticks over the fire. A child threw the remains into the air, the back and wings and head. A dog caught it in mid-leap.

Britt watched as a Kiowa man across from him took up the wing feathers of a swan like a handle and ate the roasted arm muscle. Britt did the same. The Kiowa language sang in its variable tones between Tissoyo and the men across from them. As Tissoyo spoke, he laid down the grouse breast and sat straight and was grave and restrained. He augmented his faulty Kiowa with sign language in gestures made close to his chest and from time to time fell into Spanish. Britt understood that they were speaking of the prairie fire, of the flights of trumpeters skidding down onto ponds and lakes to rest in their northward migrations, of another group of Kiowa who had split off and gone north. One man among them appeared to be Mexican or half Mexican; he wore a broad-brimmed hat and a serape in a design of vibrating colors. He wore trousers and suspenders.

Britt wiped his hands on his shirt and turned to Tissoyo. "Ask him if they are all alive, and where are they?"

"That is not a good way to start," said Tissoyo. He sat very still and Britt saw a little nervous movement of his head. But after a moment's exchange he turned to Britt and said, "Yes, your wife and two children are alive and they are here. But the little girl called Mill-ee is dead. They call her Sain-to-odii. She went on north with some others and then died from some sickness."

Britt lowered his head and stared at two or three vagrant breast feathers lifting in the slight breeze and the currents of heat from the fire. For several days now he had been thinking of how to bargain from a position of strength, and that could only mean indifference. He did not look about the camp for his wife and children. His hands rested on his kneecaps.

"Tell him I have another wife. It is not allowed among the Te-janos or Americans or French or Spanish but we underwater people can have several wives and I have another wife to look after."

He waited while Tissoyo repeated this, in fragments of sign language and Kiowa and Spanish.

"And that if my first wife, this one you have, is happy here then she can stay. And the children too."

Aperian Crow stared at Britt for a moment. *Then why did you come so far to look for them?*

"I am looking for the trails that lead from the Texas country to Santa Fe. I will have a wagon made and I will carry trade goods with the Comancheros. And so since I came close to your camp I stopped to ask about them."

Tissoyo repeated their statements back and forth with a perfectly flat look, in a kind of language hypnosis, both hands lifted and occasionally making sign. Britt tried to eat heartily of what was before him but his throat shut up like a bag tied with string. His wife and children were somewhere nearby, and he was afraid for what they might have become.

Chapter 17

THE OUTPOSTS HAD seen them ten miles away. Mary knew that Britt had come, that somebody had come, because she and her children were taken away and hidden in a hollow place behind a shelf of stone above the camp. The outposts had known for a long time; little Millie had been sent away a week ago. Gonkon sat in the stone hollow with Mary and Jube and Cherry. There were two young men to guard them.

Mary rested her back against a red granite rock. Jube and Cherry beside her. If they were to be killed there would be some sort of signal first, and she would watch for it, and then protect the children until she was dead.

From the hiding place Gonkon could hear the men talking. She turned to Mary and Jube and Cherry.

"He doesn't want you," she said. Gonkon had a haughty expression because she was afraid they would find Sain-to-odii and take the girl from her. She was so afraid she was trembling and could not keep her voice as hard as she wished. She held the girl's buckskin dress against her chest. "But she is dead."

Mary and Jube would not look at Gonkon. Millie and Gonkon

had been sent away with another band of Kiowa, as soon as there was word that a search had begun for the little girl. Then Gonkon had come back alone and said that Sain-to-odii had died of a fever. But Gonkon had not slashed her arms or cut her hair or grieved aloud.

"He says he has another wife. He doesn't want you."

Mary regarded Gonkon with a blank face.

THEN IF OUR *price is too high, what will you do?*

"I will go on to Santa Fe. I can make a lot of money carrying things from Santa Fe but I will never make any money chasing around after my wife, all over this country."

Then what do you offer?

Britt turned and pulled the pack around beside himself. He set out the gold coins, the figured cloth, and the jewelry.

"I want my wife and my two children and for that I have ten dollars in gold and some other things. Necklaces and bracelets and silk and those two horses. The spotted ones."

Those are Tissoyo's horses.

"I know it. I won them at gambling."

You are a good gambler.

"Yes."

MARY CAME WALKING through the tipis with Cherry's hand held tightly in her own and two men, one on each side of her. Britt looked up but remained seated and didn't move or change expression. Her familiar face and the lovely wavy dark hair filled his entire vision for a moment and his heart thudded in one loud report that he thought must have been audible to everyone around him. She was dressed in a long, stained buckskin dress without decoration, pieced together, and high moccasins. Her hair was curled into two round knots on each side of her head. She walked with a slightly unsure step and Britt could see a deep white scar like a miniature lightning strike, forked and unraveling through her hair. Cherry hurried anxiously along at her mother's side, dressed much the same but with a glass bead necklace. They looked barbaric and comely and terrified. They stopped at a distance from the fire. Mary bent her head and regarded her feet and her hand gripped in Cherry's was white-knuckled under the brown skin.

"Where is the boy?"

Hears the Dawn lifted a worn hand to his lips and then replaced it on his knee.

Maybe he doesn't want to come back to you.

"Where is he?"

Somewhere. Maybe he is hunting with the other young men.

Aperian Crow lifted his hand for attention and then laid it in his lap again. *Now, what you have offered, the gold and the necklaces and silk and so on, the two spotted horses, we will take that for this woman and her daughter.*

Britt stood up and indicated that Mary and his daughter should come and sit behind him, and they did so, and no one stopped them. Cherry sat very close to her father and said, "Papa, Mama can't speak very well. She can't hardly talk anymore."

"All right," said Britt in a low voice. "Hush now."

GONKON CLIMBED UP between the two boulders and twisted and pushed until she was at the top and concealed by a turned juniper. Here she could hear more clearly what was being said. She could see them down below, between two tipis, and if the children running loose in the camp would shut up she could hear much better.

"Your father is stupid." She turned and called down to Jube. "He offered all he had at once. Now they say they will only give back your mother and sister and not you." Gonkon twisted her hands together as if she would ruin them. Then she pulled at the fringes on her dress. "He has nothing left to offer."

Fights in Autumn sat and stared ahead of himself at a tarantula fingering its way down a face of stone.

"Now he says he will offer his riding horse, if they will give you too, and if they tell him where Sain-to-odii died. He doesn't believe she died." Gonkon was full of hatred and rage for the man who would take her little girl away from her. "So! You will all have to walk all the way back to the Texas country and you will die on the way. Little Cherry will die on the way."

Jube had passed his tenth birthday somewhere back on the plains. Perhaps when they had passed the Antelope Hills. He was a child of two names, Kiowa and biblical, a descendant of the kings of Benin, the coinage of an afternoon and a night and a day of unspeakable violence. And now he had become a person who was respected among people who did not care about the color of his skin or anybody's skin. He was a boy on the edge of becoming a warrior among warriors, who had a foster father named Old Man Komah who was kind to him. He remembered Aperian Crow smiling as he tipped a handful of steel arrowheads into his hand and how they flashed with thin, slitting reflections from the fire.

"My husband will take his riding horse for you." She slid down and smiled. "Aperian Crow told him my daughter had died back there, and your father believes it." She pressed her long hair out of her eyes. "You can go. We will not miss you." The tip of her nose reddened as she swallowed noisily.

APERIAN CROW TURNED his head toward Britt. *I will ask someone to go and see if they can find him. We will ask him if he wants to go back with you.*

"Very well."

Your horse is that one with your saddle on him?

"Yes."

He is good-looking. He is young.

Tissoyo listened intently. In low, whispered Spanish he said to Britt, "You have him. You have them all. If the boy will come."

Jube came walking out between the tipis by himself. No one was with him. On his shaved head he wore a round fox-fur hat with small tufts of feathers on each side in front of the ears. A knife in a beaded and fringed sheath was at his side. He saw his father and stopped. His father lifted a hand with the palm flat toward him but otherwise Britt did not move.

Jube came up to the fire.

Ah, he is here after all.

"Yes."

And so, young man, do you wish to go back to Texas and live with your mother and father again?

No. I want to stay here.

Britt shifted his gaze off to the side, and then to the igneous vaulting landscape behind the village of tipis, searching among the crumbled lava stone and juniper and pine for the glint of a rifle barrel, for someone who might have Jube in his sights and would fire if he said the wrong thing.

"I don't want to go back," said Jube, in English. "I want to stay here for a while anyway. I like it here. They're pretty good to me." Then he turned to Aperian Crow and the Mexican trader and said the same in Kiowa.

Britt knew his child. He saw in Jube's eyes and the way he held himself that he was lying, but Britt did not know about what. The boy made that odd little gesture with his hand, touching his thumb to his little finger as his hand lay alongside his leg. A compulsive small tapping of the fingers together at the tips when he was caught lying or inventing tales.

"Jube. Are you sure?"

"I want to stay."

So. Aperian Crow smiled and turned to Jube, looking up from where he sat to the boy standing.

Britt said, "I can't make you come home."

"I know it."

"Do you want to grow up here? With these people?"

"Yes, I do." He did not say Pa, or Father, or Daddy. "Go on. Go on without me."

"They killed your brother. They killed Joe Carter."

Jube wavered and opened his lips to speak and didn't say anything for a moment and then he said, "I don't remember it." He looked at the ground. "Jim and Joe shouldn't have been fighting with them."

"All right."

"Go on without me."

"All right, Jube."

The boy turned and walked back between the tipis and then disappeared. Britt lifted his head to the men across from him. None of them smiled but regarded him with faces wiped clean of all expression. Britt turned slightly in his cross-legged sitting position and said, "Mary, can you understand me?"

"She can understand you, Papa," said Cherry.

"Be quiet," said Britt. "Mary, I will figure this out later, how to get Jube back. I will come back for him. And now I am looking at all these men's faces and I will remember them. When we are gone, I want you to tell me which man laid a hand on you. Which man adopted my son."

Behind him was only silence.

Tissoyo vanished among the tipis. Britt brought up the two paint horses and Aperian Crow signaled to a boy to take them away. A woman came to fold up the silk cloth. She ran her hand over it and frowned. She poured the flashing jewelry and the gold coins onto it and carried it off. Britt walked away with his wife and daughter. When he lifted Mary with great care to Cajun's saddle he heard shouting and laughter around a fire somewhere among the lodges. He turned and saw Tissoyo tossing the red-and-blue sticks in the air with a group of young men. He was going to try to win his horses back.

So they set out again to the southeast, striking directly across the red and broken plains toward the Canadian River. Two adults and a child and the packhorse and Cajun. Britt walked beside Cajun with his hand on the lead rope and Cherry turned backward with damp, wide eyes, watching the village of tipis disappear.

JUBE SAT IN Gonkon's tipi the rest of that day with his box of bones and stones and scraps of silver. He slept uneasily that night and woke up several times to listen to Aperian Crow breathing heavily beside Gonkon and then turned and closed his eyes and pretended to sleep. He did not want them to know he couldn't sleep. The hours went by like a slow drip of water. Finally he heard the night herd coming in with the older boys behind them shouting. Then the camp crier calling out that the people would play the stick game again that night with their Comanche visitor and that some Kiowa-Apache scouts had come in. The scouts would have news and stories and gossip.

Jube ran all that next day with the other boys. They turned over rocks along the thin pools of the Cimarron and found scorpions. Jube showed them how he could pick one up by snatching at its tail and imprisoning the stinger between two fingers. He threw it at Kiisah. Kiisah dodged to one side in a curved motion and fell into the cold water. They took up bows and arrows and shot at a wand. Then the hours passed and the sun threw long shadows across the lava of Black Mesa. Jube heard Gonkon calling his name in a bright and merry voice and he could smell *tamal* and burned feathers and some kind of bird roasting. Aperian Crow walked by him and laid his hand on Jube's bald head.

"Go tonight with the older boys on night herd," said Aperian Crow. "Take my black horse."

Jube looked down at the ground to hide his sudden pride and happiness.

"I'll do it," he said.

Jube sat on the black gelding and felt through his thighs and seat how easily the horse handled. This gelding was a man's horse, a warhorse, powerful and sweet to the hand. Even Jube, a lightweight ten-year-old boy, could make the gelding do as he asked. By dark he and the older boys had the horses grazing and dozing on a grassy flat between two anvil-headed mesas. There was no moon. Jube had his bow and shafts in a quiver at his back and his knife, and buckled to his belt the ancient Spanish spur. After a while he could tell he was a distance away from the other young men. He could not smell them, their woodsmoke odor, or hear their short, low whistles that they used when they shivvied the horses. Jube sat silently for a long minute and his breathing tightened like a knot, and then in a sudden motion he turned the black horse southeast, toward a gap between the anvil-headed mesas where the Cimarron had cut its way among them. He kept the horse to a quiet walk for a mile and then he pushed the gelding into a gallop. His father and mother and sister were two days ahead of him and because he had said he would stay with the Kiowa and then run off in the dark of night his father did not have to pay for him with Cajun, his only riding horse. His mother could ride. Jube had stolen himself and Aperian Crow's best horse.

He rode with the reins taut in his hands because he was afraid the gelding would get away from him, but Aperian Crow had put a severe Spanish ring bit on the bridle. The horse slowed to a skidding walk and threw Jube forward and so he rode with the reins looser. He could barely see where he was going. They galloped through the shallows of the Cimarron River to the south bank and left deep tracks in the sand, but Jube did not know what else to do. He wanted to stay on the north side for a mile or so where he would not leave clear tracks on the stony soil but on the north side cliffs crowded in close to the river with jumbled, broken rock and thick stands of short cedar that were as stiff as fencing. He had to cross to the south bank into the sand. Behind him he left deep tracks. It worried him and made the skin on his back crawl. He had seen what was done to captives who were recovered. He had helped do those things to them.

After half a mile he was out of the sand and then many hours later he came out of the broken country and now the landscape was flatter. It rolled in waves toward the southeast. Toward home. The horse stumbled on a scattered series of rocks and Jube pulled him up, then pressed him into a trot again. Seven miles an hour over this cracked earth and the occasional stands of short grass, the stars above.

By dawn he was falling forward on the horse's mane. They had come a very long way, and yet he was still afraid. He wanted to be with his father, who carried a Henry repeating rifle and a big Smith and Wesson police revolver. He was only ten and a captive and he had stolen a Koitsenko's horse. They could well catch him and kill him and his mother and father and Cherry. It was too late to turn back. He was jouncing now on the back of the trotting horse, too tired to swing with the slight jars of the trot. After a while he fell off, holding tight to the reins.

The black horse stopped. He was breathing hard. He moved toward Jube's prone body to ease the pressure of the ring bit. Jube sat up and stared at the horse's legs. He sat on the ground as dumb as if he had been drugged, tired beyond caring. They had covered dozens of miles. It was not enough. It would never be enough.

Jube crawled to his feet and then threw himself over the horse's back on his stomach and then righted himself. He pulled out his bow and unstrung it and tied the looped reins to his wrist with the bowstring. They went on at a walk under the flat rays of the rising sun. It was spring and the sun rose more and more to the north. He reckoned that his father would cross the level country between the Cimarron and the Canadian and then when he struck upon the Canadian he would follow it south and east. Jube would catch them somewhere on the Canadian River.

If he tried to remember, it seemed that when he had come north as a captive they had traveled for four days between the two rivers. Now he was alone and could travel faster, but also he had no adult to tell him which way to go. Maybe it was a hundred, or two hundred, or five hundred miles between the two rivers. He had forgotten how far a mile was. But he remembered long ago his father saying that even a strong man could not make fifty miles a day, or maybe he had said forty, or thirty or seventy. Jube wobbled and swayed on the horse's back. If anything happened he would crawl flat-bellied into the grass and lie very still until he could get his bow strung. He would die before they took him again.

Jube's mind sifted quickly among several images; Susan Durgan's body with one leg cut off at the pelvis and her head a bony skull ringed by a few strands of curls; his brother Jim's body jerking backward, a blossoming cloud of gunsmoke at his chest. The man who reached for him with a hand as big as a wagon wheel. These images were thrown out like face cards and then disappeared. In a few miles he forgot that he had thought them.

Other images came to him. His father's alert and searching eyes and the Henry breech-loader. The feel of the percussion caps and the powder measure in the hand, the clicking noise the measure made. If anything happened, if they came to capture him and rip at his flesh and tear off the soles of his feet for trying to escape, he and his father would kill them. He and his father would wait in ambush behind some cover of stone and sotol, lying still on their stomachs. With a sudden flush in his cheeks he saw Aperian Crow in his sights. But the trigger seized up and would not pull. Then Old Man Komah appeared before him and said in a sad voice, *Son, son, listen to me, you are a clever boy. I will look out for you.*

Jube awakened suddenly and his hand went to his mouth. It was dry as rawhide and his hands were full of minute cactus spines and his lips were bleeding.

Chapter 18

❧

SAMUEL HAMMOND WALKED among the tipis as some of
the Comanche came in for their rations. He tried to remember
their faces, who was there and who was not. A cold front, a norther,
had fallen upon the springtime plains, and it was wet and chilling
and the force of it shivered the pointed smoke flaps of the Comanche tipis.

Samuel came to the campfire of a headman named Kicking
Bird, and asked him to come with him to see the new shipment of
farming tools that had come from Lawrence, Kansas. Corn plant-
ers, double-shovel plows, rakes and harrows. Onofrio walked to one
side, a slight linguistic shadow, and repeated whatever was said in a
kind of trance.

Kicking Bird ran his hand down the skeletal tines of a hay rake
in the bars of sunlight that came through the loose boards of the
drive shed. His hand was weathered dark and worn as driftwood.
A thick callus lay on the insides of his right forefinger and middle
finger from drawing a bowstring, and there was a high muscle on
the upper left arm that had come about from holding a bow at full
length.

He regarded the plow blades with a kind of confused sadness. They had taken women's work and women's tools and made of them an enormous *vagina dentata*, this biting device that ate into the earth to tear up the grass roots and into the red body of the ground.

He walked slowly from one farm implement to another. They were things so alien he had no words for them. Their steel surfaces perfectly machined into curves and angles. They had claws and mechanical arms that lifted up and let down. He touched the perforated seat of a corn planter that gleamed with green paint in a shaft of sunlight. This was where a person sat to operate the machine and it seemed to him that after a while the man would do the machine's bidding. It was better to die than to become the servant of these things. They would take the core of one's self and change it to something else. They would obliterate a person before he had a chance to stand before the sun and declare aloud the name that had been given to him, and then no one could ever rescue the tenuous and wavering self from disappearance and cold and eternal emptiness.

To Onofrio he said, *This is terrible.* He walked forward a few steps and stood before the lift arm of a toothed harrow. *These are terrible things.*

Onofrio was eating peanuts out of his hat. He brushed at his mouth and then said, "He finds all this very interesting."

Samuel said, "Farming is hard work, it is true. But once the people learn how, there is a great deal of tradition to it. I myself had a farm back in the East."

Then why did you leave it?

"Because I felt a call to come here and do what I could to help. My beliefs. I felt a call from Christ to come here and speak to you, to your people, to do what I could to help."

Onofrio said, *His guardian spirit, Jesus Christ, told him to come here.*

Then perhaps Jesus Christ will tell him to go back.

I will tell him you said this.

No. Tell him that we will not farm. We will travel up to the Cana-

dian and the Cimarron and down in Texas when we please. Why does he show me these things? They would turn us into mules. Do I not stand on two feet like a man?

Onofrio said, "He says that the Comanche are human beings and only mules pull the farm equipment. Ah, um, he doesn't like them." Onofrio rubbed some peanuts together to press away the red skins and then blew on them in his cupped hands.

Samuel Hammond nodded. It had taken weeks of paperwork to purchase the equipment. More weeks for it to be shipped and then it had all been stalled at Fort Leavenworth for the entire spring season and only with the first rains had the army teamsters consented to bring it down on freight wagons. Now it was nearly beyond the planting season and it would all sit here until it rusted.

ONE EVENING AFTER supper Samuel walked down the long hall of the warehouse and saw Mr. Deaver sitting at a table, and on the table before him were his colors and inks and his enormous sketchbook. Shelf after shelf made long stripes along the walls of the warehouse and each one of them carried some remnant of the clothing that the Indians did not want or had not bothered to come in and claim when their names were called out. Empty sleeves and pants legs hung over the edges in a sloppy, abandoned way. Caps without heads sat in rows.

Mr. Deaver's shadow poured out to his left and the candlelight gleamed on his right hand. He wore narrow spectacles and they flashed with every small movement of his head. The front of his traveling coat was smeared with reds and yellows. Pieces of hardtack were crumbled on the table.

"Agent Hammond." He looked up and smiled and took off his glasses. There was a tumbler half full of some reddish liquid and a rinse jar for his brushes.

"Well, it's you," Samuel said. "Mr. Deaver, the artist."

"Yes, myself in person. Travel-weary and frayed. How do you do?"

"I'm very well." Samuel clasped his hands together. "When did you come here?"

"Got into Fort Sill yesterday." Deaver made a swift line and then looked up. "In a supply wagon from Kansas. I was merely another piece of baggage along with the horse food."

"And before that?"

"Wyoming, more or less. I hope you don't mind that I have camped on you, here." Deaver was frayed and his clothing faded from his travels. He smelled of woodsmoke and animal fats and he was wearing a pair of high-topped boots with copper toes.

"Not at all, not at all. I am glad you've come."

"You weren't at the agency house so I just made myself at home."

"You are most welcome." Samuel watched him skim his brush across the paper. "Have you brought any newspapers?"

"Yes, yes, I brought you some AP sheets. I left them inside your door, there. They are all sticky and wrinkled but otherwise sanitary."

"No matter. Where did you get AP reports?"

"Off the wire, of course, up there at the fort. Colonel Grierson subscribes. Stayed last night in the enlisted barracks and now here I am. You don't say *thee* and *thou*."

Samuel stood apart for fear of interrupting some inspiration, some moment of creativity, and observed Deaver's thick-featured face, the spatulate fingertips and his loose collar, the ends of his foulard lying loose on his lapels.

"No. I was never comfortable with it."

"You don't say." Deaver reached for another, finer brush in the jar. His eyes were intent on the paper. "How is that?"

"I'm not sure. We live in the modern world now. Some of the older people still use it."

"But you come from a Quaker family."

"Yes."

"Of Philadelphia."

"Near Philadelphia. Yes, an old Quaker family."

"An old, rich Quaker family."

"Just so." Samuel stepped forward and bent over the jar and stirred it with a brush. "Your water is dirty."

"Yes, yes, a recurrent problem. Dirty water." Deaver made another swift line and bent over to blow on it several times and then straightened up again and set out a box of colors in round palettes. He took a drink from the tumbler. The colors in the box were primary, rich, they glowed in the candlelight while all around him were the sepia tones of unpainted wood and the dull colors of the woolen clothing on the shelves that the Indians did not want. What they wanted were the sort of brilliant tones that shone out of Mr. Deaver's box, splashy calicoes and plaids. He lifted his head.

"Come and look if you like."

Samuel walked around and stood behind him. It was a picture of Mato Tope of the Mandan, his elaborate hair, his face paint and the rich tones of his dark skin contrasted strongly with the lime green and dark red of his shawl. Gold shone in his ears.

"This all means something," Mr. Deaver said. "You see here this sort of toy knife in his hair. It means he stabbed a Cheyenne chief to death. These small cylinders mean that he has been shot so many times . . ." Deaver paused. "Ah, seven times."

Samuel pressed his lips together. He looked down at the haughty, aristocratic face on the paper.

"Why?" he said.

"I don't know." Deaver smiled. "I am only the recording angel." He turned and pushed a stool toward Samuel, who sat down on the cowskin seat.

"Apparently there are captives among them," said Samuel.

"Among who?" Deaver's hand wavered for a moment over the paper and then he drew a bright yellow stripe, very fine, across the lime green and red shawl. He was making a plaid of it.

"The Indians of my agency. The Comanche and Kiowa and the others."

Deaver nodded. "And how do you come to terms with that? I wonder."

Samuel considered.

"I pity them. The red men. These are desperate measures. When I consider how we have crowded them and dispossessed them from the Atlantic on westward. They have been driven and harried and cheated. Perhaps they feel that by taking captives they will convince us to stop."

"Yes, but the Comanche originally came from the north and dispossessed others."

"How do you know that?"

"An Apache told me." Deaver ate several pieces of the crumbled hardtack. "All you have to do is ask."

Samuel was silent a moment, and then he laughed at himself. "I see."

Deaver brushed crumbs from his front. "They all take captives. They take captives from other tribes, from the Mexicans, from white people." He carefully laid aside the portrait of Mato Tope to dry and then turned over to another sheet. It was an unfinished sketch; a scaffold burial and four or five people lifting a wrapped figure onto a framework of poles. "Probably they always have." Deaver regarded the sketch and with one hand reached out to the jar of rinse water and lifted it to his lips.

"Stop," said Samuel. "You are drinking your rinse water."

"Again." Deaver put it down. "Thank you." He reached for the tumbler and drank and replaced it on the table. He began to firm up the lines of the sketch and then with his little finger he drew a smudge of charcoal inside the outline of a man and this gave the figure substance and a presence as if it actually weighed a certain number of pounds apart from the thin paper, apart from and beyond the lines in which it was constrained. A windy day and all their hair flying, they wept for this beloved now abandoned to the ravens. The ravens then appeared with four light strokes, pendant in the unfinished sky. "Like a chess game, in a way. Taking pawns."

Samuel nodded and thudded the joint of his thumb impatiently on his knee.

"Have you seen any captives?"

"I think I have. No, no, I am sure of it, now that I consider it. Up in Kansas. I was eating tamales and quail with a headman, or just a man, and a girl with blue eyes went by with a large bone."

"Among this agency's Indians?"

"Yes. They are elusive, strange creatures." He waved his brush in the air. "She ran when she saw me. They are like elves. They are not white and they are not Indian either. They seem almost artificial."

"What band was it? What was her name?"

"No idea. The band was some families of the Quahada, I think."

"They must be retrieved." Samuel shifted on the three-legged stool. "They must give them up or I will consider cutting off their rations." He looked around at the darkened spaces of the warehouse. "You need another candle in here."

"Many times they don't want to be retrieved."

"I suppose they are afraid of being killed if they tried to escape."

"That. And also, life without clothing may be a marvelous thing." Deaver smiled and placed clouds beyond the ravens with a thin white wash; vague indications of cumulus. "They become bonded and secured to their captors in some way we don't understand. Surely it is not the cuisine."

"I was never informed of this, the captives, in Philadelphia."

"No?" Deaver carried the thin white wash over to a man's figure and made two white dots on a head of black hair. Thus placing reflections on it and by inference the light of a plains sun.

"No. It is not a matter of general knowledge."

"My goodness, there are stories and published accounts going back to colonial times. Last year the Oatman girl went around lecturing with the Mojave tattoo on her chin. It looked like some big biting thing, as if she had enormous black canines. Artfully done. Willful ignorance, then." Deaver sat back and shifted a new loose page out of his portfolio. He took up a steel pen, dipped it in a bottle, and began bringing something to life with quick, calligraphic slashes. "We spend our lives in worlds remote from one another. We imagine we all live together on this round earth but we do not."

Samuel sighed and bent his head, clasped his hands together between his knees.

"Colonel Grierson seems to think it is a small matter."

"Give him time. You are only just here."

"Still." Samuel stood up and paced a few steps and turned. "Dr. Reed of the Friends' Indian Committee is determined I should not use force. But I think about it."

"Ah, Mr. Hammond. Life changes us."

"I wish you would call me Samuel."

Deaver gave a brief bow of his head. "And I am James."

"And where have you been since I saw you on the train?"

"I went among the tribes near Omaha, and then to Denver, which was very boring, and then along with an army expedition to Wyoming. War has broken out there with Red Cloud of the Sioux. The army is building forts there in Wyoming along the Bozeman and they gallop out from time to time to do punitive things. I know you don't approve but they are just the same."

"Is that why you came down here?" Samuel sat down again and regarded the pen sketch taking shape beneath Deaver's hand.

"It certainly is. Ridgeway Glover, he was an artist for *Frank Leslie's Illustrated Weekly,* just got sent to the happy hunting grounds. They found him a couple of miles from Fort Smith naked and scalped and cut in half longways. And so I decided to move on." Deaver emptied the tumbler. "Colonel Grierson gave me a bottle of sherry. Won't you have some?"

Samuel sat in silence for a few moments. "What? Oh, no, I don't drink."

"Very well. But, and this might interest you, first I went with a rather scholarly military man to the Snake River country in Idaho, that's just to the west of Wyoming." His hand was busy over the paper. Samuel knew he enjoyed astonishing him, Samuel Hammond, with stories of his relentless journeys. The danger and the discoveries. While Samuel the Quaker sat in his agency house and fussed with columns of figures. "Captain Charles Bendire, a gentleman, a naturalist, an infantryman. Yes, the Snake River country, which is where they say the Comanches came from. It is a curious thing."

"What is?"

"There are fossils of *horses* there in the valley of the Snake River. Ancient fossils of horses very like the ones the Indians ride now. There were horse skulls and leg bones falling out of a bluff over the melodious waters of the Snake. At some time in ages past the Comanche must have known them. And then they disappeared."

"Really. The horses you mean. The horses disappeared."

"Yes. And the Comanche, they say, are the most proficient horsemen in the world. The first of all Indians to take up horseback riding. They found again their long-lost brothers, their darlings, their pets. Very curious. Then back to Denver and then down here. My companion, the reporter, has covered all he wants to cover and has gone back to New York. Especially after poor Ridgeway was brought in all in tatters. Fulsome funeral obsequies, lamenting and so on. But I wanted to come down here. I didn't want to miss the Comanche."

"No, certainly not."

Samuel emerged on the paper. His face square and lined and his mouth horizontal.

"That's me."

"It is indeed." Deaver took a small brush out of the glass of rinse water and wiped it on his pants leg and then drew it across one of the little palettes and touched in pinkish flesh tones. Another palette; gray eyes.

"I look rather grim."

"You find yourself in a grim situation, Samuel, I think it is an impossible situation."

"Keeping the Texans and the Indians apart."

"And keeping your Quakers happy back in Philadelphia."

Samuel folded his arms. "I will make it clear to these people that farming, or at least keeping cattle, is far superior to the life they are living now. I don't understand why they prefer war."

"It's beyond me," said Deaver. "They raid down into Texas, where the Texans are trying to farm. And then they come up here in the winter to the reservation where it is safe." He took up a cloth and wiped his hands. The cloth was a rainbow of paint smears. "I have often wondered why they didn't just bring the Texans up here to the reservation and let them farm, eh?"

"But then there wouldn't be anybody to raid."

"There are always the Mexicans," said Deaver. He whipped up a dirty foam in the jar and then wiped his brushes and laid them in his paint box. He closed it and flicked the catch. "How many human beings remain in this world, unvanquished and at liberty in plains like these? So few, so few. Man was born free and everywhere he is in chains."

Samuel stared at the leaping candle flame and then turned in his chair. "Yes," he said. "We make them ourselves, at great trouble and expense."

"I wouldn't fool with these people too much," Deaver said. "They are not toys or dolls that one can arrange their thoughts or minds as you wish, simply give them a change of costume. They are grown men and they are lethal." Deaver took up the portrait of Mato Tope and held it horizontally to the candlelight and squinted down it as if it were a gunsight. He saw that it was dry and held it out to look at it. "A proud man," he said. "Arrogant, I would say. Handsome."

"By reasoning with them, am I treating them as toys?"

"Your reasoning only goes one way."

"Quite true. But still I will reason. They cannot take captives or kill women and children. It is insupportable."

Deaver put the portrait away and sat back with his eyes half closed. "They are our great mystery. They are America's great otherwise. People fall back in the face of an impenetrable mystery and refuse it. Yes, they take captives. Sometimes they kill women and old people. But the settlers are people who shouldn't be where they are in the first place and they know it and they take their chances."

"You are very cavalier about this."

"So are they, my friend. The Texans are cavalier as well. Perhaps we can regard this as a tragedy. Americans are not comfortable with tragedy. Because of its insolubility. Tragedy is not amenable to reason and we are fixers, aren't we? We can fix everything."

"This is not a matter of abstract argument for me," Samuel said. "I am the Indian agent." He put on his hat. "I have to do something." He started toward the door. "I am in a position of authority for the first time in my life. Come and have supper. There is a room for you."

"I thought there would be." Deaver got up. "I am coming."

He blew on the watercolor sketch of Samuel's face and then folded him in with the mourning Comanche and closed the workbook.

Chapter 19

J UBE HAD BEEN sleeping curled up on his left side. The black horse stood over him patiently. The bowstring and reins were tied to his wrist and he lay at the edge of a forest of smooth dead trees whose lead-colored branches bent to the ground in circle after circle like a city of fossils. The naked forest was extensive and far off to the horizon they printed on the sky and the land their repeated black curves. Waves of new grass shimmered throughout this unshaded woods. A dead forest of mesquite that had grown up a century ago after years of rains and then the capricious rain time had evaporated and the trees died.

The black horse stood with his head down as if it were too heavy to raise. He breathed slowly and his eyes were closed. A horse could not travel for two days without water. Nor could he. The horizon all around was level, the air thin with a high, silting dust in the sky. He remembered the day when he was captured that the men had stopped and burned off cactus needles and fed the flat green pads to the horses. So Jube broke off dead limbs and the dry grass stems among the new green growth, and took his flint and steel and chipped some sparks into the pile. He broke off another limb and with it beat down a patch of prickly pear, picked up the flat pads with two sticks and threw them in the fire. The needles burned with quick flashes.

The horse ate them, one by one. Jube ate one as well. He sat and looked around himself. He did not know where he was on these broad plains. For the second time in his young life the knowledge that he could die came upon him but it was strangely thrilling, the thought took him in an exciting sort of tremor. The very fear of dying itself was intoxicating. It made him feel as if he had expanded and were large and cunning and adult. He understood there were great issues at stake and he had taken a perilous gamble like a grown man.

He had to find water. He was not a child that somebody had to find water for him. He had to find it himself or die.

He walked on, leading the black horse, through the waves of grass toward the southeast. Before the sun went down he made another fire in a dry wash and threw on more cactus pads and fed some to the horse and ate some himself. He lay down with the horse tied to his wrist and the slimy cactus fiber clinging and sticky in his mouth, like glycerin.

The next day very early he heard thunder toward the east. He sat up and listened. He could now barely walk and so he decided to sit where he was for a while. The black horse tried to graze with its dry mouth, one step at a time. The world grew lighter. Jube sat in the bed of grass where he had slept the night and watched as a heavy layer of rain cloud gathered and moved and strung itself out and gathered again in blue-gray foam to the east, dragging after it long, bending columns of rain.

With the increasing light the clouds moved over a series of flat-topped formations that had no tree or brush on them. They were perfectly bare. They were draped in short green grass that lay like velvet over every angle and rise.

"Those are the Antelope Hills," he said. He began to walk toward them. He thought he remembered that the Canadian River ran on this side of the Antelopes. If he could keep on walking toward them, he would come upon the river.

It took him a long time to walk a mile, a mile and a half. Milk-weed plants stood scattered through the stands of Indian Blanket flowers of rich oranges and garnet. It began to rain in fine, thin mists. Jube held his hand out to it and licked his palm and kept walking. The Antelope Hills seemed plush, a paradise of water. Their tops were as flat as if they had been sheared off with a sword. Then Jube came to the white sands and stunted cottonwoods of the upper Canadian River and the Antelopes on the far side of it. He saw the sparkling braided water while the rain fell on him and the horse. They dragged through the fine sand and willows and at last drank together from the shallow clear water. Then he sat up and wiped his mouth and got to his feet and waded the main current. The flat crests of the Antelopes rose above him. He would lie there the day and drink and drink and then go on. When he pissed his urine was dark brown. The next morning the black horse grazed nearby, eating steadily. Jube went to the river and drank again.

Now he could follow the Canadian southeastward. Somewhere along that stream he would find his father and mother and sister and he would be able to prove that he had not betrayed them, that he loved them even more than the wild life on the plains.

When he saw them they were walking slowly across a sunlit level of bent grass striped yellow and new green. "Papa," he said. "Papa!" His father was walking with his hand on his mother's knee. Cherry's small dark head bobbed behind her. They drifted defense-less through the morning air, measuring out every slow step toward home.

"Dad!" he shouted. "Dad!"

BRITT AND MARY slept with the two children between them. They lay in their blankets like parentheses around the two lives in their care, as if the rest of humanity had been destroyed by a volcanic explosion or a flood and only they four were left to start the world again. They slept all day and traveled in the night along the route Britt had come to know in its rivercourses with their long galleries of trees alongside and the stars overhead and the rising sun.

Mary spoke to the children in sign, and often Cherry and Jube called to one another in Kiowa. Britt rode with Jube on the saddle behind, and Mary and his daughter rode together on the pack-horse, whose pack was now light. As they rode, he asked Mary for the descriptions of the men who had laid hands on her. She told him. It took a long time. There had been two of her, one enduring and one looking on. The one looking on was not much moved or disturbed by what was happening to the other. She said she remembered two, one was a man with a sun tattoo on his chin. The other a tall man with a receding chin. They were the only two she could remember.

When they reached the house on Elm Creek, the dust had sifted in the door, the trumpet vine snarled around the windows and hinges. Britt made up a fire and swept out the house and watched silently as Mary went to sit beside young Jim's grave, holding her hands over her face. She seemed to have just now remembered all that had happened in the Fitzgerald house.

Jube and Cherry came to stand beside her with confused looks as they carefully read the words on the headboard and came up against the fact that the gates of life had closed behind their older brother with a final shutting and all that remained was his name and brief, fissured images of him in some other life. They seemed to have been in a dream for all these past eight months or perhaps to have become some other persons who had to be reminded that they had former selves who lived on Elm Creek in a house with a roof, that they had worn hats on their heads and shoes with heels. That they had cooked in a kettle in a fireplace and had windows to look out of. That they must now come back and inhabit those selves.

Britt worked to prepare his provisions and equipment for the trip north to search for Elizabeth Fitzgerald and her granddaughter Lottie. Jube sat watching. He had almost become a warrior. He had been on the war road to becoming a fighting man. He refused to carry water for his mother. He sat against the hard walls of their house; walls that were fixed and immovable. There were no people now. Only them. Mother, father, his sister and himself, all alone.

"Do what I tell you," said Britt. "Your mother needs the water."

"That's women's work," said Jube. He leaned back against the house wall with his hands in his pockets.

"Not here it ain't," said Britt. "Not on Elm Creek."

"It's not right," said Jube.

"Move," said Britt. "You are going with me when I go for Mrs. Fitzgerald."

Jube looked up, alarmed. "They'll see me."

"Yes, they will," said Britt. "I want them to see you. I want them to see I got my own back. You'll ride beside me and carry a rifle if I can get one for you."

Jube stared at his father out of his round eyes, and suddenly his lips were dry. He stood up and took off his hat and beat the dust from it to cover the shaking in his hands.

"*That* is man's work," said Britt. He smiled. "Get the damn water."

Britt sat with Mary at night in front of the tall fireplace. He put the Bible in her hands and opened it to her favorite passages. She stared at the letters and put her finger on a line and followed it and then closed her eyes and shook her head.

"Yes, you can," said Britt.

"I was dekan," she whispered. "Dna you cloth-ed em."

"Good!" cried Britt. He turned to the children. "Did you hear that?"

"Yes, sir," said Jube. He was subdued now and lived with an hourly, unnerving fear of having to ride back north, among the Comanche and perhaps the Kiowa again after he had stolen himself and the black horse. All he could think about was the rifle his father would get for him. If he had the rifle and if anything happened, he could defend himself.

Cherry was twisting her wavy hair into ringlets and tying them with pieces of ribbon. She smiled a bright, encouraging smile.

"Oh, Mama, that's good. *Eeshona-ta, eeshona.*"

"Stop it," said Britt. He leaned forward and placed his big hand on the Bible. They had all gone with the Johnson family to the Episcopal church in Kentucky and it was all Britt knew or cared to know about church matters but he did not want that language spoken in his house. Especially not in front of an open Bible. It seemed wrong, unholy.

"Stop what?" Cherry raised innocent and startled brown eyes to her father.

"I won't hear that language in my house."

"Yes, Papa." She stuck out her lower lip and twisted sideways in her chair and pulled her dress down over her knees. "I guess."

Britt lowered his head. He took up the poker and jammed it at the coals. Ribbons of flame jumped upward and wavered into long tatters. They were all different. It chilled him. He had brought back a family of changelings.

THE SPRING NIGHT air poured in through the window. Britt lay on his side facing Mary and watched her eyes shift in random movements beneath her closed lids. She was more frail than she had ever been; now her thin arms lay outside the coverlet and her fingers opened and closed. No, she said. No. He raised himself on one elbow and rested his head on his hand. With his other hand he reached out and tucked the fretted and disordered hair away from her face.

She opened her eyes and stared for a moment at the boards of the loft above them and then turned to him. He lay back and pulled her onto his chest and held her. He patted her back in a slow rhythm.

"You were having a bad dream," he said. "Mary?"

She sat up and regarded him. Her eyes were dulled with sleep.

"What was it about, Britt?"

How would I know? But he didn't say it. Then he realized she had spoken a complete sentence clear as a bell.

He pressed her down on his chest again and stroked her hair. He would invent a dream for her. He would make one up.

It was about rain. You were dreaming about rain. The sound it makes running off the roof. You were dreaming about the Ohio River running out of the eastern mountains and how wide and brown it is. The dream was about flocks of cranes turning all together in the darkening world and how their wings catch the light which is the light of your heart. You were dreaming about who you were before it all happened. Who you will be again. You were dreaming about a girl named Mary sitting in the gin shed in Kentucky while the rain spouted off the roof in streams, where I first saw you. That was the first time I ever saw you. The first time I ever dreamed we could be free and that freedom with you was worth anything, anything. Listen to me. The dream was about rain, water, blood, this terrible baptism. Listen.

Chapter 20

THE HEADMEN SAT on the floor of the warehouse and behind them women and children. Only a few headmen had come in. They were treating it like a council. The women were there to carry away the rations.

The wind made a low tuneless howling at the small windows. They were willing to sit and speak with Samuel but not for long. Grierson had sent a platoon of twenty men with a first lieutenant and his sergeant to barbecue a fat steer and make coffee in washpots. Troopers were dragging the bones and the head of the steer toward the disposal ditch behind the stables. Two others were picking up cups and plates to drop them in a soap kettle of boiling water. The lieutenant glanced occasionally toward the warehouse. The soldiers were not armed.

Women and children packed in behind the headmen and they turned to look up at the goods and foodstuffs on the shelves. Children crawled over the women to come to grips with one another. Two young boys fought over a brass button and their mothers silently pried them apart with strong hands. A two-year-old girl climbed up her mother's back to stare at the men in the council circle, pulling the woman's hair until the woman swung the child around to her lap. A fawn-colored dog crept in at the door and lay beside a woman with several children, beating its tail on the floor.

A pipe was handed around. Samuel took it and raised it upward, and then pointed the stem toward the earth. He put it to his lips but did not smoke and passed it on. The next man took it and made the careful gestures and then drew on it and handed it to his left. The smoke rose until it came to a layer of cooler air somewhere near the rafters and then flattened out. Samuel sat in his charcoal-colored suit with his hat beside him. Squares of light from the windows gilded the splintered planks of the floor and set the air alight with a mist of windy dust. The Kiowa and Comanche seemed Oriental to Samuel, with their still faces and pitch-black hair, beardless and agile with eyes like dark almonds. Though the headmen regarded him without expression, he knew they were impatient. They smelled of woodsmoke and sweated horses and gunpowder. The Kiowa moccasins were splashed with bright beading in floral designs, but the designs on Comanche moccasins were geometric and severe. They were all as weathered as sailors and not one of them wore a hat, as if they would defy the sun itself and the raw carnivorous wind.

Esa Havey gestured toward Onofrio.

We are waiting to hear what he has to say and then the women want the coffee and sugar. Also some calico.

Samuel turned to Onofrio. "Would you translate that?"

Onofrio squinted and nodded his narrow face. "They are happy to hear what you have to say."

"Very well." Samuel placed his hands on his knees. "Say that I am glad to see them come here, but Colonel Grierson says the band called Quahada has not come in."

Onofrio Santa Cruz moved his hand in a diffident gesture around the circle and repeated what Samuel had said, in Comanche. Behind the headmen sat a young man translating rapidly from Comanche to Kiowa for both the three Kiowa leaders and the Kiowa women in the group behind. He wore a soldier's blue coat and a bandolier and two silver earrings in his ears that had been made from the bowls of silver spoons. Stripes of blue-black paint ran from his mouth to his ears.

That is Quanah's *band. They never come in,* said Satank. *They never will. They detest white people. White people have diseases.*

Onofrio said, "This man is Satank. He is a Koitsenko of the Kiowa. Great warrior society. He says they are still hunting. The buffalo have been scarce. Few."

Samuel nodded. "But then where will the Quahada get coffee and sugar and ammunition? Their saddles and blankets?"

Onofrio leaned forward. *He understands they trade stolen horses to the Comancheros for the things they want. The colonel told him this. He is not a newborn.*

Eaten Alive made an irritated, quick motion with his hand. His long hair was wrapped in otter, and a beautiful plaque of multicolored quillwork was sewn to the breast of his buckskin shirt. It had a glassy and intricate glinting surface.

What business is it of his what the Quahada do? Peta Nocona does not go to Washantun and tell their headmen to come here, go there. These things are given us because we signed a treaty. Or some Nemernah did, and these are gifts. We can come and claim them or not.

The Kiowa named First Wolf took up the long-stemmed pipe and knocked the dottle out onto a smooth stone in his hand. He then packed it again with tobacco and lit it. He lifted the stem upward and then bent it toward the earth and then drew on it and sent it off on a second round.

Onofrio paused and then said, "He says they are owed these things because of the treaty and they can come and claim them or stay away, either one."

Samuel held up one hand. "Yes, but the treaty they signed gave them a certain amount of land to be theirs. A very large tract of land. From the Wichita Mountains to the Red River. They are not to go south of the Red River. In exchange for this promise they are to receive the annuity goods every year and other supplies every two weeks. There are plenty of buffalo and water and wood within the bounds of the land given to them."

Onofrio sighed and cleared his throat and repeated it. There was a low, incessant murmuring as the young warrior translated from Comanche to Kiowa.

Satank said, *No one gives land to anyone else. This was not Washan-tun's to give. It is ours. I never touched the pen to any paper where that was written. We told that to Big Pants who was here before him and we will tell him as well.*

Eaten Alive snorted out smoke. *We came down long ago from very far to the north, from the Snake River, a very long time ago. We drove out the Wichita and the Osage and the Lipan Apache and the Tonkawa from Texas. And so it is ours. I know the country, every canyon and cave from the Canadian River to the Rio Grande. I could travel that country in the dark. I have done so. I could tell you every spring of water from here and on beyond the Mexican towns. Why should we stay here? Big Pants wanted us to stay here too. Now he is gone. This man will go too, sometime in the future. I am not a man to turn over dirt. He is going to ask us to stay here and turn over dirt.*

Onofrio pressed his fingertips around the brim of his hat. He cleared his throat and squinted at Samuel. "Well, he said they had some battles around here and this is their sacred ground and the Great Spirit gave it to them and so it's theirs. The Great Spirit meant them to live on it."

"Is that all he said?"

"That's about it." Onofrio knew that agents and commissioners and army officers liked to hear references to the Great Spirit.

Samuel said, "This is good grass country and many people have begun to herd cattle."

Esa Havey gestured toward the window and the horizon beyond. *The buffalo take care of themselves without herding. You ask us to live inside houses like the Tewa. For more years than I can think, they have always been asking us this.*

Onofrio wiggled his fingers and squinted and again cleared his throat.

"Well, he said the buffalo don't need herding."

Samuel nodded. There was a long, hostile silence.

"Very well. Tell them whether they personally signed or not, the treaty is law and they must abide by it. Their chiefs agreed to cease raiding and learn to farm."

The headmen listened and Satank said, *Now he is going to give us the talk about farming.*

Onofrio writhed on his seat bones and said, *I know it.*

Satank drew on the pipe. *He's going to talk about how the Iroquois settled down and started farming and the Cherokees and so on. It will take him a long time.*

Onofrio nodded. *Ahuh.*

And how the Wichita farm. If I went up to a Wichita and blew on him he would die of terror. The Cherokee started to farm and look what happened, they ran them out of that country. Now they shit in little houses. They wear hats and eat pumpkins.

Onofrio had grown nervous in several stages and now he had reached the stage where he was turning his hat around in his hands by the brim. He turned to Samuel. The warehouse smelled of wet fur and dust. The low murmur of Kiowa went on for a moment and then there was laughter from the Kiowa women and headmen.

"He says they were not meant to stay in one place." Onofrio had translated for so many of these councils he knew the stock phrases by rote. He could have conducted an entire council alone, doing voices in two languages, by himself.

Samuel heard the tones in the headmen's voices. They were clear as telegrams. He held up his hand. "Please consider. The Wichita farm, as do the Iroquois in the country I come from, in the East. As well as the Cherokee. They sleep well at night, they do not worry about food supplies, their women do not mourn their deaths in battle. They sit at night in front of their own fireplaces and read newspapers in their own language. Farming is not easy, but many red men have done it and I will help any way I can. Plowing is a skill, but I am prepared to have land plowed for you."

Onofrio closed his eyes briefly and considered. Then he turned to Eaten Alive and said, *And so how is your aunt?*

She is all right. It is just her little finger is numb. Eaten Alive wriggled the little finger on his right hand.

I heard it broke her arm, said Onofrio.

No, nothing broken. I told her not to get near that horse but she paid no attention to me. I am going to shoot him or give him away before he kicks one of the children.

The young dandy who was translating from Comanche into Kiowa said they were talking about Eaten Alive's buff-colored horse that kicked his aunt and *He wants to give it away.* Two men made signs that they would take it. Another said, *Shoot it,* and another said, *Hitch him to one of those plow things.*

Samuel listened to the fragmented sounds of languages breaking up all around him and the laughter. He raised his voice.

"And also, tell him I could bring some Pueblo people to speak with them about raising crops and how it is done. They have always farmed, they were not made to do so by the white man. As the year goes around it is very beautiful. The green shoots come up and the bud and then the fruit, then the harvest." Against the blank and polite silence he felt his words falter and his voice weaken and grow thin. "We will hold another council soon, with the Pueblo if they will come and they will talk about how they farm in the dry country. They have much to teach us. To teach me."

Onofrio started to translate but Esa Havey said, *Who is he talking about, that word* Pueblo?

He means the Tewa.

Oh, the filthy Tewa. They hide in their little square dwellings like rats. They stink. We kill some of them every year. I took three captives last year, I dragged them out of their square doors. Now they carry my water.

Samuel did not need this to be translated.

"And you will no longer go down and raid the Texans. You must stay north of the Red River, you must look for another way to live. This is how it is. This will happen whether you want it or not." His voice was hard. He knew how to speak in a hard voice.

Onofrio took a breath and translated. The Kiowa language in

its floating tones murmured in the background against Onofrio's Comanche with its hard and frequent r's.

The Kiowa chief Satank said, *If you don't want us to raid in Texas then move Texas to some other place far away so the young men are not tempted.* A laugh ran around the agency storehouse.

Samuel said, "I am the agent here and I am charged with discretionary powers. I want the stolen horses and mules returned. If I hear of more raids there will be no more rations. I mean that."

The clutter of languages started up again, startled and rapid. The Kiowa and Comanche women spoke to one another and the children fell silent.

Eaten Alive said, *An agent cannot do this. You talk about the paper that was signed, the agent and Washatun signed it as well.*

"It is being done now." Samuel stood up.

I don't want the mules. You cannot run buffalo on them. Satank stood up as well, an old man but a dangerous one.

"Then bring them back." Samuel and the elderly Satank were on their feet, facing one another.

If the young men feel like it, they might.

"We will speak again when you have taken thought and considered."

We don't need this. Esa Havey waved his hand toward the goods on the shelves. *And if we do we can get it from the Comancheros.*

"I will stop the Comancheros. And their whiskey and arms."

You will not. We have traded with them from the time they carried the banner of the king of Spain. Felipe Quinto.

"I have the power to stop them, and I will. By tomorrow morning I want to see my buggy team here at the agency. Then I will distribute the rations."

Samuel turned and walked out of the warehouse.

SOME TIME IN the dark of night they brought his team in and tied the horses to the white picket fence in front of the agency house. They had placed hats on the horses' heads. Someone had taken the hats distributed to the Indians, unwanted headgear, had cut holes in them for the ears. The dispirited team stood with hat brims drooping over their forelocks and their great ears turning as if upon hinges.

More paperwork, another report.

He wrote slowly with a fraying pen nib in the light of his lamp. He spoke aloud from time to time. "No need to mention the hats," he said in a low and private voice.

He walked up and down the agency house and realized he was listening for the sound of galloping horses. He washed in a basin of hot water as quietly as possible so that the noise of his splashing would not cover any sound from outside. He sat at the edge of his bed for a while in his wool long johns, clasping and unclasping his hands, and knew he would not sleep.

He had imagined himself teaching young men how to harness horses to a plow and then the red earth turning over in shining plates. The young men interested and attentive. A spring rain and the green spears lifting above the rows like the headdresses of little underground spirits bearing as their traveling loads the rich heads of mature wheat. It was difficult to let this go. Very difficult. He said a long and confused prayer and then at last lit the lamp and took his Bible from the mantel.

Thou visitest the earth, and waterest it: thou greatly enrichest it with the river of God, which is full of water: thou preparest them corn, when thou hast so provided for it. Thou waterest the ridges thereof abundantly: thou settlest the furrows thereof: thou makest it soft with showers: thou blessest the springing thereof. Thou crownest the year with thy goodness; and thy paths drop fatness. They drop upon the pastures of the wilderness: and the little hills rejoice on every side.

And still he was angry.

Chapter 21

❧

BRITT AND HIS son rode north with a white man named Ferguson who came from a forted-up farm on the Brazos River in Palo Pinto County. Ferguson was seeking news of his two daughters who had been taken in January, five months ago. He said the war is done for them other people back east but it is not done for us. He had buried his wife and his aged mother.

They went on toward the Red River. They passed the Stone Houses on the second night out. Traveling at night and all the next day they came to the gentle bluffs of the Red River. They found the crossing at the gravelly shoal but Britt knew better than to try it, and so he led them downstream until he could see a solid bank on the far side. They rode wet and streaming through the breast-high water, and then onto reaches of white sand and then into the tall bottomland trees. Jube came through the currents riding the black horse, with his rifle held high over his head. He thought, if anything happened he would throw himself into the river and let the horse go. He was convinced that bullets could not strike him if he were under water.

The man with them slept badly. At night sitting in his blankets in a fireless camp he said he hoped he would have a chance to kill an Indian, he would kill as many as he could for the rest of the time that he was alive. Then he went to sleep, and in the middle of the night he called out in a low, inhuman voice the names of his daughters. It was as if he had left his body and had turned into a ghost and had gone out across the earth to haunt them.

Within the week they arrived at the Indian Agency. There were some Comanche and Kiowa camped around the agency. Maybe they had come for rations or perhaps they liked to be near the cool water of Cache Creek or some spirit had moved them to erect their tipis for a time near the agency merely to see what the soldiers and the agent would do next. The men watched as Britt rode past the tipis with his son on the black horse beside him. Father and son both looked straight ahead and regarded no one. The word would pass from one person to another. Britt was flushed with a feeling of triumph, of defiance. There was such a thing as Fate and these people were its agents and he had defied them all.

Ferguson said the agent was a Quaker and that Quakers do not believe in fighting or carrying weapons or that kind of thing.

"Then why the hell have they sent him to be an agent for the Comanche and the Kiowa?" said Britt. "They should have sent him to the Cherokee."

"Got me," said Ferguson. "It's the government."

The agent seemed a delicate man with a serious way of slightly dropping his head and looking up at them. He wore a suit of heavy woolens and a hat with a great wide brim. Britt watched him carefully for signs and signals as to how he would treat a black man, but there was no hesitation in his manner. He was an easterner by his way of speaking. He looked up at Britt.

"The slaves are free now," said Hammond. He glanced from Britt to Ferguson. The white man lifted both hands in the air.

"Don't look at me."

"I am a free man," said Britt. "Have been for years."

Hammond brightened. "Excellent! A free Negro! In Texas!"

Britt's face was still. He said, "Are you?"

Hammond was silent a moment. "Am I what?"

"Free."

Hammond was silent for a moment. Then he gave Britt a quick nod. "An excellent question. One worthy of pondering."

"Yes, sir."

Then Britt stood down from his horse and drew the reins together. Hammond called for someone to take their horses and see to their unsaddling and feed and water and Britt handed over the reins to a boy in a coarse suit of clothes and a flat, billed cap.

Jube slid down from his black horse. His war booty. He turned to the boy in the suit and said, "You get that saddle off first thing," he said. "Hear me?"

The boy lifted his chin and stared, but Jube stepped toward him one step, his black eyes fixed and intent, and the boy backed off. Jube shifted his rifle under his arm.

Hammond said, "Young man, I would ask you to unload that weapon if you would. We are trying to practice nonviolence here, and just as a small beginning we try to keep weapons unloaded."

Britt nodded to his son. Jube lowered his head and shifted his jaw from side to side and then opened the breech and extracted the load. If anything happened he would use the rifle as a club.

Hammond asked them to come into the agency house. It was chill and impersonal and strictly clean. They passed through the little decorative gate in the white picket fence and then Britt stood in the doorway, tall and bulky in his heavy boots and the revolver he did not unload. He stood with his hat in his hand until he was offered a chair. Ferguson sat with his hands in fists. He was choked with contained anger.

Samuel brought out a ledger and wrote down the names and description of the girls that Ferguson was seeking. His daughters. He asked Ferguson to stay at the agency until he, Samuel, could try for information from the Indians that were camped at Cache Creek. The man stared at him a moment and then nodded and got up and went out.

Britt said, "Agent Hammond, I am going to look for Elizabeth

Fitzgerald and her granddaughter Lottie. I would like a cavalry escort. I know where I'm going."

"Very well." Samuel smiled. "You seem very confident."

"I think I can do it." Britt turned to his son. "Jube, I want you to stay here at the agency while I go on to the Wichitas."

"Yes, sir." Jube was relieved. It was enough that the Kiowa and the Comanche who stayed around the agency would see him. They would talk about it when they went out again, they would unroll this gossip like a many-colored serape. The word would come to Old Man Komah and to Aperian Crow and all the others that he was with his own father again.

Britt turned to the Indian agent.

"Mr. Hammond, could my son stay here with you until I come back? He speaks some Kiowa."

"Of course." The agent regarded Jube. "Why does he speak Kiowa?"

"He was captive eight months."

"Really! How did you get him back?"

Britt lifted one shoulder. "Well, I met a Comanche who helped me." He put his hand on Jube's shoulder. "And they had his mother and sister as well. I got them all back."

Hammond put one knuckle to his lips and then dropped his hand onto his knee. "That is astonishing." He reached out and patted Jube on the shoulder. "He is very welcome. I am not, as you pointed out, free to go myself. I will send the men with you as you asked. It will show that you are on agency business."

"All right." Britt sat carefully on the edge of the chair.

"What do you need?"

"Whatever they want in trade," said Britt. "Whatever it is they like."

"I will find some supplies, some nice things."

Britt put on his hat and touched his son's shoulder and said good day and without another word walked out the door.

❧

LOTTIE WORE HER Indian name in a kind of verbal badge
blazoned on the spring air. She liked to hear Pakumah use it, calling her to come and eat, come and see something. Elizabeth did
not pronounce the name correctly and had no intention of doing
so. *Sikkydee*, Elizabeth said. *Sockadee. Sackado.* Elizabeth's knuckles
were growing large and swollen from the work but she kept on. She
broke up the elk shoulder bones into hoes, the antlers into rakes.
She learned to fasten the candelabra of bone to staffs. She cultivated
corn in the valley of Cache Creek high in the Wichitas. She and the
other women had poured in squash and corn seed early in the year.
Seed carefully saved in bags in each woman's tipi and left against the
tipi walls during the winter. For each kind of seed a reverent name.
The legends and the origins of the divine personages who belonged
to each kind of seed had been lost but the seed names remained; all
the more mysterious for being without provenance. The air was now
full of oak pollen and Elizabeth sneezed and dug, wiped her nose on
her arm and carried water from the pools of Cache Creek to throw
on the rows of tasseling corn. She took up her antler rake and ripped
out snarling nets of love vine as if they were entrails.

Pakumah was afraid of Elizabeth and her power to drive people
to suicide. Her power of life, her ability to survive and hoard her
fury like a treasure, like seeds in a bag that would later bloom out
into someone's death. Her sheer furious life force. Her husband said
they ought to kill Elizabeth, then, if she was such trouble, but Pakumah and three other wives cried No! No! because they had become
convinced of Elizabeth's ability to rise up out of water, earth, out
of the moonlit nights, to strike at them even from the spirit world.
To harry and hate until her victims hung themselves. She would be
twice as dangerous if she were dead.

Elizabeth knew that as long as she kept her bullying ways to the
society of women, she was safe. From time to time Elizabeth's mind
was overcome with images of herself driving a knife into Pakumah's
sternum, the resisting bone, the flash of blood. Of shooting somebody, an unspecified Comanche man, with a rifle or pistol. When
this happened, she stopped what she was doing for a moment and

got hold of herself and then went on slamming the antler into the earth and raking out the tangling wild buckwheat and greenbrier. On a fire nearby the women had taken the ripest of the ears and laid them on a green-stick grill over the coals to roast. They were ears with red and purple and blue-black kernels, Indian corn.

Elizabeth knew that they had driven off most of her cattle and horses. She saw her own horses now in the Comanche herd as the young men and boys took them to grazing and to water. She wrapped her swollen knuckles in strips of scrap buckskin and turned weeds out of the red earth. She would get it all back. Her anger was like sweet water to her, her plans of revenge a biblical text that she read over to herself every night, and Lottie would become herself again when they got back to Elm Creek and not the Comanche princess she was now. Petted and strung with glass beads. *Lottie girl, things are going to change.* Above Elizabeth the metallurgical peaks of the Wichitas rose in a blue early-summer sky, their red granite boulders rounded and smooth, studded with juniper and live oak and pine. She could smell the roasting ears. When she returned to her own house she would have her own roasting ears with butter and salt and pepper.

Several Comanche men came riding up the valley toward them. Elizabeth turned with the rake in her hand to watch them. Their hair looped behind them as they trotted their horses. A feeling of dread crawled up her back with a thousand legs. Something told her to prepare to defend herself against them. That the end might have come. The other women stopped and straightened up with their worn bone hoes glittering. All of them turned to look at Elizabeth.

Taibo, they said. Soldiers.

Elizabeth immediately thought of Lottie, and where she might be. If there were to be a fight with the soldiers, would they come and kill her and Lottie.

One of the men on horseback gestured to Elizabeth and told her to follow. His eyes were a thin hazel color with a fixed look.

They have come for you. They will decide your price.

She only understood part of what was said. "Sackado," she said. "Sikkydoo where?"

The man's look of contempt did not change. He gestured for her to come along and then they turned and rode back at a walk. Elizabeth ran after him. Then in a moment, so did Pakumah.

BRITT SAT DOWN on his heels in front of the fire. He did not look at Major Semple or the soldiers. He regarded only the Comanche across from him and their bright trade blankets and serapes from the Mexican settlements, their earrings and the rosary beads worn as necklaces. When the sentries had brought in word of their coming, the Comanche headmen put on their best ornaments and prepared for a day of bargaining and food, a pleasant amusement.

In the Wichita Mountains the Comanche had come upon some others who had just arrived from the agency with flour and sugar, baking soda and coffee, and they had traded for these things with ammunition and tobacco from the Comancheros.

Thus the smell of baking bannocks that turned lightly brown in skillets, the odor of coffee and bacon. Britt sat down on the ground cross-legged and removed his spurs and buckled the straps together through his belt. If there were trouble he did not want to jump to his feet and get caught up in his own spurs. The Comanche men across from him saw him do it and noted it and Britt did not care one way or the other. The soldiers did not sit down but stood behind Britt and the major with their arms grounded. A pipe was brought to mark the meeting as a social occasion. Britt sat in the familiar smells of burning sumac and tobacco leaves, the coffee and woodsmoke. He passed the pipe to his left, holding the bowl in his hand, and the carved face on the bowl looked out from between his fingers.

Then food came and Britt ate what was given him with good appetite. The major sat beside him and after a moment, seeing that what he had been handed on a wooden tray was not raw liver or intestines or eyes, ate as well.

"Ah, Brreet, Brreet!"

Britt looked up. Tissoyo strode across the beaten red earth between the tipis. Tissoyo had a burst of snowy egret feathers on the top of his head like a minor white explosion of down and plumes. His arms jangled with silver bracelets and he wore an enormous, ostentatious rosary around his neck.

"There you are," Britt said in Spanish. He smiled. Tissoyo sat down beside Eaten Alive. He settled himself gracefully and dusted his hands. Eaten Alive glanced at him with a faint trace of annoyance and a bannock in one hand.

"Yes, here I am." Tissoyo gracefully opened one hand as if to present himself.

"Did you win your horses back?"

"They would not put them up, the cowards. The Medicine Hat stallion, they wanted him to make babies. But I won a great deal of other things." He jangled the silver bracelets. They were wide and beautifully chased. They had crawled up his arm almost to the elbow and Tissoyo shook them down to his wrist. "Now, I will translate." Tissoyo was then quiet and deferential because most of the Comanche understood at least some Spanish and so Tissoyo was limited in his desire to make remarks, to relay secrets, inside information. "This man is called Horseback, and this one Eaten Alive, and this is Toshana. I don't know how to say Toshana in Spanish." Then Tissoyo turned to the headmen and said the names of Major Semple and Britt, and, far away, in a wave of his hand to the south, the name of Hammond, the Indian agent who was called Keeps-All-the-Stuff because he was refusing rations if captives were not brought in. By making these introductions Tissoyo had effectively taken over the meeting.

The major said, "I would appreciate a translation."

"You don't speak Spanish?" Britt half turned to him.

"No, I don't. You know this young Indian here? With the bracelets?"

"I do," said Britt. "I will translate as we go on."

"Very well," said the major. "But please first indicate that we, ah, come in peace. We are only interested in the captives and nothing else."

It was too soon to start mentioning the captives. Britt had come to understand they should finish the food first, but after a pause he relayed this in Spanish to Tissoyo.

Eaten Alive refused to speak Spanish but turned instead to Tissoyo and spoke in Comanche.

Tissoyo pushed a wedge of bannock into his mouth and swallowed, and then straightened his back to a perfect horizontal and became erect and dignified.

"He says, you, the underwater man, you went to the Kiowa and you paid very well for your wife and your girl child." He made the sign for *Kiowa,* a cupping gesture at the right side of the head where they cut their hair short. "You did not pay for the boy. Later the boy ran away and joined you. He says this was a trick and it was not a good one. He said you had it planned out that way so you did not have to pay for the boy."

Britt said, "My son is very brave and clever. He came on his own. He is very strong. He crossed the country between the Cimarron and the Canadian by himself in three days."

Toshana said, *He took Aperian Crow's best horse. The black one. It was a warhorse.*

Britt said, "Too bad for Aperian Crow."

Toshana snorted in a short, surprised laugh. He turned the carved pipe over in his hand and knocked the dottle from it on a smooth stone. Then he spoke again.

Tissoyo listened and then said in Spanish, "He says there are captives here with us Comanche, it's true. The soldiers know there are captives here." He signed as he spoke in Spanish. It was a habit of many translators. It was a way of gesturing and also so that everyone would know what he was saying. He made the sign for *Comanche,* a wavering snakelike motion for the Snake River far away in Idaho where the Comanche had come from in centuries past and still retained that territorial name.

Britt turned to the major and told him what had been said so far. The major nodded in an agreeable way.

Britt said, "Where is the two-year-old girl that the Kiowa took? Her name is Millie. Do you have her?"

Eaten Alive shook his head. *She is dead. The Kiowa told us she got sick and died.*

"Where did she die?"

Up near the Cimarron. By Black Mesa.

Britt kept his eyes on Eaten Alive for several blank and dubious seconds. Then with a small movement of his hand he said, "Now, a grown *taibo* woman and a *taibo* girl about three or four years old. Are they here?"

Eaten Alive nodded. Before he could speak a small boy ran up and fell to his knees in the dirt beside him and whispered anxiously in Comanche. The headman nodded. He waved his hand at the boy to send him away. The boy retreated behind Eaten Alive's back where he could not be seen and stood listening. Eaten Alive then turned his attention back to Britt and the soldiers.

They are here. The woman is mine, she is a slave. I want a rifle and ammunition and three horses, two packages apiece of coffee and sugar. He indicated the size of the packages; to Britt it looked like about twenty pounds each. *And a hundred dollars.*

Tissoyo bent over and spoke to Britt rapidly in Spanish, so quick that Eaten Alive could not keep up. "The little boy has come from Eaten Alive's wife with a message. She says sell the *taibo* woman for anything at all, just sell her." Then to cover his words Tissoyo opened and shut both hands twice, indicating twenty. "That many in pounds." He turned innocently to Eaten Alive. "Is that right?"

"Hm." Eaten Alive fixed Tissoyo with a stare for a moment and then over his shoulder he handed the carved pipe to a thin adolescent boy to clean and put back in its case. The young man flushed with pride and carried it carefully away between his two hands as if it were explosive.

Tissoyo said, "He wants to know if you will give this for the big loud woman."

"No," said Britt. "I will give twenty-five dollars in silver money for her."

That's not enough.

"Then keep her."

The boy behind Eaten Alive listened and then turned quietly and walked back toward the village and after a few moments began to run and disappeared among the tipis.

I will think about that, said Eaten Alive. *And now the girl. My wife loves the little girl very much.*

To give himself time to think, Britt turned to the major and told him what had been said so far. The major nodded. He shifted on the ground. His hip joints were hurting from sitting cross-legged.

Major Semple said, "Britt, you have a future in the army."

"Maybe so." Then Britt said to Eaten Alive, "For the little girl, I have some jewelry for your wife and two mirrors and a serape and a horse. To make Eaten Alive's wife feel better about giving up the girl, I will add the coffee and sugar and fifty dollars. This is to wipe away her tears."

Britt turned and made a motion to one of the soldiers to bring the trade pack and open it. All of them sat and watched as two soldiers opened the pack and spread out the ornate jewelry, the two framed mirrors, the serape, and the coffee and sugar. The serape was of that design called *jorongo,* a brilliant series of red and white stripes in varying widths overwoven with black diamonds. This was to wipe away Pakumah's tears and in truth Pakumah sat in the farthest tipi stroking Siikadeah's hair and weeping as if she would never stop. She wiped her face on her shoulder and then sent the boy out again with another message.

"Don't open the money," said Britt.

Eaten Alive rested his hands on his kneecaps and bent forward over the jewelry and serapes. Then he heard behind him the footsteps of the small boy. The boy again dropped to his knees behind the war leader and Britt heard the rapid whispering. Eaten Alive made a waving motion of his hand and the boy rose and stood off a few paces.

Britt could tell that Tissoyo was longing to tell him what the message was but he was waiting for Eaten Alive to answer.

"He says to give him two serapes instead of one, and the other things and the horse and the fifty dollars in silver and then that would be all right as payment for the little girl." Then Tissoyo spoke to Britt in rapid, slangy Spanish. "The wife sent a message to pay the underwater man to take her away, if he has to." Tissoyo shook down his bracelets again. They had crept up his arm as he translated because he made sign to accompany his words but in an amazing display of double-speak he had signed one thing and said another. Eaten Alive watched the signing and so did not pay any attention to the quick Spanish. Tissoyo had signed *His wife is sad to hear her husband will sell the little girl, and so you must add another serape,* even as he told Britt in Spanish that the wife was willing to pay him to take Elizabeth away.

Britt held one wrist in the other hand and rested his forearm on his thigh. He leaned on the forearm and stretched his back muscles. His admiration for Tissoyo's ability to deal in intrigue had increased greatly in the last fifteen minutes.

"As you say, I will give an extra serape for the little girl and the other things and fifty dollars in silver Spanish milled dollars," he said. He turned to the soldier standing behind him. "Open the other pack and get out the black and yellow *jorongo.*"

Good.

Eaten Alive and Wolf Escaping and the other men nodded. The soldier brought out the black and yellow *jorongo;* it was newly made and the fine wool shone. And so that, at least, was settled.

"And so we are agreed? I will take the little girl, and you will keep the woman." Britt reached to his belt to unbuckle the spurs.

"Wait." Tissoyo lifted a hand. "He wants you to wait a moment."

"What's going on?" said the major.

Britt said, "I closed the deal on Lottie Durgan and we are talking about her grandmother, Elizabeth Fitzgerald. I can get her cheap."

"Jesus," said the major. Here was a black man bargaining for the price of a white woman. The world had turned upside down. He shifted his eyes sideways to the pile of goods being laid on the serape, the bags of coffee and the sugar, the ornate mirrors. Britt was still holding back the money.

Britt turned to Tissoyo. "Tell him I know the woman. She works hard, she is strong. I know he will be glad to keep her."

Tissoyo translated and then listened to what Eaten Alive had to say to this. He said to Britt, "He says that the little girl was the one they loved the most. The woman they don't care all that much about. They already stole all her cattle and horses so they got all the good out of her."

Britt thought about this for a long moment. He had been watching Tissoyo to see if he would pull that trick again, of signing one thing and saying another. It was admirable, amazing. But Tissoyo translated straightforwardly and in a modest manner.

Britt was not sure of how much advantage he had. They could always kill Elizabeth. They did not need to sell her to get rid of her. "Twenty-five dollars."

Then Tissoyo said in that quick, slurred Spanish, "They think she is a witch, she frightens them." And at the same time he signed *Eaten Alive will think about the twenty-five dollars.*

"Damn," said Britt.

"What?" said the major. His hip joints felt like they were on fire.

"Later," said Britt to the major, in English, and then turned to Tissoyo and said in slow, measured Spanish, "Tell him that I will pay twenty-five dollars but I also want the big bay horses, the ones that sweat in leopard spots. The ones you took from her ranch." Britt saw subtle changes in Eaten Alive's face. They knew his thoughts. They knew he was thinking about when they had killed his son and raped his wife. Thoughts have power. They can drift through the air unhindered. Ill will and hatred, the lust for revenge, can detach itself from the person who generates these thoughts if that person has a certain power from some being. Even after the person is dead.

Eaten Alive lifted both palms to the air and said something in an exasperated voice.

Tissoyo took on a light and somewhat haughty expression. "He says, soon you will ask him to pay you, to take her away."

"Tell him I was thinking about it."

Tissoyo did not laugh, with some difficulty. "He says you can have her, and the horses, for twenty-five dollars, but then you have to give him a four-point Hudson's Bay blanket."

Britt turned to the soldiers. "Give them the red blanket and seventy-five dollars in silver. Do it nicely." The sergeant glanced at the major, and the major gave a brief nod. The sergeant brought out the four-point Hudson's Bay blanket and laid it out on the ground, bright red with its four wide stripes. Then he sat on his boot heels and counted out seventy-five dollars in silver Spanish milled dollars, stacked in three piles.

To Major Britt said, "We're done. Let's go."

"Did you get both of them?"

"Yes. And he gave me two draft horses into the bargain."

ELIZABETH DID NOT believe she was free and safe even when she and Lottie were seated in the wagon with soldiers riding on either side of them. She would never feel safe again. The major glanced down at her; a raped woman, a captive redeemed. Lottie sat silent and staring. What was happening to her now? There was no telling. The four-year-old watched the soldiers in a state of fear with her thin hands clutched in the remains of Elizabeth's skirt. Two soldiers led the big bay horses, now much reduced in weight. The draft horses turned constantly and called back to the herd of Comanche horses.

Elizabeth said, "What did you have to pay for me?"

Britt rode alongside.

"Twenty-five dollars and that red four-point blanket."

"What?" Elizabeth shouted and Lottie closed her eyes. "Only twenty-five dollars?"

"That's it," said Britt.

"Goddamnit, I'm worth more than that!" Elizabeth glared at the major.

"I got you cheap, Mrs. Fitzgerald," said Britt. "But remember the horses."

"You can have them," said Elizabeth. "Take both of them. They're yours."

"Thank you, ma'am," said Britt. "Much appreciated."

"Twenty-five dollars," Elizabeth said. "If they paid me by the hour for all the skinning I did there wouldn't be enough money in the goddamn federal mint to get me back."

"Yes, ma'am."

"I've paid more than that for a boar pig."

Britt kept his eyes steadily on Cajun's mane. Finally he said, "Actually, it was twenty-six."

"That don't make me feel a bit better, Britt Johnson." Elizabeth wiped her hands on her dress. "So just shut up."

Chapter 22

THE CAPTIVE GIRL was about fourteen. Maybe older. She spoke no English and sat in the office of Samuel Hammond, in the agency house, stiff as a pasteboard figure on the edge of a wooden chair. She was packaged in a corset and long stockings and a dress with a tight waist over the corset and her thin neck thrust up out of the collar of the dress with its tiny lace band edging. She had that wide fixed look in her eyes that Samuel had come to see in the Indian people themselves when they thought they were in danger. When they were disturbed and angry and frightened. The Mexican-Comanche housekeeper sat beside her but it did not comfort her. The woman had come from Fort Sill to help, and there was no way to help her.

A band of Kiowa had come in for rations. They were hungry and thin. They had been in some kind of a conflict out on the plains. Samuel told them through Onofrio that there would be no more rations nor beef nor issue of any kind until they brought in whatever captives they had. He heard himself withholding supplies from those in need. His own voice refusing food to starving people.

Then they had brought her in, with her hair loose and muddy, barefoot. They said the girl had come from somewhere far south in Texas where there was timbered country when she was very young, very young, but her adoptive parents had died in the battle with the Utes, which was just last month out on the plains. Then they had come through a great burned area and could not find buffalo and they came out of it black to the knees and starving. Now there was no one to take care of the girl and so they handed her over for two horses and several brass kettles and a supply of flour and lard and several beef cows that they killed on the spot and ate.

The girl walked behind Samuel with a stony expression and tears running down her face. The laundresses at the fort had bathed her and dressed her. For the second time she had been torn from a culture and a language she knew, from people she loved. Once by violence, once from the bitter necessities of hunger.

Samuel had a list in front of him of all the captives' names that he was able to garner. The black child named Jube, Britt Johnson's only surviving son, sat on a chair beside him, a thin cap of tight black hair on his head and his booted feet placed precisely together.

"Tell her we only want to help her," said Samuel. "We will help her go back to her own home, her own parents."

Jube translated this and listened to the reply and said, "She says her parents, the Utes killed them a month ago."

"No, I mean her real mother and father."

But they died.

"All right." Samuel paused and then smiled. "What is your name?" Samuel listened as the young black boy spoke in the tonal language of Kiowa, with several explosive consonants, clicking glottal stops, rising and falling tones.

"She says her name is Good Medicine. They say in Kiowa the name of a plant, Good Medicine."

"Her English name, Jube."

"She doesn't know."

Samuel smiled again. "I will read these names and see if she recalls one." Jube nodded and spoke to the girl. Samuel pronounced each name several times, slowly and carefully. "Alice Todd." A blank stare. "Mahala Fussell." Nothing. "Susan Murdoch." The girl's eyes shifted to Jube and then back in a wide, dry stare at the Indian agent. "Susan Forster. Mary Ann Findlay. Charlotte Sanger. Frances Lee. Vera Mae Grandin."

"Ah," said the girl. She turned her eyes to Jube and spoke quickly in the musical notes of Kiowa, those strange lifts and the explosive unvoiced *th!*, the descending tones.

Tell him that was my name. Vela Mae Glandin, Vela Mae Glandin, yes.

"Where did she come from?"

I remember a very tall bluff of stone down south in Texas. We lived on a river. Sabinal, Sabinal. That was the name of the river. It was clear water. Up above our house there was a very tall cliff.

"Do you remember what happened when they took you captive?"

The horses came running in, they were frightened. They came running toward the house. Then the Koiguh came in the house and shot my father and mother. They took me and my little brother and my aunt. My little brother would not stop crying and so they killed him. They did things to my aunt and then they killed her.

The girl's face was impassive as she said this. Jube flushed a little at his cheekbones as he hesitated a moment and then finished her last sentence.

"What were your parents' names?"

Mama and Papa.

"Oh. Yes. Well, what was your aunt's name?"

The girl frowned slightly and stared at the floral carpet. *Aun-tie Flo.*

Samuel watched the girl for signs that she was tiring, or too frightened to reply coherently. That he should stop the questioning. The girl's hair trembled in raw, newly washed locks around her neck.

"You said your last name was Grandin. Or Glandin."

"They can't say 'r,'" said Jube.

"All right. Your last name was Grandin, and what was your aunt's last name?"

I don't know. Aun-tie Flo.

Samuel lowered his head for a moment, resting it on his hand. He said a small, brief prayer for help. How to do the right thing. The girl lifted her hand to Jube and went on speaking.

Jube said, "She wants to know if she can go back to the Kiowa. And if not, can she go and live with the Comanche."

Samuel stared at the boy for a moment. "They killed her little brother and her mother and father, and then mistreated her aunt and killed her too. Why does she want to go back?"

Jube did not address this to the girl. He considered it himself. "It's all right, sometimes," he said. "It's hard but it's kind of fun."

Samuel folded his hands together between his knees. "Yes?"

"The Indians, they don't ever whip their kids. You can kind of do what you want."

"I see," said Samuel. "And what you want to do is not very complicated, is it?"

Jube tipped his head to one side and shrugged. "Well, we ran around on horses all the time. Us boys." He sighed nervously and searched for words. "And we could hunt whenever we wanted to. Us boys. The girls carried the water and stuff."

Samuel sat and waited for a moment. Jube fell silent.

"Then why didn't you want to stay?"

Jube said, "Because my mother was with us the whole time. They didn't kill her. My mother was with me and Cherry. She did everything to help us. No Indian woman came to be our mother. This girl here, you know, she didn't have a mother and father anymore after they killed them, so then she got an Indian mother and father."

Samuel leaned back in his chair with folded hands to think about this. He said, "And wasn't there another little girl with the Kiowa? About two years old?" Samuel bent his head to his list. "Yes, Millie Durgan."

"She died," Jube said. He tapped his fingertips and the tip of his thumb together. "Some others took her away north and she died."

"All right." Samuel put the list away. "Ask her if she remembers how long it took for her to be carried to the camps of the Indians."

I don't know. We rode a long time. My father wrapped me up in a blanket and kept me warm and when we got there, there was a lot to eat.

Samuel nodded. A second birth of a kind; bloody, violent, noisy, appalling. And there you were, a new terrified person in a new and terrifying world and somebody gives you something to eat.

He placed his hands on his kneecaps and turned his gaze out the window. He did not want to stare at the girl but she was so odd and anomalous. It was hot inside the agency house and he thought about going with the two children to sit beside Cache Creek. Maybe they would feel more at ease in the shade of the cedar elms.

The girl's hair was medium brown now that it was freshly washed and her eyes a watered gray, her eyelashes dense and black. Her face and hands burned brown. It was the expression on her face, the way she held herself, that he had never seen in a white person. A wary stillness in the eyes, a silent withheld aggression. She was utterly unaware of her own appearance and face, uninterested in the image she projected and not concerned with impressing him by gesture or posture. She had no interest in appearing fashionable or charming. White children, white people in general, had expressive faces, their thoughts reflected instantly. The children were winsome and eager to please. This girl had faced death and starvation at a very young age. She had never been corrected or denied anything her adoptive parents had in their power to give. She had never been struck or spanked. She was both spoiled and underprivileged, famished and indulged, her emotions sheared off as if with a knife or kept in silence and secrecy like an irreplaceable treasure. She was elfin, otherworldly.

"Jube, ask her if she would like to have a white mother and father again. If she does not want to go back to her old home and have nice dresses like she has now, and a roof over her head and good food."

No. I don't like to sleep in a house. I don't like the roof. It makes me afraid.

"Why are you afraid of the roof?"

It might fall down. It might catch fire and I could not get out.

"Do you like your new dress?"

No.

Samuel Hammond closed his eyes briefly. He ran his hand through his pale, thin hair and patted it down. She could not go back. She was not Kiowa. She had been stolen from her culture and her religion. Hammond went to his desk and took up a pen and paper. He dipped ink and began to write down the particulars for the Austin and Fredericksburg newspapers. Any of the new journals that had just started up in towns where the populace still might be attacked by bands of young men from the Comanche and Kiowa, where the newspaper offices themselves might be burned, the windows shot full of holes and the typecases scattered.

"Jube, ask her for anything she might remember of the place and the time when she was taken." Hammond lifted his head to the two children from behind his desk. "Did she ever have a birthday party?"

"A what, sir?"

"Ah, let's see. That's where you celebrate when you become a year older. Every year your parents make a cake, and put candles on it, and you get presents."

Jube appeared very interested. "Are they supposed to do that?"

"Well, some people do."

"Well, I had better tell my mama." Jube's face took on a firm and censorious expression. "She never did that and here she is supposed to."

Hammond laughed. "I didn't mean to start a family quarrel."

"No, sir, but I will just tell her."

"Yes, Jube, but just ask her if she ever had a birthday party."

He wants to know if you remember when you were little if your mother and father had a sing and a dance and sweet bannock with lights on it for you when you became a year older.

Good Medicine stared flatly at Hammond for a moment with her open gray eyes. Then she said, *My mother and father had a sing and a feast and a dance all night when the time came when I was a woman.*

No, he means your Tejano mother and father.

Oh, them. Good Medicine bent her eyes to the carpet and tried to remember. She had seen many people die, so the images that came to her of her Tejano mother and father lying on their faces dead, with stripped and bony skulls, and lakes of blood on the floor that quickly drained off down the cracks of the floorboards, did not bother her unduly. But then in her segmented and disjointed memory came an image that attached itself to the Kiowa words *sweet bannock* and *lights on it.* These then became the English words *happy birthday to you,* which were particularly pleasing to her because they were sung like Kiowa words.

Good Medicine said, *There were some lights on it. Maybe this many.* She held up her hand and spread her fingers so the agent could understand. *They sang a song.* Then, hesitantly, she began to sing. *Happi biltday to you, happi biltday.* Then the song faded away.

Hammond listened. His eyes grew wet. He walked to the window and cleared his throat and stared out at the sifting branches of the trees along the creek and a milk cow grazing at the end of a rope. Then he turned back and smiled.

"Good, good. So she was five or six when she was taken. If she is fifteen now, it was ten years ago, in 'fifty-six. And it was down on the Sabinal River. I will look on a map but I think there are some settler communities down there. I will put a notice in whatever newspapers there are." He turned to Jube. "Tell her she will not go hungry again. Tell her there will always be plenty of food for her. She need not worry."

Jube repeated this. Even though he knew she was not afraid of going hungry, or of starvation. She was afraid of the slow death of confinement. Of being trapped inside immovable houses and stiff clothing. Of the sky shuttered away from her sight, herself hidden from the operatic excitement of the constant wind and the high spirits that came when they struck out like cheerful vagabonds across the wide earth with all of life in front of them and unfolding and perpetually new. And now herself shut in a wooden cave. She could not go out at dawn alone and sing, she would not be seen and known by the rising sun.

Chapter 23

❧

BRITT WATCHED FROM horseback as the soldiers ran the United States flag up the pole at Fort Belknap. It was the spring of 1867. The Stars and Stripes streamed out into the wind for the first time in seven years. It had taken the federal government that long to reoccupy the Texas frontier forts.

It was a very windy day. The army band played "The Battle Hymn of the Republic" with the grit blowing around them. The trumpeters squinted their eyes shut, and the man with the tuba had his coat collar turned up. They had dust on their lips and the tips of their fingers. They stood resolutely in their blue wool ranks and blew on their instruments while the stone buildings of Fort Belknap appeared and disappeared in the clouded air; the barracks and the officers' quarters and the stables, the granary and the workshops. The bandsmen turned from one side to another; with the wind and the snare drums they could hardly hear one another but fixed their eyes on the major with his baton who led them all to the final Glory Glory Hallelujah.

Those standing around were men and women from the outlying ranches and young cowboys and scouts and those who had continued to live at Fort Belknap even after it was abandoned by Union troops. They kept their personal loyalties to themselves. They did not cheer nor did they call out derisive remarks. The men in broad hats leaned their elbows back on the corral rails, boys sat on the roof of the powder magazine, staring silently. The wagonmaker stood in the doorway of the wagon shop, and when it was over he turned back inside. His name was Nathan Finch. A painted board over the wide stone doorway said

Nate Finch Wagonmaker Wheelwright

Britt followed him into the shop and ran his hand over the heavy planks of Osage orange. It was also called bois d'arc. Bodark. The wood was an orange-yellow, neatly fitted together to form the truck and the running gear, the axles and tongue hounds. The wheels were made of hickory aged four years in the bark and brought from Arkansas. Britt had sent off for the fifth wheel, a single-perch, short turn. This was the steel half-circle that allowed the front axle to swivel one way and another, and Britt had ordered the best to be had from Houston.

The wheelwright and his helper lifted the 150-pound wheel onto the lathe to bore out the hub box. The wheelwright stepped on the pedal and the wheel began to spin. He left the pedal to the assistant and pressed the bore into the hickory hub. It was one of the tall rear wheels, fifty-four inches. The front ones were thirty-seven inches. Sawdust spun out of the hub box, hot and golden.

Britt took three pennies out of his pocket and walked over to the workbench by the forge and dropped them on the splintered wood. He took up the bottle of hot sauce where the wagonmaker had left his lunch and poured the red mixture over the pennies.

"Britt, you going to eat them pennies?" The wheelwright stopped the spin and then he and the apprentice lifted the wheel off and turned it to the other side.

"No, sir, Mr. Finch. They're for my boy." Britt waited a moment and then picked them up in his hand and dipped them in the quenching vat and rinsed them off. He dried the brightened pennies on his pants. The copper was now brilliant and gleaming. He put them in his pocket and wiped his hands on his shirt. "You just think what that stuff is doing to your stomach."

"I like it." The wheelwright lifted another wheel to the lathe. They had two more to go. Britt regarded the shining felloe plates, all the new metal gear that held the wheels and the wagon itself together. The iron rims were already on the wheels. They would not spin correctly on the lathe were they not shod. This was his best wagon, new-made from tongue to tailgate. He had purchased another used one from Elizabeth Fitzgerald. He had the good big bays and then Duke and a borrowed mare, and Cajun for his saddle horse. With this wagon loaded with ten thousand pounds, about four tons, he would have to use all four horses on the one wagon. If he was carrying something lighter—army blankets, the uniform issue, Indian trade goods—he could put two horses to a wagon and use both.

"There's a lot of work here now," said Finch. He spoke in a half-shout over the noise of the boring bit and the racket of the revolving wheel. Their voices boomed in the hollows of the stone building. "I've been told the army may keep me on."

"Well, good," said Britt.

"Now, the officers are going to need their washing done. Your wife might find a lot of work here too."

Britt didn't answer for a moment. Then he lifted his head to Nathan Finch. "She's not well," he said. "And I don't want to see another man's drawers hanging on my clothesline."

"Well, excuse me," said Finch. Then to his assistant, "Take aholt and stop that shit-eating grin."

He and the boy took hold of both sides of the third wheel and lifted it off and then heaved up the fourth one.

"This wagon, it would take a lot of knocking around," said the wheelwright. "Like Indian attacks." Finch pressed in with the bore and the drill spun and bit its way into the hub box. "But they say you got a friend there with the Indians."

"My time will come," said Britt. "Friends with one Indian ain't friends with all of them."

"Yes, well, some people are just lucky."

Britt listened to the tone of the man's words and didn't say anything. He put his hand in his pocket and jingled the pennies. Then he said, "I'm going to find Paint and Dennis."

"I ain't going nowhere," said the wheelwright.

Britt stood outside and watched the regimental band straggling back to the barracks with their instruments in hand. Troopers of the new black Ninth Cavalry had been dismissed and were housing their guidons in the long leather cases. They walked back to the stables, leading their horses. All bays. Brown shoe polish had been used on those horses with white blazes or socks and so they all looked alike. He walked on toward Nance's store. The store was made of upright pickets and a sheet-metal roof like a big cowshed.

He saw Paint Crawford sitting at one of the little wooden tables out in front of the store with a piece of paper on the table between his hands and a quill pen being held out to him by a black man in uniform.

"No, you don't, Paint," said Britt. "Put that pen down before I break your arm."

Paint looked up. The random splatters of pink-white skin across one side of his face and on his hands made him look as if he were disappearing piecemeal. His eyes grew round when he saw Britt.

"Aw, Britt," he said.

"I'll be damned if you join up," said Britt. "Put it down."

Jube ran up to his father from the parade ground where he had been watching the black soldiers. Britt took hold of the boy's sleeve.

"Son, look, I have three pennies for you."

Jube took them and regarded them in all their brilliant copper gleaming in his hand.

"Thank you, Pa." He shut his hand over them. He looked up at the black sergeant with his neat uniform and his shining cap-bill, the yellow cavalry insignia on his shoulder.

"Is he army?"

"Yes, I am," said the recruiting sergeant. "Regular army. Not scouts. Not orderlies. Regular soldiers."

Jube shut his fingers around the coins in a tight fist. Black men were now soldiers too to chase after the Koiguh, people like Kiisah and Gonkon and Aperian Crow. He did not know how to think about this.

"You see," the sergeant said. He tapped his pants stripes. "Yellow is for cavalry, and a blue stripe is for infantry, and a red stripe would be for artillery."

"Yes, sir," said Jube. He looked at the ground and then up at his father. "Can I buy something now?"

"Yes. Stand at the door and ask Mr. Nance for three cents' worth of whatever you want. Horehound, licorice. He has peppermints."

The black sergeant stood back with his arms crossed and regarded Britt. Behind him, sitting at another table, was a white officer who swayed very slightly in a battered kitchen chair. The white officer had a sweet and heart-shaped face. The hair under his brimmed hat was fine, drifting, and reddish. His eyes were very round, like doorknobs. A glass of Nance's whiskey sat in front of him.

"There is no life like the army life," the white officer said. "The biscuits are mighty fine."

The sergeant said, "Sir, I am Sergeant Elijah Earl. This is Major Pinney. Charles Pinney."

Britt nodded, once, to the white officer and then turned back to Earl. "How do you do. My name is Britt Johnson."

"Delighted. Now, I have no idea why this man should not join an all-black cavalry unit and become a credit to his race." He uncrossed his arms. "Do you have something against the military?"

"He can do that later," said Britt. "Right now he's my driver. We are starting a freighting outfit." Britt stared at Paint until he finally laid the pen down without signing.

"I myself have done very well in the army," said the sergeant. "There are advantages."

The white officer nodded and stared at the glass and finally lifted it. He drank it off. "I was sort of blown up a little bit at Vicksburg myself," he said. "Other than that, I enjoy military life. Don't we, Susan?"

"Susan is his dog," said Sergeant Earl, and cleared his throat. Britt saw a fluffy beige tail lifted up and down politely under the table.

"Paint, you better come with me," said Britt. "You ain't signing nothing."

"All right, Britt." Paint's shoulders fell. "It sounded so good."

Jube ran up to his father and tugged at his shirtsleeve.

"What?" said Britt.

"Mr. Nance says I got to go around to the back door and ask."

"Then go around to the back door." Britt felt the flush rise to his head. The saddle-colored skin at his cheekbones and then at the tips of his ears. But you had to choose your fights. This was not one Britt was going to choose at the moment. Jube bit his lower lip and then turned away.

Elijah Earl lifted one hand in the air. "Well, Paint can always reconsider." Paint stood up and walked away a few steps and then turned back. Elijah Earl turned to Britt, moving his entire body in one motion, and removed his billed cap, wiped his head, and put it on again. "Do you have other children?"

"Yes," said Britt. "A girl besides. Why?"

"I am starting a colored school. We'll hold it at the fort here. So there's no trouble." He paused. "In the storehouse at the east end. I have permission from the colonel."

Britt lifted his eyebrows and then nodded. "My wife wanted to teach at one time."

"Excellent!" Elijah Earl's severe, lengthy face brightened. "She can certainly help teach."

Paint stood behind Britt and waved his hands at Sergeant Earl and shook his head. *No, no.* Earl refused to look at him.

"I'm not sure she could," said Britt.

"And why not?"

Paint shook his head with his eyes squinched shut. The sergeant ignored him.

"She's had a head injury. She was taken captive by the Comanche and took a hard blow to the side of her head." Britt shifted his weight to one foot and made a small gesture with his hand. "She's starting to piece words together out of the Bible."

"Well, good God, man," said Earl.

There was a long silence. The white officer called in a quiet and diffident voice for another glass of whiskey. Dutch Nance brought it out. Britt knew he and the sergeant were sitting outside because black people were not allowed inside Nance's store. Life on the road was going to be very good.

"Let her come anyway," said Earl. "Let her come and see if she can teach the simplest things. That would perhaps help her regain her ability. Don't you think?"

Britt said, "That's possible." He turned and looked out onto the dirt street. For a moment he asked himself where it would be better. Cities of the North, with their sections for blacks only. The South in ruins and seething with bitter ex-Confederates and confused and rootless freedmen. Unknown places with unknown rules, and all in a perilous state of flux.

Jube came around from behind the store with a handful of peppermints. He offered them to the grown men as a matter of good manners, but the men all refused politely except for the white officer, who took one and cracked it between his teeth.

"I'll ask her. I don't know if I would like her and the children in town, here. At the fort."

The white officer rested his head on one hand and said, "Susan, this is a hellhole. This fort is a hellhole." He lifted his wobbling head. "If any of these crackers shoot one of my black troopers there is a certain question of jurisdiction. Of juries. Of steaming lawyers quoting the black laws of days of yore." He crunched the peppermint and swallowed a drink of his whiskey.

"I understand," said Sergeant Earl. "But they must learn to read and write." He laid his hand on Jube's shoulder.

"When are you going to have this school?"

Earl gestured toward the immense stone warehouse where men were ripping up shingles and throwing them out into the air where they sailed like leather-winged bats and then fell onto a growing heap. Seven years of neglect, and the roof leaked like a sieve.

"Two days a week is all I can get off from my duties. Do bring them in."

Britt nodded and absentmindedly ran his hand over Jube's head. "Where could she and the children stay?"

"You mean, where safe, where out of the way of drunks," said Earl. "And others."

"Yes."

Earl thought for a moment. "She could probably stay with old man Sutton, a carpenter here. He has a wife and his four children are coming to the school. He is a good, sober man."

"All right."

And so it was decided.

Britt turned to go with one hand on Paint's shoulder and a gesture to his son. A white man in cattleman's boots and a broad hat came under the veranda roof of Nance's store and strode toward Elijah Earl.

"Get out of the way, nigger."

The white officer looked up with his round doorknob eyes. He said, "That's sergeant nigger to you, cracker."

The man said, "All right then. Get out of my way, sergeant nigger."

Elijah Earl had not moved, nor had Britt and Paint.

"Don't mess with me," said the white officer. "That's my sergeant." His head wavered. "Get used to it."

The man stood without speaking or moving for a moment. He had a tanned and simple face and he was young and might yet learn to mend his manners. Britt and Paint and Earl had all turned to face him, and Jube stood beside his father with his handful of candies. Dutch Nance leaned against the doorframe of his dirt-floored store with his head lifted and watched carefully.

Jube looked all around without turning his head to see who had a weapon. If anything happened he would run inside the store no matter what old man Nance said. Nance had a shotgun on the floor behind the grain bin, and Jube wondered if it were loaded or not. If he could get his hands on it. If anything happened.

The black soldier said, "My name is Elijah Earl. Sergeant Elijah Earl."

"Get ushed to it," said the major. "I mean, used to it."

The cattleman moved his jaw to one side and then closed his eyes and opened them again.

"What kind of a world have we come to," he said. "What a world." He shifted from right to left on his knee-high boots and their undecorated leather. "All right then. Would you let me by, Sergeant Earl?"

"Happy to." Earl and Britt and Paint all stood to one side. The man passed between them into the dark of the store.

Chapter 24

❧

THE LEAN AND resilient young men of the Kiowa and the Comanche had trained relentlessly as warriors from the time they were very young. They were graceful beyond description, and their speech and symbolism and dreams were of war, ardent soldiers in an anarchic, leaderless army. The Kiowa-Apache had developed a form of speech used only during raids and conflicts, the backward language. In which all precepts of peace were turned around and all concept of human behavior was reversed. The shout for *retreat* meant *Stand your ground*. And through this fearful country and this state of undeclared war Britt was determined to drive his freight wagons.

Britt and Dennis made most of the new harness themselves. Britt bought the metal parts in Weatherford on a trip for flour in borrowed harness, and then Dennis Cureton sat with him at the little ranch on Elm Creek and cut leather to Britt's direction. Dennis's long, thin fingers rambled over the cowhide with chalk and then cut, following the grain, smoothing the edges. He had a gift for shaping. The horse collars were generously padded and every seam tucked in. The stitches were minuscule and almost invisible. Every buckle was double-stitched to hold against runaways and wear. The back and hip strap and the breeching carefully folded and stitched down. Britt wanted to decorate them with studs and rivets, the blinds and winker stays, the breast straps; but Dennis sat and shook his head. *Don't get too fancy,* he said. *No showing out. Look what happened to old man Carter. He shot dead, Britt. No showing out.*

Britt Johnson ran his wagons during times of raids and on routes no other freighter would take. He did it because he wanted them to know he was not afraid. That he had got back his wife and children and would not be made to cower around the forts and hide behind the soldiers, the black Ninth Cavalry or the white troops, either one. And the money was very good.

His drivers and guards were Paint Crawford and Vesey Smith and Dennis Cureton. Britt drove his horses hard. The Fitzgerald bays as wheelers and four others trapped on the plains, mustangs who left bruises on himself and Vesey Smith when they were broken to harness but served very well as leaders, light and agile. Two more heavy horses traded for in Weatherford. That gave him two complete teams of four each with the heavy wheelers next the wagon who took most of the load, and two quick leaders in front, who could shift direction easily and were responsive to the reins. Two extras in case one or two of the other horses were injured or galled or shot. Britt fed them on field corn and broken barley shorts and powdered molasses until they were in good flesh and strong.

Britt often stood in the driver's well so the jolting would not affect his vision, where he could take the shocks in his knees. Dennis or Paint or Vesey and sometimes all three of them rode with loaded rifles. He traveled with both wagons when he could get the orders and he got many orders because there were so few who would chance the road at that time. Britt carried replacement uniforms in strapped bales and ammunition and grain on the long and empty roads to Fort Concho, Fort Griffin, Fort Belknap. They rattled along to Jacksboro and Weatherford, the White Settlement. They carried supplies and tools to Palo Pinto and salt from Graham. They went as far as Fort Worth, where they picked up two barber's chairs for Sergeant Earl. They were the heaviest things they had ever tried to shift. Four grown men and they could barely lift them.

"What the hell does he want these things for?" said Paint.

"Starting a barbershop," said Dennis and rubbed his long, thin hands together. They hurt from the grip he had taken on the underside of the chair.

"Ain't he a busy man," said Paint. "Full-time army and a school and now a barbershop."

"He's paying for the school with barbering money," said Britt. "The women volunteered to do his linen." Britt dipped a cloth in the water bucket and went to wipe down the horse's eyes.

Paint climbed up the tailgate and seated himself in a barber chair and gazed about himself at the dusty plank buildings of Fort Worth like royalty on a throne.

"I am his majesty the king of Appalachicola!" he shouted and threw out both spotted hands. "Bow down to me, you peons! Off with your hats! Off with your heads!"

"Paint, Paint, Paint," said Britt and the horses leaned their heads against him as he stroked the cool cloth over their eyes, wiping away the fly dirt and dust and sweat.

THAT YEAR OF 1867 the Comanche raided down across the Red River and once again struck Elm Creek and killed three young men, all of them nineteen years old. Rice Carleton, Patrick Profitt, Reuben Johnson. One of them was Moses Johnson's grandson. They are buried in the Profitt graveyard where their bones lie together in the same grave to this day. The Kiowa and Comanche raiders drove off more than a thousand head of cattle. In their battle joy the young men struck one ranch and settlement after another. Britt carried headstones to the Profitt graveyard, and metal tools to rebuild the houses they had burned down. He and Mary and the children stood among the others at the graveside as the words were said and the dirt shoveled in. Old man Moses Johnson stood silent and fragile with strange lines of prophecies from the minor prophets coursing through his head in unrelated fragments but did not trust himself to speak. He was shaking inside his heavy woolens and now he leaned on a cane.

Britt's wagons continued to carry their loads among the very small towns and forts of north Texas. They were thinly scattered and open to attack. He did not build a fine house. He let the log cabin stand. It would not do to show out. Look at what happened to old man Carter. And old man Goyens from Nacogdoches, who was half black and who had also married a white woman and became rich and was the subject of lawsuit after lawsuit as white people tried to lawyer him into poverty. At least nobody shot him. The man had died wealthy and in the fullness of his years. Britt hired a survey crew to survey his quarter-section and a lawyer from far away, from the small town of Dallas, to see to it that his deed and his survey were properly registered and witnessed and notarized.

He and Mary and the children visited the Elm Creek house very seldom. It was too dangerous. But they went there in early April of 1867 after the Medicine Lodge Treaty had been signed up in Kansas, between the Comanche, Kiowa, Cheyenne, and Sioux and the federal government, a document stating firmly that the plains horse tribes would stay north of the Red and that they would abandon their way of life and take up plowing and immobility. Which proved a futile hope. So Britt, with Vesey helping, put two of his mustang leaders to a double shovel plow and laid in fifty acres of corn and Mary planted her garden with quiet, hidden efforts to walk perfectly straight and lay her seeds in straight rows and then they went off and left it to the mercies of the climate.

Britt carried ammunition to Fort Belknap for the Ninth Cavalry, who were allowed to gallop after the Comanche raiders as far north as the Red. They stopped and watered their horses from the silky oranges and reds of the river. The black Ninth Cavalrymen slapped their hands together in frustration. They wanted a fight. They wanted to prove themselves. Instead they had a boil-up of coffee and ate some biscuits. Then they tightened their cinches on the hated McClellan army saddles and turned around and came back. Britt and Paint and Dennis and Vesey stopped off at Elizabeth Fitzgerald's to unload bolts of dark green duck and her hair dye and a twelve-gauge shotgun with powder and shot, a carpet, window glass, a crosscut saw, and bar lead. The woman was making a fortress of her big house and the corrals and barns. Men worked on a palisade around the entire headquarters. The air hummed with the noise of saws and the chopping of mattocks into the earth for the footing ditch of the palisade. Elizabeth now employed six men in gathering wild cattle out in the Brazos Valley. She paid them with some bottomless source of money left to her by her first husband, Alex Carter.

"Britt, bring Mary and the children here, you hear me?" she said. "I'm lonesome here. I don't have my Susan anymore. Millie died. That's what them lying sons of bitches said anyhow." She sat on the veranda where she was making a straw hat. It would have a big purple fabric flower on it. She was not making it for herself but to place on Susan's grave there at the edge of the creek. Susan had always liked big hats. "When I'm lonesome I'm just damned dangerous."

"I might," said Britt.

"God knows what I owe Mary. Did all she could for Millie. And I owe you my life." She stood up in the pile of loose straw and placed her hands on her hips. The yellow-and-pink-checkered dress was long gone. She was now wearing a heliotrope brocade with flounces of black velvet and a stained apron over it that made her seem even broader. She had regained every pound she had lost. No one had ever mentioned capture to her, or the word *outraged,* and this silence on the matter was what she wanted. "I got something for you. Hold on." She went into the house and came back out with her dress flouncing around her heavy men's shoes. "This here belonged to Alex." She held out a brass spyglass. "So you can see them sorry bastards coming."

Britt stepped up under the veranda roof and took it and slid the brass sleeves out to their full length. He put it to his eye and turned it to the workmen. He saw in its circle a man splashing water into his face from a basin and his two-day beard and the rough weave of his shirt and every bright drop running down his cheeks.

"Jesus," he said. "It's powerful." He collapsed it and put it in his pocket. "Much appreciated. Now I can spy on you," he said. "I can blackmail you."

"I wish," she said. "I ain't that lucky. If you run onto a loose man tie him up and deliver him. But not if he's married. I don't believe in bigamy. I never did." She sat down again. "Only twenty-five dollars. I'll show them goddamned savages."

Britt looked down. He lifted a hand to his mouth and coughed. "I'll bring Mary and the children. Then they can go into Belknap two days a week for the black school."

"By God if that woman don't have a spine. Bashed in the head and ever word she ever knew knocked right out of her brain pan and here she is teaching school."

"Yes, ma'am," said Britt. The gate of the palisade as yet had no upright logs around it but stood alone like a doorway to nowhere. Dennis and Paint yelled at him. Paint wanted to know if he was going to stand there and talk all day. Dennis added that the world was waiting on them with money in its hand. Vesey Smith in the second wagon lifted his head to the sky and sang a song about Appalacky Town.

And so they went on in the hammering brutal heat of the sun on the broad open plains, the wagon wheels and axles rumbling down into the valley of the Brazos with its obscuring timber. They skirted Indian Mound Mountain to deliver their load of tools and hay and grain to Fort Concho and then turned around without rest to drive to Weatherford carrying buffalo hides in unfleshed stinking bales. In Weatherford they unloaded the hides and took on barrels of flour and a shipment of eight-day clocks in crates, loads of slaked lime and cement in paper sacks and cedar poles, the Fort Griffin regimental surgeon's trunk of drugs and medications.

Britt bought a Smith and Wesson .44 revolver that took readymade metallic cartridges. For Paint and Dennis and himself he bought the new Spencers out of the surplus firearms market that came about after the war ended. They were .52 caliber and loaded seven shots and also took the new self-contained metallic cartridges and so they no longer had to mess with loose powder and percussion caps. Britt watched the horizon as he drove; the long thin galleries of timber along the Brazos and Elm Creek and the lifts of sandstone rises. He had the wind in his face and the shimmering broad grassy world rolling under his wheels and ahead of him the pointed ears of the Fitzgerald bays nodding in their hard, racketing gallop.

Chapter 25

❧

MARY SAT IN the front room and shelled the Indian corn into a white bowl and then separated the kernels according to their color. All the blue-black ones in one place and the red ones in another heap and the yellow ones she poured out of her hand into an ironstone cup. The school needed them for counters. This was how Sergeant Earl taught the scholars arithmetic. The dark ones were tens and the red ones fives and the yellows were one. Mary sat beneath the advertisement for Jaguar Varmint Traps that Elizabeth had framed and fixed to the plastered wall. Mary did not know why Elizabeth treasured this colored lithograph of a snarling, spotted great cat but did not feel she ought to ask.

Lottie stood in the doorway and watched Mary counting out the kernels. It was a damp December with a low cloud cover. A strong gust of wind shot impelled streams of cold air under the doors and through the spaces around the windows. The bitter air made the girl's skin pale and so the tattoo in the middle of her forehead stood out like a dense and secretive third eye the color of a blue-black grain of corn. She was seven now, or eight.

"Lot-tie," said Mary. "How old years are you now don't you?"

Lottie stared at her. "You talk funny."

Mary smiled and nodded. "Yup," she said. "How old?"

"I am seven," said Lottie. "Grandma wants me to wear that apron." Mary kept on separating grains. "So I don't get my dress dirty."

"Hmmm," said Mary. She picked up another cob of corn and the sheller and began to tear off the grains into a wooden dough tray.

"She wants me to wash dishes."

"Well, dishes need wash," said Mary. "Wash and wash. Every day."

Lottie's nose grew red and her eyes filled with water and she stared with a blank face at Mary. Then she turned and ran away and sometime later Mary heard Lottie scream *No!* And the dishpan turned over and dishes smashing on the floor and Elizabeth's voice in a howl.

Jube and Cherry walked silently into the feed barn to see the calves. There were three of them standing behind their mothers and smelling of milk. Jube wanted to shoot them. He wanted to drive an arrow into their thin sides and see them go down in the straw and manure. To cut them open and eat the clotted milk from their stomachs. Cherry whispered in Kiowa that he should not and Jube strolled through the barn strumming on his bowstring as if it were a harp. The two of them also seemed to have developed a light, hidden contempt for all the devices of civilization.

For a life that must be maintained by washing things made of textiles and china and wood in water that had to be heated and soap that had to be made, for the elaborate techniques of making bread and fermenting vinegar and protecting chickens from predators when wild eggs lay in nests for the gathering. Contempt for the digging in the ground to make outhouses, for the footings of palisades, furrows, postholes, to extract rock for permanent and immovable walls. They seemed to have forgotten the years of childhood that preceded their life with the Kiowa as if it had only been a time of exile from their true lives in movement across the face of the great high-hearted plains and its sky and its winds. The smell of horse, the spartan lives, the unaccountable gifts of food that fell to the hand from nowhere. The men in a state of war from the moment they were born as if there were no other proper human occupation. Jube would have grown to be an aristocrat on horseback, silent and honed and lethal, and yet he had been returned to the nation of houses with roofs and white men, to the country of devices and printed books.

Mary heard from a distance the singing tones of Kiowa and knew it had only been her presence with them during that time that held them here with her. Only for her had they come back.

Mary put the sheller down. She was beginning to see little flashes of light. It happened when she turned her head too quickly. When she was worried. When she remembered.

She stood up. She would put a cloth of cool water on her forehead. When she dreamed now it was of herself speaking. Talking unrestrained. In her dreams words came to her in an intricately and perfectly linked series of constructions called grammar. She knew she could do it again if she dreamed it, if she prayed. She dreamed of herself praying.

Elizabeth came in snorting.

"I am the only parent she has. And I will smack the child if she does something like that again. I can't stand to smack her."

Her loud, harsh voice made the small flashes of light wink on and off in Mary's vision.

"Tell me," said Mary, and waved her hand as if bidding the rest of the sentence to come to her.

Elizabeth softened.

"Yes, Mary, tell you what?"

Mary pointed to the tintype over the mantelpiece. A great fire was burning. It was the winter of 1869. A sudden and distant crack of thunder came to them and they both hesitated.

Then Elizabeth said, "That was Mr. Carter."

"I know," said Mary. "Tell me him."

"Ah." Elizabeth put her fists on her hips and stared at the tintype as if Mr. Carter had done everybody a deliberate disservice by getting himself killed. "He was half black and half white. As you can see. My daddy was a preacher and when I run off and married Mr. Carter I thought he was going to set himself on fire. That was back in East Texas. So I come out here where a person can live the life they want." She sat down. "If they live." Elizabeth pulled heavily at the heliotrope brocade skirts to settle herself in the chair. She spilled over the edges. "Mr. Carter's father and him, the two of them was more interested in getting rich than looking out for themselves. They took a lot of chances. His daddy married a white woman too, and his grandfather before him. In New Orleans. They was all half black and half white for a bunch of generations. I don't like that word *mulatto*. Sounds like some kind of a pudding."

Mary laughed. Elizabeth looked over at her and was surprised, and smiled.

"So they got rich. Like old man Goyens. I had the best of whatever they could buy but before long somebody laid in wait for them and shot my husband and his father deader than Santa Ana." She stood up again and pulled at the strings of her apron. "And I got fixed on the proposition of staying here anyway with my boy and girl. And the Comanche got both of them." She lifted her broad, stained hand and wiped at her eyes. "And I am rich and they can all go to hell." She lifted her shoulders and held them there for a moment and then turned to Mary again. "Now I want you to practice talking."

The daylight diminished moment by moment and the faint tumbling roar of thunder somewhere to the south sounded again. Mary nodded. The lights were blazing through her vision like comets. There was the matter of Mr. Fitzgerald but Mary was now beyond curiosity and no longer cared about Elizabeth's succession of disappearing husbands.

"Don't just nod. Just talk. Say anything. I don't care if it makes sense or not, just talk. Talk a lot." Elizabeth turned her head to the sound of thunder. It made her hands sweat. "You hear."

Mary felt the familiar trembling now all through her body. It would go on when the unbearable headache came upon her and then it would go away.

"I have lights and they are going," said Mary. "Lights in my eyes and going hurt and the day and see when everything can see." She put her hand to her forehead. "Hurt."

"Oh dear," said Elizabeth. "The affliction has come upon her."

She went outside in the increasing wind to the water butt and soaked a cloth in the freezing water. She was suddenly afraid to be outside. She needed to be inside under a roof and with strong immovable walls around her. To the south, beyond the stiff live oak, a long light flashed sideways on the horizon and disappeared and then the thunder spoke again. In the back bedroom Elizabeth placed the wet cloth over Mary's forehead and then went and shook out the last three drops of laudanum into a glass of water. Mary drank it with her eyes closed and lay back down. She was trembling in a high vibrato of muscle and nerve.

"It's because Britt is a day late, isn't it?"

Mary nodded.

"He's all right, Mary. He'll come home."

Mary placed her hands together, palm to palm.

"Yes. I am praying too." The thunder was like distant gunfire or some atmospheric traveling herd of horses that proceeded toward them in a low rumble. The windows lit up and then were dark again and then the thunder came again. "Mary, do you and Britt have a married life?"

Mary lay with her eyes closed and then shook her head.

Elizabeth sat in heavy silence with the cold cloth in her hands. She dipped it in the basin and wrung it out. "What do you remember?"

"It all," said Mary. "So many days there was two of me and I wasn't one but I was the other one."

It was strange weather. A cold wind and the lightning and no rain.

"All right," said Elizabeth.

"And for Britt I can't." Mary shut her hands together like hinges closing. "I can't."

"All right."

Mary set herself to think of when the headache and shaking would be over, to think to the other side of it when she would feel very well and would get up and help Elizabeth and sing and talk and when Britt came she would try to read out loud to him from the newspaper, chasing the print with her eyes as it crawled in an insect stream off to the margins. When the headache and shaking were over with, she thought of all the good things that would happen.

After the children ate their supper they carried blankets and quilts to sleep in front of the fireplace where it was warmest.

As it grew on to black dark the wind increased. It shook every-thing that was not secure. Mary listened to it. She began to be afraid and the fear came on her like something creeping. Something she could not make go away. It was a spreading stain across her mind. She could not make the fear go away with prayer nor memorized verses of Saint Luke nor counting. In the uproar of the windstorm she thought she heard the sound of a hundred horses at a full gal-lop. She heard the door splintering on its hinges and all the precious civilized collection of objects thrown against the wall, everything broken, everything smashed, people and dishes and bottles and pic-tures and windows and clocks and dresses and bone and brains and tables and chairs. Her fear was so intense it was like being struck by lightning. They are coming, they are coming.

She sat up, alone in the small bedroom. It was very cold and she was sweating. Her headache had been reduced to a light tinny singing in her head. She darted out of bed and pulled off a quilt pieced in a confusing pattern called Broken Dishes and wrapped it around herself and felt her way to the door. Then on her cold bare feet through the main room where the children slept in the last dim glow of the fire in the fireplace and to the other side, to Elizabeth's bedroom where she slept each night alone and fat in her tentlike nightgown.

"Elizabeth, Elizabeth."

The big woman was sitting up on a chair in the dark. Mary could see her by the dim light from the fireplace. Elizabeth wiped her sweated palms on her striped nightgown.

"I got six men staying and working on this place. It's just the wind. Lightning."

"We must guns," said Mary. She sat down on Elizabeth's bed. "Load the guns."

"It's just the wind making us crazy."

"They could come in the wind."

"I know it." Elizabeth reached to the wall where her heavy wool overcoat hung on a nail. "It's stupid but I got to do it."

So Elizabeth struck a light to her kerosene lamp and went out to the front room where her long guns were kept on pegs over the door. She took down the twelve-gauge shotgun. It was a muzzle-loader. She poured in a good charge of powder and then rammed home a load of double-aught buck. She took up the heavy revolver from the mantelpiece as well and then walked back to the bedroom and handed Mary the revolver and sat with the loaded shotgun between her knees. And so they sat all night while the windstorm tore like a Viking at the edges of the roof. Sat with their loaded arms and felt safe for a while with their weapons in their hands.

THERE WERE TEN pupils in Sergeant Earl's black school and they held a Christmas pageant at one end of the warehouse. A girl fourteen or fifteen years old sang "Battle Hymn of the Republic" with a black trooper of the Ninth Cavalry playing the German flute and Paint with a fiddle under his chin. The parents sat on sacks of grain and a few broken chairs. A spattering of snow blew down on Fort Belknap in a sheer and fraying curtain. Britt stood like some piece of taxidermists' work with a tight boiled collar and a black cravat and his large, scarred hands held demurely in front of him. Dennis was also fastened into a five-button cutaway; his long neck packaged in a sort of striped tie. He lifted his hands to it and readjusted it every five minutes.

He stood beside Britt and turned and regarded him.

"This is what happens when you get married?" he said. "You got to dress up and come to school meetings?"

"Yes," said Britt. "You see some pretty thing smiling at you and little do you know what's awaiting you."

"Man. I just come for the cake."

After the children had recited and Paint had played "Lorena" on his fiddle Dennis stood up nervously and then wiped his hands on his pants and walked forward. When he was up on the foot-high stage, made of unsteady logs and planks from packing crates, he suddenly turned to the audience of nearly thirty people and threw out his hand. He began to tramp in place, and recited a comic piece of the period about a man trying to sell a cow to a preacher. He became the cow, and then turned into the rigid and offended preacher, and then the profane farmer, and then the farmer's dog. His long hands were like lines of elaborate writing. He stood in the eruptions of laughter without smiling and when it ended he bowed like a pump handle to the applause.

Outside, three enlisted men walked down the sloppy ruts between Nance's store and the quartermaster's building. It was dark. They were beginning to sober up but were still unsteady. One of them carried a heavy piece of fruitcake in one hand and his revolver in the other. They had promised to keep in mind their immortal souls and had been read the relevant passages of the season from Luke but the Methodist chaplain's kindly urging had been forgotten with a bottle of brandy from Dutch Nance. They felt obligated to do something western. Something intemperate and unwise. So the man with the fruitcake jammed it in his pocket and lifted his revolver to the air and fired three times and ducked and shrank away from his own noisy pistol shots. The two men with him made whooping noises and did the same.

Mary snatched Cherry to her side and turned and fled to the stacked bales of shingles at the far end of the warehouse. Several women went after her. Britt crowded past them and told them to go away.

He sat beside her on a small pony keg. He put his hand on her shoulder. Mary looked down and swallowed noisily but she would not move. Cherry looked out from under her mother's arm. People turned and whispered and the music came to a halt.

"Mary, it's just some of the boys," said Britt. "It's all right."

Mary was shaking. She shut her eyes.

Britt reached over and took her hand. "Let's just wait here a while until you feel better." He saw her nod her lowered head and shut her fingers around his in a fierce grip. She took her other hand from Cherry's shoulder and carefully wiped away the tears that had splattered on the back of Britt's knuckles.

"Cherry, go on back," said Britt. His daughter, now ten years old, with the face of something carefully carved into a look of unshakable calm, nodded and got up and took up her skirts in both hands and walked gracefully back to the other end of the warehouse, among the candles and swags of cedar boughs.

Sergeant Earl cleared his throat and nodded to the flute player. "Go on," he said. "Paint? Let's do 'O Little Town of Bethlehem.' "

Dennis Cureton's thin fingers wandered over his coat buttons. "Yes, Paint," he said. "Hit that fiddle."

Mary lifted her head to the music. *How still we see thee lie, above thy deep and dreamless sleep the silent stars go by.* She kept a tight grip on Britt's hand. There was something inside her heart waiting to be born out of all that violence. Perhaps it was a donkey or an ox or a sheep that stood around a cradle staring mesmerized and empty of speech until the newborn presence came to itself like the smoking blood clot, the great gift to the Kiowa and Comanche, the clot of blood that in ages past had formed itself into a young man who was the buffalo. The young man in clothes of glory who stood before the starving old people, abandoned in the snow in the great wall of stone called the Wind River Mountains, and spread both hands and said, I am your sustenance, kill me and eat me.

She felt a turning in her heart. Britt's large hand with its planing of bone and muscle still held hers. He was waiting with great patience. He would wait all night. Mary thought, *It is only a recurring illness like malaria.* That was all. It was chronic. It would come and then like the headaches she would think about when it would be gone. Think through to the other end of it. She slid her hand from under Britt's hand and stood up.

She put her hand on Britt's arm and they came back to watch Sergeant Earl hand out the handmade certificates for best pupil recitation, best attendance, first in arithmetic, the most memorized Bible verses, and for Jube the prize of a small metal toy with whirling arms for the most silent child in class.

Chapter 26

❧

THEY CAME TO the crossing of the Clear Fork of the Brazos
on a chill winter day, in late February of 1869. As they came to
the low and gentle slope down to the river valley, Dennis stood up
and said, "There's a fire."

In the middle of the road below them a buggy was burning. A
light four-wheeled buggy with a top made of oiled canvas, and it was
on fire. It stood there and burned all by itself. The oiled canvas top
burned brightly and collapsed and the shafts were outlined in small
upright flames. Clothing was scattered around. A shoe, a hat, books,
eyeglasses. They pulled up and stared at it. Pieces of chopped-up
harness lay on the ground. The leather upholstery shrank and blackened and the flames were nearly transparent in the sun.

Britt saw a boy step out of the naked white and green sycamore
trunks of the crossing. The boy held up both hands. It was a white
boy. Maybe eleven or twelve years of age. He wore a hat far too big
for him that fell down around his ears, and a wool coat, also too big,
and a bare chest underneath it. Around his neck a cravat was loosely
tied in some clumsy imitation of the dress of the white men of the
towns. He wore leggings over a pair of flowered Kiowa moccasins.

His fair hair in two thick braids and a waving cut edge where it was shorn short on the right side of his face.

"Estop," the boy called. "Help me!"

"Decoy," said Britt, and threw the reins to Dennis.

He stood up and stared down the barrel of the Spencer and fired. The boy hunched over and like a pinkish salamander writhed into the brush. Paint began to fire at random into the dull green of the Carrizo cane and grapevines on the south bank. Then a large-caliber round hit the lock of a box of farrier's tools and bells. It knocked the box into flying splinters and the bells jumped ringing onto the floorboards, they rolled like open mouths with their clappers spilling out. Cowbells, sheep bells, and several heavy school bells sang in metallic tones all over the wagon bed.

Dennis laid the whip hard on the big bays and they charged into the red water, throwing circular sprays in giant pinwheels. The bells clanged and sang out. Paint laid flat behind the bales of cedar shingles and five pony kegs of molasses. Britt threw himself over the driver's backrest and laid himself behind the shingles on the opposite side and watched for a target.

"One of them's got a Sharps fifty," Paint said and fired again. They watched anxiously for the powder smoke of the big buffalo gun.

There it came drifting in a solid, glutinous gray bank from the south shore, but whoever fired it would no longer be there. Shining hides of horses in splashy colors faded and shifted behind the screen of sycamore trunks. Britt fired and heard a horse's brief, impelled scream and shouts in Kiowa. A bullet cracked past his head and smashed into the shingles and a millisecond later the report of the muzzle blast. He fired again and again and reloaded and kept firing. The horses clawed up the sloping red sand of the south bank dragging the wagon behind them like condemned things born to flee all danger bearing heavy loads they could not jettison. Dennis whipped them on while the loose bells rang in a hundred different tones. Ahead of them near the road was the ruins of the place called the Old Stone Ranch House.

"Want me to pull off?" shouted Dennis.

"Yes!" Britt sighted down the Spencer, the barrel wavering, looking for a clear shot. "Paint, do something about those damn bells, they'll hear us."

Paint sat up to lever the top off one of the kegs of molasses with a farrier's file and began to jam the cowbells, the school bells, and all the small copper sheep bells into the molasses, where they sank with dull clicks.

Behind a fallen stone wall they pulled up and vaulted over the sides of the wagon. Before them lay the ruined two-story house with its roof gone. They fell on their knees at the empty windows. Dennis crept low to run his hands over the horses, to look for wounds. Britt began to make a hole in the dried mortar between two stones just to the left of a window frame. He chipped at it with the point of his knife and then found a thin metal rod lying to hand and ran it into the hole and then back and forth until he had a peephole.

Paint sat at his back facing the other direction over the remains of a collapsed wall, among pieces of a cookstove and its rusty pipe. His hands were thick with molasses. He tried to lick it off and wipe his hands on his shirt. His hands were sticking to the gun stock. Bees came, and made a sound like *zone zone zone* around his head. Winter bees, hungry. There were broken bits of stone jugs and pickle jars lying around. Britt looked down and saw three chessmen, a king and two pawns, lying in the dirt. Also a broken mirror. It lay just as it had been knocked from the wall long ago and its pieces lay slightly apart from each other. He wrapped his right hand in his handkerchief and took up the largest piece and tilted it from behind the safety of the stone wall and saw in it the grassy landscape broken here and there by upthrust layers of red sandstone, a stand of bare cottonwoods near the river and a low and spiky plum thicket. He heard the flat smack of Paint killing bees.

"Hey, hey, you Britt," called a voice from a long distance. And then after a moment, "You Britt," the voice said again from a different place altogether. From behind a massed growth of prickly pear whose flat pads were crowned with red fruit.

"Here I am," Britt called.

"You thief, you cheat, you steal that underwater boy." This time the voice was closer.

"Too bad," said Britt. "Come on."

Paint whispered, *Where is he?*

Somewhere close. Britt sat utterly still except for the hand that held the mirror and this he tilted one way and then another.

Then Britt said in Spanish, *"Ven y muere, pendejo."*

A man's voice called out to him in reply, *"Donde está mi hijito negrito? Ladron."*

Britt laid his rifle barrel on the window frame and fired into the stand of cactus. He fired three times, in spaced shots, moving each shot steadily to the right. Cactus fruit sprayed in bright red explosions. Paint stayed where he was but turned slightly and fired through an empty window to let them know that another rifle was present and in working condition.

After a while Britt heard them beginning to move away. He heard the soft thud of unshod horses and the tearing sound of someone forcing their way through brush. Perhaps Aperian Crow and a band of young Kiowa warriors and the Kiowa-Apache white renegade. Maybe some Comanche had joined them, maybe Tissoyo. Come to take his boy again. His only boy.

They sat until nightfall. It was the dark of the moon. A dry wind swept the sky clean and the starlight was enough to see by and the vast scattering of the constellations burned overhead, random streams of remote blue-white gems. The horses shifted and were restless under their sweaty harness. After a while Britt stepped out from behind the wall, trusting to his own dark face in the dark night, and went ahead at a walk along the dim trail. His night vision came to him easily, his footfalls soft on the stony road. Then he turned and whistled. Paint and Dennis came in the wagon, the horses thirsty and tired. Britt walked a hundred yards ahead of them all the way to Fort Griffin.

Major Pinney at Fort Griffin told him that the burned buggy belonged to Dr. Seagram and that the doctor had been killed and cut up in so many pieces they could not find all of him. Somewhere out on the plains coyotes carried these pieces away, trotting importantly through the grasses like it was a job of work.

THEY PICKED UP flour in barrels and crates of bottled beer and whiskey, skillets and peppermints and tools and ready-made over-coats, to deliver them at Nance's store in Fort Belknap, a store they could not enter. Each time before they pulled out Britt checked the toolbox to one side of the wagon to see that the big wrenches were there, and the wagon jack, an extra king bolt and carriage bolts of various sizes. He saw that the grease bucket hung behind was full. Paint and Vesey unloaded while Dennis checked off the items and made an X for payment.

Jube rode down the street. The boy had thrown down his slate when he heard Dennis blowing the dented bugle upon their arrival and shot out the door. He rode his black horse on an old dragoon saddle through the searing summer heat and dust. He carried the ancient Spanish spur buckled to his belt in the belief that one day he would find a mate for it.

Jube jumped off and then scrambled up the high back wheel and then into the driver's well.

Britt stepped down from Cajun. From time to time he rode alongside the wagons, or far out in front, scouting. He tied the big bay to an upright under their small warehouse. Then he climbed into the wagon to help unload.

"What are you doing out of school?" Britt said. "Isn't this a school day?"

Jube stood in silence. His father had not even greeted him. Then he said, "Yes, sir."

Then it seemed Britt came to himself and he put his arms around the boy and held him for a moment.

"I want you to stay in school, is all," he said.

"I hate school."

"Why?"

"I feel shut up." Jube twisted inside his tight collar. "There's too many white people here." He took his father's hand. "Did you have to go to school?"

"When I was young we were not allowed," said Britt. "But I learned anyway. In secret. And here you got your own school right out in the open."

"Yes, sir."

"Now, did I ask you if you wanted to go to school or not?"

"No, sir."

Britt took off his hat and wiped the tight, short hair of his sweating head and then put it back on. "Where is your mother?"

"At Sergeant Earl's barbershop. It's the day they wash all his linen for him. Because he puts the money in the school."

"I'm glad you know that," said Britt. "And I guess you consider the work your mother does and I do so you and Cherry and the rest of them can have a damn school. So get back there. Apologize. Sergeant Earl ain't there for his health."

Britt walked through the fort, past the parade ground and out the south entrance to the town. His shadow was a deep black intensity in the bald sun. Hackberry trees whose rough leaves were perpetually noisy even in the springtime shaded small houses of picket and frame and in the shade of one particularly large tree was a miniature building painted dark green with white trim and a striped barber pole in front.

Mary stood up and turned to him. Three of her came to their feet in the broad mirrors and they all had an expression of delight. Several other women turned to him as well in greeting and the tiny barbershop seemed a vast hall of moving figures in bright calicoes.

Mary stood on her toes and stretched up to kiss him. He stood with his hat in his hand and said hello to Mrs. Earl and Mrs. Sutton and Miss Thrim. These three glanced at one another with significant glances and stepped significantly on one another's toes and said they had to get the linens and towels ironed and so they left. The bright white linens were bundled in wads in their arms.

Britt sat down in the barber chair.

"They are hauling themselves out of here to give us time alone," he said. He glanced into the mirror at Mary where she stood behind him, her hand laid on his shoulder. Mary would not look at herself in a mirror. Had not done so for a long time. "We need some time alone, baby girl." He reached up to his shoulder and touched her hand. "Mary, say something. Anything."

Her eyes shone and she lifted her hands and retied the ends of the headcloth. All the mirrors made this gesture seem that of an eight-armed Hindu goddess lifting in some mysterious sign or gesture. The bottles of bay rum and Tiger Balm glittered in the bevels.

"I can't much," she said. "The McGuffey blue already I said. I did."

"Good!" Britt said this in a false, bright tone as if to a child and then heard himself. He closed his eyes for a moment. He took her hand again. He heard the bugle's stuttering music for pay call and a dim and general roaring emerge from around the stone barracks. It would not be long before some of the men were here for hot water and haircuts and shaves and lotions. "I will sit and you will read it to me," he said.

"All right," she said. She stood behind him, very still. Her hand closed on his shoulder and he could feel that it was cold. "Britt, they are shooting at you."

"No, Mary. No, baby. We are so armed we scare ourselves. They tried once and they won't try again." He drew her around to face him. "We need some time alone."

Mary looked at the floor. "Britt, Britt." She slowly leaned forward until her head and its white headcloth pressed on his shoulder. "I can't."

Over the big mirror facing him was an advertisement for Niagara Star Bitters. He studiously read it. He lifted his hand to the back of her neck. Felt her sweet, moist breath on his shoulder and the fine bones beneath his hand. A breeze washed through the hackberry leaves and then it was still again. "It's all right," he said. He longed for his wife and yet she was wounded and damaged and only she could say when those wounds had healed and still he wanted her. She knew it.

In a whisper she said, "There are women some you know. Britt are others than me."

"Hush." She stepped back and he stood up out of the barber chair. "No." He put one hand on her upper arm and with the other hand flicked a small dry leaf from her collar. "Not ever."

She caught the leaf and crushed it in her hand. A sparrow flew onto the doorstep and spied around itself out of the irregular black stripes that streamed down from its bill as if it had been feasting on roofing tar. Mary pulled off her white headcloth and shook it.

"Bad luck," she said. "That bird in the house, go, go."

Britt waited until the sparrow flew away. Then he said, "Mary?"

She lifted her head. "Oh Britt, find another," she said. She pressed her hands to her eyes.

He took her arm and sat her down in the barber chair. "You saved my children." He held her upper arms in both hands. "If you had not been there with them they would have died, or they would never have come back to us. I owe you everything." She closed her eyes and shook her head. He let go of her and stepped back. "You are very beautiful. When I saw you and Cherry in the camp up there walking to me I almost broke down. In front of those men."

She took hold of the arm of the barber chair. "And I saw you, I saw you."

"I'll wait as long as I have to wait." He did not raise his hands to her again. "Forever if that's how it is."

She said nothing but she ran her hand down his shirtsleeve. Then she took his arm with both hands and leaned her head against it.

"Britt."

He smiled and then stepped on the pedal again and again and the chair rose in jerks into the air. "How far does this thing go up?"

"Stop! Stop!" She began to laugh.

He took hold of the chair arm and spun her around and in all the mirrors Mary's laughing face and the figured blue print of her dress whirled as if she were a merry-go-round of eight women with lifted hands and flying skirts.

He caught her and stopped the chair. "I'll wait," he said. "Hard work takes your mind off things."

Chapter 27

❧

AND SO HE kept on. Britt asked seventy-five cents a hundredweight and he got it because of the danger of the roads. Sometimes they had orders to carry to Fort Worth where the stagecoaches of the Butterfield route laid over and repaired. For the stagecoaches they brought thoroughbraces and window blinds and new wheels from Waco and then they took on mail and packages for the forts. They loaded an organ for the Methodist church in Palo Pinto and bales of red drapery for Lottie Deno's establishment in Jacksboro. In that town they rested for two days once when it was raining so hard that the creeks were up and they could not move. Dennis and Paint watched from under their hat brims to see if Britt would go to seek out some other woman, being so long separated from Mary, but he stayed with them under the wagon covers, laid back atop the load, reading a seed catalogue. He licked his thumb and turned the damp pages from rutabagas to Red Chief tomatoes. There were four other freight outfits also marooned there, the men bored and impatient, smoking behind the running curtains of rain that poured from the eaves of the buildings. The streets were channeled with slow-moving lava flows of red mud.

Britt was restless when they had to stay in town for any length of time. He was wary of the white men. It was better on the road, traveling free of any rules and away from ex-Confederates and strange men come into the country from distant places. It was better to travel and sleep under the wagons with no company but their own. The road was like a very long and thin nation to itself, a country whose citizens were isolate and untrammeled, whose passports were all carte blanche.

Britt and Dennis and Paint stood at the open window of the large frame building where people had gathered to hear Captain Kidd recite the news of the day. The building was used for town meetings and storing wool and voting. It was still misting rain and they kept their hats on.

Captain Kidd was an elderly man who read all the newspapers he could find in Dallas and then he traveled from town to town and told the news both foreign and domestic. The crowd smelled of damp fabrics and tobacco. They were silent and intent.

Captain Kidd sat on a high stool and called out to the crowd that the Franco-Prussian War had begun. That the delicate Frenchmen with their thin mustaches and ancient guns were whipped soundly at Wissembourg by the Germans, who wore no toilet water scents and slept in the rain. Huge blond men grown strong on pork sausages had made mincemeat of the French army. Also the French could not traverse their guns. He said that a canal called Suez had been driven between the land of the Israelites and the valley of the Pharaohs and now the great ships were sailing on salt water to the land of Punt, where there were spices and turquoises and exotic diseases.

"Are the pharaohs still there?" whispered Paint.

Dennis lifted his thin shoulders. "I don't know."

A white man in the doorway signed to them to come in. "You boys better hear this," he said. "Shem, Ham, and Japeth are all a-sailing down the Suez Canal."

The three black men entered cautiously and stood against the back wall with their hats in their hands, looking at no one.

Captain Kidd had a white chin beard and a five-dollar hat. He sat in a shaft of faint rainy light pouring through the window, through the gaps in the boards of the wall. Cascades of water spanged on the roof. The tall stool made him seem an illuminated figure in a waxworks. Beside him on the floor his pile of newspapers, the *New York Herald*, the *New York Times*, the *Chicago Times*, the *Philadelphia Inquirer*, the *London Daily News*, the *Cincinnati Times*, and the *Boston Morning Journal*. All of them of varying dates and full of maps, engraved illustrations, and advertisements.

"And now an amendment has been got up between the several states," said Captain Kidd. He stared out over the men and the women with their pancake hats, their bonnets, as if in a trance. He seemed to be receiving messages from another world. "It is the Fifteenth Amendment to our glorious Constitution which Constitution was written under threat of arrest and execution by our forefathers who signed their names and their honor and their sacred fortunes. This Fifteenth Amendment allows the vote to all men qualified to vote without regard to race or color or previous condition of servitude. That means colored gentlemen. That means the sons of Ham. And now a report from the joining of the Union Pacific and the Central Pacific Railroads where Progress has lifted the locomotives on Her Mighty Wings to traverse the land of the savages despite their murders of survey crews and the small Chinese people toiling and toiling with the laying of the ties and so on."

Captain Kidd continued straight on with fact after fact and reports one after the other as if he had been wound up and set to working despite murmurs or cheers or boos or hissing from the crowd. Dennis and Paint and Britt slipped out and went to their wagons. Heavy wagon sheets waxed and waterproofed were tied over the loads, and other sheets laid over the horses where they stood in a faint aura of steam from their warm bodies as water ran off the sheet hems.

"Let's try the crossing at Keechi Creek," said Britt. "It might be down." He stroked the wet necks of the leaders, checked the trace chains and the tongue hounds. The wood of the wagons and all their complex parts had swollen with the rains and so were tight and secure. The sides of the wagons and the horse's rain sheets were dotted with mud. Men went past in flapping slickers with rain running from their hat brims.

"What do you think, Britt?" said Dennis. He stood long and thin, very dark and drenched in his black coat and hat. All the dim houses of Jacksboro were blurred lines in the rain and mist, the occasional yellow lamp at a window.

"About Keechi?"

"No."

Britt nodded. "About the Fifteenth Amendment. I don't know. It may take a while before I can put a ballot in a box."

"It's legal."

"Wait," said Britt. "Wait and see how things turn out."

Chapter 28

S'AMUEL STEPPED DOWN from his buggy in front of the adjutant's office where several enlisted men sat on the veranda steps opening envelopes. It was mail day. One man was reading aloud to another in a halting Irish voice the way a child reads; he studiously pronounced *the* and *a* and hesitated over *nuptials*. Samuel tied his buggy horse by the lead rope and walked up the steps. The men looked up and were not sure whether to stand up or not.

"It's all right," said Samuel. "Good day, men."

"Good day to you, sir," the soldier with the letter in his hand said. "And could you tell me then, sir, what is a nuptial?"

"A wedding," said Samuel.

"It is as I thought," said the one being read to. *"Biodh se amhlaid."*

All the buildings were completed now and they were bright with the uneven surfaces of new-cut limestone in the cream color of the stone of the Indian Territory. Each had a veranda against the sun and the weather. It was the spring of 1870. A rainy winter behind them. The long parade ground was lined on one side by the enlisted men's barracks with a fireplace at one end and private quarters for a sergeant at the other. On the opposite side were detached houses for the officers and out of one of them came Colonel Grierson. He was pulling on his uniform coat and in a hurry for he had heard nothing from his family for several months.

The adjutant's hands were full of envelopes and the squared and folded packets of the eastern papers. Samuel took up a letter from Dr. Reed of the Indian Committee and another from his supervisor in Fort Leavenworth and a copy of the *Chicago Tribune*. He flipped the newspaper open and stood reading the front page.

"Samuel, there you are," said Grierson. He took the packet handed to him by the adjutant. "Come and eat with me. Mail day. My cook makes a pudding with dates in it on every mail day. It's like some kind of paste with little dead things in it."

Samuel looked up from the front page. "Thank you, I will. Here I see one of your colored sergeants has been awarded the Medal of Honor. A man of the Ninth."

"Oh, is it in the papers? Good Lord!" Grierson avidly read the covers of two letters and then shoved them in his blouse front. "We're having the ceremony tomorrow. It was Sergeant Emmanuel Stance. How did they get hold of the news?" Grierson came to stand and read over his shoulder. "Well, they went to the War Department for news, of course." He stared at the illustration where colored men charged forward on horses that had all four feet stretched out front and back and their guidons rippling. Indians fled in every direction. They fell from their horses and lay facedown on a rocky earth. "I do believe the illustration is quite accurate. You see there, I swear that is Two Hatchet. Look at the receding chin."

Samuel nodded. The illustration was so lifelike he too recognized the face of Two Hatchet; the tall bony warrior who had held the little boy on his lap at his first meeting with the Comanche and Kiowa. The little boy with the toilet seat around his neck. "Yes, I know him. That is him. But there seems to be some problem with the uniforms."

"I think you are right." The colonel took the paper from Samuel's hand and looked closely at the engraving. "They have the chevrons on upside down. Well. Come and have dinner with me."

They sat across from one another at Grierson's dining table, silently reading their mail. The cook brought in plates of green beans and a sort of beef hash. She stood briefly behind Samuel with a glass of water suspended in her hand and he turned and wondered what she wanted him to do with the water, held there in the air. He saw she was intent on the illustration in the *Tribune*.

"Yes, sir, I was just looking at the picture." She set the glass down in front of his plate.

"Well, that is Sergeant Stance," said Samuel.

"A picture of him in the newspapers from back east," said the cook.

"Yes," said Samuel. "I think this one is him." He put his finger on the charging figure on the left. The cook said nothing but stood fixed and intent and then shook her head.

"In a newspaper from back east," she said. "I never."

"I will make sure Sergeant Stance gets the illustration," said Grierson. He turned to Samuel. "He's her brother."

"They got his chevrons on upside down," said the cook. She gathered up the bread basket and the butter plates. "But it doesn't matter, it doesn't matter." She walked in a dignified way back to the kitchen but then from behind the closed doors came the sound of several voices in subdued and joyful screaming.

Grierson read his letters silently and Samuel unfolded his own. The letter from Dr. Reed concerned the efforts of the Friends' Indian Committee to see that supplies were delivered on time from Fort Leavenworth but he, Samuel, must remember that fishes and loaves were only a small part of the effort to be expended in bringing the red men to the light of Christ. Samuel forged on through the lines of small handwriting. Dr. Reed once again pointed out the futility of using military force to keep the Indians on their reservations. The reports of Custer's dreadful behavior at the battle of the Washita last year were becoming clear now that there was an investigation into the matter and it is evident that women and children were killed and no one could be sure that Mrs. Blinn and her son, the captives, were not hit by errant gunfire.

"But the boy's head was smashed in," Samuel said to himself.

"Excuse me?" Colonel Grierson looked up.

"Oh, just talking to myself," said Samuel.

"Always happens on mail day."

Thus force always brings about unintended consequences, but a contrite heart brings great blessings. Samuel glanced up briefly as Grierson read the *Tribune* report of the action at Kickapoo Springs, and from time to time the colonel snorted. Samuel went back to his letter. Dr. Reed wished to remind Samuel of the centurion who begged Christ to heal his servant. *For I am a man under authority, having soldiers under me, and I say to this man, Go, and he goeth; and to another, Come, and he cometh.* And yet he humbled himself before Jesus Christ our Lord with a contrite heart. Samuel shifted in his chair and turned the page for a better light. He hoped Dr. Reed was not enjoining him to attempt to bear witness to military commanders.

"Here is more coffee, Samuel."

"Thank you."

He read on. Dr. Reed commended him for refusing guards. It illustrated both personal bravery and good judgment. Their confidence in him was unabated and he sent greetings from the entire committee and from Henry Morgan as well. Samuel folded the letter.

"And they recovered the captives?" he said.

Grierson said, "One. One boy. Sergeant Stance took after a group of Apache who were bearing down on a train of freight wagons there at Kickapoo Springs, and ran them off. Then they were attacked and Stance charged, overran them, and killed the leader. Went on and broke up their camp. Apparently they had the boys with them, but the youngest one fell off a horse and went wandering around. Willie Lehmann. He was picked up by one of the freighters."

"Where is he now?"

"The boy?"

"Yes."

"The freighter arranged for him to go home. Now, the other boy, Herman, they still have him."

Samuel folded Dr. Reed's letter into a small packet. "New Mexico Apaches or Kiowa-Apaches?"

"Kiowa-Apache." Grierson drank off his water. "Stance is determined to run the rest of them down. He is an outstanding soldier."

Samuel nodded. "The Medal of Honor is an amazing distinction," he said. "The men of the Ninth must be quite proud."

"They are indeed." Grierson sat back as the cook laid the soup plates with the date pudding in front of them. "They have every reason to be. Proof that colored troops do very well. And the Indians were beyond the limits of the reservation, you know."

"Yes, Kickapoo Springs is certainly south of the Red."

And all his efforts of kindness and understanding, of gifts, long speeches, rations and rewards for bringing in captives, had come to little. A feeling of shame washed over him; very raw, very hot. And grief for the children. The white captive children and Indian children who might have been in the camp that was overrun. He drank his coffee and again bent to the illustration in the newspaper. "I believe the reason this illustration is so accurate is that the artist is James Deaver. He has spent quite a lot of time among the Indians."

"Oh, is that him?" Grierson read the reporter's name, Simonton, and then the artist's signature. "Indeed it is. James Deaver. Well, he could have got the damn chevrons right. I'll never hear the end of it."

Samuel did not stay overnight to see the ceremony the next day. He could not bear it. But from the agency he could hear the regimental band and the shouting, borne down on the ceaseless wind.

Chapter 29

❧

ONCE WHEN BRITT was traveling on horseback between Fort
Belknap and the Red River on a mission of his own, he came
upon the Medicine Hat paint.

He had gone alone and quietly into the woven, shifting grass of
the summer plains to find a route that would take him to the Indian
Agency with his wagons. To the Indian Agency and then beyond
to the new Fort Sill. He wanted a route that would carry him from
one defensible position to another. From timber in the Brazos River
Valley with its easy crossings, to the Stone Houses, where he and
his teamsters could fort up if they were attacked. Beyond the Stone
Houses he intended to look for ravines, bluffs, any cover that they
could easily get into and none farther than a few miles apart. Places
where he could put the horses into a full gallop and reach cover
before any of them were killed or disabled. How strange this land
had appeared to him five years ago. Alien, unknown. How quickly
he had learned.

He rode along in the light summer winds, in the early morning,
and noted the grass. It was a good year. The Comanche and Kiowa
would not have to range very far to find grass for their horses.

The day wore on and late in the afternoon he came to one of those low, slow rises that would stop at a short ridge no higher than fifteen or twenty feet, and anyone to the north would see him sky-lighted when he reached the top of it, so Britt swung down from Cajun and walked the last quarter mile of the easy rise. When he neared the top and could see beyond to the far horizon he wrenched up a large flat stone and tied Cajun's reins to it, and then went on bent over. At the top of the rise he lay flat on his stomach and un-slipped the neat brass sleeves of the spyglass.

He trusted his own sight at first. He searched each quadrant of this grassy, blowing world, one after another. It was June, and the sun standing at its farthest south, and so the light came from behind him. It made cactus pads in the land below bright as round metal cutouts, and the tissue of grass flowed in a glittering sili-cate river under the wind. A few hundred yards distant a stand of twisted post oaks in a creek valley tossed their coarse, rimed leaves. They were like an island in a sea. Then he saw among the short trees a bright whiplash of some silky stuff fly up into the air and then subside.

A horse's tail. Britt narrowed his eyes and lifted his chin slightly and watched with a deep and abiding interest. It flashed again, a horse whipping its tail like a hurricane against the summer flies. It was by itself. Which meant there was a man with it, otherwise the horse would have gone wandering off to join up with a band of mustangs. Horses did not remain alone of their own free will. It was either tied or hobbled.

Somebody was laid up down there, sleeping during the day and traveling at night. He pulled out his large bandana and wrapped the spyglass in it to hide the shining brass.

He put it to his right eye and watched. The horse slowly moved out of the screening post oaks with short steps. Hobbled. The red and white splashes of the Medicine Hat paint came into the round gelatinous lens, a blue edge trembling around it. The horse grazed busily, its ears turning, picking up every sound. The wind was com-ing from the north, so it would not smell Cajun. However it was possible that Cajun would smell the paint and would call out a long-ing and quavering welcome. But they had had a hard day's ride. Cajun was willing to stand downslope tied to a rock and rest. He was probably asleep. Britt watched a few more minutes; he was sure it was Tissoyo's Medicine Hat. The perfect shield of red on its chest, the red cap and ears on the white face.

Britt wanted the horse very badly. He wanted him to give back to Tissoyo. Britt lay quietly, willing to watch all day if need be.

After a space of time during which Britt lay with the spyglass held steadily in his long hands, the sun burning his back and sweat running in crawling small streams down his ribs, something moved behind the screen of the trees. A man came clear in a space between two post oaks and looked around himself. He walked to the Medicine Hat and stroked his neck. He had his black hair cut short on the right side, and two long braids. Kiowa. Britt noticed a quick, jerky movement as he tossed his braids back. A black fig-ure of some kind tattooed on his chin. A cold feeling came over Britt. This was one of the men who had laid hands on Mary. He had smashed her head in with a rock, perhaps he had shot his son. Britt's heart slowed down to an even and deliberate beat. He felt very still. He did not know if he could bring the man down with the Spencer at this distance or if he could get a clear shot. He guessed the distance at nearly three hundred yards, which was the limit of the Spencer's effective range. If the wind would lay and not deflect his bullet he might do it.

He lowered the glass for a moment. He could try to take the Indian there where he was, or wait until he picked up and moved on. Which would probably be during the night. It was coming on to evening, and so Britt would have to make up his mind very soon. If he shot and missed there would be a running fight in the darkness. The Kiowa knew the land better than Britt would ever know it. The sun poured down the sky in a shimmering furnace heat, setting into some very high, thin clouds to the north of west so that now the angle of reflection would not so readily reveal the spyglass or the rifle barrel to the Kiowa. If he waited until the sun was on the horizon it would not reveal any reflection at all. Then he would have about ten minutes to take his shot.

The man would be busy with preparations to move. He would unhobble the Medicine Hat and beat out his saddle blankets and knock the grass and dirt from his saddle fleecing. Pack his saddlebags. Eat something.

Britt backed downhill on his stomach and then walked unhurriedly toward Cajun and patted him on the neck. He pulled out the halter and slipped off Cajun's bridle and put the halter on and re-tied him. Britt slid the Spencer out of the scabbard and checked his loads, made sure that there was one up the pipe. He left the spyglass in his saddlebags.

When he returned to the edge of the ridge he slid forward on his stomach. He laid his hat down beside him. He sifted dust over the barrel just in case. The sun melted into the northwestern horizon and had lost its shape in the dusty atmosphere until it was an egg of creamy, violent red. Britt put his right eye to the barrel and the V of the sights on the post oaks, so much smaller now and more distant than when he had seen them through the spyglass, and the shadows of the short trees fell in a pouring dark stain for a long way out onto the grass. The slashing tail of the Medicine Hat flew in a silky red banner and tiny biting insects became glowing points of light in the sun's last rays.

The Kiowa moved among the trees. Now he was very small, seen with the naked eye, and the oaks were a fussy gathering of indistinguishable leaves and branches. But the man was clear enough. Britt breathed slowly and followed the Kiowa's movements with the barrel. The sun was reduced to a red spreading light. He had another minute or two at the most.

Then the Kiowa came and stood near the paint and lifted his hands to firmly set the spray of hawk feathers on his head. Each feather took on a tip of luminous sunset light above his hair. The signature and promise of his guardian spirit. Britt drew in and held his breath. He fixed the V of the sights on the hawk feathers glowing so brilliantly backlit. Enough to allow for drop. The man was very close to the horse.

He squeezed the trigger slowly. The explosion kicked the barrel into the air and made his ears ring. There was a short, wet, animal scream from the stand of trees. Gunpowder smoke drifted down the ridge in front of him. He flattened himself on the ground, the trigger guard under his hand.

Britt slid back downhill a few yards and jacked another round into the chamber. He moved westward along the ridge. He did not want to remain in the same place where he had taken his shot. Cajun stood alert and nervous, his eyes fixed on the ridge. Now the world was all black shadows and vagrant deep reds and only a thin arc of light showed above the horizon. In the eastern sky the shadow of the earth itself was cast into space. Then the light was gone and all was dark.

He waited. There was no sound from the distant group of trees. Still he waited. The major stars developed in the sky one by one. The wind sighed and sifted among the grasses. Now he was in the night world, which was another, different universe. He waited for the narrow moon to slide up out of the east.

As he lay there he saw in the remote distance, to the north, ahead of him, a point of red light. It was the burning rock oil at the edge of its ravine, leaking its black slime and burning perpetually.

There was neither movement nor sound from the island of trees. Britt decided to wait out the night. If he went downhill in the dark he would stumble. He might not be able to find his way back to his horse. He lay there with one hand on the Spencer and his revolver bulky on his hip. He was unable to find a comfortable place to lie but not very troubled about that either. He was sorry to leave Cajun tied and saddled with sweaty blankets, but that's how it was. From time to time he woke up out of a doze and lifted his head to watch the trees. The moonlight was dim and overhead a powdering of uncounted millions of stars both small and large. Britt was hungry and thirsty. So was his horse. He woke when he heard a thin nicker.

The bay was desperate for water. He woke when he heard a click-ing sound and sat upright in the dawn light with the carbine in his hand and saw that Cajun had come to him, dragging the rock with his lead rope.

Britt turned. He could see the paint horse out away from the trees in a white blur. The horse was still hobbled and grazing in a desultory way. Often the horse seemed to stop with uneaten grass still in his mouth, which showed that he was very thirsty.

In a few minutes Britt could read the lettering on the barrel; *Spencer Repeating Rifle Boston Mass.* Britt left the carbine on the ground and carried his revolver in his hand and made his way down the slope. There was no cover between him and the trees. He ran the distance zigzagging and bent over, and at last reached the edge of the copse and slid down a layer of red sandstone that guarded the depression like a well curb.

The paint saw him and called out. The horse stood where it was, nodding, running his tongue out.

The Kiowa lay with both arms outflung and his hands slightly lifted and stiff. A large section of his neck and jaw was missing, and Britt could see the pieces of teeth scattered and the white puzzle of the man's neck bones and all around his head a dark pool of dried blood. Britt stepped closer and saw the sun tattoo on the man's chin, the deep, short scars from his self-torture at the Sun Dance.

So much for you, Britt thought.

He walked around the man's campsite, looking for signs that there were others. He did not expect to find any and he did not. The man had been alone. Why, Britt would never know. He was not on a raid, or there would have been others. He might have been exiled from the band, perhaps, for some infraction, like Tissoyo. Perhaps he had stolen the paint from someone else and was fleeing with it. At any rate, he had come to his end.

There was nothing Britt wanted from him other than the horse and his death.

He walked back upslope in the early-morning light to Cajun and put the bridle on and slid the Spencer into his scabbard. He tightened his cinch and stood up in the stirrup. He rode down again and loosed the hobbles on the Medicine Hat and rode on. The paint followed. They could not be far from water because the Kiowa would not have made night camp too far from water. He would have watered his horse and then ridden away a short distance to camp in case someone else came to the same source. Britt saw, from time to time, the tracks of the paint coming from the north but too scattered on the occasional patches of bare ground to follow. Then he smelled the odor of the burning rock oil and at the same time saw the paint's tracks clearly leading down a small bluff of red stone that broke off in squares like thin bricks, and a patch of bright greenery. And there was a spring.

He stripped Cajun of his saddle and blankets and let him drink, and the paint thrust his head in beside the bay and drank as well. The horses sucked in vast draughts of clear water. Downslope from the spring a thin edge of grass grew, and horseweed and maidenhair fern. He let them eat and sat with his rifle between his two hands and watched and listened. Swallows darted around his head. Now he knew where the water was, between the Stone Houses and the Red. If he waited until nightfall and looked for the thin point of light of the burning rock oil, and caught its odor on the wind, he could always find it. This made him feel very good. And there was one down for Mary.

WHEN HE ARRIVED at the agency he removed his broad-brimmed hat and then put it back on. The agent was glad to see him again. He remembered him as the colored man who had retrieved his wife and children and the other white woman and her grandchild from the Kiowa and the Comanche, whose boy Jube had translated for the Grandin girl. They stood at the prim white picket fence that surrounded the agency house. Hammond saw something in the light of Britt's eyes and the way he carried himself that the man was deeply restrained. That he bore a hidden self. That something had happened.

"I want to leave this horse for a man named Tissoyo whenever he comes in."

"Tissoyo." Samuel regarded the horse and its colorful markings. "You know him?"

"Yes. He's a Comanche. I think he is with Esa Havey's band."

"Very well," said Samuel. "I will see to it. And maybe you would like to come in and eat something? I could have some dinner made for you."

"No sir, thank you." Britt did not want to cause trouble for himself or the Indian agent. The white soldiers or employees might see him walking in the front door of the house and sitting down at a white man's table to eat, and then there would be resentment, anger, hard words. He had enough trouble as it was. One trouble at a time.

"You are welcome to stay all night, then," said Samuel. "There is the wagon shed, I am sorry to say." He paused. "Is there something I can do for you?"

"I started up freighting, Mr. Hammond. I come to see if I could carry loads for the agency."

"Why yes, Mr. Johnson, I would be happy to place an order with you." He smiled. Samuel's hair blew in the hot June breeze and he wished he had put his hat on. "It's dangerous. You know it is dangerous." He put a hand on the hip of the Medicine Hat paint and stroked him. The horse shifted his feet and nodded. He was tired. His red forelock scattered over his white face.

"I can make it, sir," said Britt. "I just been laying out my route."

Samuel considered this. "You won't travel alone?"

"No sir. I got two men to come with me. We will be well armed." There was still a shifting and restless air about Britt and the way his eyes took in every building and the shadows of these buildings at the agency and every object or person that stood in the shadows as if even here the present world were infused with lethal forces. He carried a heavy Smith and Wesson revolver in a holster that was slick with use.

Samuel held his hand over his eyes and looked up at Britt. "I need tools, flour, horseshoes and ox shoes, those are the immediate things." He thought for a moment and then said, "If you could bring several loads from Fort Worth it would be quicker than ever I could get it from Fort Leavenworth."

"Yes sir, you just write me out a list."

"I am happy to do so. And you're sure you can cross the plains area between Fort Worth and here?"

"Yes sir," said Britt. "I can pull a trigger as well as they can."

Chapter 30

❦

IN THE LATE spring of 1870 Britt and Paint drove to the Graham salt works fifteen miles to the east of Elm Creek to carry wallpaper and surveyor's equipment and an entire box full of accountant's ledgers plus the steel pens and a jug of ink to go with the ledgers and ten barrels of flour. It was unseasonable weather, a hundred degrees at noon. Dennis was in Fort Belknap taking orders and filling up their small storage shed behind Nance's store. The shed was made of upright logs from the Brazos bottoms, and clean yellow rods of sunlight came through the chinks between them, swarming with dust motes, falling across Dennis's long black spider fingers as he wrote carefully in the ledger. When people came in with eggs and butter and venison hams to be sold in Weatherford, he noted down each item. He checked to be sure the eggs were covered with lime or grease so they would not be held accountable for spoilage. Then he presented the ledger to be signed and dated.

Sometimes Jube sat with him. His black horse was tied outside and sleeping in the sun. He had been sent away from the school in the warehouse for beating up the other boys. Jube had nearly become a warrior among the Kiowa, he would have ridden fast horses into mortal danger, carrying weapons on raids to kill other men, and now he must sit quietly and chant his ABCs in a mindless sing-song. Play gentle children's games and hold hands and dance the schottische. He felt exiled. Even with his mother there in the dusty warehouse chalking sprawled letters on a board. When a boy imitated her confused speech, Jube drove the boy down with his fists, knocking over chairs. He kicked the boy when he was down, heavy solid kicks. Sergeant Earl took Jube by the front of his shirt and marched him out the door.

Dennis found it hard to make the boy go back to this and so instead he asked Jube if he could read what was written, and do the sums, and when he had difficulty Dennis taught him with great patience. Jube understood the figures more easily because there were the summer melons before him in a pile at fifty cents each, thirty melons equals fifteen dollars. They had to account for these fifteen dollars and then subtract the haulage, which was seventy-five cents the hundredweight. And so there Jube, now you figure me that out.

AS PAINT AND Britt came along the Graham road across the flat country they saw ahead of them a wagon to one side and a man standing beside it. Another freighter. His team was unhitched and moving restlessly.

"What is it?" said Britt. They pulled up. The long Y-lines pooled at Paint's feet. They came to a halt in the middle of their own dust. It rose into the air and hung there untroubled by any wind.

The man wore a broad-brimmed hat against the sun. He leaned against his axle-grease bucket and wiped his face.

"They are colicking," he said. "Something they ate back there in Belknap."

The horses were wet with sweat and yet cold to the touch. One snapped at his flanks in pain and the other was about to go down. Britt and Paint jumped off the wagon.

"Hitch on behind us," said Britt. "Then tie the horses behind, you got to keep them moving."

The three men stripped most of the harness from the two grays and Paint walked them up and down the dusty road. Paint had to drag at their bits to keep them moving. Britt and the other freighter emptied his load of sacks of grain onto the roadside and then with great effort ran the wagon behind Britt's wagon and shoved the tongue into the blocks and tied it there. It was a simple one-ton farm wagon or they could not have moved it. They threw the harness into the second wagon.

Paint tied the man's team behind the second wagon and Britt got his own team moving at a trot. This concentration of wagons and horses filled the air with the dust of their passage that could have been seen miles away.

"What'd they eat?" said Britt.

The man sat backward on the mess box, watching his horses.

"Some of that army grain," he said. "Last year's oats. They was selling it cheap."

The team of grays did not want to move because of the pain in their guts but Britt's two sorrel leaders and the Fitzgerald bays bent to their collars and dragged them along the road in the stifling heat. Far ahead was the line of broken hills and the Graham salt works smoking the air in high pillars.

"That'll shake their guts down," said Britt.

The man stood up. "Bella is going down," he said. "Keep moving."

The man jumped off the wagon and when his faltering gray mare came alongside with her knees buckling he took hold of her tail and cranked it to one side like a windlass. Her head fell forward and then her neck stretched out as she was dragged onward.

"God, don't let her go down," called Paint.

"What the hell do you think I'm doing?" said the man. His dirty whitish shirt was wet with sweat. Then she was down in an explosion of dust and was being dragged. The thick, square blinkers of her driving bridle scooped up the red dust of the road. "Stop!"

Paint and Britt brought their team to a halt and jumped out.

"I can't get her up," he said. He twisted her tail and slapped her on the hindquarters. "Come on girl, get up, get up, Bella." The gray mare groaned where she lay and she threw her head back again and again, along the ground, until she had made an angel wing in the dirt. "Damn, I am going to lose her."

"Look here," said Paint. "Here's how." He knelt his stocky body down beside the mare's head. He clamped his black-and-white fingers around the mare's mouth and nostrils and shut off her wind entirely. "Wait," he said. After a moment of suffocation the mare fought wildly to her feet and Paint jumped out of the way. Britt was already in the driver's seat and touched the bays with the whip and Paint and the man kept after the grays, slapping them, encouraging them. After a few minutes there was the sound of spurting, trumpeting farts that were as loud as steam whistles.

"Thank God!" the man said.

"There you go," said Britt.

"Whew." Paint waved his hand in front of his face. "I am being knocked out, here."

After another mile the man and Paint climbed up into the seat beside Britt and the grays came along behind, nodding. They had lost their sweat and were still farting. So they came into Graham, down the gentle slope on the far side of the Brazos among the hills that the river had carved out of the plains in ages past.

"Now what else is going to happen?" said Britt. He shifted the reins between one large callused hand and another.

"Well, what else has happened?" said the man. "My name is Barton Calloway."

"Yes sir. My name is Britt Johnson, this here is Paint Crawford."

"Britt Johnson," the man said and looked at him.

"Well," Britt said. "We slept in the warehouse there at Belknap and this morning a dog or something ran off with one of my boots. Damn, I looked all over." He shifted his feet. On one foot he had a lace-up and on the other a pull-up boot. "Could have been a goat."

"You're Britt Johnson," said Calloway.

"Uh-huh."

There was a wowing, clattering sound as the right forward tire came loose from its wheel, and even though Britt stood up and pulled on the reins they could not stop in time. The wood of the wheel had shrunk under the tire in the summer heat and long travels and so the iron hoop sidled off the wheel rim and went bounding down the hill into the Graham salt works. It struck a stone and leaped into the air and bowled on downhill, gaining speed. There was nothing they could do but shout.

The iron tire hurled in great bounds and among the smoke and boilings of the salt works some men stood up and yelled. The tire bounced onto a kettle rim and jumped into the air. Hot drops of brine bolted upward and then the tire ran on through the salt works to the one street of Graham, the warehouse and two buildings of upright pickets, into an open space, and struck full into a trader's wagon. The trader was a man who dealt in mirrors and shawls and pins and fashion dolls and sheet music and little blue china teapots. The tire hit the backcloth against which these things were displayed, and pieces of china and the heads of porcelain dolls sprayed. The peddler was shouting and swearing when they pulled in. He took off his bowler hat and hit it against the rail of his trader's cart, shouting unknown words in an unknown language. His hand was shaking.

Britt walked up to him with his large hands gently patting the air. "Mister, I'll make it good."

The man was from some far country across the ocean, and he spoke in a language Britt could not understand as he set up the table and gathered up smashed teacups and loose sheets of music. Men came out of the warehouse to watch. The little trader was furious and there were tears in his eyes as if this strange visitation of a loose iron hoop smashing into his small stock of cheap and delicate treasures was the last in a long series of insults and failures. He looked up at Britt, who was at least a foot taller, with a suddenly frightened expression. He had a thin small face with black mustaches, and the drooping points of his mustaches were trembling. A sweating fat man at one of the boiling kettles watched and cried out, "Hor hor hor, Britt! You bought yourself a dollie! Hor hor hor!"

Brit reached out and patted the trader's arm.

"It's all right, it's all right."

The man calmed down a little. Britt came to stand beside him. The foreigner looked up at him with round black eyes. Britt pretended to write with his right hand on his left palm. "What do I owe you?"

The man wiped his face with his sleeve. It was possible that the writing gesture meant, *I am a huge black outlaw and I am going to kill you so write out your last will and testament right now.* But after a moment the small man fished a pencil out of his pocket and a little pad of paper. The man went over the damage and wrote everything down in a shaky script and then added it up. It came to seven dollars. He showed Britt the writing and the sums. Britt took off his laced boot and opened a small packet that had been sewn to the upper and handed him the seven dollars in paper. The man stared at Britt's two different boots for a moment and then nodded and put the bills in his pocket. Britt held out his hand. The man stared at it with his mouth slightly open and so Britt reached down and took his hand and shook it carefully.

"It's all right," Britt said.

"Yes yes."

Then Britt looked over the undamaged articles tangled up in the fallen backcloth and found a small hand mirror.

"This too," he said. "For my wife."

"You wife? Wife."

"Yes. How? Much?"

The small foreigner hesitated. He had just sold more articles than he would normally have sold in a week and he had the money in his pocket. He did not have to tramp about with his handcart in the hot sun for a whole day if he didn't feel like it. He could sit in the cooling shade and repair things. He smiled and said, "Gift, gift. I gift you."

"Nah," said Britt.

"Yes yes! I gift you! You wife. Take it, take it."

Britt turned the mirror over in his large hand. The man's lips trembled as he nodded and smiled once more. Britt could not know that the little man had at one time been to a Shakespearean play translated into Romanian and had seen an actor painted coal black named Othello, who strangled a little blond actress until her eyes bulged in the footlights. Britt would not have known the name Shakespeare, or Othello.

"Thank you," said Britt.

"Yes yes," said the man.

Britt wiped the dusty mirror off on his shirtsleeves. It had a wooden frame that had been figured and gilded. He put it inside his shirt in the hopes that Mary might look at herself again. To make up for a mirror once thrown and smashed on the floor. That she might look at herself and see once again that she was beautiful and loved and desired. The small foreign man would never know what the mirror meant to Britt, or the extravagant hopes he put in it. The terrible damage he was asking it to undo.

So Britt found himself in possession of broken teapots and a doll that was nearly whole except for a chip off the right side of her head and some torn sheet music as well as the mirror. He took the clinking bag of destroyed gewgaws back to the wagon. They untied Calloway's team and backed his wagon off. Fire flared in the broad daylight. The wooded hills around Graham were slowly being stripped of timber for the salt boiling.

Britt and Paint nodded to the men and turned to unload the delivery. Britt took the end of the long crate of surveyor's equipment and began to back away. Paint jumped down to take the other end. The wagon wheel that had thrown its tire was frayed on every felloe, and it would take an hour to reset the tire.

The man Calloway stood and watched.

"You was the one went and got Elizabeth Fitzgerald and her granddaughter from the Indians up there."

"Yes sir." Britt staggered backward with his end of the crate. They dropped it at the door of the building. Dust billowed up. He straightened and beat the dust from his hands. "And my wife and my two children."

"Well, we just got word they went down to Legion Valley, south of here, and murdered three white women and a baby. Five days ago. They took a boy named Dot Babb and a girl, Bianca Babb. They call her Banc." The man took off his hat and wiped his hair and put the hat back on. He decided not to go into the details of that extravagant butchery, a woman seven months pregnant and left without a head. "Is there any way you could look for them? If you been there twice you can go three times."

"Maybe," said Britt.

"I'd make it worth your while." He beat dust from his hat. "The whole family would."

"I got work to do," said Britt. "But I would keep an eye out for them. What do they look like?"

Tears stood out in the man's eyes. "They're my niece and nephew." He paused and cleared his throat. "I will write down their description and names and everything." He paused. "Can you read and write?"

"Yes," said Britt.

"All right." The man felt in his shirt pocket. "Just a minute. I got to borrow something to write with from old man Graham."

"I'll ask about them," said Britt. "If I can."

Chapter 31

❦

*I*N THE FALL of 1870 the only children who came to the agency school were Caddo, a tribe that had settled down near the agency in fear of the Comanche, and also they came because their mothers were busy and did not want them underfoot. Two boys and a girl. The children took up their pencils and pretended to draw the letters of the alphabet.

The schoolhouse was a cheerless place. It was so seldom used now that it had become a place where washing was done when it was not in use as a classroom and the teacher's desk had to be cleared and the washtubs and pans and buckets of grainy soap squares put back in place after the lessons. Sometimes there were clothes soaking in a bucket and the one girl who attended was interested in whose clothes they might be. She held up a heavy cotton shawl that dripped all over the floor and said something in Caddo to one of the boys and they all laughed. Storms grumbled outside and they looked nervously out the window as the predatory thing they knew as Walking Thunder stalked up and down impatiently in the west, his interior fires streaking like incandescent wires across the clotted, pendant clouds.

The children seemed strangely mature. They seemed to under-

stand that life was a serious matter and often fatal. The teacher felt
an air of contempt from them when they stared blankly at his enormous letters chalked on a black-painted board. A, this is A. There
was a fierce rivalry between the two boys, who were of the same age
or nearly the same age, and once a fight broke out over something
the teacher did not understand and they hammered at one another
with a silent and total commitment to doing damage to one another.
He sat down between the two of them and asked what it was.

The girl translated. It was about one of the boys' arrows that
had been retrieved from a hornet's nest and not given back. The
teacher asked the girl to tell the boys that sharing was a good thing,
because then other people would share with you. An arrow was a
small thing, wasn't it? Peace between people is a very big thing, a
thing that wise men of all ages had considered, but they could have
it if they wanted, even though it was very grand and its value beyond
price.

The two boys drew off from one another and nodded and sat
down again at the long bench and drew A's. Their rules of sharing
and property were very complicated and sacred. Certain parts of the
buffalo were shared with father's brother's son and other parts with
grandparents on the mother's side and arrows carried one's mark
of right into the air like an announcement and this was a form of
signaling and war speech that should never be taken by another, but
the teacher could not know that and did not think to ask.

SAMUEL SAT AT his desk beside his glowing sheet-iron stove
and its crisp, tinking coal fire that shone through the isinglass.
There were stacks of requests from Texas, for reparations from those
who had had horses stolen, houses burned, crops destroyed. Some of
these were honest and others were not. He marked with an X those
that were dubious. When there was government money to be had,
people did all sorts of strange things. Honest men would lie. He
turned down a request from an Oklahoma man to come and grow
hay and corn on reservation land that would be used for the Kiowa

and Comanche rations. He refused the request because he knew the Comanche would destroy the crop, and the man knew it too, but he would then apply for reparations at two or three times what the crop was worth. The Comanche would be doing him a favor if they set it on fire. Then not only would the man have deceived the federal government but Samuel would have more paperwork.

Samuel very much wished to prosecute a thin young fellow with long yellow hair and an extravagant vest who had been taken up by soldiers and delivered to a sheriff for sharpshooting into a Comanche encampment up near the Cheyenne Agency. He had killed a woman and a young girl and got away with stolen horses. A vivid and malignant young man whose boots had two-inch heels. However, since the incident occurred on reservation land it was a federal crime, and the closest federal courthouse was Fort Smith, Arkansas. Samuel had two witnesses who might testify against the young dandy, but it was a month's trip there and back and he must send in a request to the superintendent at Fort Leavenworth for a daily stipend and travel money for these witnesses and that would take several months if it were even granted. The witnesses had no intention of taking on two weeks' travel to Fort Smith, Arkansas, at their own expense to testify against someone whom they then had to live near if he got out on bail. And he would get out on bail.

The last Samuel heard the prospective witnesses and the alleged killer were drinking together in some sleazy saloon in a crossroads town in the Sans Bois Mountains. They laughed in fruity alcoholic voices and retold the story of how the woman and girl were shot down. How their hair flew. Neither Samuel nor Colonel Grierson had the authority to arrest and detain United States citizens if they were not on reservation land. Grierson would have been horrified if Samuel had asked him to. He would have said, *We are not under martial law here, sir.*

There were days when work on the sawmill went slowly. Samuel took the wagon reins himself to carry logs to the sawpit and shifted stone with the stonemasons. They will have houses, he said. I will see that they have houses. If we ask them to abandon life out there, then they must have houses to come to. They will get used to roofs. They must.

He filled out more paperwork to pay a man to raise a rail fence around ten acres of plowed ground. He went to inspect the fence, and when he stood on the rail in the middle of its span it gave way. Samuel told the man, "You will do it again and do it right. Tear this down. Start over." Then he drove the small one-ton farm wagon to the banks of Cache Creek and helped to dig coal for his own fire and for the forge in the blacksmith shop. He bought a herd of two hundred head of Texas cattle for the beef ration but had to send them out to graze under the protection of several Caddo men to keep the Comanche from riding down and issuing to themselves the beef whenever they felt like it. The cattle had to be kept away from the Comanche and Kiowa so that Samuel could then hand them out or withhold them as he saw fit. To withhold them if they did not bring in the captives. It was insane. He drummed his fingers on the shelves of the warehouse and thought how demented it was.

A band of young Comanche men rode in at night and sent several shots through the agency windows and carried off a team of mules and took several bales of bright calico from the warehouse. Samuel was not awake when the rounds came through the front windows but he shot off the bed and found himself lying flat on the floor when he did awaken. The result of a year under fire.

They did not want the calico or the mules but they took them for trophies. Samuel rode out looking for them and found the mules wandering around the Keechi Hills draped in yards of flowered cloth. Afterward Samuel sent a message to Colonel Grierson saying that he wanted guards. He would now use armed guards at the warehouse. He wrote to the Friends' Indian Committee that this should be permissible in their beliefs, because the guards, though they were soldiers, were under his civil authority and were therefore acting as policemen. Did they not have a police force there in Philadelphia? He was not using military force.

In his nightly prayers Samuel asked only that he be made to understand why he was here. What to do. He had no doubt that there was some greater design, but he fell into a deep sadness as he knew he could not understand this design. It made him feel shallow. A ship holed in some vital strakes and sunk to the gunnels and adrift. He was lonely and from time to time he felt the intensity of this loneliness, the strange questing feeling that comes from abandonment, that were he to keep on searching about in his mind and memory he would find someone or something to comfort him. The Holy Spirit was hidden in the vast plains and would not come to him even though he asked and asked again. It was because he was no longer a servant to his fellow men but an authority. A man with authority who must apply that power.

The world of Philadelphia faded and slipped from his mind. The concerns with the refitted *Monongahela* were the concerns of another time and place. She was out somewhere on the other side of the world carrying oil and flour from Argentina to California, they said, with money invested on his behalf. Letters from his parents and his brother's wife told him of that other world called Philadelphia, and the harvests near Lancaster. The brittle and haughty young woman who in some other age had sent back his ring wrote in a beautiful hand to say she was sorry. Sorry for what? Samuel had to think for a moment about what it was she was sorry about. He did not answer the letter.

He got into his bed at night with a feeling that he was being besieged by hostile forces that sang without words just at the edge of the horizon, and one night he dreamed of an enormous moon lifting over the Washita Mountains. It was swollen and it covered half the sky. This was deeply frightening and also the moon itself seemed terrified, with its round O of a mouth, as if something even more fell was following the moon from behind.

AND SO THE Kiowa and the Comanche lived and raided and hunted out on the long rolling plains while the telegraph and the railroad approached from the east, bringing news of the corruptions of Washington and the Communards of Paris and the street fighting there.

Samuel Hammond still refused to issue the orders that would have sent the army after the Kiowa and Comanche and bring them back by force to the reservation. So a band of Comanche rode down on Ledbetter's Salt Works west of Fort Belknap. The men left the hot salt pans and retreated behind a palisade and charged their small field cannon. They knew they had no help from either the Rangers or the army nor would they go back to where they had come from in the southern states, now an occupied country, and so they fought until they ran out of ammunition. Then old man Ledbetter shoved the king bolt from a wagon into the twelve-pound Napoleon field piece and fired it. The hissing bolt socked into Esa Havey's war horse and the stallion dropped like a stone. The Comanche turned and rode away. They laughed at Esa Havey running behind on foot until Hears the Dawn took pity on him and pulled him up behind.

On a dark night they infiltrated the town of Fredericksburg and took horses, and as they galloped away they overturned haystacks and set them afire and shot down a man who was walking out in the early morning singing and looking for his cattle. On the way home, on the plains, they came upon four men herding cattle and killed all four of them.

They struck at settlements far south of the Red River, far down in the Hill Country. They rode four hundred miles straight south to the ancient Spanish town of San Antonio, a town now grown up with theaters, paved streets, bakeries and candy stores and suburbs. Fifteen miles from San Antonio they captured two boys who within a year forgot every rule of behavior they knew and became skilled Comanche warriors. Throughout the winter of 1869 and the year 1870 the young men of the Comanche and the Kiowa rode with their hair floating in the night wind and their faces painted in beautiful colors of red and black and yellow, with hail marks and lightning strokes. Always there came that impeccable and otherworldly moment when they closed with the enemy, when they took the enemy's women and children captive, whose faces were distorted in mortal terror and their eyes as round as dollars.

In the late fall of 1870 Samuel at last rode out onto the plains to

search out the Kiowa and Comanche camps and to see the people of
his agency where they lived. He did not think they would kill him.
They might, but it was unlikely. He wore his broad-brimmed hat
and a heavy coat and a muffler because in late October the wind was
bitter. The annuity goods were two months behind coming from
Fort Leavenworth in Kansas. It was probable that the months would
go on without their delivery. The army sent a message saying they
had other priorities at the moment. There were forts out in Kansas
and Colorado and Wyoming that had to be provisioned because the
Sioux and the Cheyenne had broken out and were killing settlers
like chickens in a run. They would send the annual goods for the
Comanche and Kiowa at the earliest possible time. Your obedient
servant, Major T. J. Kinnel.

But Samuel got his goods in his own way. He rode to the post to
tell the colonel he had a shipment coming in. Bales of bright calicoes
and brass bells, ship's biscuit and kettles and salt. Things he could
withhold or grant to the Kiowa and Comanche in return for meek-
ness, good behavior, surrendered captives.

"You have a freighter coming up from Fort Worth?" said
Grierson.

"Yes, it's faster. I'll deal with the paperwork later. The delays are
unforgivable. A colored man named Britt Johnson."

"How does he get through?"

"He has a friend among the Comanche. Apparently this friend
looks out for him somehow. And I am leaving for a few weeks to go
out to the plains."

Samuel rode north and west into the Wichita Mountains with
his schoolteacher and Onofrio for companions. They dragged a
packhorse behind them. They had given up on the agency school.
They rode through the red stone mountains and here and there they
caught sight of elk galloping away into the canyons with their noses
stretched out, bearing the heavy weight of their candelabra horns
without effort. A bear's shining agitated hide hurried up a mountainside. Samuel shut his coat tight against the wind and bent his
head down to keep his hat from flying off.

His schoolteacher was a Friend named Thomas Beatty, and he was a good young man with an infinite supply of cheer who wanted more than life itself to go and live with the Kiowa to teach the children there in the lodges. Sooner or later Samuel would have to let him go and risk himself in that task.

They rode through broad valleys of dry grass. The stones of the Wichita Mountains had fallen wholesale into red heaps, and some stood isolated on the skyline in odd sentinels. One was very tall with a stone hat on its head. It regarded them from a sharp ridge as they rode by and when Samuel looked up with his hand on the crown of his hat it released them from its stone gaze and turned to wait for some other travelers. They slept beside a ragged fire that spit and cracked with mountain pine and in the morning they ate hot bannock and drank sugared coffee for breakfast. They saddled their horses and went on.

Every day was a gift of peace. Samuel listened to the quiet as they rode. The silky grass pale as champagne lifting and falling in currents. Once when they stopped at noon to eat he saw a cactus fruit on the tip of a prickly-pear pad glowing like a candle. He stared at it. It seemed that it had some sort of small light inside. Then he saw that sunlight was pouring through a hole in the red fruit and that the fruit itself was hollowed out. He stood up and bent over it. Two bees were at work inside the cactus fruit, scouring away the sweet pulp. Sunlight coming in through the hole had lit up the thin and transparent walls of the fruit and made it glow in a deep carmine red. He found Onofrio standing beside him. "Pretty," said Onofrio. "Very pretty." Then they rode on toward Mount Scott.

The Kiowa of Kicking Bird's band welcomed them and took them in. Kicking Bird spoke to Onofrio in Spanish. He said they had not heard of any captives whatever. None. Perhaps here and there a Mexican child, but these they purchased from the Apaches who raided in New Mexico. There was no harm in buying a Mexican captive. The Apaches treated them like dogs. They had a better life with the Kiowa. They married and had children. Here in this camp is a man named Komah, they call him Old Man Komah, the son of a Mexican captive, he has a wife and children. He translates for us and trades to San Idlefonso. Aperian Crow gestured toward the tipi wall to some direction where he thought Old Man Komah might be at the moment. Crowds of wiry-haired children stood outside and tried to see in the tipi door. A little girl in a soft hide dress with a necklace of glass beads farted with a shrill noise and the other children hissed and cried out *Nyyyah!* and slapped her lightly until she began to cry.

A young woman named Gonkon came in and laid blankets on their laps and then brought wooden trenchers of tongue and tamales wrapped in shucks and sat these on their laps over the blankets. The tipi was the first he had ever seen with a liner inside. It was very comfortable. He ate and listened to the odd and pleasing sounds of a tonal language.

Kicking Bird and many others were going out in the spring to meet the Comancheros near the Alibates flint quarries and did not understand why they should not. It was a great fair, a festival on the open plains, and when the two-wheeled carts came from New Mexico there were horse races and gambling games and shooting at targets. The Comancheros sometimes tried to trade for one of the Mexican captives, tried to redeem them. They had to know the person's name, however, and often it was too late, the captive had become Kiowa like us. The captive had forgotten his name, and it was too late.

Samuel listened attentively as Onofrio translated. He told them that it did not matter what the customs were. They were now under United States law under the Treaty of Medicine Lodge, and the United States had just fought a great war against slavery so that the taking of captives and selling them was not allowed. *Raiding is not allowed because it is murder. I have said this many times. The soldiers have not bothered you before. But my heart has hardened. Where is the girl named Millie Durgan? She would be eight or nine years old now.*

Kicking Bird shook his head. They did not know of any girl named Millie Durgan. Not alive. There had been a captive taken five years ago, but the girl died from some disease a long time ago. There were no white captives with the Kiowa.

"What about Elias Sheppard, thirteen years old, taken near the town of Blanco? Clinton and Jeff Smith, Adolph Korn, Alice Todd? The Lehmann boy, Temple Field? And many others."

I will ask here and there. Perhaps some other bands have some captives.

Samuel was silent when he heard this translated. The silence lay between them like a delicate invisible structure that no one wanted to disturb. And finally Samuel said that he would withhold all rations until they were brought in, and if not, he had the soldiers at his orders.

They went on into the country around Rainy Mountain and then on to the Antelope Hills. From the crest of the hills Samuel saw a herd of mustangs in full flight across the undulating plain. They ran with nodding heads, and their thick wavy tails streamed behind them. They had trim legs and small hooves, crested necks and long flowing manes. They bore within themselves the Andalusian and Soraya blood from the horses who had escaped from the Spaniards centuries ago. He wondered what they were running from. There had to have been two hundred or more. Then he knew they were running because they wanted to, because the plains were open and level and they were made to run. The herd broke apart around a breakwater of standing stones and came together again and then they bolted through the belt of trees, the cottonwoods and willows. Through the bare limbs Samuel saw the stream of flashing tails and ribs and backs plush with winter hair. Then the wild horses splashed snorting into the Canadian River.

They rode through a herd of sedate buffalo with long winter pelts. The cows moved away with their half-grown calves and the bulls with their elderly beards turned slowly in a studied way with their eyes on the riders. Their fat split hooves ground circles in the snow as they turned to keep the travelers fixed in their line of sight. The next day with Onofrio's help they found a Comanche village near the tall spires of limestone on the south bank of the Canadian. The tipis smoked like ovens from their conical tops.

Onofrio went ahead with one hand lifted and calling out in

Comanche. Samuel and Beatty hung back. Samuel looked all about himself on the bare plains and thought what a miracle of endurance it was to live like this solely on God's bounty, on whatever came to hand, in this sere country. To find their way across it from the Wichita Mountains up to Colorado and even on to Wyoming, and south to the Rio Grande. People of great courage and fortitude, born with an unsatisfied wanderlust so that their greatest joy was to break down the tipis and move on. They traveled alongside the rivers of the plains with their belts of trees and then crossed from one river to another and found things they had left behind in some other camp, or with delight they came upon a garden they had planted last year and was now bearing fruit. They did not live in the same world of time that Samuel did. There were no hours. No birthdays.

And he must bring this to an end. That was his job. That was why he was here.

The headman of the band was a man named Toshana. The man smiled and said, *Ah, here is Keeps All the Stuff, come to visit us.* He sent out the camp crier to call out that they had an honored visitor, for the men to come. He offered his pipe and so they went through the ritual of smoking and then ate. Toshana said they had no captives either. That if the agent wanted them to stop taking captives he should tell the army to come to them and they would settle it by force. But that was the only way it would ever be settled. He smiled as he said it.

"It is known everywhere that you have *taibo* captives," said Samuel. His face was still. He felt as if there were a band around his throat, frustration and anger.

Yes, perhaps some Mexicans.

Then Eaten Alive came into the tipi with a five- or six-year-old child. The boy's brown skin was broken with sores and lacerations, he was thin and shivering and dressed in a piece of bed-ticking that nearly enveloped him.

You see here, said Toshana. *We just got him from the Apache, see how they treat them. If you want to take him with you, you can. I will not ask you to pay.*

"Where did he come from?" Samuel held his hand out to the boy and felt an anguish in his heart at the sight of the child. The boy ducked his head and shrank away.

We don't know. The Apaches didn't say where he came from.

"I will contact the military in Santa Fe. Maybe they have a report of a missing child."

Toshana was silent for a while, and then he said, *But there are thousands.*

Samuel nodded. Thousands. He gathered his thoughts and said that there were several white captives, at least four or five young boys and one who would be grown up now, perhaps eighteen, and several girls. They were United States citizens and could not be abandoned.

We are only Comanche here, said Toshana. *Only Comanche.*

Hears the Dawn spoke in a low assenting voice. He said that the people to the south were Texans anyway. They were not Americans. There were the Spanish in New Mexico, and the old people spoke of the French coming from far to the east and south, and then there were Americans north of the Red and Texans to the south. Beyond the Texans were the Mexicans. *Isn't that right?*

Samuel turned to Onofrio and said, "Tell him that they are all white people and there are different nations among the white people. The Texans are now Americans."

Onofrio spun a thin shred of bark between his fingers.

He said, "There is no name for white people. Nobody says 'white.' Only white people say 'white people.' In Comanche the name means something like 'a captive.' *Taibo.* In Kiowa they say 'the hairy mouth people.' Beards, you see. I think the Sioux say *Wasichu* but it does not mean white. And I have heard from others that the Chippewa and the Cree call you-all Long Knives. *Kitche-mokoman.*"

Samuel listened with his head to one side, watching the flames that burned sedately on a layer of flat sandstone. The Comanche men around him listened as well with great patience to a language they could not understand.

Toshana said, *I am chief now that the Texans killed Peta Nocona.*

His wife was Nautdah, and they took her away. They said her name was Cynthia Ann Parker.

Samuel heard Siinti-on Parkar, but he knew who it was. She had starved herself to death in the house of her white relatives.

They took her captive and Peta Nocona's child Topsannah and they both died in the house where they kept them. She was with us for twenty-five years. You take captives too and so it is hard to listen to what you have to say. She was my aunt, the girl my cousin, and now they are dead.

"That's different," said Samuel. "We only took her back again."

But you did not get back her brother. His taibo *name was Chon Parkar, and they took him but he got away and came back to us, his people.*

"I know." Samuel nodded politely and made a conciliatory gesture. "Adults who have spent their lives with you will be able to make their choices. It is only fair. But they must be brought in so we can see they are not being held against their will."

We are only Comanche here.

Samuel said, "Nonetheless, I have come to warn you. The Texans are now Americans. So are the people of New Mexico. They have all become Americans and they are under American law. This is the last time. You will stop raiding and you will bring in the captives. If not I will send the soldiers."

Toshana laughed. *But you are Gai-ker. You do not fight.*

"You will see."

Samuel stood up to leave. The fire had burned down and the woman named Gonkon came in with more firewood. Before he left he said that he knew there were at least four boys with the Comanche, and if they were not brought in he would have the headmen arrested and thrown in jail. In a jail with stone walls, and there would be manacles and chains.

Eaten Alive started to speak but then shut his lips around his words and sat and thought for a moment. He was very angry. He would come in for rations in a few weeks since it was a cold fall and the grass was poor. He expected to be given his live beef and his sugar and coffee. If he had a captive he would bring him. He said that he would raid when he pleased. That he knew the Indian agent had goods brought to the agency in wagons from Forta Wurt but he himself would not raid the wagons. That the wagons were driven by a man named Breet, and the only reason that man was still alive was because he was a good friend to a Comanche named Tissoyo but this kind of thing cannot last forever.

"Bring them in," said Samuel. He took the wordless young Mexican captive and put a blanket around him. "Or you will go to prison. My heart has hardened."

Chapter 32

❧

BRITT ASKED ALL three men, Dennis and Paint and Vesey, to ride with him as guards and drivers to take a load of trade goods from Fort Worth up to Oklahoma to the agency. He asked Major Pinney for an escort from the Ninth, and so three black soldiers came as well. Britt took both wagons and asked four heavy horses of Elizabeth Fitzgerald so that he had six to a wagon. Elizabeth asked only five dollars for the teams' use. He could carry nearly twenty tons with two wagons and six-horse teams. They would carry mostly metal goods. Angle irons, plow blades, and massive rolls of copper wire for messages of some kind that would come down these wires from Kansas to Oklahoma. They carried crates of the strange bulbous glass cups that were somehow supposed to help this process.

It was the last week of November of 1870 and cold. Better than the heat. Better for men and horses. They made it in five days from Fort Worth to the agency without trouble. They arrived at the burning rock oil and the spring near it in good time early in the evening. Britt was pleased. During the night Britt had two men standing guard for four hours each. He slept with the quiet, secret speech of the running spring water in his dreams. A spring in the desert plains. He awoke with a blanket wrapped around his head and his nose cold and his breath smoking in the thin winter air. He listened to the sound of Vesey and Dennis laughing and the horses grinding up corn from their feed box on a wagon tongue. He had dreamed he was sitting alone in the cabin at Elm Creek and that the Medicine Hat paint had come up to him out of the tangled winter grapevines and spoke to him. The paint wanted to tell him something, something urgent. *What, what?* said Britt in his dream. He sat up in his clothes and the shadow of the little ravine was chill, the lines of thin strata like bricks a strange puzzle.

One of the soldiers with them played something on the harmonica as Paint shifted the crisping bacon from one side of the skillet to the other.

"What's that song?" said Britt.

" 'Annie Laurie,' sir," said the soldier.

"My wife wants to hear a harmonica," said Britt. "It's a new thing."

"Yes sir, my cousin sent me this from Chicago. A Chicago company makes them."

They came into the agency with a loud noise and much calling and shouting. Britt stood in the wagon seat with the reins of the front team in his hands and nodded as men came out from the sawpit and the stables and wagon sheds to meet him. He signed the receipt for the accountant. He unloaded at the agency warehouse.

Then they reset the load for Fort Sill; kerosene in barrels and the lamps themselves packed in straw, the sacks of rolled barley and corn for the cavalry horses and a church bell for the chaplain's new small stone church. It was a heavy load. The cavalry was preparing to move, they said. Before long they were to take to the field and come to grips with the horse Indians of the plains.

Britt and his men and the two wagons passed by Cache Creek on the south bank. At one of the wide places, on the north side, the Kiowa were camped. They had the wide plains around them and the long galleria of the timber on Cache Creek to one side. They did not bother him because he and the men with him were well armed, although they came to watch him arrive and then pass by. The heavy wagons and twelve horses jangled and thudded across the dry earth and then went down the slope into the water. They stood in a long line drinking in the roiled water, and the men with him, Dennis and Paint as well as the three enlisted men from the Ninth, sat with their rifles in their hands. As Britt stood knee-deep in the water, checking harness, he saw a boy come down to the bank with a buffalo-stomach bucket. His feet in moccasins that patted the red dust lightly and the bucket swinging from one hand. Then the boy looked up and stopped. Although he had black hair, Britt saw that he was a white boy.

"Who are you?" said Britt.

The boy stared at him with narrow blue eyes. He stepped back a few paces into the brush.

"Do you know your name?" asked Britt.

"Chon," the boy said. "I Chon Digasun." The wind tore at his hair. The boy stood rigid with water slopping on his shins. "You leave me alone."

"John Dickson," said Britt. "I will come back. When I come back from Fort Sill, I will come by here and I'll have money to exchange for you."

"You leave me alone."

The boy turned and ran back to the tipis. He left the bucket where it fell.

ONE BY ONE, captives were brought in. Samuel checked his lists. There was no word of little Alice Todd, the Whitlock boy still unaccounted for, the names Kuykendall and Massengill and Dickson, the two Smith boys, Herman Lehmann, written out clean and accusing. A distant band of Comanche brought in a boy with a thin, sensitive face, a wide mouth, and hooded eyes. He never looked at anyone from the moment he was brought in. He kept his head high and stiff and his eyes half closed and his gaze on the floorboards. He moved slowly and carefully. He seemed to be injured in some obscure way. His adopted father had bargained over his price, holding out for one more pound of coffee, another blanket. The Comanche had been traders for a century or more, and they were skilled at it. The boy listened with his beautiful eyes on the windowsill. Listened as he was sold by the man he had adored and whom he had imitated in everything. Followed across the hot plains, the man who had given him his Comanche name and approved of his aim with a rifle and his torture of a Mexican captive.

He stood up like an automaton and followed the Indian agent, expecting to be killed, and when he was not killed, he was flooded by a feeling of contempt. He was crushed into whiteman's clothing and led to a building.

By late November there were four of them. All of them boys and angry and silent in the stone schoolhouse. Samuel was not sure who they were. He sat with each of them alone and tried to find out their names but they had trouble pronouncing the words. *Kleenton, Haydoff, Tempah*. The smallest one only knew his Comanche name, Toppish. The soldiers plunged them into tin bathtubs and took away their weapons and their buckskins and cut their hair and they all looked like thin unfinished wraiths with uneven haircuts and mistrusting expressions. They refused to sleep in the schoolhouse and so Samuel had an army tent placed in the schoolyard and they settled in there; they slept on the bare dirt floor of the tent in the cold, in their new woolen clothes and their shoes beside their heads. They were afraid of the schoolhouse walls.

He asked for the names of their parents, but they had forgotten. He asked them to remember where they were from, but they had only vague images of a double-log cabin and a truck patch and sisters or mothers or fathers who were dead. Samuel guessed that one of them might be Clinton Smith, whose brother Jeff was still missing. Another was Adolph Korn, who spoke only Comanche and German. The third boy with the thin and sensitive face might be Temple Field who was taken in the Legion Valley massacre, but the last and smallest did not match any information he had. They were smaller than they had been described in the circulars, they appeared four or five years younger, as if the prairie sun and wind had shrunk them or held them in suspension from the time they had been captured. The schoolteacher showed them how to hold pencils in their hands, but Clinton seemed to think of the pencil as a weapon and held it like a knife until Beatty placed it in his fingers correctly and held his own hand over the boy's callused hand and drew the point across a sheet of paper.

Temple watched with his half-closed eyes and whispered, "What for? What for?"

"For messages," said Beatty. "To make messages."

They drew great slash marks across sheets of paper. They listened carefully as the young Quaker explained that soon they would go home to their own people. He tried to get them to sing, but they could not hit the note and had no sense of the musical rhythm of white people, but only the subtle and constantly varying beat of Comanche songs, the floating tenor.

Samuel counted out pennies into their hands and sent them to the sutler's store for hard candy so they could understand the meaning of money but when they came back they put the hard candies beneath their blankets in the army tent and did not eat them. They were afraid of being poisoned.

IN THE BITING cold that came in the last of December of 1870, Samuel saw a man in a light buggy driving up from the south along Cache Creek. A little man, bowed over his hard hands that held the reins in a knot. Samuel met him at the door of the agency house and brought him inside out of the wind.

"Mr. Hammond, I am Sam Kilgore," the man said. "My boy was taken in Clay County. Martin. Last week. There was a big raid, they killed old man Koozer and took his wife and two daughters. They killed some of the Maxeys. The Maxey baby. They took the Maxey boy."

Samuel tried to take notes but the man's account was rambling and repetitive and once he wept, briefly, with his hand to his forehead.

"Koozer was a Quaker, like you," Kilgore said. He wiped his nose with his sleeve. "Like you."

Samuel turned away from Kilgore to watch the trembling low light behind the isinglass. This was the fourth bereaved parent and relative who had driven or ridden across the dangerous stretch of open plains to ask for his children. He put his head in his hand and for a few moments listened to the wind scouring away the putty in the window frames and said a brief prayer.

"Let me see what I can do." Samuel reached out and touched the man's arm. "They are coming in in three or four days for rations. Just wait here. You can sleep in the enlisted barracks at the fort."

"What will you do?" the man asked. "I know of people that came here to the agent before you, and he said he could do nothing. He said he couldn't do a damn thing. People went and ransomed the children themselves. The Babbs did, paid hard money and a good gray horse to get them back. Y'all are useless as tits on a boar."

"Let's calm down," said Samuel. "Calm down. I understand how you feel. You are right to be angry. I will get them back. I will. No matter what."

A week later Samuel saw a column of dust toward the northwest. He stood with one of the men from the sawmill, the man who worked the big crosscut saw. His name was Frenchy Robideaux, and he watched the Indians coming with narrowed eyes. Before Samuel could tell one horseman from the other, Onofrio rode up at a gallop.

As they watched the Indians approach, Onofrio tried to calm himself. To get his breath back. He held to the reins tightly, and the alarmed horse danced to one side and then the other. "They come by the old hayfield. At Caddo George's place. They killed that Caddo boy you set to watching the cattle."

"Well, God save us," said the sawyer. "The sons of bitches."

They stood together in the cold December wind and saw the dust storming off to one side of the approaching horses and loose hair streaming in the wind. The spiky black design of lodgepoles heaped on either side of a mule. Dust boiled away from the hooves of their horses as if with every step they took they set the ground on fire.

Samuel had a can of coal oil in one hand. He had been on his way to burn a pile of cut brush. He set it down and opened the white picket fence gate.

"Why?" he said.

Onofrio lifted both shoulders. "The Comanche and the Caddo have been fighting one another forever," he said. "They just fight."

"Frenchy, take Onofrio's horse and go to the post, go to the commander's house, and tell Colonel Grierson to come with a detachment of soldiers. Go now."

"They'll see me," said the sawyer. He wavered. His hand went to his hat and then to the reins. The horse shifted and turned his head to look at the approaching Comanche and Kiowa horses. "They'll know. They'll follow me."

"Hurry," said Samuel. "Just go."

"Give me a pistol."

"I don't have one," said Samuel. He threw the reins over the horse's neck and turned the stirrup for the sawyer. Finally the man stepped into the stirrup and rode away at an innocent and casual walk and when he was out of sight behind the new sawmill he spurred the horse into a gallop.

The headmen came to the agency house. They dismounted in simple, fluid motions and looked about themselves, and one turned back to call to the women. The women and children stayed on their horses. Samuel saw Two Hatchet, a handsome man despite his receding chin, with delicate, long eyes. A man whom Samuel recognized as Satank, old and weathered, spoke to Onofrio.

"They have come for the rations," said Onofrio. He swallowed several times. "They want them now. They don't need any beef. They already got their beef."

Samuel said, "Come inside." He opened the little white picket gate with its ornate, turned gatepost and made a welcoming motion.

The men stood reserved and hostile among the chairs and desks, their moccasins leaving dusty impressions on the carpet like bare feet. Two Hatchet picked up a steel pen from the desk and turned it up to look at the point. They all wore revolvers. The old man Satank stood beside Eaten Alive and regarded Samuel beneath drooping eyelids.

"You killed young Jesse George," said Samuel. "The one who was looking after the cattle. That is murder."

The young men went after him, said Satank. *The Caddo always fight us.*

And Eaten Alive laughed at Samuel and said there was no controlling the young men. It was foolish to ask him to do so. He could not.

"You have taken yet more captives," said Samuel.

Yes, we have some captives out on the plains, a long way away. Eaten Alive said it easily, with a wave of his hand.

Onofrio's voice ran along behind the sound of the Comanche language in a relentless monotone. There was no one to translate for the Kiowa but the time had passed for translations and for considered words. Tones of voice and gestures said everything that needed to be said.

"Bring them in. Bring them in now."

Eaten Alive said, *They are having a good time. They want to be Comanche. Who would not want to be a Comanche?*

Samuel turned to Satank. "Bring in any captives you have. Any and all. I will not issue you rations, and this is the last time I will say this. Bring them in or you will be taken prisoner."

Satank said something in a high, loud voice that was not translated. Onofrio stood silent with a shocked look on his face. If fighting started it was going to be at very close quarters. Onofrio stepped back. Satank shouted again, and bent forward toward Samuel, his finger stabbing the air. Then he reached inside his four-point blanket with his right hand. Onofrio threw out his arm in front of Samuel. Two Hatchet stepped backward and knocked over the water pitcher. It shattered. Satank brought out two human scalps and flung them at Samuel.

There are your captives. That is all you will ever get of them.

The scalps fell at his feet. One was light brown hair, and the other was black and long and wavy. They lay with scattered locks on the flowered carpet.

Samuel reached down and picked up the streaming hair and for a second or two considered the agony of these two deaths among so many others. Death by random violence, by intent. Death and violence seem to have sprung up all around him like demon weeds. This was not like marching and ordered armies. It was different and ancient beyond time. He heard the sound of horses and commands coming from the north road.

"I am telling you my patience has come to an end. There are soldiers here and I will use them. I will send them after you and the Quahada. Our force is much greater than yours. I wish you to understand this."

He is done talking, said Onofrio.

Satank and Setanta and Aperian Crow stared at Samuel for a moment. Then Satank made a dismissive gesture, and they turned to go.

When the headmen walked out of the gate in front, beyond the delicate and civilized little white fence, they were met and surrounded by soldiers and the soldiers reached out to them in a moving confusion of blue woolen arms and boots. The headmen were disarmed and handcuffed. A man named Big Tree fought for a short while but three soldiers flattened him on the ground and cuffed his hands behind him. A revolver fell from beneath the buffalo robe of Eaten Alive and it went off with a startling bang but nobody was hit. A soldier picked it up delicately by the grip between thumb and forefinger. He said that Agent Hammond might want to make out a receipt for this but the sergeant told him to shut up. The men walked away between the soldiers quietly and stepped into the army transport wagon. It was not dignified to struggle. The women and children had scattered to the horses and within moments they were gone.

Samuel sat in Grierson's office in the stone commandant's building and signed the arrest warrants. Grierson reached across the desk and took the papers from him.

"I know this runs against your every belief," he said. "I am sorry."

They were to be tried in a Texas court, since homicide was a state and not a federal crime. An engraving of President Grant hung in a dark frame over the fireplace, and an American flag hung limply from its staff. The colonel's windows were open several inches despite the cold. He was using ox shoes for paperweights, each half-shoe an iron comma from some giant's alphabet.

"That is neither here nor there," said Samuel.

"I am sending a detachment to the agency," said Grierson. "I will take the women and children into custody until they return the captives. They will be well treated."

"Yes, I suppose they will be." He turned in the chair and reached for his coat. "They have provoked me into this."

"This is not going to be easy, Samuel."

"I know it." Samuel stood up and jammed on his heavy wool coat with fierce and punitive thrusts of his arms. "Don't sympathize with me, Colonel. I have lost all goodwill, here."

"You will need all your resolve," said Grierson. "The Texans will want them executed by cannon, or machete or something."

"Oh yes, I have thought of that many times." Samuel put on the brown felt hat that he had bought so long ago at Wanamaker's on Market Street. "I am grateful for your prompt response."

"My duty," said Grierson. "And I think a friend of yours is here. James Deaver."

"What, he's here?"

"Yes, he is. And another reporter from somewhere. Chicago or somewhere." Grierson turned to the window and threw it open. He leaned out to the chips and kindling of the carpenter's yard behind the commandant's building. The men were constructing a great stone beehive kiln for drying lumber. He shouted, "Mr. Deaver!"

A faint voice called out, "Here!"

Chapter 33

"ELL, WELL, NOW it begins!" cried Deaver. He grasped Samuel by the coat sleeve. "We got reports of all the captives, and here we are at the crucial moment of arrest." Deaver forged on through the cold air toward the sergeant's quarters. "How kind of the army to put us up in its drafty barracks." They walked down the quadrangle; stone buildings arranged around the long parade ground. On the verandas of the enlisted men's barracks soldiers stood staring toward the guardhouse. "And you will refuse them food and blankets while they starve."

"I can forbid you the agency," said Samuel.

"But you will not, you will not." Deaver walked on with one hand on Samuel's sleeve. His muffler tossed in the cold wind. His breath smoked. "I am your conscience, I am the recording angel. I shall do sketches of our brave military riding into the enemy camps and the women and children held prisoners, we will be here on the spot when it happens."

The enlisted men's barracks was one long hall with a great fireplace at one end, and a sergeant's private quarters at the other end. The correspondents had somehow requisitioned it; Deaver and another man were in the room along with carpetbags and portfolios that were much the worse for wear. Samuel sat on a spindly chair in front of a long table with bottles on it. Lone Star Bitters and London Royal Nectar Gin, Ayers Compound Extract of Sarsparilla. The stone walls had recently been plastered white, but they had been keeping their card scores on the wall near the table with penciled totals in Roman numerals. The cards were on a bed; slightly racy. The picture on the backs was of a girl standing on a stream bank, fishing; she had hooked her own skirt hem and drawn it up so that her drawers and garters showed.

"This is Charley Simonton," said Deaver. "He's AP. Charley, Agent Hammond."

"Delighted," said Simonton. He nodded. He still wore his slouch hat. He had clearly finished some report and was now in a slight daze of thought. Written sheets lay to one side of his hand. "Ran into Jim here when we were on the first run of the Kansas City–Denver railroad. Just inaugurated. We were on the inaugural run."

"How are you here so quickly?" said Samuel.

"The telegraph," said Simonton. "We listen in with a router box."

Deaver turned the pages of a newspaper. "Here it is," he said. "*New York Times.* They did a good job with it." The wood engraving was delicately lined and the background an intelligent balance of blacks and whites. An Indian warrior on a horse galloped beside the smoking locomotive. "We got to ride in the parlor car with the railroad nabobs. Treated to antelope chops and cold Krug, and I sat and observed starving Indians begging at the Wichita station." Deaver slammed the newspaper down on top of his sketchbook. "How is it?" he asked. "How is it we do this to the original inhabitants of this continent?" Deaver ran his hand through his thick, dark brown hair as if he would tear at it.

"I don't have any answers," said Samuel. He sat quietly in the ruin of his own personal philosophies as if they were smoking timbers in a heap and felt as if he had just murdered someone, or perhaps abandoned someone in a burning building.

Simonton looked at Deaver and then back to Samuel. "So you're the Indian agent," he said. "Honored."

"I am that," said Samuel.

"A Quaker."

"Yes."

"Well, well." Simonton nodded. "You came here to bring peace and brotherly love, and you are going to preside over their destruction. My my."

"I have merely arrested four men who have admitted to murder and kidnapping." Samuel sat with both hands loose in his lap. "There was nothing else I could do."

"Why should they be charged with murder? This is a war. They are at war with the Texas settlers, and now you are handing them over to Texas juries. Have you heard the news from Washington?"

"Tell me, then."

"The Peace Policy might be rescinded." Simonton searched in his pockets and found half a cigar. He lit it. "You must regret that. Or maybe not."

"Why do you want to talk to me?" said Samuel. "I must thank James for introducing us, but I don't keep much of a social life and I find matters are pressing."

"Wait, wait," said Simonton. He put out a hand. "Jim is an old friend. He makes interesting acquaintances. His sketches are renowned. I depend on him for the interesting acquaintances he makes."

"You owe me," said Deaver. He had poured himself a shot of gin and sipped at it and with the other hand sifted through a loose-leaf pile of ink drawings. "I am looking at the mementos of a destroyed people, here."

"And you are the Friend in authority," said Simonton. "The other Quakers of the Indian Committee are far away. You can do as you like."

"That's quite untrue," said Samuel. He tried to think of something to calm himself, to reply politely. He was the Indian agent and could not indulge in personal hostilities. He was a representative of the federal government and also of the Society of Friends.

"But the Quakers and the red men are alike, in some way."

"I used to think that," said Samuel. "But experience has taught me otherwise."

"But think. The young Comanche men go alone to the mountains or some deserted place and fast and cry for a spirit to guide them. Do you not seek the Inner Light?" Simonton leaned forward in the chair. He was interested.

Samuel glanced up at Simonton from beneath his eyebrows. "You know very well we do."

"So do the horse Indians. Now, consider. Both Quakers and Comanche stand alone before the Divine Presence and seek to be taken, or moved, by the spirit."

Samuel threaded his fingers together and regarded his shoes. "Mr. Simonton, this is the sort of conversation Harvard divinity students have with each other when drinking brandy in their rooms."

"But the question must be considered, were you to dispute theology with a Comanche medicine man, or a Kiowa priest of the Sun Dance."

"I have no intention of disputing my beliefs with anyone."

"Ah, you will miss one of the great pleasures of life. As well as London Royal Gin."

"I will concede that."

"The free life on the plains. No other people like them anywhere," said Deaver. He turned to Samuel, and Samuel saw that his eyes were glistening. "You will send the army after them. You know they kill the women and children. You know about Sand Creek and the battle on the Washita. Will you preside at the hangings?"

"What hangings?" Samuel stood up and reached for his old brown wide-brimmed hat. "Are you quite sober, James?"

"No, I am not," said Deaver. Simonton silently poured out another measure of gin for the illustrator. "I am merely here to see them tried and then strangled on a rope. A carnival of crime on both sides. Which side are you on?" Deaver wiped at his face and took up his glass. "You are going to force them to live within the reservation," said Deaver. "I find this melancholy. It will kill them."

"It can't be helped," said Samuel. "You spoke once of tragedy. That Americans were uncomfortable with tragedy. And here it is. We are regarding it. Like an audience."

He walked outside into the cold. The cavalrymen were forming in ranks, and their guidons stood out stiff in the wind and all their brasses glittered even though the sun was dim under a screen of high, thin clouds. The black Ninth Cavalry were serious and reserved and conscious of their recent honor. The horses moved against their bits and their tails blew between their legs and Samuel watched as a kind of great ordering took place, as if the union of men and horses made them more than themselves, something they were meant to be from the moment they were born. Their bugles a hazy harsh gold and their carbines sheathed at their left stirrups and the flag boots creaking on their slings and so they stood silently in the beauty of their weapons.

SAMUEL DROVE THE mile and a half to the agency, watching the winking of the horses' shoes as they trotted on. He set the brake block as they started down the rocky slope to the valley of Cache Creek. The horses minced their way down, and the fixed wheels spewed dust. The agency appeared in the crawling weaves of ground-blow, the sandy wind poured through the white picket fence and around the warehouse and corrals. The place was empty and lifeless, devoid of red men or white men either one. Here and there a bit of ribbon and a rawhide box where things had been dropped as the Kiowa and Comanche women were taken captive. A sense of something about to happen. The stubborn brush unmoved by the wind. The wind's scouring howl as it poured across Oklahoma.

Samuel did not know what to do with the scalps. They lay in loose sheaves of hair on his flowered carpet. Finally he buried them like kitchen trash in the manure pile behind the wagon shed.

He paced the agency house from one end to another. He felt he was turning into someone else. Or perhaps someone he had always been. He was hardening like pottery fired in a kiln. Hard angry words in his head carrying an abrasive silt. He did not like the sounds of the words in his own head. Outside he saw two Caddo boys digging the scalps out of the manure pile and turning them over in their hands. They threw them at each other and then one of them put the brown scalp on his own head and pranced in a circle. Samuel sat down in front of his coal stove. He did not like the chemical smell of it but wood was scarce. He was within seconds of going outside and taking the boy by the back of his jacket and beating him with the buggy whip.

He got up and walked through the door and slammed it behind him and went to stand in front of the new water mill, arising stone by stone, the masons snapping their chalked strings along the courses of sandstone. Others were constructing the dam. Shouts and songs. Mexicans and soldiers working side by side.

He stopped to watch two stonemasons with a scorpion. One shot down his hand with a knife and cut off its poisonous tail. It began to run in confused circles. The men squatted down to watch it and laughed.

He went back into the agency house and washed his face and hands and sat down in front of a plate of hominy grits and prairie chicken. He could not eat.

He sat at his desk and flipped through Isaiah as if through a law dictionary, searching out the right words, the right terms.

I have trodden the winepress alone, and from the peoples no one was with Me. For I have trodden them in My anger, and trampled them in My fury; their blood is sprinkled upon My garments and I have stained all My robes. For the day of vengeance is in My heart, and the year of My redeemed has come. I have trodden down the peoples in My anger, made them drunk in My fury, and brought down their strength to the earth.

JAMES DEAVER TOOK a bath in a horse trough after the horses had been led to water in the late, cold evening. He had sent his clothes to the post laundresses. He had the impression of himself and all the horse Indians of the plains shut up in a frame and drifting away in thin colors on scattered sheets of paper. It was because of the gin that sat in its glass in the dirt beside the water trough. He got out and dried himself and did not feel the cold. He finished the gin and put on his shirt and then went to the barracks carrying his pants. He clodded across the parade ground with bare legs and wet shoes.

He sat at the table beside the fire and composed a long telegram to Dr. Reed of the Friends' Indian Committee in Philadelphia. In it he stated that Samuel Hammond had abandoned all precepts of his Quaker upbringing. Imprisoned several Indian men in the guardhouse in Fort Sill to be sent to Texas justice. Indian women and children held in horse corral. Refused rations to the families that had come in who were destitute and starving. Imprisoned young boys in the schoolhouse whose only crime was that they had been captives and were not yet capable of accustoming themselves to the ways of white people. Discouraging thing that men could so change and alter. Red men wanted only a life of freedom on the plains and to hunt the bison there as God meant them to else why did he place them there. Agent Hammond ignoring all precepts of Peace Policy. Still time to stop conflict. Soldiers preparing to campaign. Your obedient sv't, James Nathan Deaver.

IT WAS A week later, the first week of January of the New Year, that the letter came from Dr. Reed. Samuel sat close to the window to read it as the light faded from a world that was glistening with windblown dust.

Our dear Samuel Friend in Christ;
    We have with dismay read a report to this Committee that thou hast imprisoned five men of the Kiowa and Comanche tribes inclusive

of their women and small children despite our professed desire to treat the Red Man as our brother and as a being deeply wronged over the centuries that we have inhabited this continent. Whatever the desperate measures taken by these people remember that they have been cheated and dispossessed of those things most dear to them. Is it not to be expected that the Kiowa and Comanche and others under thy charge are reduced to such measures?

If thou has stood resolutely by our agreement in that the Texans and others who have incrementally stolen the lands of these people be prevented from mistreating them then those for whom thou art responsible should have understood our feelings of love, of admiration, of brotherly regard and come to settle themselves on the vast reservation that has been set aside for them.

If thou hadst been attentive to thy duties then the saving truths of the Scripture would have been communicated to them. If the Red Men have not seen the advantages of peace then thou hast somehow been amiss, Samuel. Unless our reliance is on that which comes from above, we shall fail.

Samuel put the letter down. It was clear he would have to resign. He would be glad to go. He did not know how to use authority, he was not good at it. Let someone else come and take on this terrible task. He had only a few things left to do. War with the Comanche and Kiowa was coming as sure as the sun rose in the east. As the sparks fly upward. It would take his letter of resignation several weeks to reach Dr. Reed in Philadelphia, and in the meantime he must complete every task he could.

And after that he would take the overland route for San Francisco, where at some time the *Monongahela* would come in and he would board his own ship as supercargo and go with her round the Horn. How could he have known this was something he had always wanted to do? A private and obscure longing to be on the surface of the great oceans suddenly appeared as a complete and accomplished thought. He had been obligated to a life of service from his earliest upbringing and he had done his best. Now he wanted to take ship around Cape Horn and serve no earthly power whatever.

THE BOYS' RELATIVES had at last been found, and until they came to claim them the boys lived like shadows in their army tent. Sometimes the soldiers came to teach them how to gamble with dice, and they liked that. They were in an empty space between their Comanche names and the names Clinton Smith and Adolph Korn and Temple Field and Valentine Maxey. It made them feel as if they were made of some other substance than flesh and blood. They often sat and gazed at the Speckled Blue-Faced Mountains behind the agency and the fort. Yes people were good to them. No they had not learned their alphabet. Yes they would try.

Samuel sent for a photographer to take their portraits. The boys watched with rigid and fixed expressions when the man set up the scaffolding and then placed the camera and the dark cloth over his head. When he turned the brass lens tube toward them like the barrel of some weapon, they shouted aloud and fled. All that remained on the glass plates were blurred streaks like smoke, or the impression of fugitive spirits caught in the flash powder.

Samuel sat and thought of how to reach them. How to describe anew their lives to them before they were taken, how to help them know who they were. He had the feeling that they might never again know who they were. That their identity might be held as some distant, lucid secret in the heart of God until the day they died.

Like his own. Like his own.

Beyond the windows the blue loom of the Wichita Mountains, a sanctuary of iron and granite and clean water. Temple Field regarded them from his half-closed eyes. No one knew what he thought. The other boy captives spoke to him but he refused to answer. Samuel handed him over to his grandfather, shook the old man's hand, and handed him a handkerchief to soak up his tears.

Two years after Temple Field was returned to his family near De Soto, Kansas, he died of self-starvation, in complete silence.

Chapter 34

❧

*I*N LATE DECEMBER of 1870 Britt rode in front of a herd of horses at a slow trot to bring them in to Fort Belknap. The army had bought them from a rancher named George Daley who lived in a large log house that was constructed like a fort out beyond the Old Stone Ranch House. In return for bringing them in, he was to have four of the best of them. Paint and Dennis were moving northeast from Elm Creek toward Jacksboro with a load of hay and butter in small kegs and salted beef. They would meet back in Fort Belknap and begin to break in the four horses to harness. Britt trotted Cajun at a slow and steady pace in the front, and as long as he kept this up, they would follow him.

It was very still. Fog shifted in low banks in the valley of the Clear Fork of the Brazos and he and the horses he was leading rode down into these and inside the fog he could only see a few nodding heads behind him with the manes tossing along their necks in damp strands. Then they came up and were clear for a while and then they trotted forward into another fog bank and the horses followed him by scent and sound.

Before long he came to the remains of the Old Stone Ranch

House, where he and Paint and Dennis had sat behind the walls and fired at Kiowa and where he had heard someone in a taunting rage calling to him to give up his only son. The walls were indistinct in the heavy fog. If the temperature dropped, the fog would change to ice. The world would turn to glass.

Britt turned inside the remains of the wall that had once surrounded the ruined house, and the loose horses, eleven in number, followed and stood with round eyes and nostrils smelling of it all, the strange walls and the remains of the cookstove with its faint meat odors. He felt he had best stay within the broken wall and near the old house to see what the weather would do.

He unsaddled Cajun to give the horse's back a rest and sat the saddle down on its fork and laid the saddle blankets over. He unstrapped the rifle scabbard to set the Spencer upright on its butt plate so that moisture would not leak down into the breech-loading mechanism. He leaned it against the wall.

The sound of his own footsteps was blurred and then silenced in the quiet noises of horses moving about, murmuring to one another. They would not stay within the ruined walls for long, but they would go no farther than the riverbed and its dried grasses and pools of water and he could easily collect them. They had been content with Cajun as their leader, but the gelding was now tied and resting. Before long they would choose another leader, most likely the oldest mare, the one with the glass eye, and she would soon set off toward the river.

Britt stood and listened. It was possible that the Kiowa crossed here often; a place that they had marked in their memory as a crossing that promised good fortune on their raids. A place on the northwest border of the rolling plains. He could hear nothing but the stamping and the breathing of the horses. He walked forward into the blank mystery of the fog toward the rear of the house where he knew the far wall was and beyond that a stone spring house. There was a good hiding place back there. A good place to lie in ambush.

What did he have that they wanted? His life. His horses, his weapons, and his gear. Or it could be as Tissoyo told him; when a loved one was killed, then you must go out on the roads and trails and kill the first person you came upon to send that person's soul to be a slave to the one you loved in the world beyond. Britt never understood what that world would be like. Maybe like this one where unformed beings crept step by step in a cold and blinding fog.

He stood at the front wall of the house with its sashless windows and doorless doorway out of which the mist drifted like breath from an open mouth. He walked around behind. Reefs of fallen rock where the back walls had come down. Each stone squared and marked with a chisel. The cookstove where Paint had taken shelter. From it came a scent of cold grease and wet iron. His footfalls were muffled by the damp dried grass and soaked litter from the bare hackberry trees. He stopped beside the fallen wall and listened.

In the distance he heard someone singing. It was a lifting, chanting falsetto. A song of grief and parting sung in some Indian language, in the dense mists of the river valley. Britt stood very still for some time. The song never faltered or stopped but went on and on with a thin insistence coming from a great distance through the fog. Finally he slid the revolver from its holster and checked to see that there was a round in the chamber. The big metal horse head of the six-shot revolver was comforting in his hand. A new Smith and Wesson that took ready-made rimfire cartridges.

He could not smell woodsmoke. He moved forward toward the singing. Always move forward toward the enemy. Toward those who would kill you and take your son and your wife and turn the minds of the children against their parents until they were recovered as shucked and empty shells. He came to a stand of trees with slaty trunks and limbs like black nerves dissolving into the mist. Beyond that a bank descending into a cut.

The singing had stopped. He had been heard. He took one long step that brought him under an anacua tree, and his boots pressed without sound on the dead sandpaper leaves and he laid his shoulder against the bark with the revolver's barrel raised.

He took each breath slowly. After a moment his heart quieted. He saw a drop of moisture on his hat brim appear and then grow pendant with a condensed seed of light from the pale fog in its center, and then it dropped. A stone tumbled in a damp clatter down a bank he could not see. Still he did not move. He shifted the joint of his thumb over the hammer and then laid his left hand over it to deaden the sound and cocked the revolver. He took his left hand away and then stood with the weapon cocked and the barrel raised.

The man appeared out of the mist like something being inflated. Like something tiny that within seconds expanded and filled all the world in the space of a deafening shriek and bore down on him with a face painted half black and dotted with hailstones. Britt fired. Then a bullet clubbed his upper thigh and blood and flesh and fragments of cloth sprayed. The brilliant muzzle flashes exploded into strange prismatic rays in the fog. The gunsmoke billowed dark and burnt against it. Britt dropped to the ground with his left hand over his crotch. He lay flat. There was a blundering noise as the man fell or rolled down the bank beyond into a deep pool of dark mist and then stillness.

Britt listened intently. A few stones cascaded down the bank after the man. In a few moments there was no other sound. Far away he could hear the horses as they snorted in a rattling noise and blew and shifted at the sound of gunshots. He could feel himself bleeding into his heavy wool trousers. He shifted slowly onto his side and unbuckled his belt and felt for the wound and was swept by a kind of melting relief when he knew he had not been hit in his private parts. The round was embedded in his upper thigh an inch away. He brought his hand away bloody and wiped it on his shirt.

He lay for a long time in the dry anacua leaves. He lay on one side with the revolver against his chest, unmoving. The slightest shift would give him away. With infinite care he once again cocked the forty-four revolver and put his left hand over the hammer and his thumb as he did so, but still the slow *click click* seemed very loud, still there was a rustling noise among the leaves as he moved.

Long rays shot through the fog and it thinned. It was nearing midday. Still cold. He began to shake. He had to move. He was leaking blood. Had he been hit in an artery, he would have been dead by now.

He rose to his feet and was forced to hold to the trunk of the anacua for a moment and then limped forward into the tangle of brush and vines that guarded the bank. Leaves stuck to him. It had to be some cutoff of the Clear Fork. There was a torn place in the brush where the man had run through, and Britt came to it and held the cocked revolver high and slid down among the red and black stones.

At the bottom the man lay in the wet red soil faceup with his black hair scattered around him and bone fragments and a fan of brain tissue like thrown soup. His arms flung out with the silver bracelets shining. Britt saw that beyond the black face paint the man was Tissoyo, and that he had hit him in the left eye.

He uncocked the revolver and laid it down and fell to his knees. In a hopeless gesture he placed his hand around the side of Tissoyo's neck to check for the thumping of that great artery in the throat but there was none. He tore off the breastplate of pipe beads and put his ear against Tissoyo's warm chest but there was no sound.

Britt fell back to a sitting position against a shelf of rock and stared at him. Tissoyo's face with its one eye was turned to the invisible sky overhead. His skull wrecked and scattered over the common earth. Britt sat there for a few moments beside the body and looked at Tissoyo in a way we are not allowed to look at people when they are alive. Searching desperately for a sign of life where there is none. The black hair was cut short around the left side of the head where he had shorn it off with a knife in grief for someone he loved who was dead, and now he was dead too. Britt felt a peculiar fullness in his head and his chest as if he were swelling up, and his ears were painfully blocked. He was weeping. Weeping and bleeding into his wool trousers and onto the stones and leaves around him.

What a sweet, high-hearted man he was. So openhanded, so dead. Wasted, wasted. Britt could not stop himself from reaching out to Tissoyo's body once more. He got to his knees and bent forward and against all reason took the limp wrist in his hand and felt again for a pulse. He held it for a long time. A faint hope that the pulse might be buried down in the muscle somewhere, secretly pumping. Even though the brain and nerves inside the skull that had driven it were destroyed. But Tissoyo lay utterly still in his brave face paint and his silver bracelets in circles up his brown arms and his old Walker Colt in the red mud.

After a while Britt released the dead hand and stood up and took off his jacket and then his shirt. With his hunting knife he cut his shirt into strips and dropped his trousers and bound up his wound, around and around the top of his thigh. His boot sloshed quietly.

He did not know if Tissoyo had been alone, so he limped down the long draw in the fog, step by step, until he came to the place where it joined the main valley of the Clear Fork, and there he found Tissoyo's camp. Sloppy and disorganized, still a bachelor. A burned-out campfire and a bag of brown sugar, a rawhide packet of stiff jerky to pour the brown sugar on, a rawhide box and in it Elizabeth Fitzgerald's sausage grinder and a small package of coffee beans. A tin cup hung on a branch, the Hudson's Bay four-point blanket and buffalo robes.

Looking at him from a stand of live oak were the Medicine Hat paint and the black mare with her white nose, the splash of white on her side. They were hobbled, strands of grass in their mouths.

Britt carried Tissoyo to the scaffold later that day. He had built it far away from the wagon trail so that the white men could not rob it. He placed Tissoyo on it and covered him with the four-point blanket and the buffalo robe. He pulled the firing pin and the cylinder from the revolver and threw them away and then placed the revolver in Tissoyo's hand. He limped over to the Medicine Hat paint and led him to the scaffold and shot him between the eyes and the mare afterward.

Chapter 35

THEY CAME BACK to the house on Elm Creek for a day and
a night, and they expected to sleep late the day afterward. It
was just before Christmas, and they came early in the morning. It
was the time of year when the Comanche and Kiowa kept to their
winter camps.

They left the children at Elizabeth's fort. It had been a long time
since they had been together with each other in solitude and only
themselves for company, even for a few hours. Britt took a shovel
and dug out the barbecue pit and broke up mesquite for the fire.
He found a small hickory tree of the kind that grew in the north of
Texas, and even though it was not like the great hickories of Kentucky it would burn well and long. Then he started the fire and
placed a section of heavy hog wire nearby to lay over it when the fire
was down to coals. Britt had rigged sections of canvas for awnings
and his Spencer rifle stood leaning against the live oak fully loaded
and one in the chamber.

A calf carcass hung from the long limb of the live oak, glinting
blue with sheath tissue and marbled red and white with fat. On the
rise downstream young Jim lay in his eternal cold bed of earth with

the words on his headboard fading into pale gray and a small glass vase of *ekasonip* tops in a cottony spray before it. Mary thought of her oldest son as a prince frozen in some icy cavern far below the earth who would lie there until the Second Coming, and then Jesus would place his hand upon the boy's closed eyelids and say, *Arise and come into thy kingdom.*

All those in the black community of Elm Creek and Fort Belknap and others even farther away were to come. For music they had Paint with his fiddle and the enlisted man of the Ninth who played a flute and a corporal named Henry Thrim who had acquired, and could play, the new instrument called a harmonica. Mary walked over to the wall and looked at herself, turning her head, in the small mirror. It belonged to the Elm Creek house because this was home and someday they would come back here to live and so she would have it nowhere else. She unfolded borrowed sheets to throw on the long sawbuck and plank tables. She waved Britt away from the dishes. She would not let him pick them up. His great callused hands were dirty with sap and charcoal. So he bent forward from his height of six foot one and kissed her with his hands out to each side.

"Britt," she said.

Why now was his touch so vivid and sparkling? His touch was a tiny point of fire and her skin was alight. She thought of what had changed and when. When she had seen him lying on the surgeon's table with his pants torn off and his boot thick with coagulated blood like shredded liver and the surgeon taping his private parts out of the way and plunging in with his probe for the bullet. His body suddenly her own and so vital that she would have given anything to spare him the steel instruments. How vital he was to her, how loved. The tongs probing muscle and fat with a wet clicking and then the bullet drawn out with strings of tissue clinging to it. The hissing carbide lamp. Mary on the opposite side of the table with her hands on Britt's hands, which were clasped together like a construction of metal. She could not touch him enough, then.

She put on the five-gallon kettle full of water to boil for his bath and then went to take the broom and beat on the devil's trumpet vine that crowded the front of the house and looped over the door. She beat on it until all the dead leaves had fallen off and it no longer looked so untidy. She sent the dead leaves flying into the yard. As she stood there a massive cloud bank engulfed the northern horizon like a silent and uninvited guest of gigantic proportions that hesitated on the threshold of the world but would come in whether or no. It was a deep marine blue and in front of it raced white squall lines in blowing lather. She went back in and arranged coals in the fireplace. She took up lids and squinted at the seething contents and then lifted coals onto the tops of the two heavy Dutch ovens and the spider skillet.

Britt sectioned the ribs and backstraps and set them to barbecue slowly. From time to time he straightened and looked at the northern horizon and watched the long clean plains of dried grasses that spread beyond the heavy trees of Elm Creek. He stood very still and searched each stand of trees carefully. He listened. Then he dipped a small brush of dried sage into an ironstone cup of sauce made of brown sugar and the catsup Mary and Elizabeth had made and bottled, a sauce simmered with wild chili petins and half a cup of broth. He stood upright with the sweet-smelling brush in his hand and did a quick tap step.

"Mary," he said. "You going to read something."

"No," she said. She walked over to him to look at the crisping meat. "You know anyhow people want to dance and dancing and not listen. Me up there words words words people falling over sleeping."

"They'll listen or I will make them listen."

"No, Britt." She did some steps beside him. The steps were precise and quick and she did not falter. "I am dancing too."

He watched her with a quiet expression and then she turned around in four steps and made her skirts fly out and then took his arm for a second or two. He smiled a slight, hesitant smile because he saw she was happier than he had seen her since she had been rescued, and he was afraid it might evaporate, be burned away when a headache and the tremors arrived again. He reached out and took her upper arm to steady her, and the newly made plaid cotton of her dress crinkled under his hand.

"Britt, when will you stop going?" She laid her hand over his.

"When they quit coming," he said. He put his other hand to the crown of his hat because the increasing wind threatened to get under his hat brim and skim it way. "If they quit coming then the more people won't be afraid to carry freight. Right now I hardly got no competition. There ain't many of us on the road." He lifted his hand from her forearm and touched her cheek. "It's all right, baby." He turned up his coat collar. "By that time all my cows will have twins each and we'll be rich as old man Goyens." He smiled. "But we won't let anybody know. I went and sent all the money to a bank in New Mexico."

She lifted both eyebrows with wide eyes.

"I been told it's best." Britt splashed sauce on the ribs so that they sizzled and blackened. "Sergeant Earl fixed it for me."

She gazed at him for a moment, thinking, and then lifted both hands to her bright headcloth in a sudden gust of wind. He took off his hat and set it over her head, cloth, and all. He laughed. It sank down around her ears. "Go inside, baby."

"Come in and wash." She ran her hand over his rough shirt-sleeve. It smelled like woodsmoke. "Wash up and a clean shirt and everything."

She poured the boiling water into the tub in front of the fireplace and then the cold water. He carried the Spencer in with him and stood it against the wall and then stripped off his clothes. He stepped into the tub and stood naked and turned up a pitcher of water over himself and then took the brush from her and scrubbed at his hands. He looked at them closely in the light from the window.

"How's that?" he said. Runnels of soapsuds poured down his forearms and dripped off his elbows. "Can I sit in the front row now?"

"Yes."

She handed him the cotton towels made in a rough tabby weave and he scrubbed at his short, tight hair and ran the towel behind

himself and then between his legs and over the thinly healed hole
in his upper thigh where the Fort Belknap surgeon had dug out the
.44 round and had taken sections of flesh with it. He turned himself
in front of the fire and all the damp evaporated from his skin. Mary
started to grip the sides of the tub to throw the water out, but Britt
took it from her and opened the door and stepped out into the cold
naked and flung the water and yelled, "Hoowee, God almighty!"

He dropped the galvanized tub and ran back in. Mary wrapped
a quilt around his shoulders and he stood again in front of the roaring fire until he had warmed. He reached for her, but Mary firmly
handed him his underwear and socks and shirt.

"People coming," she said. "But after and so on."

"And so on," he said.

They stood inside at the windows and watched the storm arrive.
On the stone hearth sat the brass barber's basin that they had borrowed from Sergeant Earl to pass around for school money. On a
long table the steaming trifle in its blue-willow bowl, jars of stuffed
peppers.

"Mary," he said. "They aren't coming." The wind struck the
house like a hammer. Every pane in the windows jumped. It had
grown very dark. It was perhaps two in the afternoon of a short
winter day. Between the bare limbs of the cedar elm they saw the
storm ballooning across the plains to the north of them. The columns of snow drifted down from the overburden of cloud and were
then blown horizontal. The windowpanes shivered and the blown
snow lifted up the canvas awnings to throw them in manic flights
across the open lands or plaster them against the tree trunks of Elm
Creek. The smoke of the fireplace was sucked up the chimney in a
solid column.

"Maybe some."

"Nobody's going to travel in this."

"Oh." Mary's lower lip stuck out. "Dancing. I was dancing and
that new thing of some music."

"Harmonica," said Britt.

"Don't talk for me," she said.

"All right. You wanted to hear that new thing of some music."

"A harmonica," she said. Her eyes were large and round at the bottoms and very black. She had brushed out her wavy hair until it shone and pinned it in a decorative knot with a black net over the knot and then set a starched headcloth in a taffeta plaid on the back of her head. The long scar that forked and raveled like lightning into her scalp had diminished in color and her hair grew over it. She snapped her fingers. "Damn."

"Listen to you," he said. "You cussing like a freighter." He put his arm around her shoulders. "Never mind. The Comanche or the Kiowa won't be coming either." He tucked back a strand of her hair. "It's been a while since it was just you and me." He dropped his hands and went and bent over the spider skillet. "No kids. And plenty of firewood for all night and the morning." He spooned up some of the apple mixture with its crisp topping and blew on it and tasted it. "All this for us." He put the spoon down. "All that barbecue for us." He set off the Dutch ovens and the skillet so the apple crisp and the potatoes would not burn.

Mary bit her lip and looked at the floor. In a low and mournful voice she said, "I was going to dancing, Britt."

"Here." He took her in his arms and moved her around the floor singing "Appalacky Town." "When all the gents and the ladies come down, going to have a walk around Appalacky Town." They danced sedately around the floor in front of the fire for as long as Britt had breath to sing but he could not carry a tune in his hat, and Mary started laughing at him and so they stopped.

She said, "Remember the sorghum coming in? Old man Chessman and lost his load."

He lifted his hand to her hair and gently took off the taffeta headcloth. "Yes. In Kentucky. They let us have a dance that night and old man Chessman sat in a corner and pouted. Spilled it all over the Findlay road." He laid the headcloth on the table beside the trifle. "They said he was going to get whipped for it, but Mr. Burkett never did nothing." He lifted his hand once again to her hairnet and carefully disengaged it, and her hair fell down. "We danced all night." Snow built a shelf of white on the sills and the windowlights jumped with every blast of wind so that they sent out planes of altering red reflections from the fire.

And between that time and this Britt had become a different man than the one who was polite and grateful to be allowed a dance, who had stood silent and diffident behind Moses Johnson as his freedom papers were written out in Little Egypt. That self had disappeared as if in the heavy spring fogs of the Ohio and this person he was now had appeared, someone who had been there all along. A man with land and a house and a family and a Spencer rifle to hold it all.

Mary lighted a candle at the coals and stood gazing at the flame with the faint curl of wick smoke rising past her hand. "Remember the whistle boats and that rock of fog river?"

The great bluff of stone that stood out over the Ohio River and in a deep fog you could stand on it and look down into a drifting mist and hear far upstream on the wide river the steamboats laying on their whistles and the cry of it was like something calling for help or guidance in a dangerous, lightless world. When all was wet and damp and rich with water.

"Yes, I remember."

The snow fell upon the house and the trees beyond the window and ran in manic circles between the washhouse and the leaping fire in the pit. He turned to look at her where she stood still with her hair falling down on the shoulders of her plaid dress and the small gold dots in her ears that glinted in the firelight. Somehow neither one of them wanted to eat.

He moved past her to the heavy bedstead in the far corner and sat down on it. "All we need now is some of Paint's godawful wine." He lay his heavy hand down on the coverlet with the palm open to her. "Mary girl."

She turned her head slightly to one side and looked at him out of the side of her eyes and smiled a small, questioning smile that was somewhat sly. She held up one finger. She went to the tall safe that stood against the wall and held their cookware and the heavy steel canisters of flour and baking soda and cornmeal and brought out a glass jug that sloshed with a deep purple liquid and a living, gelatinous sediment that wavered in the bottom.

"God damn don't shake it up," he said. "They'll find us dead in the morning." He took the ironstone cup from her and drank it down. She made an attempt but after one drink her eyes began to water and she put it down on the floor.

"Mary, do you want me?"

She bent forward and laid her hand on his neck and kissed his cheek. So he began to unbutton her dress button by button and they made their own world again between them. He laid his hands on that warm skin he had not touched for so long. They lay in the light of the fire in their own house. Snow thickened on the windowsills. The tumbled sheets and her small body warmed him to the center of himself. They had come home, if only for a short while. Every moment and every touch of her hands on his back was like stolen riches. The treasonous world tapped at their windows, dots of snow against the black night.

Chapter 36

❧

IN LATE JANUARY of 1871 Britt decided to set up a route past Fort Worth and on into Dallas. The two towns were thirty miles apart. When Britt and Paint and Dennis started out they went with two wagons and four horses to a wagon and they were already loaded with forage and grain for the horses for this long trip, but even so they picked up several tons of salt from the Graham Salt Works in heavy burlap sacks and two tons of cut limestone from the quarry in the White Settlement. Named for some people named White.

Dallas had nearly five thousand people, and they said a railroad was coming in. It had freedmen's towns in small neighborhoods at the fringes. Britt intended to drive straight into the ford over the Trinity River and then up the bluff road and onto Peachtree Street without any delays. Dallas was a stronghold of the Ku Klux Klan, and the town was like some hostile nation that had within its borders treasures of cloth and bales of gloves and kegs of kerosene and lightning rods and he had to go in and deliver the salt and limestone and pick up the return load and get out before anything happened. They kept the horses at a trot until they came to Peachtree and then walked the horses carefully through the traffic. They left the salt and the limestone at the depot where the Curry brothers waited for them in the freezing, drafty air of the warehouse. They then went on and came away from the Sheridan's Supply warehouse with part of the return load; cases of Brandon and Kilmeyer beer in amber bottles brought from Leavenworth to go to Nance's store. Then they went on to Poindexter's Ironworks for wagon tires and tools and ox yokes.

Paint wandered into the blacksmith shop with his noonday meal in his hand. He watched as the smith reset a tire. An old man sat on a bench with his feet in the shavings and the hoof clippings and shorn bits of metal. He was thin in a sort of collapsed way and his skin was like old paper and his lower lids drooped and were very red.

The old man said, "I seen one other nigger that was turning white like that." He nodded toward Paint's arm. "In splashes." He held out a skeletal hand toward the forge fire to warm it. The smith dropped the tire into the quenching vat and steam shot up in gouts.

Paint looked over at the man and then away again with a polite smile.

"Well sir, where was that?" Paint finished his biscuit and salted ham and then turned up a bottle of beer. He shook the crumbs from the cloth wrapping and put it in his pocket.

"Alabama." The old man shifted his tattered shoes. It was very warm in the blacksmith shop and the slight wind fluted at the dirty windowpanes. The old man had a heavy wool coat closed around him.

Paint clasped his hands between his knees and pushed at a hoof clipping with his boot. "Well sir, did he turn all white or what?"

"I don't know," said the old man. "We left."

"Well, it seems to always get bigger." Paint lifted his forearm and looked at it. "I tried to color myself with hair dye but I couldn't get the color right. It was always darker or lighter. So I give up."

The old man nodded. "The Lord sends to each of us some chastisement. Some burden, so that we may turn to him."

"Yes sir," said Paint.

"Yours is to turn into a white man."

Paint nodded slowly and thoughtfully but he had no idea what to say. The smith smashed his five-pound hammer onto the hot and glowing tire. After a few moments Paint thought of something to say and turned to the old man, but he was deeply asleep where he sat.

They got out of Dallas without incident.

The thirty miles between Dallas and Fort Worth was a long and pleasant drive. Britt knew it was a place where they would not have trouble from either Comanche or Kiowa or white men. It was a good feeling. He did not have that kind of feeling very often. The prairies between the two towns were damp with apricot-colored grasses that steamed in the noon sun, and the frost shadows of isolated live oaks shrank and wilted. Britt wished he had brought a saddle horse with him to ride through the shallow sunlight and the crisp air. He sat in the front wagon and drove with Dennis beside him and Paint coming alone behind in the second wagon. Vesey Smith had joined the Ninth Cavalry. He said he wanted to go hunting Indians.

As they passed through Fort Worth with its few scattered buildings, Britt saw coming up from the south along Rucker Street a long tattered stream of cattle with men in broad hats riding alongside. He stood up in the seat to watch. There had to be more than a thousand head. It was too far away for him to see their road brands. Britt stood up with the ends of his muffler dangling over his chest.

"What the hell are they doing?" he said.

"Beats me," said Dennis. "Maybe folks here in Fort Worth are hungry. Real hungry."

Britt saw ahead a black man walking alongside the road with a king of clubs playing card stuck in his hat band.

"Hey you nigger," he said. "Talk to me."

The man turned. "You speaking to me?"

"Yes," said Britt. "You the only man on the road."

"Then what?"

Britt and Dennis on the wagon drew abreast. The harness jingled. "How come you got that card in your hat?"

The man said, "Witches."

Britt pursed his lips and nodded and then said, "Tell me something."

The man was dressed in a threadbare coat and a dimly white shirt without a collar. "Just ast me."

"What are all those cattle coming up the road for?"

The man turned and looked down Rucker Street and even as they stood the noise of cattle bawling at one another increased. The sound of their immense horns knocking together with a myriad clicking, an incessant running clatter, sounded like an avalanche of some small brittle things that never ended. The entire road was a field of moving horns. The men on horseback shouted at the cattle and at one another.

"They going on up north. Way up north. I don't know where exactly."

"What the hell for?" Britt stood on the wagon seat and watched.

"So up north people can eat them."

Britt turned from the man with the card in his hat brim and spoke to Dennis and Paint. "They are going to hold them here till March. That's what they're going to do. And throw a bunch more together and then move them up to Kansas. I bet that's what they're doing. They are going to fat them up there where there's rain. I'll be damned. A whole herd. Man, that is a good idea."

The man turned and began walking on down the road.

"If you knew how come you ast me?"

Britt signaled to Dennis to get the horses moving and Britt said, "You want a ride? Get up here."

"Nah. I like walking."

"Where you going?"

"I don't have no idea."

THEY OVERNIGHTED AT the outskirts of the White Settlement and slept under the wagons. They got up to the sound of Paint singing "Marching through Georgia" over a brisk cookfire and banging the skillet and coffeepot. They fed the horses and then themselves and loaded their mess box and the bedding, and then started home.

They stopped at the Graham Salt Works and paid old man Graham his money and he returned to Britt the money in gold pieces that made up his freighting fee. They headed on toward Fort Belknap. On the way they would pass Elm Creek and spend the night there. As they came out of the hilly country around the salt works and onto a level plain tall with yellow grasses, a place called Salt Fork Prairie, Dennis turned to the north.

He said, "Yonder they come, Britt."

They flowed like a school of fish through the grasses in a cascade of shining paint hides. They were crying out in loud voices and riding through their own bank of gunsmoke. Their hair was cut short on the right side, tossing sheaves of blunt short hair, and some with unbound braids.

Britt screamed for Paint to abandon his wagon and come on. Leave it, leave it! he shouted. It was not defensible. Maybe they would stop and loot the wagon and take the horses. They had been caught in the one unprotected stretch between Graham and Indian Mound.

Paint threw away the reins and jumped and with his rifle over his head came running toward Britt and Dennis and the high-sided freight wagon. He ran alongside and laid one hand on the gunnel and vaulted over the side among the bales. Britt jumped back to join him and began firing. Dennis came over the driver's seat as well and kept the reins in his hand and screamed at the horses. The Fitzgerald bays lunged into a full gallop within seconds and briefly slammed against the doubletrees and hit the leaders in the hocks with them until the leaders were also plunging forward. Crescents of dirt and sod flew up from their hooves.

"Maybe we can make Indian Mound!" Britt yelled.

"Too far!" Dennis half-lay behind the driver's seat with the reins in his hands. He could not see where they were going. The wagon careened on from one small drainage to another and the horses lunged against the load.

"Throw the shit out!" Britt shouted. The Kiowa had started their charge too soon and were still half a mile away but on the other hand on this open prairie they would have been seen at any distance. Britt and Paint tore open boxes and hurled out the loads of gloves and hats and mirrors, then tossed over the crates they had been packed in. They ripped open grain sacks and spilled barley and oats over the side in a long yellow waterfall of grain and then tossed the sacks in the air. Far behind Britt saw that some of them had stopped to jump into the abandoned wagon and begin rifling through the load. Bottles of beer shot into the air, strings of amber molasses flew in arcs. They were cutting the horses out of the harness.

They had to get somewhere to protect at least one side. Indian Mound Mountain with its timbered oak slopes and broken architecture of red stone lay ahead on the horizon, too far. On a slight rolling rise was a stand of brush and stunted live oak growing up around a tipped layer of stone.

"Drive into it!" Britt called to Dennis. "Drive straight into it!"

"There's rock!"

"Do as I tell you!"

Dennis stood up despite the cracking shots around him and aimed the horses for the stand of brush and small trees. The horses crashed into the dense and wiry stand and tore their forelegs and clawed over rock and the wagon straddled the bank of stone and tipped. The bays lunged on in a powerful striving that pulled the wagon bed over the flat table of stone and crowned it, but the horses kept on clawing for purchase until it was clear the wagon would go no farther. Britt jumped out and carried with him the box of Spencer rimfire ammunition under one arm. The stiff, small limbs of the live oak saplings tore off his hat and ripped a gash in his hand.

"Cut them loose, Dennis!" He dragged the ammunition box into the low trees. "Cut them loose and tie them somewhere. Tie them to the wagon tongue." He slapped his hat back on his head.

Paint and Britt tipped over one of the trunks that carried hair dye and another with carboys of carbolic acid. A round plowed into the hair dye with a loud smash and flung it all over Britt's hands and it ran down along with the blood from the gash in his hand. He shoved a trunk to one side of the copse and the trunk with the carboys in it to the other side. They had at least some protection on three sides. Not much. But some.

Dennis crawled over to the wagon and then to the horses but he could not get them unharnessed. Bullets and one arrow struck so close that his face was powdered with tiny splinters. The arrow had hit the hard planks of the wagon with such force that it buried its steel head almost to the barbs. He left off grappling with the buckles and crawled back into the wiry brush and yelled for ammunition.

The Kiowa galloped like circus riders in an invisible ring. They called out and sang and there was a kind of fire streaming around them. They were lethal and beautiful and they had come bearing the mystery of death for mankind to puzzle over. They were adorned with the flight feathers of eagles and their horses were outlined in sunlit manes. One man wore an ancient Spanish coat of mail slapping over his chest and he shouted at the men forted up in the stand of live oak and brush in a merry voice. The horsemen wove and circled and turned and spun, incessantly moving targets. Britt felt the brush all around him jumping with bullets. He looked for the young white renegade and then the boy rode past, a small shield on his arm and on the boss of the shield a scalp of light brown hair tossed in dirty strands.

Britt aimed for the boy's ribs and fired. The boy shot sideways off the horse's back and a blossom of blood sprayed over his horse's withers. He went down and stayed down.

"I got the little son of a bitch," said Britt.

Paint crawled through the brush and rocks to shove a hatful of cartridges to Dennis and then fought his way back to where the banks of heavy gunpowder smoke threaded among the stiff wire of yaupon holly and live oak saplings and it was all lit up by repeated muzzle flashes. They kept firing until their barrels were too hot and the cartridges were cooking off before they could be fired. Sweat ran into their eyes and they could hardly see one another for the gunsmoke and their own shots deafened them. It seemed like hours had passed or that they had been thrown into some eternity of strife that would never end. Britt shifted to his revolver but he had only one bandolier of ammunition for it so he became very careful. Paint turned over one of the bottles of acid on his rifle barrel and it hissed and stank.

"What the hell are you doing?" said Britt.

"I'm cooling it."

"You're going to gas us."

The Kiowa knew what was happening. They knew their barrels were overheated. Britt saw in the distance two men standing outside of pistol range and holding two horses each. This meant that several Kiowa were on the ground and crawling toward them. They could not see them unless they stood up and then they would be exposed.

Dennis stood up with his Spencer and saw two men coming forward on their hands and knees in a stand of wild buckwheat. He fired over the dancing, nervous backs of the bays and as he did a round struck him in the throat and he fell back onto the stiff brush and was tangled in it and half held there a foot above the ground. Bright red blood leaped out of his throat in regular, pulsing sprays and painted the live oak leaves with a startling color. After a few moments he lifted one hand and then dropped it and his rifle fell beside him.

"Dennis is hit," said Paint. He lay down behind the trunk of acid bottles. He fired twice and saw a young man with a beautiful long brown body spin around on his horse and fling off the far side and come to lie on his face.

"Is he dead?" Britt sat up and began to feed rounds into the magazine. Bright brass casings lay all around him.

"Yeah, Britt."

And then Britt was hit in the center of his chest. He threw up his hands into the air and his rifle somersaulted forward and fell at his feet. His eyes drifted and then in the middle of all the shouting and dust and noise and the sound of a hundred horses galloping his eyelids slowly closed. The hole in his shirt was dark and absolute. He fell forward with his hands opening like flowers. A long brilliant sun moved on toward the afternoon and its change of color in the air and overhead the vultures rose tier upon tier, riding the updrafts. How beautiful is the sky over the rolling plains. How far away.

"Aw, Britt," said Paint. "Britt."

The two lead horses were brought down. The light sorrel horses jerked and stiffened and then fell straight down in the harness; it seemed they had lain down with their legs folded under them and their necks bent forward in a graceful curve so that their noses touched the ground, bowing. They were both dead. The Indians could now hear only one rifle replying.

Paint shoved himself backward over the stone and clawing brush and laid his hand on Britt's collar and drew him down. Britt's hat fell off and his unmoving eyes looked upward toward the building clouds and the vultures that rose higher and higher on some rising column of air into the white ices of the cumulus until they reached such altitudes that they winked out like dark stars. Paint touched Britt's eyeball but there was no movement, no blink, and the ribs under the shirt had ceased to move and draw breath.

"Aw, Britt."

A certain calm overcame Paint. A strange thought came to him for one second and that thought was that the random splashes of white that flowed over his face and his arms made him very beautiful. That they were not random at all but that there was a pattern underlying them he had never seen before. He decided he would go out to them. He would present himself to them. Like a Medicine Hat paint.

And so he reloaded his Spencer. The barrel had cooled. He laid Britt's rifle across his chest and covered the handsome face in its saddle-colored skin, now strangely pale, with his coat. The long hands with their smooth heavy muscle lying each to one side empty as clothes without people in them. Paint stood up without a hat on his bullet head so that the Kiowa could see the startling markings on his bald skull. Both the black and white parts of his arms were streaked with blood from the brush and cactus but he was un-wounded. He would present himself to them as a whole person. He shouted something. He walked past where Dennis lay suspended in the ironlike brush and the dead sorrels bowing to the earth and the trembling Fitzgerald bays.

He stood up in the river of savory grasses with their colors of sepia and slate and the drifting phantoms of powder smoke. He began firing. His rifle muzzle followed each target, hungry and seeking. The brass cartridge shells leaped from the breech like jewelry thrown to the wind. He made of himself a gift. He shot and cocked and shot again. He was hit many times. *Ahó, ahó,* they shouted. The Kiowa words with the rising tone that meant *Kill him, kill him.* Or perhaps one of them said it in the falling tone *ahô, ahô* that meant *Thank you, thank you.*

Epilogue

B RITT, DENNIS, AND Paint were found the following day by fellow teamsters and were buried where they had fallen. Their grave marker was cut by hand into native stone and it is in the middle of a field and it is not easy to find. Some reminiscences taken down in the early 1900s say that the men were scalped, other accounts say they were not. Some say the cavalry found them and buried them and others say they were found by other freighters. No one knows who made the headstone.

In May of 1871 General William Tecumseh Sherman arrived in Texas to investigate the endless complaints of Texans concerning Indian depredations. His entourage passed near the place where Britt and his companions had been killed five months before and was watched, from a distance, by Setanta, Satank, Horseback, and other Kiowa and Comanche on a raiding party. They let Sherman's column go unmolested, but the day following, the war party rode down on a train of freight wagons and killed Nathan Long, N. J. Baxter, Jesse Bowman, James and Samuel Elliot, James and Thomas Williams, all freighters for Henry Warren, government contractor. The wounded were brought in to Fort Richardson, where Sherman was staying. A fort with stone barracks and a dusty parade ground at the edge of the Red River Valley. When Sherman got the news and realized the attack had missed him by a matter of hours, he rode out to the site and saw the bodies of men who had been tied to wheels and burned alive. There was no mention of Britt Johnson and his black companions. The men of the Warren massacre were all white men, and a Texas state marker in good gray granite has been erected and their names carved into it.

Because of the Warren Wagon Train Massacre, President Grant rescinded the Peace Policy and the Quakers were removed from their position on the board of the Indian Bureau. Thus the long Red River War began and was finished only when the buffalo were destroyed and Ranald MacKenzie ran Quanah Parker to earth in Palo Duro Canyon in 1874 and shot seven hundred of his horses. When Quanah Parker surrendered, there were at least two white warriors with his small band, who had fought alongside him for many years. And so it ended.

Mary, Jube, and Cherry lived out their lives in the turbulent frontier era of cattle drives and land disputes. They did nothing that made the white community take note of them but went quietly on with the school and the barbershop, and Mary died in her mid-eighties without ever marrying again. It has been said by neighbors that she was faithful in visiting Britt's grave and tending to its upkeep until she was very old and became bedridden. Despite genealogical research, it is not known what happened to Cherry and Jube.

Millie Durgan returned to the Elm Creek community at the age of eighty, traveling south from the Kiowa reservation with her Kiowa children and grandchildren. Sain-to-odii was unable to speak English, but she was polite and somewhat bemused by the community's efforts to bring forward a birthday cake. She remembered almost nothing of her life before her capture.

Except for three pieces of hard evidence, Britt's history is entirely oral; stories of his courageous journey to retrieve his wife and children, his rescue of other captives, his freighting endeavor, and his companions remained in the memories of the people of north

Texas long enough to be recorded and written down. He is invari-
ably spoken of in terms of respect and admiration. One man described him as "a magnificent physical specimen," and others told of
his travels and his freighting business. The elements of legend have
collected around his historical figure, and its image remains bright
and untarnished. He left nothing that could be traced either in land
or written material or heirlooms. Only his gravestone, on which is
written, *Britt Johnson, Dennis Cureton, Paint Crawford, Killed By
Indians 1871*. All he had was the story of his life, which was as good
as any other man's, and in the end it is all we have.

Author's Note

❧

I CAME UPON BRITT Johnson's story while researching
Enemy Women. An early draft of that book ended with the
protagonist's journey into north Texas immediately after the Civil
War. Britt Johnson is mentioned in many histories of north Texas,
and the accounts are often contradictory or confusing. They all come
down to two or three oral histories taken down in the early 1900s,
and three pieces of hard evidence; a census of 1860, an 1864 muster
of a scouting company, and the diary of Samuel A. Kingman, who
was present at the signing of the Medicine Lodge Treaty of 1867
and whose diary mentions Britt Johnson in search of captives. The
story of Britt's journey to rescue his wife and children from captivity
is beyond doubt, as are the brief accounts of his life afterward.
Entering Britt's name in a search engine will lead to several good
Web sites.

This is a work of fiction, but any full rendering of Britt's story
would of necessity be close to fiction since there is so little to go
on, but that little is arresting and quite moving. I have sorted out
the names of his children and of his former "owner" as best I could.
Many of the Comanche and Kiowa people named here were real

people, such as Kicking Bird, Toshana, Hears the Dawn, Aperian Crow, Esa Havey, Setanta, Satank, and Old Man Komah. Others are invented. Sergeant Elijah Earl was a real person, as were Dennis Cureton, Vesey Smith, Paint Crawford, and Medal of Honor winner Emmanuel Stance. I have tried to give them all a living presence and dreams and daily speech.

The character of Samuel Hammond is in no way a portrait of the remarkable Lawrie Tatum but is an exploration of Tatum's dilemma; a Quaker sent as agent to warlike tribes of the south plains. Colonel Grierson was a real person, the first commander of Fort Sill. With one exception, the names of the captives are genuine, including Elizabeth Fitzgerald, who led a charmed life, and all of those taken in the Elm Creek raid of 1864.

This book is a novel, but it's backbone—Britt's story—is true. Britt's story returned to me repeatedly as I read through north Texas histories over the years, and I often wondered why no one had taken it up. And so I did.

Bibliography

Axtell, James. *The Invasion Within: The Contest of Cultures in Colonial North America*. New York: Oxford University Press, 1985.

Baker, T. Lindsay, and Billy R. Harrison. *Adobe Walls: The History and Archaeology of the 1874 Trading Post*. College Station: Texas A&M University Press, 1986.

Beatty, Thomas C. *The Life and Adventures of a Quaker among the Indians*. Facsimile reproduction. New York: Corner House, 1972.

Brant, Charles, ed. *Jim White Wolf: The Life of a Kiowa-Apache Indian*. New York: Dover, 1969.

Brooks, James F. *Confounding the Color Line: The Indian-Black Experience in North America*. Lincoln: University of Nebraska Press, 2002.

Brooks, James. *Captives and Cousins*. Chapel Hill: University of North Carolina Press, 2002.

Cashion, Ty. *A Texas Frontier: The Clear Fork Country and Fort Griffin, 1849–1887*. Norman: University of Oklahoma Press, 1996.

Cope, Thomas P. *Philadelphia Merchant: The Diary of Thomas P. Cope, 1800–1851*. Edited by Eliza Cope Harrison. South Bend, Ind.: Gateway, 1978.

Custer, Elizabeth. *Boots and Saddles; or, Life in Dakota with General Custer*. New York: Harper and Brothers, 1901.

Drimmer, Frederick. *Captured by the Indians: Fifteen First-Hand Accounts*. New York: Dover, 1985.

"Early Days of Freighting." *Frontier Times Magazine* (Bandera, Texas) 6, no. 4 (1929).

Fehrenbach, T. R. *Comanche: The Destruction of a People*. New York: Da Capo Press, 1994.

———. *Lone Star*. New York: Da Capo Press, 2000.

Finley, Florence. *Oldtimers: Frontier Days in the Uvalde Section of South West Texas*. Uvalde, Texas: Hornby Press, 1939.

Foster, Morris. *Being Comanche*. Tucson: University of Arizona Press, 1998.

Goodrich, Thomas. *Scalp Dance: Indian Warfare on the High Plains*. Mechanicsburg, Pa.: Stackpole Books, 1997.

Hamm, Thomas D. *The Quakers in America*. New York: Columbia University Press, 2003.

Katz, William Loren. *The Black West*. New York: Harlem Moon/Broadway, 2005.

Lehmann, Herman. *Nine Years with the Indians, 1870–1879*. Facsimile reproduction. San Antonio, Texas: Lebco Graphics, 1985.

Liveremore, Mary. *My Story of the War: A Woman's Narrative*. Hartford, Conn.: Worthington, 1889.

London, Marvin F. *Indian Raids in Montague County*. St. Jo, Texas: S.S.T. Printers, n.d.

Lott, Dale F. *American Bison: A Natural History*. Berkeley and Los Angeles: University of California Press, 2003.

McGinty, Brian. *The Oatman Massacre*. Norman: University of Oklahoma Press, 1998.

McMurtry, Larry, and Stanley Noyes, eds. *Comanches in the New West: Historic Photographs*. Austin: University of Texas Press, 1999.

Methvin, J. J. *Andele, the Mexican Kiowa Captive*. Albuquerque: University of New Mexico Press, 1996.

Momaday, Scott. *The Way to Rainy Mountain*. Albuquerque: University of New Mexico Press, 1969.

Perry, James. *A Bohemian Brigade: The Civil War Correspondents*. New York: John Wiley and Sons, 2000.

Rister, Carl Coke, ed. *Comanche Bondage: The Captivity of Mrs. Harper*. Lincoln: University of Nebraska Press, 1989.

Russel, Evalu Ware. *Kiowa*. Audiocassette. Richardson, Texas: Various Indian Peoples Publishing, 1991.

Stodola, Kathryn. *Women's Indian Captivity Narratives*. New York: Penguin, 1998.

Tatum, Lawrie. *Our Red Brothers*. Facsimile reproduction. Lincoln: University of Nebraska Press, 1970.

Tocakut (Harlan Hall). *Remember, We Are Kiowas: 101 Kiowa Indian Stories.* Bloomington, Ind.: Authorhouse, 2000.

Wallace, Ernest, and E. Adamson Hoebel. *The Comanches: Lords of the South Plains.* Norman: University of Oklahoma Press, 1986.

White, Leslie, ed. *Lewis Henry Morgan: The Indian Journals, 1859–1862.* Ann Arbor: University of Michigan Press, 1959.

Wilbarger, J. W. *Indian Depredations in Texas.* Austin, Texas: Hutchings Printing House, 1889. Facsimile reproduction, Austin, Texas: Eakin Press, 1985.

Zesch, Scott. *The Captured: A True Story of Abduction by Indians on the Texas Frontier.* New York: St. Martin's Press, 2007.